THE WHISPERER

THE WHISPERER

FIONA McINTOSH

ALFRED A. KNOPF

NEW YORK

THIS IS A BORZOI BOOK PUBLISHED BY ALFRED A. KNOPF

All rights reserved. Published in the United States by Alfred A. Knopf,
an imprint of Random House Children's Books, a division of Random House LLC,
a Penguin Random House Company, New York. Originally published in
hardcover by HarperCollins Publishers, Australia Pty Ltd., in 2009.

Visit us on the Web! randomhousekids.com

Educators and librarians, for a variety of teaching tools,
visit us at RHTeachersLibrarians.com

Library of Congress Cataloging-in-Publication Data
McIntosh, Fiona.
The Whisperer / Fiona McIntosh.—First American edition.
p. cm.
Originally published by HarperCollins Publishers, Australia, in 2009.
Summary: "Two boys with a mysterious connection
find a way to save each other." —Provided by publisher
ISBN 978-0-553-49827-1 (trade) — ISBN 978-0-553-49833-2 (lib. bdg.) —
ISBN 978-0-553-49834-9 (ebook)
[1. Fantasy.] I. Title.
PZ7.M4786557Wh 2015
[Fic]—dc23
2014003767

The text of this book is set in 12-point Goudy.

Printed in the United States of America

April 2015

10 9 8 7 6 5 4 3 2 1

First American Edition

For my beautiful nieces,
Ellie Rogers and Gracie Hughes

1

Master Tyren squinted into the sun as he looked up to scan the rickety scaffolding. It always made him feel dizzy to see the grunters running around on the dangerous wooden skeleton that would form the grand tent. It was scary work, needing courage and confident, sure-footed movements. He was looking for Griffin, young brother of the Twisted Twins, a popular contortionist act. Tyren had originally assumed the boy possessed the same brilliant skills as his brothers. Unfortunately, Griffin did not, and had shown he was good for little else but the physical labor associated with the setting up of the famous Master Tyren's Marvels of Nature Traveling Show.

The showmaster prided himself on presenting some of the rarest beasts—human and creature—that existed in the land, and he was very excited at the prospect of his latest acquisitions . . . because it meant wealth. Tyren cared little for the people and creatures in his acts, but their potential to make him rich was unquestionable. This latest group of creatures was special, and the reason he was seeking the lad. He needed Griff's help to make the newcomers feel part of the family as quickly as possible.

Tyren grumbled to himself, and then his gaze locked onto the boy. "Ah, there you are," he murmured, noticing that the boy was assembling the top of the timber structure for the Grand Beracca, or main tent, that audiences filled each evening. "Griff!" he bellowed.

The boy stopped hammering and lifted a hand in salutation. "Ho, Master Tyren," he called back, a look of query on his face, shining with the sweat of his effort.

"Come down. I need to speak with you," Tyren yelled up.

He watched the boy nod, and then, like one of the new Myrrh Monkeys, which Tyren had recently acquired at huge personal expense, Griff scampered down the creaking skeleton of struts that would soon be a tented wonderland of light and color, activity and fantasy.

He arrived, breathing hard from all his exertions. "You wanted to see me, Master Tyren," Griff said, wiping dusty hands against his working clothes, his sleeve a convenient cloth to mop the beads of sweat from his forehead.

Tyren nodded. "Yes, it's about—"

"It's just that I like what I do, Master Tyren. It's quiet up there, and hard work, so it keeps my mind blank—" His outpouring of rushed words stopped abruptly.

Tyren frowned. This was precisely why Griffin would never amount to much more than a lackey. The boy was feeble-minded, he was sure of it. Always prattling on about keeping his mind quiet or not being able to stand the noise in his head. "But you don't even know what I've called you for," he said.

"I know you want to take me off the Grand Beracca and give me a new task."

Another of Griffin's quirks was his strange ability to guess what someone else might be about to do or say. The three brothers had been with the traveling show for a few moons, but Tyren had become aware of the boy's uncanny ability only recently, when some of the other showfolk had grumbled about it. He decided to test this curious skill that others claimed the boy appeared to possess.

"Well, that's right. I need you to help Chauncey with the new act. One that needs very special handling."

"What is the act?" Griff asked, and then answered for himself. "Oh, enchanted creatures," he said suddenly, his brow creasing.

Tyren stared at the dark-haired boy in amazement. "Now, that's a secret, Griff. Who told you about it?" Tyren was irritated that this guarded information had been leaked to the general gypsy folk. If a mere grunter knew, then surely everyone did. Although they were a relatively close community, these people worked for Tyren and he had to ensure that respect for the chain of command existed. He was the boss, after all, the man who paid their wages and took all the risks. He glared at Griff. "Well? Who else knows?"

Griff suddenly looked awkward. "Er, no one, Master Tyren. I don't think so, anyway."

"To my knowledge, only three people know. I am one of them, but you are not. That means Chauncey or Jasper is the culprit. I'll be talking to them," Tyren blustered, his face coloring with his rising irritation.

"Master Tyren, no!" Griff cried. "I mean, sir, it's not either of them. They haven't said anything."

"Then how do you know?" The large man's eyes narrowed. "Have you been spying?"

Griff shook his head.

Now Tyren's plump cheeks wobbled as he shook his own head with growing exasperation. "Eavesdropping, then? I'll cut an ear off for that."

"No, Master Tyren. I promise you."

The master of the Traveling Show straightened, puffing out his vast chest. "Then, Griffin, unless you tell me how you know such a thing, I'll have no option but to punish others on the suspicion that they have been spreading my private affairs when they should know better. Rules are rules, boy. I make them to keep control or the whole show will suffer."

Griff looked beaten. "They haven't said a word, sir. I'll tell you how I know, but you won't believe me."

"Try me, boy." Tyren's anger was cooling, replaced by confusion. "Are you protecting someone?"

This was met by silence and another shake of the head. "Not someone," he murmured.

"Then what?" Tyren demanded.

"I hear things," Griff mumbled.

"As I thought, eavesdropping and—"

"No, Master Tyren," the boy interrupted. "Forgive me," he said, lowering his voice and eyes. "I don't listen in on conversations. I hear thoughts." He kicked at a pebble, and the showmaster could see the frustration of that action.

Tyren looked at the gangly child quizzically. "I don't understand. What do you mean, you 'hear thoughts'?"

Griff shrugged. "Exactly that. I don't mean to and I don't want to. But I hear them all the same."

4

"So you can hear my thoughts?"

"Sometimes. I . . . I do try to block it out, stay busy, get as far away from people as possible so I don't have to listen."

Tyren couldn't believe what he was hearing. "So what am I thinking now? I'll concentrate on something particular," he challenged, looking up and across the field where the Traveling Show was sprawling as it was set up for the performances that would take place the following day.

Griff's mouth twisted. "That you wish Madam Tyren weren't wearing that see-through dress today because it shows how big her backside is."

Tyren took a step back, his hand lifting from his side, ready to give the upstart a clout for mentioning his wife's rear, but shock prevented him from making any further move. He gasped. "How did you do that?"

Griff shrugged again. "I don't know, sir. It's an affliction. I wish it would go or I could heal myself of it. But I'm cursed with it."

"You mean you can do this all the time?"

The boy nodded miserably. "I've learned to put up walls in my mind and to ignore it, but sometimes people's worries or anger, their sorrow or even happiness, can bubble through very strongly and I can't help but hear their thoughts." He looked anxiously at the showman. "That's why I love my work, Master Tyren. Up there on the scaffold I can distance myself from people. It helps. It doesn't stop it, but it makes it easier for me to be distracted. Concentrating on not falling off keeps my mind away from other people's thoughts."

Tyren just stared at the boy, perplexed and confused by the suggestion that such a talent existed, but also slightly excited by what he was hearing. "People have complained." It was all he could think to say as his mind began to rush in various directions.

Griff looked apologetic. "I've done my best to hide it since we joined the traveling show, sir. Sometimes I forget and things slip out. I . . . I shall be more careful, I promise."

"Just let me understand this correctly now, young man. You can hear what people think?"

Griff nodded. "Not everything, Master Tyren. Only thoughts that they're casting out, er . . . things that they feel strongly about."

"I still don't understand," Tyren said, shaking his head.

Griff's expression became earnest. "Well, there is deliberate thought, I suppose, and then there's just random thought that has no real purpose."

"Oh, so I was deliberately looking at my wife's backside and thinking how big it looked so obviously that you could hear it."

"Exactly," Griff said, grinning. "And you were concentrating on that thought. But if you walked beneath the scaffolding and were simply thinking that you must remember to remind Jasper to do something or that you were thirsty, I don't tend to hear those things."

"Only important thoughts, then?"

"Well, you could see it that way, but"—Griff shrugged—"I think of it as more forceful thoughts. Rather than the endless stream that we all have each day, such as it may rain today, I feel a bit cold, I wish we weren't performing tonight—that sort of thing—I hear the thoughts that are worrying people or seem to be occupying them."

"How fascinating," the showman said, twirling the waxed tips of his long, luxuriant mustache.

"You won't tell anyone, will you, Master Tyren? Our secret, all right? I give you my word that I will never use it against anyone."

Tyren's eyes narrowed and an idea formed in his mind as he watched the anxious boy shifting from foot to foot. "Fine, Griff. Don't worry. Our secret. Now go and see Chauncey. The new act arrived this morning—the creatures are jumpy and their owner is grumpy. I've picked you—you're about her age—to help settle her nerves and help Chauncey secure the beasts, that sort of thing. Run along, lad," he said, the new act forgotten for the time being as another one began to coalesce in his thoughts. It was priceless. He could make so much money!

Griff leaped to his task, clearly glad to be let off the hook. "Thank you, Master Tyren. I won't let you down, sir."

"No, I'm sure you won't, young man," Tyren agreed. He turned away and muttered beneath his breath, "In fact, you may be the answer to my prayers."

Griff was angry with himself for slipping up with Master Tyren. He wondered what the repercussions might be for his error in revealing the truth. But the showmaster sounded genuine enough when he said he would keep Griff's secret. It was a curious skill he'd lived with since he was old enough to scamper unaided around his father and knew what the man was thinking before he said anything aloud to Griff or the twins. Phineas and Matthias weren't really twins. Phineas was older, but they looked so alike in height and coloring, even down to the freckles on their bright, open faces, that they passed as twins. Griff's dark looks were the opposite of theirs, and his father always said he looked like his mother. He was told she had died when he was born, so he had no memory of her and he noticed his father's mind closed like a vault whenever any of the boys mentioned their mother, Griff's looks or the day he was born.

When Master Tyren's Traveling Show had come to the town a day's ride from where they lived, the boys had badgered their father to take them to the Beracca. After much pleading by his three sons he had agreed, although it was Phineas and Matthias who had been mesmerized by the man with no legs, who got around on his fingers; and the amazing Swallowing Sweeney, who eased burning swords down his gullet, sometimes six and seven at a time. The blind woman whose empty eye sockets could still see the dead and terrified everyone in the tent was, nevertheless, no match for the Lizard Man, born with scales, or the performing dog with two heads. Griff had been dizzied by the smell of the oil lamps and so many people crammed into the tent. The aroma of hair oil mingled with perfume and sweat, soap and bad breath, liquor and the sweet lavender that the ladies waved beneath their noses. Far worse for Griff was the sense of being crowded by the audience's thoughts, which had assaulted him inside the vast tent. The showman's calls for talent had captured his elder brothers' attention, and once they'd displayed their extraordinary skills of strength, balance and bendy bodies, Master Tyren had made an offer of work that even their father could not fail to see was irresistible. What he perhaps hadn't anticipated was that Griff would also beg to be allowed to join his brothers. Tyren had welcomed the suggestion, for another working hand was well worth a couple of plates of food a day. In his mind Griff had heard his father's despair, although his father had simply nodded at Tyren and said it was entirely his boys' decision. He was no farmer or blacksmith who needed his sons: he made his income from falconry, breeding and training the hunting birds for local lords and nobles. Although his father kept it to himself, Griff heard his pride that his sons were being offered a way to earn their own income, but behind it lay the anguish that his family was being taken from him. Instead of voicing this, though, he had simply added, "The boys have to grow up and earn their keep sometime." Phineas and Matthias had whooped with delight at what sounded to them like the go-ahead, but Griff felt hollow. Nevertheless, he wanted to be like his brothers: to help his father and earn his keep, no matter how little his wages were. No one had bothered to correct Master Tyren's mistaken assumption that Phineas and Matthias were twins either, and so the Twisted Twins were born.

Griff sighed. The shows were everything to his brothers. It's how this small community of traveling folk existed. Each town looked forward to their arrival as the show passed up and down the realm of Drestonia. Right now they were headed east to west across the realm, leaving behind Griff's home on the rugged far mideastern coast for the soft scenic beauty of the west, almost at the capital, Floris. Griff couldn't imagine being in the city; in fact, this town of Tarrymonger was busy enough for his senses and yet Jasper had called it sleepy when they'd arrived, rolling into the main square with their brightly painted wagons and lots of noise and fanfare.

He wondered how things might change once Duke Janko

returned to the capital from the wars in the far north. Griff had no interest in politics, but he listened to the adults talking around the fires late at night and it seemed Tyren was concerned with Janko's presence in Floris. Only last night the showmaster had been bemoaning that the King's brother would likely threaten the peace and stability of the realm.

"He's the Duke! Why would his return create problems?" his wife had chided.

"Well, my dear, because not just I—but many of Drestonia's thinkers—believe that Janko has dreams of kingship."

"Rubbish!" Madam Tyren had countered. And other heads had nodded. "The man's a hero. He's been securing our northern borders for years. He should have statues carved in his likeness, festivals pronounced in his honor," she had carried on.

"I don't doubt it," Tyren had murmured sagely, taking a long suck on his babble pipe and allowing the smoke to drift slowly from the corner of his mouth. "But I still think he fancies himself as ruler, not just general of our army and servant to the King."

"But the King has an heir now. Janko has to accept that the boy is next in line," someone had commented.

"Acknowledge, perhaps," Tyren had said quietly, "but not necessarily accept. The son is now, what, around thirteen summers? They didn't expect him to live past his second. You'll recall whenever we passed through the capital we heard stories that he was a sickly infant, not that I've ever seen him. Have you?"

People around the fire shook their heads.

Tyren continued. "What's more, we never saw the Queen

during her pregnancy. We never saw the lad when he was born. They've been so careful with that boy."

"We haven't been to Floris in many years, Tyren. He could be a strapping lad by now," his wife said, reaching for the still-warm lekka biscuits, spiced with cinnamon. "Besides, we did hear that Her Majesty's confinement was touch and go. They didn't want to risk the child. The physicians thought it better to keep her still and not allow her out and about."

Tyren gave a sound of disgust. "It's all a bit strange, if you ask me."

"Oh, hush," his wife admonished. "We know the boy is hale and healthy now—it's half the reason we're appearing in the capital, isn't it? To celebrate his birthday?"

Tyren grunted. "Well, if he's all grown-up, then it's all the more reason for Janko to hate him."

"There's a darkness in his soul," Blind Pippin added, even though he hadn't been part of the conversation. "I sense it whenever we're in the north. I can feel that man's shadowy presence."

Madam Tyren snorted her disgust at this and several others around the fire clearly agreed.

But Griffin had stored away the blind old man's insights and paid careful attention to Master Tyren's warning. He himself had never even had Duke Janko's shadow cross his path, so he didn't consider himself a judge of the man. But the stories of his ferocious battle skills and courage were legendary in Drestonia. Griff wasn't sure he needed to meet any royalty anyway. He was happy with the simple life on the road, although he missed home deeply. Griff always dismissed thoughts of home before they could take hold and upset him.

It was best to forget the past, banish the memory of his father's sorrowful face when they had left him and to simply look forward—to try his utmost to enjoy this new life traveling the realm.

Tomorrow evening the performances at Tarrymonger would take place. Newcomers to Master Tyren's shows were never sure what to expect. This was not a circus, nor was it a fairground. The Marvels of Nature were essentially the curious oddities of life that people rarely got to view. He wondered about Tyren's new act that he was to help with and got a hurry on, keen to please the showmaster and secure their bargain, because the absolute last thing on earth Griff wanted was for his secret to get out.

2

L ute watched his mother's skirts billow in a circle as she swung around at her husband's suggestion. He had always enjoyed the rustle and swish of her silks and taffetas. It was the sound he associated with his beautiful mother, the Queen. He hadn't taken much active interest in the politics of the realm, but he liked to listen to his parents, and, as Pilo had counseled, the less he spoke and the more he listened, the more he learned. He bit silently into the juicy pinky-orange flesh of the garalba, its sweet fresh flavor exploding into his mouth.

"A hero's welcome?" Queen Miralda said, eyebrows arching with surprise.

Lute glanced toward his father, who shrugged. "Why not?"

The recently turned thirteen-year-old watched the Queen join the King at the window of the King's private salon. They both looked out across the city. Lute wondered if they'd forgotten he was there, curled up on a soft chair. Unlikely, he decided, but he had worked out long ago that to be still and relatively quiet meant that he could linger longer amongst the adults.

He knew the scene that his parents looked down upon very well indeed, having stared out of the same window every day since he was old enough to stand. He loved his father's private salon and didn't need to join his parents to know that right now they had a wonderful vantage from on high and could look straight down the long, wide street all the way to the grand royal fountain a full mile away. He also knew that, at this moment, the street was lined on either side with crowds of Florians, eager to glimpse their brave general—Lute's uncle—and his triumphant return to the capital.

"It's the least I can do under the circumstances," King Rodin added, putting his arm around his wife. "Janko is a hero. He's quashed every rebellion that the mountain horde has thrown at us. They may not fear our army, testing it at every turn, but they fear Janko and his reprisals."

"Are you sure his brutality is always the answer?" Miralda questioned gently, leaning against the King's broad shoulder.

"Diplomacy has failed me, my love. That old rogue King Besler clearly has nothing better to do with his time than sacrifice his young men in pointless war with us. Janko's got every pass through the mountains covered. Besler should have taken my offer last time. It was a good bargain for his people. Now he makes a bitter enemy of us."

"But Janko's so ruthless, Rodin. Why does he have to fling healthy young men off the mountains, for instance?"

Lute's attention was riveted. Suddenly the fruit and his vague thoughts held little interest in comparison to what his parents were discussing. He began to believe that maybe this time they had forgotten his presence, to be talking this openly.

"He has to kill them, my love, because those young men want to see me dead. They want to overrun our realm and claim Floris as their own. It's us or them."

Miralda sighed and turned her head slightly, and now Lute knew she stared out across the magnificent lush gardens of the palace and further—to the fountains where dragons spouted water in which the children of Floris loved to play. "But what if it were our son, Rodin? What if it were Lute? Could you condone such murder, then? It's your mercy that people will remember your reign for, not Janko your henchman and his cruel lessons. I'm just so glad that our land permits a child—blood kin or otherwise—to be lawfully deemed your heir."

Lute was now convinced. They *had* overlooked that he was in the room, although he had always known of his mother's displeasure of Janko as an heir. Perhaps his parents should have had several children, or even adopted them, because the realm permitted any named child of the sovereign to be considered an heir to the throne. He felt suddenly embarrassed, rose from the chair he'd been reclining in and tiptoed across the salon. He glanced behind and was pleased to see they had not noticed him. He stood at the room's entrance, not wanting to intrude but too curious now to leave the conversation entirely. On an impulse he hid in the hallway but peeped from behind the doorway.

He watched his father kiss his mother's hair and knew how sweet it smelled. "Lute is thirteen summers, Miralda. I think you worry too much over that boy." The King stole a glance behind him, as though checking no one was listening.

His mother's face creased into a frown. "You know why I am so protective, Rodin."

"Of course I do. Lute's situation is made all the more fragile because of our secret."

It was Lute's turn to frown. His mother covered her husband's mouth with her hand. "Hush, Rodin. We agreed never to speak of it openly."

The King sighed. "I just want to assure you that I do understand, no matter how distant I seem sometimes, and that he will not be involved in war, I promise."

Lute bit his lip as he considered what his father had just said. What could he have meant about Lute being fragile? And a secret? What secret? His mother's response dragged his attention back.

"And in a few years Lute will be sixteen summers, the very age of the young men that Janko considers it perfectly fine to execute in such barbaric style."

"They are soldiers."

"They are boys!" she beseeched. "When Lute comes of age—and that's only one more summer away—he will become an honorary member of our army. His head's already full of weaponry and combat."

"Like any boy," Rodin reminded her. "I'm glad he's a strong youth now."

Lute's frown deepened when he heard his father admit his early frailty.

"Lute *was* fragile, but that's all changed now." Rodin nodded his agreement as Miralda continued. "He considers himself invincible."

"I'm proud of him."

Lute felt a spike of pleasure to learn this.

"But he is technically a soldier of your army from next summer," his mother countered. "And say he were to be captured by your enemy, you would expect him to be ransomed, am I right?"

"It's the honorable way. It's how all royals are treated."

"Well, don't be too sure of Janko. If Besler captures him, I hope you don't expect any compassion."

"It's not compassion, Miralda; it's just how it's done. No royalty is squandered. Captors simply make money from royal captives, and I would pay anything they asked for Lute—does that reassure you?"

"No. Because he is still just a young man. You're missing my point. He's no different from any other boy who is being flung off those escarpments. We have to remember that although Besler is our enemy, his men are simply following their king's orders."

Rodin sighed. "We could argue this all day—it is a matter of principle. There is no right or wrong. It's just how war is handled, my love."

Lute watched his mother round on his father and grab his shoulders. "But you can change it," she begged. "You can order Janko—"

"No!" The King shook his head. "He is in charge of our army and our security. Believe me, you would not enjoy life if Besler were the emperor he dreams of being."

"And you're comfortable about Stalkers roaming the realm? They were Janko's idea as well."

"They're our domestic law enforcers."

Miralda gave him an arch look. "They follow their own

law, Rodin. You yourself have said that you don't like them having so much freedom. You said you'd talk to him."

"And I will! Now, Miralda, this is state business and I will raise it with my brother when I see him. No, I don't like the Stalkers having so much freedom but when they were initiated they had a strict purpose. Janko had good reason to ensure we had some sort of domestic law enforcement. I suspect, with him away, their leader has probably allowed his own enthusiasm to take control."

"Then order them to stand down, Rodin! You're king!"

"I will not usurp my brother's role. Miralda, we are very close in age, Janko and I. But for a year or so he would have been king. I am sensitive to this. We complement each other well. The Stalkers originated through good sense and it was a clever idea of Janko's. It's all part of our realm's progress. It is his duty, his responsibility to rein them back in if they're not following his strict orders. I don't feel it's right for me to step across his area of supervision, which is the security of our realm."

"They are bullies, Rodin. That's what I'm hearing, anyway."

"And I'm sure everything you hear is very reliable, Miralda," Rodin replied, unable to fully disguise his sarcasm. "Let it be. I will discuss the Stalkers with Janko at the right time in the right setting. The day of his homecoming after years of being away at war is not that time."

The Queen gave Rodin a sad look and pulled away from him.

"Don't be like this," the King cajoled gently. "He's coming home today. I'd like us to welcome him together. We are family, after all."

"He is your family, Rodin. Not mine—not in my heart, anyway," the Queen said bitterly. "But I shall be at your side as you wish."

"Make sure Lute is present also," the King said, running out of patience. There was no mistaking his tone.

"Janko does not like Lute."

At this admission Lute's eyes narrowed. He had forgotten about the hunting incident but he felt sure the Duke had caused the horse to bolt. As if she could hear his thoughts, Miralda added, "Did you not notice how rough Janko was with Lute when he was really young? He was barely out of infancy but he was left bruised and screaming, you may recall, although your brother claimed he'd just been playing with him." Miralda gave a loud snort of disgust. "I'm not sure Lute remembers but he certainly didn't go near Janko for the rest of his visit."

"But Janko doesn't understand children, not being a father," said Rodin, moving away from the window.

"But there's more to this," Miralda said tartly. "You've forgotten the hunting accident."

Lute watched the King purse his lips before he spoke again. "Lute doesn't know his uncle very well at all. This is an opportunity for them to get closer. You three are all I have. I'd like to think we can all get on."

Miralda switched topics. Lute knew his mother tended to do this whenever she felt beaten in any discussion. She flicked at some lint on her clothes as she spoke casually. "I'd hoped we'd have discussed the betrothal to the young Lady Ara by now."

"Yes, forgive me, I have not paid it sufficient attention, but you know I have had war on my mind."

Miralda persisted. "You know why I want that marriage promise sealed. Lute and Ara are very suited. It is especially comforting to me that they like each other so much. We have only one son. I want him to be happy but I also want his line to the throne secure. A betrothal helps."

Betrothal? Marriage! Ugh, Lute thought. That was the last thing he wanted to listen to them talk about. He had liked Ara very much on the two occasions they'd met, but he had plenty to do before he wanted his mother pushing him into marrying the young princess of a distant realm. He wondered why the Queen was so insistent but his query was answered immediately by his father.

"Because it threatens Janko with heirs, you mean?"

Miralda looked abashed. Lute knew his father was right, just by the expression on his mother's face. Still she pressed ahead. "It secures the line, Rodin—the *right* line."

The King nodded. "Just make sure Lute is there to greet his uncle with all the other noble well-wishers."

Lute pursed his lips. He had different ideas.

The atmosphere on the streets of Floris was akin to a festival. King Rodin had already declared it a public holiday and ordered Crown coffers to provide a quart of ale for each adult, and the palace had organized vast amounts of food to be cooked in all the local inns and eating houses at its expense. None of Rodin's people would go hungry tonight in this city. The revelers were already in high spirits and people lined the main thoroughfare leading to the palace and waved purple-and-green squares of fabric—the royal colors.

Lute, entranced by the festivity, had been careful to grab a couple of the linen squares that were freely available to the city folk; there was no doubt that his father was making the long-awaited return of the Duke as triumphant and as splendid as possible.

Getting out of the palace had been easier than he'd anticipated. Guilt-ridden that he'd stolen a jacket from one of the stableboys, he'd left a silver frenk in its place to more than cover the loss. It was his best intention to return it surreptitiously, but in case he couldn't, he felt better for leaving payment. Unless he counted the honey cakes he regularly removed with uncannily light fingers from the kitchens, he had never stolen anything before. But this was an exceptional occasion. Lute wanted to see his famous uncle before he was properly reacquainted with him in the more formal atmosphere of the palace. As it was, the tension was obvious between his parents over the Duke's victorious return. His mother clearly disliked Janko, while his father revered him. Family sensitivity and her own good grace prevented his mother from coming right out and saying that she didn't want her son around the Duke, Lute realized. In contrast it appeared his father couldn't wait to get nephew and uncle together again. Lute didn't know what to think; he trusted both his parents, but as they were so divided on this issue, he was determined to work out the Duke for himself.

He had been tempted to discuss it with Pilo, his guardian, although "guard" might be a better way to describe him, Lute thought as he wended his way through the happy mob. He loved Pilo, who was, if Lute was very honest, more of a father to him than was his own. He shared the King with an entire realm, and Rodin was often away. Even when he was at home, he appeared distracted, almost absent. The only person who could hold Rodin's attention from matters of state for any length of time was Lute's mother. He tried to imagine how the Duke felt about being the younger son, by only a year. Lute would have loved a brother but he was intelligent enough to understand that Janko might well feel competitive toward Rodin, who was, his mother had once mentioned, just eleven moons older. He remembered how she'd arched an eyebrow when she'd said it because eleven was a superstitious number in Floris. It was said to hold bad luck and it was another reason Miralda was suspicious of the man. The number was significant. Mothers became smotheringly protective of their children during the moons between turning eleven and reaching twelve. Lute could remember how ferociously careful the Queen had become when he was living through that time. In fact, that was really when Pilo became so important in his life.

"Get off, lad!" a large woman groaned, and gave him a shove; she grimaced, pointing at her big toe.

"Sorry," he said, shocked by being pushed around, stopping himself from adding "madam," or even saying "Please excuse me" or any other overly gracious statement. He might be the Crown Prince but right now he was simply a boy in the crowd. Pilo's head would start to spin on the spot if he knew where Lute was right now. It made Lute inwardly grin just thinking about it—the heavens had granted him a wonderful opportunity for escape. His mother had summoned Pilo when he and Lute were on their way out for some horse-riding practice. Pilo was training Lute on how to take his filly up to a full gallop over rough terrain. They'd been practicing this for so many days now he'd lost count, but Pilo was determined that the Prince be not just proficient but an expert in the saddle from a young age. And so, while Pilo could hardly fail to answer the Queen's summons, and thought Lute was saddling up to take a more sedate ride within palace grounds, Lute had deliberately dirtied his shirt, ripped a couple of holes in his riding breeches, made sure he'd worn his muddiest boots, stolen the grubby jacket that was a fraction too large for him and pulled on an old cap he also found in the stables. He could pass for a commoner if he kept his language simple and his good grooming hidden.

He glanced behind himself again. The woman was still scowling but she'd forgotten about him already, he was relieved to note. He pushed on, deeper into the crowd and closer to the front so he could get a look at the Duke when he made his spectacular arrival in this adoring city.

For the next hour Lute had to cool his heels. He killed the time by joining in the merrymaking as best he could without being found out as an interloper, and at one point even joined in a jig with a few of the young men, who were trying to impress the girls with their fancy footwork. He knew the formal steps of the Terillo backward and forward but pretended to be as clumsy as the other boys. He enjoyed the easy camaraderie and the laughter and clapping. Plus he could hardly fail to notice one girl, who smiled just for him, right at him! . . . he was sure of it.

But with the dancing finished for now and the pretty girl gone at the call of her mother, and despite the general frivolity still bubbling around him, Lute was becoming increasingly anxious about the length of time he'd been gone. Pilo was a man of few words and always calm, but Lute could imagine both of those qualities he admired so much about his guardian would disappear once Pilo discovered Lute's absence . . . and the lie.

"He's coming!" someone suddenly yelled, diverting Lute's attention, and the crowd erupted into mad cheering.

Lute couldn't see much. He wasn't at the front and there was no way of pushing through any further. He'd just have to wait until his heroic uncle passed by and hope to catch a glimpse. Everyone was waving their colors, and a man not far away from where Lute struggled to remain upright began a rousing chorus of the royal anthem. Before long all were joining in. It was so stirring to hear his people singing their realm's special song with such gusto and joy that Lute felt his breath catch with pride. If only his father could be here with him now to witness this. In fact, he promised himself that when he next got the chance, he would talk to his father about perhaps doing some royal "walks," as some of the neighboring realms called it. It was becoming increasingly fashionable with the various royal families to be more accessible by touring amidst their people at far closer range than ever before.

He could just glimpse the horses of the army in the distance. He felt the excitement level lift around him and Lute was carried along on it—suddenly he was just as eager to see the great, courageous leader of the army enjoy an uproarious welcome home.

Finally, the Duke drew close and Lute could see him. He looked so much like Lute's father in his features and yet he was broader, sat taller in his saddle and was leaner, perhaps meaner, in his countenance. But it was the mouth that brought Lute the most surprise. Where Rodin's smile was all radiance and joy, there was something about Janko's smile, so achingly similar, that rang false. To Lute—who knew that expression so well—it was definitely not real. There was none of the sun in Janko's smile. In fact, the smile struck Lute as being cold, almost wintry.

As the Duke drew level with Lute's part of the crowd, the people surged forward in adoring fashion and Lute lost his balance. He was pushed ahead by the swarm and before he knew it he was sprawled on the dust and the Duke's horse reared. Lute fully anticipated the crunch of the animal's hooves somewhere on his body and instinctively covered his head with his hands, but it seemed the expert skills of the Duke guided the horse away from him.

"What the—" he heard someone roar close by, presumably the Duke himself. "Get him away from here" came next and Lute felt himself hauled up and literally dragged back into the crowd. His uncle didn't look back, but with his face in profile, Lute saw the same fake smile frozen in place.

"All right, boy?" a man asked, dusting Lute off. "Nothing hurt?"

Lute knew that voice. His head snapped up in an instant and he was staring into a face he knew all too well.

"I'm old, not senile," the man said in response to Lute's shocked silence.

Lute opened his mouth to speak but the man held a finger up. "Not now. Come on," he said, and grabbed Lute by the sleeve.

They walked but said nothing, shouldering their way out to where the crowd thinned. Now that the Duke had passed by, most people had turned their attention to the celebrations and feasting anyway, so they went unnoticed.

"I'm sorry, Pilo," Lute finally said.

"I'm sure you are. You certainly should be."

"I just wanted to see him."

"You're due to meet him shortly. Why the hurry?"

Lute shrugged. It did seem rather pointless all of a sudden. "I don't know, I wanted to see him alone and not in a formal situation. My mother's creating such tension around his homecoming that I know it's going to be all stiff and difficult when I meet him."

His guardian stared ahead, his stride long, his strong jaw clenched. Lute knew Pilo, always so careful to shield his emotions, was disturbed. Anything could have happened in the crowd, he realized. He felt immediately ashamed of his reckless behavior. "Mother seems to hate him," he added, the memory of his uncle's cold expression fresh in his mind.

"No doubt your mother has her reasons," Pilo replied.

"Well, what are they?"

"You should ask the Queen. I am not privy to her innermost thoughts."

"She shares plenty of them with you."

"Yes, like how good-looking you are, how well you sit your horse, how tall you are suddenly, how—"

"Oh, stop, that's not fair."

"Isn't it? Your parents have put in place measures to keep you safe, Lute. They're not doing that for fun. One of those things in place is me. I'm disappointed you made the choice you did today. It could have ended badly."

"But it didn't!" Lute argued, knowing Pilo was completely

entitled to be angry but feeling obliged to make a stand for his decision. He was tired of the adults always making all of his decisions.

"Right," Pilo said sarcastically. "I suppose being trampled by a horse is inconsequential. Apologies, Majesty."

"I wasn't even nearly trampled," Lute replied, his tone sour.

"You weren't watching. You were rightly cowering. And if not for the Duke's speed and agility and fine horsemanship, you might well be lying in the street with a broken head right now."

Lute's mouth twisted at the reprimand. He kept it shut. He knew that was the best decision he'd made today. They strode on in silence until they were nearly at the palace, no doubt easily reaching it before Janko's entourage, because Pilo had led them around the shorter back way.

Lute paused. "How did you know?"

Pilo turned back to face him. He sighed. "I have eyes everywhere, Lute, especially for you. You've got to understand that the only heir to the throne is never going to be without companions, shall we say."

"You had me followed?" Lute asked indignantly, moving again and pushing through one of the smaller gates. In his irritation he inadvertently ignored the guards, who, suddenly realizing who was moving past them, bowed.

Pilo's nod acknowledged the men for both of them. "I just had someone keep an eye on you. There's no saying what mischief a thirteen-year-old boy—who spends all of his time being told what to do—will get up to when left to his own devices."

Lute stole a glance at Pilo and realized the man was wearing a soft grin. He was relieved and it was time to be mature rather than keep arguing. "I'm sorry again."

"I know you are. You forget, I was thirteen once; so was your father. And he knows better than most what it is to be groomed for kingship, the restraints and the constant monitoring that goes on. I understand, Prince Lute, really I do, but this is your life. You must accept your responsibilities. You will never be alone—much as you crave it. The royal title demands that you are always carefully guarded." He frowned. "That surely isn't your jacket?"

"No, I think it's Berk's," Lute replied, embarrassed.

"Then return it. I'll see you upstairs, and be quick. Your parents want you present to greet your uncle. Hurry."

Lute nodded and watched Pilo disappear into the palace, his long legs covering the distance across the bailey with ease. He sighed. His adventure was over but the taste of freedom had been fun while it lasted. As he trudged toward the stables, he wondered when he'd ever taste such delicious freedom again.

The bailey was brimming with men. It seemed Duke Janko's party had arrived. Lute knew his uncle would still be moving through the welcome delegation, including the mayor and endless dignitaries whose hands he would need to shake. Lute wondered how that smile of his uncle's would hold up. He frowned as he remembered its hollowness. He heard a few of the newly arrived men talking; they were senior officers, from what he could tell from their uniforms.

". . . and said he can't wait to be getting on with the matter at hand," one man said.

"Plenty of time for that. I thought he'd revel in all of this attention," his companion replied. "You, boy!"

Lute froze. He turned slightly to regard the two officers.

"Yes, you!" The man pointed. "Hurry up when I call you, boy."

Lute was trapped. He walked over, keeping his eyes lowered. "Er, yes, sir?" he asked, unused to those words rolling off his tongue.

"Where are you headed?"

Lute put on his best stableboy brogue. "The stables, sir."

"Thought so. Take this horse, will you. I think he's got a stone trapped in his shoe. Have the stable master sort it out and be readied in a few hours."

Lute pulled at his cap and took the reins. "Yes, sir."

"And have the saddle oiled," the man growled as Lute began turning the horse. He didn't wait for Lute's reply. "What were we saying?" he said to the other officers.

"Well, it's true, anyone would love the attention but Janko hates his brother, you know that. He wants to get it over and done with" was all Lute heard as he led the horse away, stunned.

3

Griff ran across the main staging areas. The activity felt frantic as people made their preparations for the first performance in years in this region. Griff loved the color of the Traveling Show. Life had been tough for a lot of the inhabitants from around these parts—in fact, it was the crop failure of the past two seasons that had encouraged the show not to do the vast journey from east to west—but this year it was different. Griff had heard the showfolk talking excitedly about this being a bumper year for crops and the whole realm was feeling brighter. Master Tyren had nevertheless taken the precaution of basing the show at Tarrymonger, which meant he could lure the country people but also pull some good audiences out of the capital—they were so close now to Floris. In the capital city, of course, they would settle down and run nightly performances for perhaps two moons.

"Ho, Griff," someone called.

He slowed his trot to a stride and looked over to see Jeb with his flock of rare pufferbirds. Most people would never have seen one of the birds, whose lives could be measured in moons rather than years. The man had raised most of the now-trained troupe from newly hatched bappies and Jeb was very proud of the pale rainbow colors of his flock, which now numbered at least thirty, Griff was sure.

"Ho, Jeb. How's Horis?"

"He's better. That little welt on his beak has healed and all his feathers are back."

"Any new chicks?"

"Another batch soon, I reckon. Any day now."

"And another year of training," Griff finished, and Jeb grinned.

"I've got a new trick. Tell me what you think."

Griff paused. "All right." He was in a hurry but Jeb was a nice old man, one of the few people in the Traveling Show, Griff had decided, who cared about giving the audience the best performance every time he took to the ring. Some of the others only cared about the takings for the day.

Jeb gave a command to the babbling birds and they all blew up into their full puffed size on cue, then lifted as one to settle on Jeb's head. He looked like he was wearing a bonnet of fluffy feathers. And then they sang.

Griff laughed. "The audience, especially the children, will love it, Jeb."

Jeb's chest swelled. "Ah, you're too kind, young Griff. Glad you like it but I see you're in a hurry."

"I am a bit, sorry to rush off."

"Go, go." Jeb flapped at him, looking much like a puffer-bird himself.

Griff trotted off, resisting the aroma of freshly brewed

keraff and the smell of newly baked bread that instantly caused his belly to rumble. It wasn't even nearly noon and he felt famished. It would have to wait. He ran by the dining tent and saw cook Gwen already ladling out bowls of steaming soup to hungry grunters like him, who had been up before dawn to start erecting the Beracca. Although theirs was the lowliest of work, it was the hardest, most demanding of all. It was also the most invisible—no one paid much attention to the grunting team. Without it there would be no colorful, amazing Traveling Show . . . yet few stopped to acknowledge or praise them for their efforts.

He shrugged off that gripe as he saw Chauncey in the near distance, directing the unloading of crates. Strange, unhappy sounds emanated from the timber-slatted boxes.

"Master Tyren asked me to help with the setup of the new act," he said as Chauncey wiped his lips from swigging a cup of water from a nearby pail. "Did you want me to help with the unloading, Chauncey?"

The man grimaced. And they both looked toward where the loudest howling was coming from. "No."

"What's in there?" Griff asked, unable to contain his curiosity any longer.

"It's a centaur."

"What?"

Chauncey nodded smugly. "Didn't think they existed, did you?"

Griff shook his head, openmouthed.

"You'll be even more surprised when you see all the other new creatures we've got in. Hurry up, though, lad. Their owner's over there. We've given her Ilbo's old place."

"Her?"

"Her name's Tess. She's your age and Madam Tyren thought your quieter manner would suit her. She's a bit of a strange one, I'm told. You're to be a friend to her until she settles in."

"Don't you think Abby or one of the other girls in the show would—"

"They're all too old to be bothered with her. She needs someone her own age. You're it."

Griff nodded unhappily and, glancing again at the crate where a doleful whine had now cranked up, he moved toward the blue-painted wagon where Ilbo the Hairy Man had been accommodated. He had died quietly in his sleep on the night of the last full moon, and not only had it upset all the show-folk but Tyren had lost one of his most popular acts.

Griff knocked gently on the door.

"Who is it?" demanded a female voice.

"My name's Griff, I've been—"

The door was flung open and he was confronted by a girl, smaller and much skinnier than himself, with golden hair, slightly sun-browned skin and a sprinkling of freckles across her nose. Her large gray-green eyes regarded him with interest. "You've been sent to mind me, have you?" She sounded hostile.

Griff didn't answer immediately, entranced by the partially striped, hissing creature in her arms.

"Is that a veercat?" he asked, his tone filled with awe. He wanted to stroke its light-red fur but it gave him a look of warning. "I saw one once," he continued, his fingers twitching to touch it. "A black one. My brothers never believed me. They say veercats are just myth."

"Well, they're not." Her tone had softened. "Tell your

brothers you've just seen your second veercat and the rarest kind, the red one."

Griff shook his head with wonder. "Can I see his wings?"

He sensed she was warming to him. The girl, who had soothed the veercat's surprise at Griff's arrival, stretched out the animal's shiny, almost transparent wings, revealing the patterned network of dark, threadlike veins. "They don't fly, you know," she said. "They glide."

"Like bats?"

"Better than bats. But they are related to the winged dragoncats. And those do fly."

"You've seen one?" Griff asked, incredulous.

She grinned at his eagerness but then sighed. "No. But I know a few still exist. I want to find one." She stepped back. "I'm Tess. I suppose you want to come in."

Griff followed her, closing the door gently behind him. He wasn't sure what he was meant to do but Chauncey had urged him to be the girl's friend. He looked around, desperate to find something meaningful to say. "Would you like me to open the windows?" He felt stupid for asking. If she'd wanted the windows open, surely she'd already have done so.

But Tess didn't dismiss him. Instead, she shook her head gently, her mouth twisting in concern. "Not immediately. Rix is not comfortable here yet," she said, stroking the cat's dark, striped tail. "He might make a dash for the woods." As if to reinforce his determination to flee, Rix's catlike whiskers twitched and his pointed feline face looked as though it was gathering up its features to snarl.

Griff looked over at Rix, noticing the veercat's huge pointed ears—the same striped dark color of his tail—erect and moving to catch every sound they could. "He seems happy."

She cocked her head to one side. "What did they tell you about me?"

He shrugged. "That you're a bit strange."

Tess grinned but Griff saw the sadness in it. "I am. Like my animals. I like your honesty. I don't trust people."

"Caution around strangers is wise. But I won't hurt you, Tess."

"But you're here to spy on me?"

His shoulders dropped slightly in resignation. "They want me to keep an eye on you, but"—he shrugged—"no, I won't spy on you. I would like to help you to be happy amongst us."

"Well, I'm not sure I could ever be happy cooped up here."

Griff looked around. "You know, if we set to and painted these walls a lighter color, it would feel bigger, less gloomy," he said. "I'll do it for you."

"That's kind, Griff. But it's not that. I'm just not sure I want to do this."

"The Traveling Show, do you mean?"

She put Rix down and the veercat immediately scurried beneath a low bench seat and into the shadows.

"I was living in a hut in the Night Forest on—"

"The Night Forest," Griff murmured, impressed. "We lived about six miles from its eastern rim. People were scared of it."

Tess made a soft sound of disgust, but she looked intrigued by him, too. "I lived there for years."

"Alone?"

Griff saw her lips purse.

35

"No, with my sister. But she died of the wasting fever. I was all right to live alone but I got careless and people saw me, saw Rix. They began to talk. They became scared and suspicious. Before long the Stalkers came looking."

"Stalkers!" he repeated. "Gosh! What a life you've lived. Weren't you scared?"

She nodded. "They're vile, just big bullies, really, in red gloves and black capes."

Griff smiled. He admired her pluck and suspected it showed. He'd heard about the cruel Stalkers and their sinister, threatening ways. "So what happened?" he asked.

"I was lucky." She shrugged, opening a canister that let out a pleasant, delicious fragrance. She brought the tin to her nose and inhaled before she continued, closing her eyes just for a second as she enjoyed the aroma. "Master Tyren got to them before I was carted off to the city orphanage. I think I would rather die than live there."

"Why, Tess? You'd have had a place to sleep, friends, regular food."

"That's just a polite way of describing what is, essentially, prison. There would be rules. Grown-up rules. And probably loads of chores. Anyway, none of that matters because I can't live without my creatures. They're my friends. They're my family. We protect each other, always have."

"Family is important."

She smiled. "Thank you for seeing them that way. Do you want some phelan tea?"

He nodded, though he had no idea what it was. "How many creature friends do you have?"

"Dozens," she said, busying herself with the task of brewing tea. "The water in this pot is already boiled," she explained, "so your timing was perfect. I carry my own leaves—I dry them myself," she continued, digging a wooden spoon into her tin.

"So Master Tyren saved you, is that right?"

She spooned dried leaves into a pot.

"Yes, he offered me a chance to travel with all of you."

"And what do you do in return?"

Her face creased into a frown. "Well, I'm not happy about it but it was the best solution. I have to show off my creatures. Master Tyren said most people have never seen a veercat or a centaur before."

"He's right. What else have you brought?"

Tess poured hot water over the leaves. "I'll just let that draw for a minute. Um, well, there's Rix. Davren, my young centaur, of course. Then there's Elph, the sagar, and Helys, my tiny califa. She won't grow much bigger. I might be able to persuade Gaston to make an appearance but he is contrary," she said, twisting the pot and sniffing its vapors. "Ah, lovely, almost ready."

"Who is Gaston?"

She laughed. "He's a gryphon. But he's always cranky and the horses would revolt if they got even the vaguest hint that he was around."

"I've heard of the others, but what's a gryphon?"

"Your namesake! Gaston is half beast, half bird. Body of a lion and the head, wings and claws of an eagle. And he's black and terrifying. He lives in the mountains in the northwest but visited me in the forest now and then."

Griff's eyes had got rounder and wider as she'd explained.

Now his jaw dropped. "Visited you?" Griff exclaimed, taking the mug of tea she offered him. "Why?"

"I told you. We're friends."

"How?"

Tess fell silent.

Griff sipped the hot tea, blowing on it first. The silence lengthened, and Griff sensed it might feel awkward for Tess, so he filled it with chatter. "I taste flowers, perhaps some bark. There's a grassy flavor, too."

She looked up, surprised, and seemed to warm still further to him. "Well done. Most people can't taste the bark or the grasses."

"It's delicious," he said, telling the truth. He had never tasted finer tea.

She smiled. They fell silent again.

"Tess. I know," Griff finally said.

"What do you know?" she mumbled, frowning.

"I know that you can talk to the creatures. That you can summon them and that they trust you completely although they don't trust any other humans."

She glared at him. Her suspicions were back and on full alert. "Well, I suppose Master Tyren would tell—"

Griff continued as though she hadn't spoken. "I know how you battled to save your sister's life. And that when she took her last breath all the creatures who love you came to pay their respects as you buried her. I know where she is buried; I can see the clearing and how at midday the sunlight filters through the leaves and lights her grave as though our god, Lo, himself is smiling upon her. I know that you wish you could be there right now with some flowers."

Tess sucked in an angry breath. "How do you know any

of this?" she demanded. "No one was there but me. I dug the grave, I wrapped her in cloth and I buried her myself. Master Tyren knows nothing of my life in the forest."

"I know. I'm sorry. I—"

They were interrupted by a knock on the door. Tess moved her tea aside and pushed past Griff angrily to open it. "Yes?"

"Ah, young Tess. Hello again. Are you settling in all right?" It was Tyren. He stared at the veercat with greed. Griff could see that the man was almost smelling the potential money to be made from showing this curious animal and its companions to an eager public. "I see young Griff is keeping you company. That's good. You two should get on famously."

Tess threw a still-angry but perhaps more confused glance in Griff's direction. "Thank you, Master Tyren," she said as politely as her bad mood would allow.

"Now, as I understand it, the creatures are unloaded, Tess, but we can't permit them to be seen roaming the enclosure. I was—"

"They wouldn't want to," she said before he could finish. "It's far too open."

Tyren nodded patiently, his fat face wobbling as he worked hard to maintain the kind smile. "Yes, indeed, much too open. So I thought we could keep them in a tented—"

She ignored the showmaster. "I was thinking we could let them go in that copse not far from here. It offers a feeling of woodland. Those few trees will mean everything to my creatures, more like their home."

"But they could escape!" Tyren argued as gently as possible, although Griff noted his smile had frozen and turned wintry.

"They won't be happy in a tent!" Tess argued.

"My dear. I have put myself out on a limb for you. I cannot risk that these creatures get lost, roam without supervision, or that you decide to leave the Traveling Show. I have given my word, paid a lot of money to the authorities to give you your freedom. You belong to me now. You understood that from the beginning. It was the bargain we made, child. Don't tell me I have to claim back my gold and return you to the Stalkers?"

Tess scowled and opened her mouth to give a retort that Griff was so sure would not be polite that he stepped in front of her and cut off whatever tirade was about to come out.

"Er, no, Master Tyren, you don't," Griff chimed in. "Tess was just telling me over some tea that she'll have to spend a few days getting used to us and our ways. And I said that this is her first day, after all." He shrugged. "She's bound to feel like a stranger at first. We'll have a think and find a solution for her creatures, sir. Leave it with me."

"Be sure you do, Griff," Tyren said, nodding firmly at him. "Tess, your creatures are our prize drawcard, now that Ilbo is gone. Don't let me down."

Much to Griff's relief Tess said nothing as the showmaster turned away. Once he was out of earshot, though, all the fight seemed to have leaked out of her. Griff closed the door.

"It won't help you to have him as an enemy."

"He's only helping me because it suits his purposes."

"It was no different for my brothers and myself. We just had to learn to fit in and make friends. I'll be your friend, Tess. This wagon will feel like a home soon, I promise. Look, Rix is already exploring," he said, and pointed.

Tess found a sad smile when she saw that the veercat was indeed sniffing around the corners of the wagon. "You're being very decent to me, Griff. I'm sure I don't deserve it."

"I know what it's like to feel like an outsider. In fact, I feel very alone a lot of the time. I will not let you down. You can trust me. I'll help you with your creatures."

He could tell that she'd spent most of her life not trusting anyone and could hear her thoughts colliding with each other. She wanted to be his friend, though; he was sure from the thoughts he could hear.

"Come on," Griff said kindly. "I'm starving and that bell you can hear means the food tent is still serving. Leave Rix locked in here. I've got an idea for the other creatures. We'll talk about it over a meal."

To his further relief Tess agreed, following him to the smell of where roasted meat was being served.

They lined up quietly to get their meals, which were being dished out onto clay plates by Madam Tyren and her team of helpers.

"That's Tyren's wife," Griff whispered. "She's all right but don't trust her completely. Her loyalties are to Tyren and the show. She likes his wealth. Ah, here come my brothers," he said, grinning crookedly. "Now I'm in for it."

The burly boys arrived, winking and grinning at their younger brother. "Who's your girlfriend, Griff?" one asked.

Gesturing at the handsome youth, Griff replied. "Tess, this is Phineas, the eldest, and Matthias," he said, pointing to the second brother. They both nodded at her, smiling widely.

Tess immediately noticed how different they were from her new friend. Unlike Griff, who was dark and swarthy with longish soft, wavy hair, they had short, scruffy golden hair and pale skin. They both regarded her through light-blue eyes, filled with what seemed to be permanent amusement. "Ah, the Twisted Twins. I've heard about you two. But you look identical. How can you be twins and not the same age?"

"They're not twins," Griff explained. "Phineas was born at the beginning of Leaf-fall and Matthias the end of the following Thaw. So there's not quite a year between them. I'm three years younger than Matthias."

She frowned, still confused.

Phineas explained. "Master Tyren decided that the Twisted Twins sounded better than the Twisted Brothers, so he just passes us off as twins."

Understanding flitted across her face. "I see; well, you could easily be twins," Tess admitted. "And what is your part in the show? I heard you were a balancing act."

"More than that, I hope," Matthias said. "Balance is a big part of it but there's strength, control, suppleness. We're contortionists. Come along to our rehearsal this evening and you'll see how much more."

"I will," she said.

"Tess is a new act. She owns beautiful, rare creatures," Griff said, proud that he had such an exotic new friend to introduce. "She's got a young centaur!"

"No!" the boys said together, intrigued.

She nodded. "It's true. He's very shy of people. I don't know how he'll ever forgive me. I couldn't bear to hear him wailing today. That's why I fled to the wagon."

"I heard him," Griff said, then turned to her. "We'll go see him straight after we've eaten," he reassured. "No, you can't push in, Mat, or trouble will befall me. You'll have to queue."

"But I'm famished," his brother groaned.

"I don't eat much. You can have my helping," Tess said, clearly liking the tall, affable brothers immediately.

Mat beamed a smile at her. "I'll look forward to that, Miss Tess, and to a special viewing of your beasts," he said, and hurried off to join his brother at the back of the queue.

"They're nice," she said, looking at Griff sideways. "You don't look at all like them. The opposite, in fact."

"I know. Apparently, I look more like my mother. She had dark hair, dark eyes."

"You're quite young to leave your mother and father, aren't you?"

He shrugged. "I'm older than you, I'm thirteen summers. Anyway, my mother died when I was born." He looked away from Tess and she saw sadness ghost across his expression although he tried to hide it, perhaps not wanting any pity. "And it was Dad who raised us."

She took a small crust of bread and balanced it on the side of her plate next to a small helping of stew. "So if he's still alive, why are you here?"

Griff pointed to a lonely bench at a table farthest from all the diners and she followed to sit down and eat. "Money became tight but Dad didn't want my brothers going off to fight in Janko's army. He worried that the general might just take them if he needed new recruits."

"So you all joined the Traveling Show," she completed.

He nodded as he chewed on his hunk of bread. "I didn't want my brothers going off without me. It felt important to have them close."

"Don't get me wrong, but they seem as though they need only each other."

43

He grinned. "I know what you mean. I'm the one who needs the brothers. I wish I had a twin. Sometimes I dream I do."

She changed topics, perhaps sensing his sorrow of parting from his father, his home. "What's your idea for the creatures—you said you had one?"

"Well, rather than letting them roam free, perhaps you could tie them up on—"

"Tie them up? Are you mad?"

"Let me finish," Griff said patiently. "Tie them on long ropes so they have lots of room but Tyren is satisfied that you are preventing the animals from roaming wild. He has to protect the money he's already paid for you, Tess. Just make it look as though they're fully secured and once you've earned everyone's trust, it will be easy to convince Tyren to allow more freedom for the creatures. Let everyone get to know you, become one of the family, so to speak."

"And are you one of the family, Griff?"

"Well, I like to think so."

Tess looked around at how isolated they appeared from the other people. "Is that why you sit apart from everyone else during mealtime? And why you were given the job of looking after the newcomer? You seem to be a bit of a loner yourself."

"I just don't like a lot of noise," Griff said unhappily, and she noticed he shook his head now and then as though trying to rid it of water.

"Well, I'm the same," she admitted, watching a gaggle of women arrive at the food tent. "In fact—" She stopped, surprised when Griff stood up, groaning.

He looked around at the group of chortling women. "Are you finished?"

Tess was confused. "Er, not quite."

"Grab your bread. You can finish it while we walk."

Tess frowned but did as he asked and soon found herself being hurried along.

"What's wrong, Griff?"

"I get there early usually. It gets a bit noisy for me otherwise."

Tess hadn't noticed. "So you never did tell me how you knew all that stuff about me," she said, running slightly to keep up with Griff, who was striding away quickly.

"No, I didn't."

When he said no more, she became indignant. "Well . . . are you going to explain?" she asked.

He began to jog. "Tess, bring Rix and have the others brought to the copse. Tell Chauncey that Tyren said it was all right. I'll explain everything there."

"But where are you going?" she yelled after him, puzzled.

He didn't reply, just ran ahead toward the safety of the trees.

4

"Miralda," Duke Janko said, before bending to touch his lips to her hand. She had to restrain herself from pulling away from his mouth or visibly flinching. "It's an honor to see you again, Majesty," he said, straightening.

"Welcome back, Janko. Congratulations on all your success in the north."

He shrugged, as if to say it was all about duty. "My brother only has to ask and I am there for him."

Miralda cocked her head to one side, ensuring the pretend smile never left her face. "That's so generous of you. You're a good brother to him," she said, the honeyed words clearly pleasing the Duke, but in her heart they were hollow, driven by scorn. Miralda hated him. She wondered if he knew this. "The city welcomes you with great excitement," she added.

He smiled and with it came an expression too close to the face of the man she loved. She hated Janko all the more for echoing his brother's looks so keenly.

"I am amazed by the enthusiasm, Rodin," Janko said, turning to the King. It irritated Miralda that the Duke never paid his brother quite the right amount of respect once he was out of earshot of the dignitaries of the palace. He should address him as King until told otherwise. She knew it never bothered Rodin, of course.

"Don't be," Rodin replied, with his usual generosity. "They love you, brother. As they should. You have kept harm from them. Old Besler must be licking his wounds in the north."

The Duke chuckled, accepting the tall goblet of wine that was presented to him by a servant. "That fat backside of his was sent scurrying into the cave network that his rabble favor. They won't surface for months now, for fear of reprisals."

"Indeed," Miralda said, taking a sip from her goblet. "I heard reprisals had already been taken."

The Duke stared at her and the feigned smile was dropped, replaced by an expression that spoke of secrets and cunning. He blinked slowly before he answered. "We must make examples of his horde. Brutality is the only language they understand."

"Have you tried any other way?" she pushed, knowing this was irritating her King, who gave her a warning glance.

"Oh, talking doesn't work, my Queen," he said, and she heard only a sneer in his tone, which she could tell was suggesting she keep her nose out of men's business. She felt her blood beginning to boil at his condescension. "I know it sounds all very nice to talk across the parley table," Janko continued, and Miralda turned off from his voice. She looked toward Rodin, apology in her glance, and felt rescued when she saw a familiar servant enter and the dark head of her son appearing nervously around the door directly after him.

"Ah, the Crown Prince is here," she said, deliberately impressing Lute's title as she cut across Janko's words. "Come in, darling. The Duke has arrived and is keen to see you."

Lute glanced once at the Duke before he was guided fully into the room by Pilo, now behaving every inch the servant. Due to all the rush of getting cleaned up and readied for presentation, Lute had not had an opportunity to speak to his companion about what he'd overheard in the bailey. It was playing on his mind, although he was beginning to believe he must have misheard the words, or misinterpreted them, because his father and uncle looked so happy. He planned to try hard to impress the Duke for his father's sake.

"Thank you, Pilo," Miralda said, and smiled softly.

Lute had sensed that Pilo had been a blessing in his mother's life, ever since he had first appeared four years ago. And since Pilo had firmly entered Lute's life, the Prince had come out of his "shell," as he'd heard his father put it. Meanwhile, his mother clearly adored Pilo for the care and effort he put into her son. They would never have more children, Lute knew this. No one had needed to tell him. He had sensed that he had been hard-won and there would be no sister or brother to share the burden of this parental love. So all the love his mother in particular had to lavish on a family was directed at Lute. But he was being groomed for a role that would require him to have the broadest of shoulders—being loved too hard would be the least of his troubles. That's what Pilo had always counseled in his reserved manner, anyway.

"Janko, this is our son, Lute. You haven't seen him for

some years now," Rodin said, both men turning to regard the boy.

Lute couldn't help but note that where one of the brothers beamed with pride, the other did not successfully hide his disdain. The memory of what he'd heard earlier was haunting him. And the look he saw flit across Janko's face suggested the Duke was not enamored of the idea that a child had shunted him from that enviable position of heir. Lute reminded himself to be careful.

"Lute?" Janko said, mock awe in his voice. "Stars save me, child, you've grown! How tall and strong you look now."

Lute darted a look at his mother and with almost imperceptible encouragement from her soft smile he nodded low at his father's brother. "Duke Janko. Yes, sir, I'm a lot older now and I love to ride, shoot, hunt, swim, fight. I hope I'll make you proud."

The Duke bowed. "Majesty," he said, more formally now and with much reverence, "do call me Uncle."

"Welcome back to Floris," Lute said carefully. "I hear you were successful in the north." He had practiced this compliment with Pilo, ensuring he got just the right amount of awe but also dignity into his words, as though spoken like a king in waiting.

"As usual," his father said, adding lightness to an otherwise bare conversation.

Another glance toward his mother told Lute that she too sensed the awkward pause, the stilted nature of their exchange.

And no doubt simply because she did so love the King, she rushed to help out. "Perhaps you'd like to go out riding with your uncle tomorrow, Lute? I'm sure Pilo would accompany and it would be a great chance for Janko to have some time with you," she tried. "Janko's an expert horseman. I'm sure he'd like to see your father's latest acquisition for your stable."

"I'd be delighted to," Lute replied, once again adopting the polite tone he had rehearsed. "Father's given me a beautiful filly."

"A filly, eh?" Janko replied. "And how well do you ride?"

"It's not a question of how well but how fast," the King said with mock weariness. "Can't get it into these boys' heads that it's about finesse not speed."

"Oh, Rodin," Miralda said with an amused glance back at her son.

"All right, all right," the King admitted. "Yes, Janko, your nephew is a talented rider. I'm sure you'll be impressed."

"You will go along, too, won't you, Rodin?" Miralda asked. Lute sensed the worry in her voice, even though she tried to disguise it from Janko.

Rodin shook his head. "Pilo will. What about you, my love?"

"Ah, that's right, you're something of a horsewoman, aren't you, Miralda?"

She smiled but Lute could see how forced it was. "I love to ride. But not tomorrow." Lute knew her too well. He could see in her eyes that she couldn't imagine anything worse than riding with Janko, while trying to remain gracious and polite throughout the conversation. "Pilo and Lute will be fine company for you."

"I can't wait," Janko said, grinning at him, and Lute

bristled at the oily sound of insincerity in his voice. "Who taught him?"

"Pilo taught me," Lute answered for himself. "Pilo is my teacher in everything. Er, sorry, Father, I meant that as no—"

"Not at all, my boy. No offense taken," Rodin said. "Janko, this is Pilo. He joined the elite servants about four years ago, was it?" Pilo nodded, said nothing. "And about two years ago took over full responsibility for Lute. He's become indispensable to us, I have to admit. And, as you can see, Lute has come along very well since you last clapped eyes on him."

"My word, you have!" Janko admitted. "The last time we met you were such a weakling, Lute. Always running behind your mother's skirts. But you're tall and look strong and healthy. I'm pleased. Almost ready for soldiering. How old are you now?"

His mother probably hoped that Janko had missed the worried glance that Pilo threw her way but Lute didn't, even as he prepared to answer. "I'm thirteen summers, Uncle."

"Bit young for your army, Janko," Rodin said, with a friendly punch to his brother's arm. "Anyway, let us go. You must be eager to settle back into your old place. I'll walk with you—I could use the exercise and we can talk on the way. I think Miralda's organized the entire west wing of the palace for you if that suits?"

"Suits perfectly. My thanks to you both," Janko said, smiling. "Tomorrow morning, then, Lute," he added. "Let's plan a ride for just after dawn."

Lute nodded. "I look forward to it, Uncle Janko."

"Until tonight, then, Majesty," the Duke said, and swept toward the main doors of the salon, the King in tow.

Miralda turned back to her son but she cast a glance Pilo's way when she spoke. "Lute, would you ask Dalz to organize some fresh watered wine, please? This is too warm for my taste, and by all means order some pastries for yourself. I happen to know Cook's made some fresh honey cakes."

Lute grinned. He went in search of the servants, who had been banished in case the King and Duke needed to speak privately. But so far everything had been very conversational and unimportant. Perhaps more would be revealed on the ride tomorrow. He left the chamber eager for cake but reminding himself to talk to Pilo about the soldier's comment.

⋈❋⋈

As soon as Lute was out of earshot, Miralda changed her lighthearted tone. "Listen to me very carefully now," she said, her expression filled with anxiety as she regarded Pilo. "That man is not nearly as friendly as he seems."

Pilo blinked and finally spoke for the first time since entering the royal chamber. "How would you like me to treat that warning, Majesty?"

"Pilo, I trust you completely, so I'm going to be candid with you and share my deepest fear. Lute is in danger. I'm sure of it but my husband is not very receptive to the hints I've dropped. He holds his brother in very high regard and I have no proof anyway. However, my instincts tell me that the Duke does not wish my son a long and happy life."

Pilo stared at her, his blue eyes darkening as he considered the Queen's fears. "Do you question his loyalty, Your Majesty?"

She had never admitted such a thing aloud, but the man's question deserved an equally direct response. "Not to Drestonia. But I don't believe he's as loyal to the family as he tries to appear. I am truly anxious."

Pilo's gaze narrowed and Miralda felt the full weight of this unfathomable man's stare. In truth, he was such an unknown quantity. She realized she entrusted her most precious possession to this quiet man, who said little. However, Lute loved him and she had absolutely no complaint about his care for her son, whom he'd helped bring out of his shell. Lute had become a far more adventurous child since Pilo had come into his life.

"I fear for Lute," she repeated.

"Then I will take precautions, Majesty."

"Thank you," Miralda replied, unsure of what else she could say to explain her seemingly irrational anxiety.

"Perhaps you should come on the ride with us?" he suggested. "You would enjoy it."

"Oh, I know I'd enjoy being out riding with Lute and yourself, but no! Definitely not with the Duke in tow. I'd struggle to keep my manners gracious around that man. Something about him brings out the worst in me. And I'd rather it was a pleasurable experience. I am uncomfortable with him being around Lute but at the same time I realize that my son must get to know Janko. The King has enormous admiration and regard for the man. And I respect that they are brothers. Family ties are important." She looked immediately embarrassed at her last words, glancing away.

Pilo frowned, clearly not understanding her sudden discomfort, and bowed his head slightly in acknowledgment as

Lute returned with the news that Cook had also made custard wafers, his favorite.

"A huge tray is on the way up now," he said, "still warm!"

"Lucky you, darling," she said, and hugged him while looking over at Pilo, impressing upon the servant that this child was everything to her. *Everything*. And she needed to secure his safety, his throne.

5

Tess stared incredulously at Griff. "You can hear my thoughts?" she repeated, her tone suggesting she didn't believe him.

"Yes," he said, embarrassed. "Only the ones that you are so aware of that you . . . well, you force them out beyond your mind, I suppose." He'd kept the secret for years and now he'd spilled it twice in the same day to different people, both relative strangers, although he felt he could trust Tess. The silence stretched until he felt uncomfortable, and was about to excuse himself when Tess surprised him.

"I believe you," she said, her expression grave.

"You do?"

Tess nodded. "No one else could know what you revealed. You had to be able to hear my thoughts to have that information about my sister." She looked shaken.

Griff took a deep, relieved breath. "I'm sorry about your sister, Tess. I'm sorry that you're alone."

"I have my creature friends," she replied sorrowfully, but

then brightened. "And now I have you. I don't envy you that skill. It must be hard to live with."

Tess was the first person who had ever sympathized. His brothers thought he was the luckiest person alive to possess such a gift, while Tyren, he sensed, was plotting to find a way he could make use of it. His father had not wanted to talk about it, had even become angry the last time Griff had mentioned his talent. That had been many years ago. He had not discussed it with anyone since then—until today. He wanted to hug Tess for feeling sympathy. "That doesn't even begin to cover it. There are times when I just want to run away, head for the forest and live alone."

"So you do know how I feel." She smiled. "Hearing others think. Hmm, that must be truly awful. Is that why you hurried away from the meal tent?"

"Yes." He shrugged. "I'm fortunate that it's only thoughts of high importance to people that I can hear. But a crowd can overwhelm me." He looked over at Rix, noticing the veercat's huge pointed ears erect and moving to catch every sound they could. "He looks content."

"He's more comfortable amongst the grasses and trees." She stroked him. "But he's not liking this rope."

"There's yards of it, Tess. He can move the full length of this clearing. They won't hurt one another, will they?"

She gave a snort. "Don't be mad. They're my friends, which means they look after each other."

Griff turned to regard the centaur with awe once again. "Will Davren let me close?" He'd been glancing at the beast, determined to get to know him better but not wanting to frighten the centaur or Tess with his eagerness. "He's magnificent," he added, noticing the creature's broad chest and muscled physique. Davren's hair was dark and shaggy, falling in soft waves to his wide shoulders. He looked like a young man to his waist, but from there on he became all beast, similar to a horse. His body was sleek and shiny, with dark chestnut-colored hair covering his withers and flanks. "He looks so strong."

She nodded and Griff edged toward the young centaur.

"Are you talking to him?"

"Yes. We have become used to using the mindlink," she replied, reassuring him. "You can't hear?"

"No. I can't listen in on conversations. I know it's hard for you to imagine but all I can do is hear a person thinking something when it's really important to them. Is Davren scared?"

"He trusts me. He knows I wouldn't do this for someone I was not sure of."

Griff felt a momentary thrill pulse through him. Tess was his first chance at real friendship. Apart from his brothers he lived on the fringe of the showfolk, not really close to anyone. That she had chosen to trust him meant everything.

"Just hold out your hand."

Griff did so, marveling at the perfectly sculpted head and torso of a boy, not very much older than himself, who possessed the body of a horse. He was lean and muscled. "He's so incredible to look at."

"He's very strong, as you've noticed. But he's not comfortable here, so he's a bit nervous."

"No parents?"

"He's an orphan. He won't talk about what happened."

Davren reached out and placed his open palm beneath Griff's hand.

"This is his formal greeting. Now, turn your hand so that his ends up on top of yours," Tess guided. "That's how you say hello properly in Centaurian."

Griff did as she suggested and won a tentative smile from Davren. "How did you learn such things?"

She shrugged. "I sense them or the creatures teach me. He likes you. He says you will be a good friend to us. He trusts you. You should talk to him. He understands, he just can't talk back to you in the normal manner but he can communicate with the others—reassure them about you." She too smiled gently. "And he can talk to you through me if you like."

"I'm pleased to hear that he likes me," Griff said, genuinely delighted. He tore his eyes from the handsome centaur and looked at the equally intriguing black-and-white-striped sagar. "Elph looks calm, too."

"Elph is *always* calm. Sagars are sleepy creatures until they're frightened or disturbed in some way. So long as Elph has food and somewhere soft to sleep, and is near us," she said, taking in herself and her creatures with a wave of her hand, "he's happy." Griff grinned at Elph's long, strong snout, which he could use as a tool for everything from feeding himself to exploring. His six thick, stumpy legs intrigued Griff.

"And Helys seems fine, too." He smiled at the small creature that reminded him of a hairless puppy—her features were fine and delicate, like a mouse's. She had very long whiskers that twitched constantly, seeking information from the surrounds, and her round ears moved equally incessantly, picking up every sound in an equally anxious manner. Her eyes were huge and dark with long, thick lashes. He thought her most beautiful.

"Yes, she seems fine but she's not, because she's pale blue today, which means she's very nervous."

"What is her happy color?"

"Normally, a buttery-yellow color signifies she's feeling safe and happy—she goes a bit orange when she's joyous. Green is her calm, content color."

"Does she get cold with no fur or feathers?"

"No. I don't really understand how her body works but she's off the purples, so this place is more to her liking. She thinks you're handsome, by the way."

Griff felt his cheeks redden. "Well, she'd be the first to think so. Trust my luck . . . a califa!"

Tess giggled. "She's incredibly pretty by califa standards."

"I can see that—even though I didn't know until now what a califa looked like. Please tell her I think she's very beautiful," Griff replied, no longer blushing. Tess must have told Helys because the little creature glowed orange momentarily. He cleared his throat. "So you feel comfortable with your friends here? I'm sorry they're tied up, Tess, but we just have to prove to Tyren that you are cooperating."

Before Tess could answer, the showmaster stomped into the clearing with Chauncey, whose mouth was slack with wonder when he sighted the animals. "You're not defying me, are you, young Tess?"

"No, Master Tyren," she replied, glancing at Chauncey, who appeared entranced. "Er, I took Griff's advice and each of the creatures is secured by a rope. They feel safer here than amongst the wagons."

"I've explained to Tess that we don't always stop in places

where woods are so near, Master Tyren," Griff lied, but he knew precisely how the showmaster's mind worked and decided he would cut off any objections before they arose. "I think if we can just win the creatures' trust in these early weeks while we're still moving along the fringe of the woods, then by the time we reach somewhere like Cupsley, or Bridgetown, they will allow us to house them beneath a tent or in a wagon."

"But what if someone should see them here?" Tyren exclaimed.

Tess shook her head. "They won't. My creatures know how to hide themselves. They are well practiced. And we're not here long enough, are we?"

Chauncey didn't reply and got a dig in the ribs from his boss to prompt him to pay attention.

"Sorry, Master Tyren," the big man said, unable to contain his astonishment. "Strike me, these beasts will fill the tent over and over."

Tyren threw him a greedy look of agreement. "How long are we here?" he repeated.

Chauncey tore his gaze from the quartet of curious creatures and shrugged. "We perform tomorrow; we're gone the next morning, boss."

Tyren's eyes narrowed, deepening into his fleshy face. "All right. I'm holding you responsible, Griff. This was your idea. If I lose a single creature, you and your brothers will go without wages for a year."

Griff nodded, hardly even hearing the threat. "You won't lose any of them, I promise."

"How can you be so sure she won't run?" Tyren demanded.

Then, as though something had dawned on him, he smiled. "Ah, of course. I understand how you know. Very good. I want to talk to you, Griff. Come see me later. It's important."

Griff did not allow his anxiety to show. He simply nodded, although he knew what it meant: Tyren was going to ask him to perform.

"Settle in, Tess, and start thinking about your act, what you're going to wear and how you're going to approach presenting the beasts," Tyren said over his shoulder. "Don't even think about escape. Griff here will tell me if you do." He left with Chauncey in tow, both chuckling quietly.

"So you're spying on me?" she asked, looking aghast and angry at the same time. She folded her arms.

"Don't be daft, Tess. That's typical Tyren, making sure none of us trusts one another. Just remember what your creatures told you about me. If you trust them, then trust me. Come on. We have to plan your act. We'd better go see Madam Tyren about some clothes for you—she's in charge of the show wardrobe."

Tess softened and threw a worried glance at her friends.

"They'll be safe," he reassured, taking her elbow. "You're right. No one knows they're here and they know how to hide should anyone stumble into the clearing. We can check up on them regularly."

"I do trust you, Griff. Just so long as you don't try to talk me out of sleeping in the woods with them tonight." She glared at his look of surprise. "I'm like Elph," Tess assured him. "I don't feel the cold."

Janko's welcome-home banquet had been a lavish affair. Rodin had ordered the most impressive royal feast the palace had seen since Lute had been born, and the kitchens had worked themselves into a frenzy of activity to impress the returning hero.

The highlight of the dinner had been what was known in the region simply as Serephon. It came from the ancient language and meant "blessed creatures" but was used to describe a complex dish that began with roasted ox. Within the carcass was a cooked deer, which was in turn stuffed with sheep that, when opened, revealed a goat that was stuffed with a small pig, and which ultimately revealed hares stuffed with tiny voles. It was a mighty achievement by Lambert, the head cook, that each of these animals was beautifully prepared and cooked to perfection within another, each bringing different flavors of meats and herbs; and, of course, it was a spectacular centerpiece for the royal banquet table.

Lute hadn't partaken of the Serephon but had nibbled on the simple roasted slices of meat that Pilo had cut from a haunch of cold beef and served with fruit chutneys, soft cheeses and thick hunks of warm bread smeared with butter. Pilo had sampled the dishes first, Lute noticed. The Prince had joined in the many toasts to the Duke and laughed politely at all his uncle's jests when the guests—all important men and women of the realm—had somehow become a willing audience for Janko to regale with stories of his adventures. It was then that Lute noticed his mother was not at all as riveted as his father and everyone else seemed to be. Her attention was wandering and she looked unimpressed when Janko's audience clapped or cheered.

Soon enough Pilo had leaned over his shoulder. "Time to go, Your Majesty."

"So soon?" Lute asked, a plea in his voice.

"You have to be up for the dawn ride, don't forget, my Prince," Pilo said. Pilo always said just the right thing, thought Lute. He could have just said *It's time for bed*, and made Lute feel as though he were a mere child being taken from the grown-up part of the banquet. Instead, Pilo made it appear as though it were Lute's duty, as Crown Prince, to get his sleep.

"Of course. I shall just wish my parents good evening."

Pilo gave an almost imperceptible nod as Lute walked over to the three adult royals.

"I must take my leave. Good night, Mother," he said, formally kissing her hand. "Father, sleep well," he said, bowing to the King. "Uncle Janko, see you in the morning."

"I'm looking forward to it, young Lute," Janko said softly over his shoulder. "I can't persuade your father. Serious affairs of state apparently await, but I'm sure we shall have a lively time nonetheless."

"My mother would—"

"Er, no, darling," Miralda said, smiling indulgently. Lute had never seen that expression before. It seemed forced, overly polite, as she tinkled a soft laugh clearly for Janko's benefit. "Both of you, and Pilo, can rise with the birds and enjoy the dawn."

Lute saw Janko throw a look of sympathy at his mother. That expression seemed equally fake. "A queen must get her beauty sleep," he said.

"Can I just thank Lambert?" Lute murmured to Pilo as they moved away from the chamber.

"In case your mother forgets to, you mean?" Pilo said, striding so quickly that Lute had to hurry to keep up.

"She won't forget," Lute assured.

"That's my point. I think you were wondering if there were any stickycakes going begging."

Lute grinned. He'd been found out. "Well, you made me leave before they were served."

Pilo gave a soft sigh that said it was all right to go via the kitchens. Inside the cavernous wing at ground level of the palace there was a soft, warm fug of food smells and people's toil. A vast assortment of servants were fetching, carrying, cleaning, tidying.

Lambert spotted the young Prince and clapped his hands furiously to get everyone's attention. The kitchen staff bowed, welcoming Lute.

"I didn't mean to interrupt your work, Master Lambert. I've just excused myself from the banquet but I wanted to quickly thank you and all the people in the kitchen for the magnificent meal that was served tonight."

Lambert beamed, his face cherry-red from his hot exertions, while his staff cheered and whistled their approval, not just of their chief's cooking prowess but mostly for the Prince's thoughtfulness at paying a visit.

"Thank you, Majesty. That's most kind of you," Lambert said, his huge body skipping up on light feet to bow with an almost feminine grace. "But you leave before the sweet courses."

"I must, I'm afraid," Lute said, contriving an expression of deep disappointment. "Duty calls. I must be up before the lark tomorrow to ride with the Duke, and Pilo here thought it best if I withdrew now . . . er, before the final courses."

"Oh, but my Prince, Sarah's made stickycakes in your honor that are just dripping with honey from the royal hives. You can't miss those," Lambert said, all his chins wobbling.

Lute shrugged, contriving misery, not daring to look at Pilo. "I'm sorry, Lambert."

"Well, Majesty, we cannot ignore your duty, but do let me have a plate of them sent up to your chamber with some warmed sweetened milk."

"Sweet dreams, indeed," Pilo said, and Lute nudged him to remain silent.

"That would be most acceptable, Master Lambert," Lute said. "Thank you."

Later, dressed for bed but on his private balcony munching on the cakes sandwiched with thick cream and dripping butterscotch and honey, Lute opened his thoughts to Pilo.

"My mother's worried about something."

"Is she?" Pilo replied, distracted, scanning the city gently lit by twinkling torches.

"Pilo, don't play dumb. I know that you notice everything, even if you don't want anyone to know that. What are you looking for out there?"

"Nothing," Pilo replied, although his eyes never stopped searching.

"So now you're behaving strangely as well. And what's all that about tasting my food? You've never done that before." He was onto his second cake.

"It was an excuse. I was hungry."

Lute made a scoffing sound. "Rubbish! You never eat. I think you exist on air."

"It's simply something your parents would like to introduce."

"Food tasting?" Lute asked incredulously. "You jest."

The man looked around and shook his head.

"But why should *you* die of poison?" he asked, reaching for another delectable cake.

"Ah, and there's the great divide between royals and servants."

"Pilo, stop. Be as direct as you normally are. What's going on?"

"Absolutely nothing that should concern you. We will now have food tasters for the King and heir. We're just taking some new precautions."

"Against what?"

"Treachery, the usual thing against royals."

It reminded Lute of the soldier's comment. "Who?"

"You never know," Pilo answered. "As I said, just a few precautions."

Lute was not satisfied with the answer. He frowned in confusion, his cake half-eaten. "So why is my mother acting so strangely?"

"I think you'll have to ask her that. She may be thinking about a new gown, for all you know."

"I'll tell her you said that," Lute threatened. They both knew Queen Miralda, although renowned for her beauty, was far more likely to be thinking politics of the realm than shallow thoughts on fashion.

Pilo sighed. "Prince Lute. There is nothing for you to worry about."

"I'm not worried. You are. And my mother is. The King

doesn't seem at all bothered, simply pleased that his brother is returned. Why do I sense that no one else close to him feels the same way?" He swallowed the remains of his fourth cake.

"Well, perhaps you should search your own heart, Prince Lute. I didn't notice you leaping out of your skin to reacquaint yourself with the Duke this morning."

Lute felt he had finally got to the bottom of what was troubling the normally unflappable Pilo. "I hardly know him," Lute said, defensive now but aware that his guide and mentor was the least chatty person in the palace and rarely wasted words. Everything Pilo said to him was usually for the benefit of teaching him, and Lute sensed this occasion was no different. Pilo was being oblique, deliberately avoiding coming out and saying what was on his mind but clearly urging Lute to work it out for himself.

Pilo turned from the cityscape at last and fixed Lute with a keen stare. "But you don't like him."

Lute shrugged. "I didn't say that." He couldn't hold Pilo's gaze and knew, by looking away, that he revealed his true thoughts to his companion.

"You don't have to," the man said gently. "But then, neither do I," he added.

Lute looked up, surprised by the admission. "Can he sense my reluctance?"

Pilo thought about this. "Possibly. But he doesn't know you nearly as well as I do and you've conducted yourself impeccably this evening. Your parents will be proud. Have you finished? Any more and you'd surely burst."

"Actually, there is something I wanted to discuss with you." He considered a fifth cake but decided four was enough.

"Oh?"

"I overheard some soldiers talking in the bailey as the Duke's party was arriving. It was probably nothing—in fact, I likely misunderstood. . . ."

"Don't justify it, Prince Lute, just tell me," Pilo suggested, closing the first of the doors to the balcony and checking the locks repeatedly.

"I just caught a snatch of conversation—a comment, really. . . ."

Pilo turned. His close-cropped beard twitched as his mouth narrowed with irritation. "Spit it out."

Lute yawned helplessly. He was tired after his early adventure in the streets of Floris and now tonight's big feast. "One of them said something about knowing that Janko disliked his brother."

"Is that so?" Pilo didn't seem surprised.

"Yes, but watching my father and the Duke tonight, you'd think they were the closest of friends."

"You would, wouldn't you," Pilo said, his tone loaded with skepticism.

Lute regarded Pilo. "You don't trust him."

"It's not my place to trust anyone, Prince Lute. I am your guardian. And I would run a sword through anyone—Duke or otherwise—who might wish you harm. Hopefully, he will hate the claustrophobic atmosphere of city life and he'll be gone as fast as he's arrived."

Lute nodded. "Let's hope so, because he makes my mother act very strangely and I think my father feels obliged to overcompensate."

"King Rodin loves his brother. And we should not forget

that Duke Janko is loyal to the realm. Without him we might well be bowing to a different king," Pilo said sagely.

"And now you admire him," Lute said dismissively.

"I admire what he's achieved for Drestonia. I'm not so sure what he plans to achieve on this visit."

"What does that mean?"

"Nothing specific. It's my job to be suspicious of everyone . . . otherwise, what's the point in giving me the role of your champion?"

Lute gave his companion a look of disdain. "And now you're just playing with words and talking around the issue. Tomorrow I'm riding with him. Should I fear that?"

"I will be there. You have nothing to fear."

"Cake?" Lute offered, changing the subject now that he knew Pilo was not going to enlighten him any further this evening.

Pilo shook his head as he ushered Lute back into his sleeping chamber.

"How can you resist them?" Lute groaned.

"Food doesn't interest me."

"But these are stickycakes, Pilo. Not just food. This is the food of the gods!"

A rare and brief smile creased Pilo's face, gone almost as soon as it arrived.

"What does interest you, anyway?" Lute asked, licking honey from his fingers.

"Plenty."

"Such as?" Lute responded, vaguely irritated that he was being urged inside and to bed. He was sure Pilo was not as anxious about the late hour as he was about his security.

"Such as riding, swordsmanship, the safety of the Crown Prince."

"My parents know almost nothing about you, do they?"

Pilo shook his head as he encouraged Lute even closer to the bedside.

"Why is that?"

"Do you remember how old you were when I joined the elite staff?"

"Several years back."

"And you were so withdrawn you hardly spoke. Now we can't make you stop speaking. There was another occasion when you were silent and constantly nervous, I'm told. It was when you were three."

Lute buttoned his nightshirt. "What's your point? I'm growing up now. I feel more confident. Surely that's normal?"

Pilo pointed to a basin of still-warm water and Lute dutifully washed his face and hands. As he handed Lute a linen to dry off with, Pilo continued. "My point, Prince Lute, is that on each occasion when you have become curiously introverted, the Duke has been present in Floris."

Lute stared at his manservant, baffled. "What are you saying?"

"I'm not sure I'm saying anything in particular, my Prince. I'm simply trying to explain why your mother may be edgy. She connects the Duke with unease for you."

"Well, I'm fine," Lute said, clambering into his huge bed. "No one should worry."

"Excellent," Pilo said brightly, although Lute was not convinced that this wasn't all part of Pilo's usual demeanor. The man was like the almost-extinct califa: able to change colors to suit his surrounds, mood and—in Pilo's case—

particularly whom he was talking to. Lute was sure no one knew the true Pilo. The man had little patience for fools and little interest in the majority of people in the palace. Pilo seemed unimpressed by just about everyone, although Lute sensed that he very much liked and was fiercely loyal to the King and Queen. And yet, Lute knew Pilo could be highly amusing on occasions, courtesy of his pithy, dry wit. Above all, Pilo made Lute feel safe. He couldn't quite pinpoint why he should ever feel threatened in his own home, but distant memories told him he had been scared at times. Though not since Pilo's arrival in his life.

"I shall be in the adjoining chamber, as usual," Pilo said.

"Do you sleep, Pilo?"

"Never," the servant replied, "so call me anytime, no matter how trivial your want may be."

"Why is Dragon here?" Lute asked, yawning, glancing down at the enormous mastiff, the largest of the royal dogs.

"Dragon does exactly as he pleases—you know that," Pilo answered, stroking the dog's enormous head.

"You're fibbing again. You've got him here on guard, haven't you?"

Pilo gave the Prince a withering look. "I think you're more tired than we thought. Dragon hates most people, as you well know, and he prefers to be here with us than around the Duke, who is, after all, a stranger to him. I presume you don't plan to send him away?"

Lute shook his head. "No, I like Dragon here, but I still think you made him come. It's all part of your strange behavior tonight." He yawned widely again. "You are coming riding tomorrow, aren't you?"

"I shall be around," Pilo replied. "Sleep well, my Prince."

He glanced down at Dragon, giving him a stern look, and it seemed the dog understood precisely what was required of him.

⋈❊⋈

The banquet was over, formal farewells had been dealt with and the musicians and performers were packing up at the end of the Great Hall. Miralda had excused herself, leaving the two royal brothers to sip a nightcap by the glowing embers of the fire. Two of Rodin's dogs were at the hearth, his guards close enough in the chamber to intimidate any visitors but not near enough to hear the conversation between the King and Duke.

No one could hear them. No one except Pilo, who had only been prepared to leave the sleeping Prince because he trusted Rodin's most feared mastiff to set up a terrible noise should it hear anything unfamiliar or untoward. Dragon was a fierce guard dog and, for some reason Pilo could never fathom, was just as happy to take commands from him as he was from his real master. Pilo had never taken advantage of this until tonight, but the mastiff had dutifully come when he called, trailed him to the Prince's suite and, even more amazingly, remained where he had been quietly ordered to stay. It bought Pilo the time he wanted to steal downstairs and eavesdrop on the royal brothers. This was not something he felt happy about doing, but for all the Queen's deep distress over Lute's vulnerability where the Duke was concerned, the King seemed equally comfortable. Pilo needed to see for himself, and the best way to catch the Duke in an unguarded moment was to spy on him.

"Thank you for today, Rodin," said Janko, wearily raising a goblet.

Rodin smiled. "Don't mention it, brother. Truly, I wish I could show our appreciation for your heroism more keenly. You know there's to be a statue sculpted in your honor—are you up to posing for it?"

"Of course," Janko said, waving a hand as though it were of no importance.

"What are your plans? Do you want to return to your estate in the country for a while? It's been years since you've been home to Longley—although you know you're welcome to stay in the palace as long as you like."

Janko pursed his lips momentarily. "You know, perhaps it's best I go to Longley. I don't think Miralda likes me being here."

"Nonsense!" Rodin dismissed Janko's theory, but from his tone it was clear to Pilo that the King was not so sure. Rodin shook his head as though baffled. "Miralda's just not one for a lot of pomp and ceremony and dressing up. You know her, happier on a horse than in a gown. We haven't held a banquet such as this in years—she was probably anxious that it should all go off well."

Janko smiled indulgently. "That's kind of you but I think I make her nervous. She watches me a lot, have you noticed?"

"You always were the good-looking one," Rodin said, feigning indignance and draining his wine.

At this Janko snorted. "I don't think you should ever worry on that score, brother."

"No, I know," Rodin said, and sighed, rubbing his eyes. "So what did you think of Lute? He's growing up into a fine young man, we think."

"He's got poise—far more than I recall."

"It's been several years. I should hope so."

"No, it's not just his age. He's gained confidence, stature."

"Well, he's growing into his role. Lo willing, he won't need to set my crown on his head for a few years yet but he's getting very good counseling from the team of trainers and advisors we have around him. He will make a good king one day—make us all proud, I'm sure."

"Indeed," Janko said. "That manservant of his sticks close."

"Pilo?"

"Is that his name?" Janko said innocently. "What's his actual role?"

Pilo leaned forward from behind the enormous velvet drapes that concealed him. He needed to hear clearly why the Duke was so interested in the relationship between Lute and himself.

Rodin chuckled. "It's funny you mention that. There's never been anything officially said but somewhere along the line Pilo became a personal aide to our son. Now he's his closest companion. His champion, in fact. There is no title that fits him, but he shadows Lute, and that's a good thing because Lute trusts him, loves him dearly."

"Like a father?" Janko responded, and although it was gently done, Pilo sensed it was a deliberate barb, meant to wound.

But it seemed that the King was too secure in Lute's affections to feel intimidated. "No," he scorned, then yawned. "More like a much older brother Lute never had."

Pilo watched Janko smile benignly, although the smile

never reached his eyes. "Have you and Miralda kept trying for more children? I'm still surprised and delighted, of course, that you were able to have Lute."

Janko watched the King move in his seat as though pricked. "Well, yes, it's no secret we struggled to have children. But we have Lute. One heir is all you need to keep the line going."

"You shall have to be very careful that nothing should happen to the boy, Rodin."

Pilo felt his muscles stiffen. He tried to tell himself he was imagining it, but all the same he heard the Duke's words as a soft threat.

The King apparently did not, although the words that Lute overheard in the bailey were now looming in Pilo's mind.

"We are being careful," Rodin replied evenly. "It's why we permit Pilo such constant access. As I say, Lute trusts him."

"And you?"

"Implicitly! I'd trust Pilo with my own life. I certainly trust him with my son's."

"I was just thinking perhaps we should throw a small elite guard around Lute. My men, I'll train them. We can—"

"Absolutely no need. Lute would hate it. Besides, there's no immediate threat."

"Rodin, you can be awfully cloud-headed sometimes. How can you possibly know when a threat might arise? That's my very point. There is threat all around him, all the time. I'm a soldier. I know a bit about fighting and cunning. If someone wanted to kill the King and his heir, they'd hardly broadcast it by making themselves obvious."

The King sat up, stung. "But who are you suggesting would want either myself or my son dead?"

Janko stared at his brother. "How about Besler?" Then he softened. "No, forget that. Besler will be quiet for a long time," he said, finally. "But that's not really the point. It doesn't mean precautions shouldn't be in place."

"Precautions *are* in place, Janko," Rodin said, sounding vexed now. "Stop fretting, for Lo's sake. You worry about the security of our borders. I'll worry about internal security. Pilo watches over Lute. My son needs nothing more."

"Nothing more?"

"You haven't seen Pilo with a sword."

Pilo knew that Rodin, who was staring into the fire, did not see how his brother's gaze had narrowed at this comment. He would only have heard the gracious words "As you wish, my King" that Janko said, and looked up to see the Duke smile in acceptance, although Pilo saw only cunning in it.

"Well, time for bed, I think. My first sleep on a soft mattress in years. I have to be up early for a ride with Lute, so forgive me for leaving you so suddenly," Janko said, getting up and giving a short bow.

"Not at all. I've finished here. Are you sure you don't want me to come along tomorrow morning?"

Pilo's ears pricked up. He hadn't realized the King wanted to join the ride. And Janko answered just as Pilo suspected he might. Pilo's lips thinned as the Duke spoke.

"No, Rodin. I think I need to get to know my nephew and the only way to do that is to have time alone with him. I'm looking forward to it." He smiled tightly again and left. Pilo was about to steal away himself when moments later a page ran up breathlessly.

"My lord King," the boy said, bowing.

"Oh, what is it now?" Rodin said, draining the last dregs of his fiery liqueur wine. "A message?"

"From Captain Drew, my King. He said it is important you receive it now."

"Very well, what is it?"

The page straightened, cleared his throat softly. "I am to tell you, King Rodin, that Captain Drew is confused by the presence of Duke Janko's troops on the outskirts of Floris."

"Well, they've just returned from the mountains. Why does he need an explanation from me?" Rodin growled.

The boy looked back at the King blankly. "I'm sorry, my lord, but I was given that message to give to you. Captain Drew did add that he would appreciate a chance to discuss this with you."

"When?"

"Now, my lord, on the battlements. He wishes to show you something."

"Lo save me! I'm a tired king who needs his sleep and you want me to climb to the top of the palace?" The boy blinked, unsure. "Well, come on then, lad. Lead the way," the King grumbled as he stood.

6

Griff knocked on Tyren's wagon door. It was his wife who opened it and stared down at him.

"Er, Master Tyren asked me to come and speak with him," Griff said in response to her glare.

"Now? It's nearing midnight."

"Is that the boy?" they heard Tyren yell from the depths of the wagon. "Tell him to come in."

Tyren's wife shrugged and stepped back so Griff could pass. He pulled off his cap. "Thank you, Madam Tyren," he mumbled, embarrassed. He'd never been inside their private wagon. Tyren normally worked out of one he called "the saloon," where he did his business dealings. This was far more salubrious. Dark velvet drapes and ruby glass lanterns lent a plush, privileged air.

Tyren ambled out of the back to where Griff stood awkwardly. "Leave us," he said to his wife. "Sit down, Griff," he added, pointing at a hard chair near the door. "Want to taste some curaj?" he asked, pouring himself a shot of the amber liquid from the etched-glass flask on a small side table.

"Er, no, sir. Um, I don't."

Tyren twitched a grin before knocking back the small glass of liquid, wincing as he swallowed. "Burns all the way down," he said, groaning softly. "Is that girl settled?"

"Tess? Yes, sir. She's going to be fine, I'm sure. Madam Tyren picked an outfit for her and we spent tonight planning how she can present the creatures in the show for maximum effect. I befriended her as you asked and will help her all I can. She's actually very nice, so it's not hard."

"I'm counting on you, boy. Keep an eye on her. I have a sneaking suspicion she's not fully committed to our cause."

Griff shrugged. "She has nowhere else to go, Master Tyren," he said carefully.

"Don't be too sure." He sat back and contemplated Griff, who squirmed beneath the scrutiny. "Anyway," Tyren continued. "I asked you here tonight to discuss you, not Tess. This quirky habit of yours. How accurate is it?"

"Habit?" Griff frowned.

"You said you listen in on people. How accurate are you?"

Griff heard alarm bells ringing in his mind. "I don't listen to them. I simply hear things. As to accuracy, I don't know, Master Tyren. I never ask people, to be able to check if I'm right or wrong."

"Well, you got my thoughts right earlier today. Surely you've practiced on your brothers?"

"No, sir. I don't practice at all. I avoid using it as much as I can."

The showmaster grinned and Griff saw cunning in his expression. "Well, you're not going to avoid it for much longer, young Griff. I want to build a new act around it."

Griff stared at Tyren as though he were speaking a different language, his face a mask of incomprehension.

"I trust you're not going to refuse," Tyren said at last, and his tone was as cold as ice.

Griff began to gabble. "I hear random thoughts, Master Tyren, only when someone's anxious and only when I am concentrating hard or I've let my guard down from shutting the voices out and they get through to me. I've taught myself—for most of the time anyway—how to block them from my mind."

"Well, unblock your mind, boy, because I plan to make many carks from you."

"Carks?" Griff didn't know whether to be amazed or horrified. "Master Tyren, I don't even earn ten sharaks each moon. It would take years to earn a cark."

"I'm going to be charging you out at five jaks a visit, young Griff. Don't you realize you're not a freak of nature with a misshapen head, an extra-long tongue, eleven fingers or one eye at the top of your nose? You're not too tall, too short, too fat, too thin or too hairy. Everyone accepts that all of these quirks, visited upon some special people as the Mother's sense of humor, are natural oddities . . . Nature taken a wrong path, you could say."

Tyren sat forward, his shirt stretching tightly over his enormous belly. Griff could see the man's hairy flesh in the spaces between the buttons as the fabric pulled. He looked down, not only repulsed by Tyren physically but repulsed by the man's greed. The showmaster continued, unaffected by Griff's anxiety, his voice dropping to a gentle, almost-liquid quality that ran over Griff thickly like honey. It felt cloying, sticky, uncomfortable, and Griff squirmed again as Tyren laid a fat hand on his arm. "But what you have is not an oddity, Griff . . . it's not even a quirk. What you possess is something we all dream of discovering in anyone, let alone ourselves. You have magic, boy. And to witness real magic at work, people will pay handsomely. I dare say we can persuade the King and Queen of Drestonia to attend our show if you are going to demonstrate your magic and tell us what our monarch is thinking." Tyren laughed, loving his own jest, and rubbed his hands gleefully. "You, young Griff, are going to make me rich."

"Master Tyren, I don't want to—"

"Did I mention that I shall pay you generously for your trouble? If the act takes off, as I suspect it will, then I shall be paying you not ten sharaks each moon, Griff, but fifty!" He beamed, very pleased with himself.

Griff rubbed at the warm spot where Master Tyren's hot hand had gripped his arm. He took a deep breath. "No, sir. I won't do it."

Tyren's expression changed in a blink. All humor left his face as his eyes narrowed above his ruddy cheeks. "Won't?" He feigned confusion.

Griff pressed on. "I'm not a performer, sir. You know me. I'm a grunter. Your best. I work hard but not in front of people, Master Tyren. Please don't ask me to do this."

Tyren's face darkened. "Oh, but I am, Griff, I am. I insist, in fact. I haven't had access to such an original act since Madam Saff and her Levitating Objects of Curiosity. That was nearly two decades ago. And now I have another unique act at my disposal and I intend to use it, make money from it."

Griff's alarm was so intense he felt dizzy. Performing was not what he had joined the Traveling Show for; he was happy to earn his wages from being a grunt. His mind raced to find excuses, ways to get out of this. Before he could construct a plausible lie, Tyren made a chilling threat.

"And if you try to stop me from making money from your talent, I'll not only send your new girlfriend to the city orphanage and have her creatures given to someone else to handle, I'll drop you and your brothers off in the next town. No money, little way of earning it. You'll starve, you three. Oh, and did I mention I'll send someone to your father? I'll want that money back that I gave him. I imagine he's spent it by now—on the new horse and that cow he needed. We'll have to beat it out of him."

Griff stared at Tyren, unable to imagine this was the same jolly showmaster he had been traveling with these past few moons. All this time he had thought Tyren to be a decent sort. How wrong he'd been. How wrong his father had been in trusting this man. The threat was real, too. He could see it in Tyren's malevolent, determined gaze. He wondered momentarily whether the showman might hurt the creatures. Probably not, because it would affect income, but he would certainly carry out the rest of the threats on Tess and on Griff's family. No, he should not call this man's bluff or say anything other than yes.

He cleared his throat. "Well, I wouldn't want to upset you, Master Tyren," Griff said carefully after finding his voice. He was pleased to hear it come out so steadily and not squeak. He had never felt so frightened.

Tyren poured himself another glass of the amber curaj. He

laughed and there was genuine mirth in it. "Looks as though you've got your head screwed on right, lad. It would be wise to pay very close attention to my warning." He held out his hand as though wanting to shake on a deal.

Griff had no choice but to offer his own in agreement, hating the sensation of Tyren pumping his hand, squeezing hard enough to let Griff know this was no jest. His warnings were not to be taken lightly.

"How would you like this to work, sir?" Griff asked, trying hard to keep his face as expressionless as possible. He could not let Tyren know how scared he was or how angry. All he wanted to do was to leave this wagon in one piece, no further threats, the showmaster believing that he had two new acts on the bill for tomorrow night.

Tyren sat back, satisfied not only that Griff was compliant but that a bargain had been reached. "Simplicity is the key, Griff—it always is where magic is concerned. And your act will be magical. It's not a trick. It's not conjuring a dove from a kerchief or a mouse from behind someone's ear. What you do cannot be explained because it is not rational. And that is everything I desire, because people will pay anything I ask to witness true magic."

While Tyren warmed to his thoughts, Griff's resolve turned wintry as he listened to the huge man continue enthusiastically.

"We shall simply sit you down at a table in a tent and your paying audience can listen to you tell them what they're thinking, or perhaps even what their friends are thinking."

"That could start some problems, Master Tyren," Griff

warned, disguising his rising fury. "Perhaps those friends don't want to share what they're thinking."

"Then they don't have to enter the tent, do they? Tell me, Griff. Are you able to tell me what Madam Tyren is thinking right now?"

He didn't want to, but of course he could. He thought about lying. But it wasn't worth the risk. "Yes, but only because it's important to her."

"And?"

"She's worried that you will drink the whole flask of curaj. You either get abusive or you snore loud enough to lift the roof off the wagon."

Tyren clapped his hands and laughed. "That's exactly how her mind works! Now I know you don't lie to me, boy. Excellent, excellent! This just gets better. People who want to know what others are thinking about them can pay double." He rubbed his hands together again.

"Master Tyren, I don't think we should—"

"You let me do the thinking, Griff. You just do the eavesdropping on their thoughts."

Griff had to rein in the tide of rage that was building. Tyren obviously believed he could hear everything and anything . . . and that simply wasn't true. "I can't guarantee you the success you want. And it would be their word against mine. They could refuse to pay."

"Oh, they'll be paying before they meet you, laddie, and who's to say there won't be a few helpful 'friends' in the queue."

"I won't cheat." It was said before Griff could stop himself.

"You'll do exactly as I say or those you care about will

take your punishment. Don't think I won't have Tess or your brothers watched. I'd suggest you don't test me either. Just do as I say, Griff, and we can all be rich and happy."

There was nothing for it but to agree to the man's face. But Griff's mind was already spinning toward ways to get Tess and his brothers away from Master Tyren's Traveling Show . . . and quickly.

7

It was a crisp early Thaw morning and a mist was rolling up the downs, the sun not yet high enough or warm enough to dissipate it quickly, but the light was sharp and a promise of Summertide not far away. Lute loved days like this one and especially quiet mornings with not too many people around yet, with only the birds for company.

Pilo had woken him when it was still dark. He had held out a steaming bowl when the Prince was dressed and Lute had quickly devoured the hot porridge and stewed fruits. Lute felt fit to burst.

"Keep this with you," Pilo had said.

"What is it?"

"At first glance it looks like an ornament on a chain. But it's actually a whistle."

Lute had looked at Pilo quizzically. "Why do I need a whistle?"

"I hope you don't, but humor me today and wear it, will you?"

Lute had shaken his head at the secretive man but he'd

been happy enough to wear the whistle, which had been fashioned from silver in the shape of a horse's head. It was beautiful and intricately crafted.

"It feels old," he had commented as he stared at it on the silver chain around his neck.

"I had it made many years ago. Now I'm giving it to you."

Lute had looked alarmed, reaching instantly to take it off. "Pilo, I can't possibly take something so precious."

"You can because I want you to. This is a gift. I have no son to give it to." He had cleared his throat. "In fact, I have no family to bequeath anything to. It looks very fine against your doublet. I shall look upon it with pride as you wear it."

"But maybe you will get married someday. Mother often says she feels guilty that your palace role keeps you from a family life."

Pilo had blinked. "She shouldn't. I am privileged to serve."

Lute had felt sure he'd missed something in their conversation; Pilo had seemed cautious. Lute had frowned. "Well, thank you. I'm honored by your gift."

Pilo had moved away. "Don't blow it recklessly, by the way."

"Why not?"

"Let's just say it's precious. Don't wear it out, eh?"

No more was said about it until they sat together, horses side by side, watching the mist stirring and rolling, slowly revealing the moors that Lute would soon be riding across.

"Should you ever need to summon me, Highness, and I am not readily available or in sight, blow that horse's head."

Lute grinned. "You're certainly in a fanciful mood this morning. Why would you not be available? You're always at my side."

Pilo shrugged. "Just a precaution, my Prince. Humor me. Agree to this plan."

"I agree," Lute replied, shaking his head. "Happy?"

"Delirious," Pilo answered as he nodded toward the stables. "Here comes the Duke," he added with a grimace.

"You really don't like him, do you?"

"Liking has no relevance. All that matters is honor and trust."

"Do you trust him?"

"Not for a second," Pilo answered, and led Lute's horse toward the Duke's approaching animal. "And neither should you," he murmured, glancing at Lute with a stern gaze. Then he looked over to the man approaching. "Greetings, Duke Janko," Pilo said. "Did you sleep well?"

"Like a babe. Good morning, young Lute. That's a fine horse you have there."

"Morning, Uncle. Her name is Tirell."

"After the wood nymph, eh?"

Lute nodded.

"She's a beauty, too," the Duke admitted.

"Duke Janko," Pilo began, "I thought you might enjoy it if we took you over the moors toward Peckering. You may recall there's a marvelous lookout at Billygoat Beacon and you can see how the city has developed."

"Excellent. But, Pilo, I would prefer to ride with my nephew alone."

Lute sensed an instant tension crackling between the two men but their tone remained polite, words carefully chosen.

"My orders are to stay alongside the Prince at all times, Duke Janko," Pilo replied cautiously.

"Even when he's with the King or the Queen?" Janko said, smiling, but Lute heard no humor in the Duke's tone.

"No, when the three royals are together, I—"

Janko didn't even wait for the man to finish. "Then it should not trouble you to leave the Prince alone with his uncle. We are family." He impaled Pilo with a cool stare. "Royal family," he added.

Again Pilo did not answer immediately and seemed to feel no embarrassment at taking his time. "Is privacy essential, Duke Janko? Because I prefer to fulfill my sworn duty."

"As a matter of fact, it is. What I have to say is not to be shared with a commoner."

Lute took exception to this. "But, Uncle Janko, Pilo is more than—"

"Pilo is a servant, Lute," Janko said firmly, not caring that he spoke so plainly before the person in question. "I know he's important to you at this stage of your life but soon you will be fourteen—a young man. And all of the trappings of childhood, including this somewhat clingy manservant, will be removed. It has already been decided that Pilo will not be with you past the next winter." He ignored Lute's look of surprise as he turned back to Pilo, whose expression gave nothing away. "Wait here. We shall be no more than one turn."

There were only twenty turns in a day, signaled by bells. That would have to be the longest time that Lute had been separated from Pilo since they had first been brought together by his mother. Lute looked at Pilo, whose hard, light-eyed gaze had now narrowed and was directed implacably at the Duke. He couldn't tell what his companion was thinking but it was obvious none of it was kindly toward the Duke.

"I shall be waiting, Duke Janko," Pilo said, his words falling like ice splinters.

The Duke had already begun to turn his horse, deliberately showing disdain for the warning in Pilo's voice. "Come, Lute. Show me what that filly can do."

Lute gave Pilo a worried backward glance and had just a second or so to see the reassuring nod from his friend before setting off at a trot, which quickly turned into a canter. Before they were even off the main grounds of the palace, they were galloping and Lute suddenly forgot the previous tension and lost himself in the exhilaration of the ride.

They galloped all the way to Billygoat Beacon, finally slowing on the rise. Both Lute and Tirell were breathing hard by the time they reached the summit, at which they arrived long before Janko guided his horse to Lute's side.

"I had no chance against her," the Duke admitted, sucking in air but laughing at the same time. "She certainly takes after her fleet-footed nymph namesake."

Lute grinned. It felt good to see his uncle happy, and he momentarily dismissed the memory of the earlier animosity between the Duke and Pilo as he enjoyed the sensation of being outdoors and carefree on horseback. He couldn't think of anything he'd rather be doing. "I suppose the city must look very different after so many years in the mountains," Lute said, trying for well-mannered conversation—as his parents would expect. "Floris has now connected several towns that were, only years ago, tiny little outposts. Fairlight, for instance, is now part of the city."

"Do you see this as your city, Lute?"

He turned to look at his uncle, unsure of the intention of such a strange question. "Mine?"

"Don't be coy. Tell me, how does it feel when you look out across this growing city, this flourishing realm?"

"I feel pride."

"Why?"

Lute looked baffled but could tell his uncle demanded an answer. "Because we're prosperous."

"What else?"

Lute shrugged. He really didn't know what else. "Well, I think it's an elegant-looking city. The—"

"Tosh!" Janko exclaimed. "That's not what I mean." He backhanded Lute in the chest. "Here, boy, in here! What does your heart, your very soul, say to you?"

Lute felt the pinpricks of suspicion return. Felt the care-free sensation of just moments ago vanish. "I'm sorry, Uncle Janko, I don't know what you mean. I've already told you that I am very proud of this city. That's how my heart feels."

His uncle sighed. "I've fought for years to keep this city safe, to watch it flourish as it does now. These days Floris in particular but also Drestonia as a whole is a very prosperous realm. It would be considered a prize catch by any marauding army and it is why old Besler would love to annex it."

Lute couldn't shake the tension but he tried again to be polite. "Well, that's why my father loves and admires you."

"Because I keep his realm safe, do you mean?"

"Because you are loyal to Drestonia and want peace for it as much as its people do."

"Ah, spoken like a true king, Lute."

"I am not a king."

"But you wish to be," Janko said, and there was a cunning note in his tone now.

"I am its Crown Prince," Lute said carefully, silently

acknowledging the turn of the conversation, alarm bells clanging in his head.

His uncle barked a harsh, brief laugh. "Indeed. Heir to the throne of Drestonia? Why, it has to be the most envied position in the whole of the Moragans."

"The Moragans is a group of nine kingdoms, Uncle Janko. We are but one of them," he replied with care.

"But your kingdom is the largest. Yours is the most powerful—it has the river network and its fine harbor. It has mineral wealth and rich black agricultural soil. Drestonia grows everything it eats, and its surplus it sells to the rest of the realms it dominates. Please don't pretend to me that you consider it one of the pack."

Lute bristled. "I don't pretend anything. I am the son of the King and Queen, nothing more, nothing less."

"The only son of King Rodin."

"I can't help that," Lute said, tiring of the banter and its curious undertone, and the need to remain polite. He wished Pilo were here to guide him. "Uncle Janko, why are you reminding me of something so obvious? I have known the Crown was mine since I was old enough to understand words."

Janko's expression lost all pretense at politeness. The man who looked so similar to the King suddenly became the lizard-like predator the Queen feared. His lips pulled back in a sneer and his voice seemed to drop a few notes into a growl. "Because, young Lute, I've no intention of allowing you that Crown, for I don't believe you are the true heir."

And he reached for Tirell's reins.

8

Miralda gestured that the servants should leave and the palace aides silently left the salon where the King and Queen had been taking their morning porridge. It was not long past first light, with the sun lifting itself to brighten the dark sky with slashes of pink cutting across the inkiness. Mists rolled away from the palace toward the hills.

"Are you feeling well, Rodin? You've hardly said a word. In fact, you've been downright broody," she said. "Is it the early hour?"

"Mmm?" Rodin seemed distracted, looking around from where he'd been staring.

She repeated her inquiry.

The King sighed. "Forgive me. I'm puzzled, that's all. Last night I received a message from Captain Drew. I thought he was misinformed but it seems he's right: Floris appears to be surrounded by soldiers."

"Pardon?" Miralda said, pushing away her bowl. "What do you mean?"

Rodin shrugged. "Exactly what I say. All the town gates were secured by the home guard at my behest last night, but fringing the capital are the soldiers of the legion. It just doesn't make sense."

"Upon whose orders?" And then she answered her own question. "Janko? Janko's done this?" she asked, her voice barely above a whisper.

Rodin seemed as incredulous as she did. He didn't sound frightened, however. "He wouldn't, though, Miralda. Think about it. This is my brother. The brother who has been fighting for our freedom and peace for probably the past dozen years. It is because of Janko and the army he commands so rigorously that we enjoy such prosperity now. This couldn't be his doing. He is lauded, loved. He is a duke. He is my brother," Rodin repeated, almost to himself, and Miralda heard the tone of desperation he tried to mask.

"It's not enough, Rodin." She stood, wringing her hands, but in anger, not fear. She was no longer prepared to be gracious toward Janko. "It's obviously never been enough. Janko wants the Crown. Don't you see? He's always wanted it. Up until now he's been patient, perhaps fighting his own inclination to go against his brother. But he knows you're getting on in years and unless he makes his move soon, Lute will become King. I tried to warn you but you never took me seriously." Miralda heard her own rage rising, trying to escape. She reined it in, determined to keep her composure. "What are you going to do?"

"Well, I came down here to talk to him this morning. I couldn't find him when I learned about it in the early hours, but naturally I thought this was some sort of mistake. I'm

94

even beginning to think this might be Janko's idea of fun, part of the festivities, you know. Perhaps he plans a parade of the army so the people can thank them."

"You're clutching at straws, Rodin. Does fringing an entire city sound friendly to you?"

Rodin closed his eyes, shook his head.

"The fact that you ordered all the city gates closed suggests to me that you don't feel fully sure of your brother's intentions. What about the drawbridge?" she asked, standing to move to the balcony to check for herself.

"I've ordered it to be raised. It should occur any moment. No one's getting into the castle, I promise."

And then Miralda felt her blood turn to ice. "Lute! Rodin, he's gone out riding with Janko."

In his shock Lute found himself doing what Pilo often did, which was to hold a silence until it felt awkward for the other person, except he wasn't doing it deliberately as Pilo might. His mouth gaped as he tried to make sense of what the Duke had just revealed.

"What makes you say such a thing?" he finally asked.

"Let me tell you a story," the Duke continued, as though their ride out were still friendly and there were no tension between them. "Before you came along, there was King Rodin, Queen Miralda, and there was me, the loyal brother. Your mother remained barren for so many years that it was quietly understood, though rarely spoken about, that an heir was not likely to come along."

Lute felt a fresh chill creep through him as his uncle continued.

"Some well-meaning people whispered to my brother that he should take a new wife, that he owed it to the Drestonian realm to produce sons—at least one heir. He wouldn't hear of such a betrayal to Miralda."

"That's a good thing, surely?" Lute offered, glancing around, wondering how he might escape this threatening situation he found himself in.

"Oh, those of a romantic inclination would think so. But politically, no, Lute. It was not a good thing to be so blinded by an attachment to someone that he put the good of the realm at risk. It's a sign of weakness."

"How dare you!" Lute exploded. "Let me go." He nudged at Tirell's ribs. But the Duke was ready for him and pulled at the reins he held.

His uncle shook his head. "I want you to listen to my tale before I permit you to leave."

Not really sure of where he found the courage to sound so regal, Lute sat straighter in his saddle and set his jaw defiantly. "Permit? I am Crown Prince. You permit me nothing."

Janko only smiled. "Ah, and here we have it. I wondered when it would surface . . . when the arrogance of status would emerge to show its true colors. Now I know you're not your father's son! He would never demonstrate such open superiority. Curiously, I admire it!" He grinned at Lute's struggles.

"I demand that you let me go." Lute twisted in the saddle but Janko's grip on the reins didn't falter.

Janko laughed openly now. "Calm down. A crown prince should have composure at all times. Never show your fear,

Lute. I'm sure your champion, the suspicious Pilo, has mentioned this." Lute's anger flared to rage and it brought him the moment of icy calm he needed. He stopped struggling. "Good. That's a nice trinket you're clutching so tightly, Lute. I noticed it earlier. It's very fine craftsmanship. May I see?"

Lute felt he had no choice. He squirmed, purse-lipped, as his uncle studied Pilo's recent gift.

"It's exquisite. What is it?"

"Simply what you see," he answered coldly. "A finely crafted head of a horse."

"But it is hollow."

Lute shrugged. He was not going to tell Janko what it was if he couldn't work it out.

"This is not Florian work and your father would not purchase anything from a silversmith outside of Floris."

"Pilo gave it to me."

"Pilo. Ah, there's that annoying name again. He's awfully close to you, isn't he?"

"He has been given his orders by the King. I have no say in his duties."

"You obviously care for one another."

"We are close friends."

"Well, Lute. He's not here now, with his grave face and searching gazes. It's just you and I . . . perhaps a few others," he said, gesturing behind.

Lute turned and was astonished to see three soldiers, two on horseback, another crouched, the reins of his horse wrapped around his fingers.

"Why are these men here?"

"Keeping watch over me," Janko said, too innocently for

Lute's liking. The chill he'd felt earlier was hardening, turning his blood to ice, it seemed. He was frightened now, and the fear overwhelmed his fury. This whole situation felt suddenly dangerous. He was outnumbered and outmuscled. He took a silent, steadying breath to clear his mind; looked back at the Duke, trying to keep his face expressionless. Pilo would demand that he not show fear.

"Shall I finish telling you my story?" the Duke asked calmly.

Lute needed time to think. Pilo was too far away to help. He'd have to fend for himself. He nodded, unable to say anything as the sense of peril escalated in his mind. Let the man talk while he figured out what to do.

"Good. So now, where were we?" Janko pondered, looking to the sky and squinting. "Ah yes, Rodin refused to take another wife. Instead, he made a bargain—not with his people, they were none the wiser—but with one person."

"A bargain? For what?"

"The Crown, of course."

"You lie! My father would never do such a thing."

"Ah well, you see, perhaps not now because he has you. But a dozen or so years ago, he would have made a deal with the devil himself, so long as he could remain married to your mother and not bow to the increasing pressure to give Drestonia an heir."

"I don't believe—"

"Let me finish, Lute. You see, the tale gets complex because although your father made his bargain, and sealed it with blood in fact, you miraculously came along and changed everything."

"Well, I don't remember seeing any rule of the realm that

forbids the King and Queen from having sons. Surely this made all the people happy?"

Janko threw back his head and laughed. "Of course it did. Yes, indeed! There was *much* celebration. I heard they were dancing in the streets and three days of festival were launched. The more far-flung realms sent their envoys with messages of congratulations and our closest neighbors sent dignitaries and even a few royals to join the festivities. I could not attend, unfortunately. I was holding off Besler's horde in the north. I was keeping our realm safe."

Lute ignored the Duke's bleating. "So where is the problem?"

"The problem, my Prince, existed with the man with whom the bargain was made. He felt cheated."

Lute shook his head as though he wasn't following the tale. "But what had he given in return?"

"His life. His loyalty."

"Well, so does every Drestonian. I'm sure he understood that the arrival of an heir would cancel all previous agreements."

"You know, I truly believe he would have understood if the heir were genuine." Janko ignored the way Lute was staring at him, as though he had gone suddenly mad. "You see, the man in question knows that the heir to the throne— that's you, Lute—is an impostor."

Lute rocked back in his saddle. It felt as though Janko had kicked him in the belly, knocked all the wind from him. Lute straightened, forced himself to breathe steadily. "I don't know why you're saying this or what mischief you're up to, Duke Janko, but I've heard enough," he said, pulling at the reins again but to no avail. He surreptitiously began to take his feet from the stirrups. He'd take his chances on foot, even though the Duke and his soldiers were faster on horses; perhaps he could take them by surprise and make it to the stand of trees, where there would surely be somewhere to hide.

But the Duke was sharper than Lute gave him credit for. "I wouldn't, Lute. That man over there will bring you down with a single arrow before you even get halfway to the trees," Janko said conversationally, and smiled when Lute became still. "Actually, I intend that you'll hear it all. Ask yourself honestly, do you look like either of your parents? Rodin is beginning to gray now but he had sandy-colored hair to go with his green eyes. Your mother is still very beautiful despite her now-fading glory, I'll admit, but she was once brightly golden-haired and blue-eyed. You, Lute, have dark hair and dark eyes. It's impossible that they conceived you."

Lute stared at the Duke, feeling his world crumble around him. Janko was right and had hit on something that had troubled Lute since he was old enough to take notice of people's appearances and his own. It was true. He looked nothing like either of his parents.

"I asked my mother about it once," he replied, surprised at how even his voice sounded. "She told me I looked like her ancestors."

Janko shook his head. "She's lying. Her people are from the south. They're a fair-haired race."

"I think *you're* lying."

"I have no reason to lie to you, Lute. I'm simply telling you what I know."

"For what purpose? What do you hope to gain?" Lute demanded, desperately wishing someone would come along who would divert their attention, just for a moment. He was a boy against four men. He was beyond fear. He felt helpless. "Why have you told me this?" he finally demanded.

"Well, I thought it would be polite to let you know that I plan to put the real heir on the throne very shortly."

"The real heir? Have you gone mad during your time in the mountains? Who do you believe is the true heir?" he asked, knowing he really didn't want to hear the answer.

"Oh, well, that would be me, young Lute. I am the true heir. I am your father's genuine family—unlike you. I am his brother and was next in line to the throne until you came along. I was the man he made a bargain with, whose skills he used in defense and whose influence he used over mercenaries and our soldiers to keep the realm safe." Duke Janko's voice began to rise in anger. "I gave my loyalty gladly, for the throne was going to be mine upon his death. We all know Rodin has a weak heart. He could go at any moment. I have been patient. I have been faithful to him. And now that the borders have been utterly secured and we are clearly the strongest of all the realms, I'm ready to claim my crown before you do. If I let it go any longer, then in a year the army will answer to you. I cannot have that. Drestonians love their royals and would instantly transfer their loyalty to you should Rodin die. As it is, I sense they are already a little in love with their young Prince. And that won't do, Lute. This is my time to seize the Crown."

Lute could barely believe what he was hearing. "What are you going to do?" he whispered, his throat so dry he couldn't even speak properly.

"Going to do?" Janko laughed mirthlessly. "It is already done, boy!"

9

Rodin tried to calm his wife's panic. "Miralda, be still. Pilo is always with Lute. You and I both know that Pilo can fend off a dozen men at once if need be. I swear Janko means the boy no harm."

Miralda was shocked. She rang for the servant but could no longer hide her anger. "Rodin, I think you are blinded by brotherly love. There is nothing vaguely sincere about Janko toward either myself or Lute. He may love you but he loves your crown more. I want a runner sent now to find Pilo. I want Lute back here immediately!" She felt as though a scream was about to escape her throat.

"I swear, Miralda, there'll be an explanation, I promise you."

"If anything should happen to Lute, I won't forgive you, Rodin. I have tried to make you understand that Janko has been a threat to Lute since his birth. On the two occasions Lute has been hurt, Janko was present. I know you can't see it and keep dismissing my concerns, but it's frighteningly plain to me that Lute didn't squirm and fall from Janko's arms; he was deliberately dropped near those stairs when he was nearly two. And the fall from the horse? Again, Janko was conveniently at the hunt. I suspect he found a way to spook Lute's horse, and then when he realized our son would survive, he disappeared again. His time has run out for contriving accidents. He is making his move before our son turns fourteen and is general-in-title of our army."

Rodin had turned ashen. "What you're suggesting is ludicrous, woman, but I have no answer for you yet, although I'll be demanding one from my brother, I can assure you! I'll order the runner now. I'm sure Janko will laugh at this accusation."

Miralda looked at her husband with sorrow, her fear for Lute taking full flight. "I don't think there will be any more laughing in this palace, my King."

At her fateful words the doors burst open and soldiers entered, followed by the King's terrified aide.

"Your Majesty, soldiers have stormed the palace."

Miralda felt her heart sink. She clasped her hands to her face and allowed herself a moment of grief, knowing it was already too late for them—Rodin looked weakened; she worried for his heart. But she refused to accept that it was too late for Lute. Pilo would save him. And if she alone lived to see this day out, then she promised herself she would avenge this outrage. She dragged her hands away from her face, drying the tears in the movement, and setting her jaw firmly to look upon their intruders.

"What is the meaning of this?" Rodin demanded.

"We are following the orders of our commander, Duke Janko," a fearsome-looking warrior said.

"You're not Florian army!"

"No, we are mercenaries. Not sure your army fully realizes what's under way yet . . . er, Your Majesty." The man loaded the title with irony. "Duke Janko plans to be King Janko before the day is out."

Rodin's already-reddened face darkened as he began to struggle to breathe.

"Rodin!" Miralda shrieked. "Help! Someone! The King's heart is giving out."

"Probably best," the huge warrior said callously.

"You brute! Call a physician. I demand it!"

"No, madam. Let him die. It will make the situation so much easier," the man replied, and, turning his back on her, he strode away.

Miralda's desperate cries rent the air.

⋈⊹⋈

"Wh-what are you t-talking about?" Lute stammered. "What's happening to my parents?"

"Well," Janko began, "about now I'd imagine my dear brother has realized that he is no longer in charge of his realm."

Lute stared at the man who was supposed to be a beloved member of the family, but was now someone he was privately vowing to seek vengeance upon . . . if he lived long enough. "What's going to happen to the King and Queen?"

"Who cares?" Janko replied, and smiled.

Lute felt a deep pain settle in his gut. "And me?"

"Ah. That is a dilemma. You are only a child but a troublesome one because you're claiming to be the heir. I'm afraid we'll just have to allow vicious Fate to take her course." He grabbed the red scarf from around Lute's neck, gave a signal, and a second later Lute heard a hard "thwack!" and then Tirell screamed.

The filly reared onto her hind hooves and Lute felt himself slide backward. Instinctively he wrapped his arms around her neck, gripping with his knees as tightly as he could. He managed to stay on and a second later she was back on all fours, then without a chance for Lute to even gather his wits, Tirell was racing away. Whatever had frightened her had also hurt her. She was making a soft noise of anguish as she rushed them both back down the hill. Lute knew no horse would move so recklessly on a descent unless it was terrified, and, his own safety aside, he was filled with fright that Tirell might break one of her legs. No soothing or handling could calm the young horse, though; all he could do was let her go while he had to work hard to stay on her back. They hit the flat ground at such speed he closed his eyes briefly to steady his panic and, in that moment, remembered Pilo's whistle.

He had no idea if it would work. The part of him that was still thinking clearly argued that even if it did, how was Pilo to hear him from so far away? It didn't matter. He had nothing else. He reached blindly for the silver horse's-head sculpture around his neck, put it to his lips and blew as hard as he could.

Curiously, he wasn't surprised when no sound came and he briefly wondered why he had ever thought something that was clearly just a beautiful ornament was ever going to have a practical use. He was alone with a panic-stricken horse that he now realized, with deep alarm, was heading straight for the ravine. He'd forgotten about the deep slash in the moors. Normally, they walked their horses gently along it if they were riding in this region but he was sure Tirell was not thinking about what was ahead.

He could hear her labored breathing, could see her eyes—wide with shock and panic—and the flecks of foam at her mouth. He knew enough about horses to realize that she wouldn't respond now to anything he did or said. They were going to run off the edge.

10

Pilo had paced angrily after Lute's departure with the Duke, banishing the other servants in his wrath. After a few minutes of helplessness—tempted to rush back to the Queen and tell her of Janko's deliberate decision to remove Lute from Pilo's care—he had ignored the Duke's couched warning and set off after the two riders.

His idea was to shadow Lute and Janko from a distance, and although he had long ago lost sight of the Prince, he knew where Lute was headed. After last night's spying, although he was now deeply suspicious of the Duke, he didn't anticipate that Janko would make any sinister move against the Crown and was lost in thought as he guided his horse along the ravine's edge toward Billygoat Beacon. He'd had no intention of going up to the lookout itself. His plan had been simply to hide in the small stand of trees at the southern edge of the lookout and to keep Lute in sight. He had been sworn to this duty and it made no difference to Pilo whether the Prince was larking about with friends or was with his revered, heroic uncle. His job was to be close to Lute at all times and he intended to stay true to that sworn oath of duty. And so it was with intense alarm that while he had been admiring the way the sun had finally chased off the mist of morning, he heard a sickening sound. He had heard it only once before but instantly recalled it.

The previous night Pilo had dreamed that he had become separated from Lute and that the Prince had been in danger. When he had awoken, the feeling of unease wouldn't leave. And so he had gone hunting for the whistle he'd had made more than a decade earlier for another child. A baby, in fact. The baby was his daughter. When she was born, he had never known such joy. He had always looked forward to a horde of sons and daughters and Ellin was his first. For her name-day celebration he had planned to give her the horse's-head whistle that he'd had fashioned in silver by a man many believed was a wizard. The man was neither old nor young, handsome nor plain, tall nor short. In fact, Pilo had always been bemused by the fact that he couldn't truly remember what the man—whose name he had since forgotten—actually looked like. Everything about the silversmith was a blur. Pilo had gone to him on a whim during his travels in the far northwest of the realm as a personal guard to a very wealthy noble. He had been on his way home and was looking for a gift to take his daughter for her special day. A local artisan in the village he was passing had told him of the man in the foothills. "Crafts silver like no one else you will ever know," she had said when he could find nothing amongst her pins and brooches that caught his eye for Ellin. Pilo's interest had been caught by the woman's description of the silversmith, and with time to spare, as the nobleman had decided to stay a bit longer with old friends, he'd gone in search of the man and found him. Reluctant at first to make any piece for Pilo, the man had finally agreed when he'd learned that the ornament was for a child.

"I want to give her something that will always remind her of me so she will know when she's touching it, I am always close," Pilo had said. He had meant it as a romantic notion, so that his daughter might keep his memory close, long after his death.

However, the silversmith had accepted his request far more literally. Two days later, when he went to fetch the piece, Pilo's breath had been taken away by its exquisite work and beauty but also by the fact that the man had made a practical item, rather than simply an ornament. At first he hadn't understood why the man had chosen a horse for a girl. He had expected something more fragile, more to feminine tastes.

"Do you not want your daughter to ride?" the man had asked.

"I intend to teach her," Pilo had replied.

The man had shrugged. "Do you not want her to love animals?"

"Of course," Pilo had said, frowning. "I want her to love horses above all others because we rely on them so much for our daily lives."

The craftsman had nodded. "Do you not want her to be able to call you at any time of the day or night . . . to know her father is always close?"

Pilo had felt cornered. "Yes, that's certainly what I asked of you."

"Then I have given you the perfect piece for your daughter."

"But what is it?"

"A whistle," the silversmith had replied, and smiled.

Something in that smile had sent a shiver through Pilo. It wasn't a shiver of fear but more like a chill of omen. It was as though the man knew something that Pilo did not.

"I have crafted this for your ears only," he had explained. "When blown by another, you alone can hear it. Does she have a sister or brother?"

"No. She is an only child." Pilo remembered how he had frowned. "So I'm the only person who can hear this?"

The man had nodded.

"But what if I'm out of earshot?"

Again the silversmith had smiled. "You will never be out of earshot because you will hear its call here," he said, pointing to Pilo's head and then prodding him in the chest over his heart. "And here." He blew the whistle and a host of sensations pulsed through Pilo's body.

"No one else can hear it?" Pilo had asked again.

"I couldn't hear it just now," the silversmith had admitted, and again he smiled at the confirmation of the whistle's magic properties. "Not even your child will hear it. It is crafted for your ears alone."

Pilo had never been able to give Ellin his special, magical gift. By the time he had returned to their home, family and friends were gathered somberly to greet him, many of them weeping. In his absence his wife and daughter had been killed in a freak accident in which horses, still attached to a wagon of beer barrels, had been startled and had bolted.

His wife, carrying his little girl, had not been able to get out of the way in time and both had been trampled. Pilo had arrived in time to bury his young family. His once open, happy heart had closed itself off to everyone and had hardened to a stonelike presence. He had never known such despair and bitterness. Pilo had considered burying the magical whistle with his daughter so that a part of him traveled with her, kept her soul company on its new journey, but something had prevented him from tossing the beautifully wrought sculpture into Ellin's tiny grave alongside her mother. To this day he wasn't sure what had forced his hand to remain clasped angrily around the silver chain rather than release it to the earth where his daughter lay.

Pilo had roamed the realm without purpose for a while. He had felt lost without his wife and child—all that happiness ripped away from him, leaving him empty and angry. He had sold his services to whoever needed anything from a guide to a guard, until he had found himself in Floris. The hum of the realm's capital had helped to ease his anguish, kept him busy. He had accepted a position in the palace as a tracker amongst the royal hunting crew. His good work and quiet, professional manner had come to the King's personal notice when Rodin was out on a hunt with his young son. An accident had occurred; the Prince was thrown from the horse he was learning to ride. Rodin had been so distressed by the boy's fall that he had not been able to think clearly. Pilo had been a pillar of strength, calming the King, and soothing the boy, refusing to let him drift into a dangerous sleep before the physicians could arrive. When Lute had become distressed at being separated from Pilo's large, comforting embrace, Pilo had carried him gently in his lap on horseback. All through the boy's next few days of observation by the royal doctors, Pilo had stayed close by, keeping the spirits of his mother positive, and entertaining the Prince during his enforced rest. A friendship had formed, and when it was time for Pilo to return to his former duties, the Prince had become frantic at losing his new friend. It was no surprise that the Queen had asked Pilo to take a new position she would create—Prince's Aide—so that he could remain a close companion to Lute.

Pilo had liked Miralda from the moment he'd met her. Liked her strength and humor; she had qualities that had reminded him of his wife and he could see how vulnerable the Queen had felt at coming so close to losing her only child. He could sympathize with this fear, having lived through the horror of such a loss. And so he had agreed to the new role.

He began to learn more about Lute and soon discovered that the boy who was being groomed for kingship was going to make a fine royal—better than his father, Pilo decided, because as much as he liked Rodin, Pilo sensed a weakness there, especially where his brother Janko was concerned. Rodin clearly idolized his younger sibling's heroics in the north. Rodin was not cut out for such activity, but he was definitely more a man of the people, and Pilo believed the realm was fortunate that Rodin had been the heir and not Janko. This had become all the more obvious when he had watched the Duke on various occasions, not that the Duke would recall him. Pilo had observed from a distance. He didn't like Janko but that was purely a personal reaction. At a more objective level Pilo could see that Janko was brave, strong and ruthless where the security of Drestonia was concerned. One could hardly criticize him for that loyalty to the Crown. But Janko's presence had created friction within the palace, and his nearness to Lute, according to his mother, had always caused the boy to withdraw. During those quiet, frightening days while Lute recovered from his fall, Miralda had explained that the Duke had never taken much notice of Lute, barely sparing a glance toward the wet nurse who had brought him, relatively newborn, to his mother on one occasion. That hadn't seemed so odd to Pilo. This was the realm's top soldier, after all—why would he bother himself with a squalling baby? She had nodded but then had argued that this was no ordinary child. This was the boy who would one day rule the land . . . rule Janko. "You'd think the Duke would have some curiosity, wouldn't you?"

Pilo had thought no more about it until he'd learned that the Duke had been in the hunting party.

"Didn't you know?" Miralda had asked. "Surely you would have been told?"

"No, my Queen. I went ahead as a scout. To my knowledge it was the King and the Prince alone. Even after the fall I never saw the Duke."

"I see. Well, he arrived unexpectedly that day, found Rodin missing and, unable to resist the opportunity for a hunt with his brother, went after him. He was one of the first back to raise the alarm, offered to guide the physicians to where Lute had fallen."

"How strange, Your Majesty. We felt the physicians took rather long to arrive and they came alone. They had no escort."

He remembered how the Queen had frowned at this news

and had said she was going to check into it, adding, "Is it mere coincidence that man is always around when Lute is injured? The last time our son was hurt, he was barely more than an infant and Janko claimed Lute squirmed and slipped. Fortunately, Lute only suffered bruising but he was scared of his uncle from then on."

Amidst the worry of her son's fall from the horse and the discovery that Janko had returned to the north the evening of that hunt, she had never found out anything else. Pilo had thought nothing more of it until she had given him her warning last night. Pilo had only the Queen's mistrust to go on, but on a whim he had dug through his old trunk of belongings and found Ellin's whistle. He had never thought he'd part with it. Never believed there would be reason to do so. But this morning it had felt right.

Pilo had just been telling himself that he should swerve away from the old riverbed that formed this ravine he was fringing and head toward the stand of trees when he heard a sound of such panic he dropped the reins.

It was similar to a pain—a scream of pain, in fact, that cut through his mind and made his heart skip a beat before it began to pound hard. He recognized the chilling sound instantly.

Lute had blown Ellin's whistle.

He straightened, alarmed, and scanned the moors. There, right ahead of him and heading straight toward him, was a horse at full gallop.

11

Unable to sleep, Griff had risen before anyone else; it was still dark enough that it felt as though it were the middle of the night. His instincts told him it was that silent time just prior to dawn and very soon—probably in just minutes—the birds would give their first chirrups, and slashes would appear across the sky as morning began yawning and stretching from her slumber.

He tiptoed around the wagon he shared with his brothers and put his boots on outside to avoid disturbing the lightly snoring pair. Sitting on the step of the wagon, Griff shivered from the chill. It was too early to expect any keraff to be brewing anywhere soon, and after Tess's home-dried phelan tea, he knew it would never match up anyway. It was too dark to begin work but he needed something to distract him. The truth was Griff wanted to think but he was too frightened about where his thinking might take him. He sensed that if he thought about it for too long, he would start down the even more perilous pathway of plotting an escape. He couldn't imagine how four of them plus a horde of exotic animals could go unnoticed for very long.

The creatures! Yes, that's where he would go. He broke into a lope and made his way to the small copse. The four companions were already well alerted to his arrival, and when he entered the now dimly lit clearing, there was no sign of them. Tess had trained them well.

"Davren, it's me, Griff. You're safe."

He listened intently because he could see nothing in the still very murky light. It felt like an age but finally he heard a soft footfall behind as the young centaur walked toward him.

Griff held out his hand in the way he remembered Tess teaching him. Davren responded in kind.

"Hello, Davren," Griff began, wishing he could talk to the centaur as Tess did. But he kept his voice even and friendly. He couldn't fully make out the centaur's features in the shadows but he was able to tell that the creature was intrigued and not fearful of him. "I couldn't sleep, so I thought I'd come and check on you, see that you're all fine. Er, wait." He dug in his pocket. "I brought Elph a biscuit. It's a bit stale but I'm sure he won't mind."

In the gloomy half-light he saw Davren smile tentatively before cupping his hands to his mouth and giving a soft hoot like an owl. Immediately Elph blundered out of the undergrowth to take the biscuit greedily. It was devoured in a blink but Elph returned to nuzzle Griff's hand with his velvety snout, and Griff took this to be the sagar's thanks.

"You're most welcome," he whispered, and stroked the strange creature's head.

"And Helys? What color is she?" he asked anxiously of the centaur.

Davren pointed to a leaf.

"Oh, good, green. She's calm, then," he replied, delighted.

Davren grinned, nodded, then touched his heart and gave a gesture that was halfway a shrug.

Griff bit his lip. He nodded. "I'm worried. I don't think we can stay with the Traveling Show for very much longer. Tyren wants me to do something that I don't wish to. I'm thinking of running away."

Davren frowned, pointed to himself and the happily groaning Elph, whom Griff was still stroking.

"I won't leave any of you, or Tess," he said, hand over his heart. "I promise. But we may have to be patient. For now I have to go along with Tyren's instructions. I can't risk angering him. Do you understand? We all have to do what he wants of us until I can figure out a plan."

The centaur nodded and looked up at the lightening sky. Dawn had arrived. Suddenly the birds were beginning to sing and the wagons of the showfolk, still gray-looking and washed-out in the bleary mist of morning, at least had an outline now. In fact, in the distance Griff thought he could see Blind Pippin picking his way very carefully to a bushed area where he could relieve himself. Davren pointed to where Helys was emerging from behind the more heavily wooded area of the copse. As Griff turned, she flashed orange, just for the briefest of moments. She was joyous!

And he felt happy for one of the rare times in his life. With the creatures—now his friends—there was peace, not a constant crowding of thoughts that he had to shut out. It was only then that he realized he was not even guarding his mind, as he usually would. For the first time in living memory he was not bombarded with the thoughts of others. Either the creatures were blank to him, or something about being with Tess's magical friends gave him relief from his own magic. He was just about to say something regarding this to Davren when he heard a shriek in his head. It hurt him, alarmed him. It sounded, of all things, like a whistle. The sound pierced his mind and shattered his calm. He was holding his head and groaning as it ripped through his mind.

And then it stopped abruptly and he heard a voice. It was no more than a whisper through his thoughts. Two words only.

Help me! the voice begged.

And Griff fell to the ground unconscious.

⛬

Pilo urged his horse into a gallop and thanked his lucky stars he was riding his stallion today. Bruno was always eager to thunder across the moors, never requiring more than a quick nudge with the heels and the sense of being given free rein. The stallion covered the ground between himself and the other horse at such a fast speed that Pilo could only pray he would be able to guide Bruno in precisely the right manner. If he could maneuver the big stallion in such a way as to frighten Tirell into slowing at least, then he had a chance of preventing her from taking the Prince down the ravine and falling to certain death.

He couldn't be sure that the Prince had seen him yet but he felt a surge of pride to note that the boy he'd taught to ride so well was still working hard to calm the bolting horse. Right now Lute looked to be bent as close to the horse's ear as he could get, no doubt talking to her, urging her to slow. It was too late, though. Even from here Pilo could see that Tirell was past reason. He knew this state of mind. In a panic like this the horse would run until she hit a large immovable object—like a tree—or until her heart gave out.

Now his fright surged further. It looked to him as though Lute was planning to jump from Tirell. He understood why but it was a flawed plan. At this speed the boy's body would be shattered, even if he did survive.

He grimly steered the stallion straight at Tirell. He could feel the big horse's indecision, his surprise at what was surely going to be a head-on collision. But Pilo forced him forward, urging him even faster. Now he was close enough to see the whites of Tirell's panicked eyes and the equally wide eyes of his Prince, who had finally seen him.

"Lute!" he yelled. "Be ready for her to rear!"

There was no time for further instructions and he couldn't even be sure Lute heard; he just had to hope the Prince remembered all his training. Furiously digging his knees into the ribs of his stallion, Pilo spurred the horse on harder still. The pair of horses seemed destined to slam into each other.

At the final second both animals lost their nerve and, as Pilo had expected, Tirell screamed her terror once again and reared up. In the meantime the stallion roared his own fury and, without Pilo's careful handling, would probably have bitten the filly, the Prince and anyone else he could sink his teeth into. Pilo reached quickly for Tirell's reins as Lute slumped forward and finally fell off his horse, breathing hard, trying to talk but not making any sense.

"Wait, my Prince. Don't speak," Pilo advised, growling

at Bruno to try to rein the angry animal back under control. "Just catch your breath." He himself was sucking in great breaths like his horse, and Tirell looked spooked: Foam flecked her flanks and fizzed at her mouth. Her nostrils flared angrily and her eyes remained white and staring. She would have bolted again if she weren't being held so determinedly by Pilo, and he knew it was angry Bruno frightening her now as much as whatever had made her so terrified in the first instance. He dismounted. "Go, Bruno," he commanded, knowing the stallion would not move too far. Tirell settled a bit more once the huge horse had wandered off, still grumbling and snorting to himself.

Without letting go of the filly, he bent to Lute. "Can you walk?" he asked.

Lute nodded.

"Then you take Bruno. Let me take Tirell."

Lute followed the instructions, taking Bruno's reins and following Pilo toward the woodland. Bruno knew Lute and didn't seem to mind the lad leading him.

"There's quiet in there and also shadows. It will help reassure her. Was anyone following?"

Lute shook his head miserably.

"Even so. It's best no one knows we're there."

"Pi-Pilo," Lute stammered.

"Wait, boy. Trust me," he said, and guided the snorting, unhappy filly ahead.

Once beneath the canopy of trees, Tirell began to quiet as Pilo had promised. A small rivulet gurgled through the wood and Tirell drank greedily, stepping into the water in her urgency to quench her thirst. Bruno was less eager to get his hooves wet, but he settled quickly and before long was grazing quietly. The filly remained skittish and anxious but Pilo could read her; he knew she would soon find some calm.

He turned to the Prince, who looked pale and shaken though his expression was nonetheless defiant. "All right. What happened?"

"Tirell bolted."

"I gathered. Do you know why?"

"She reared suddenly," Lute said angrily, "and I know who is responsible."

Pilo's eyes narrowed. He had his suspicions. "Who?"

"My uncle!" And to Pilo's surprise the Prince spat on the ground—it was a Drestonian gesture of challenge. "The Duke," he said, his tone filled with disdain.

"You're sure of it?"

"As sure as I know your beautiful whistle doesn't work. It made no sound but I thank the stars you were nearby."

Pilo blinked. "Lute, what proof do you have that the Duke caused Tirell to bolt?"

"Apart from his hostile action?" Lute growled. "There was his admission that he needs me dead."

"He *said* that to you?" Pilo said, aghast, a fresh chill moving through him. Suddenly it was very dangerous to be seen and he glanced around to be sure they were still alone.

Lute nodded and told Pilo everything that Janko had said.

Pilo began to pace as he listened, his thoughts turning darker as the Prince's story unfolded.

". . . and there were three of his men behind us, anyway. Now that I think about it, judging by their clothes, they weren't our soldiers. I could hardly take my chances and flee.

They would have run me down easily enough, or shot me with an arrow. One of them probably targeted Tirell with a pebble from a catapult or something that really hurt her."

"Cowards!" Pilo spat. "But their cravenness is their undoing," he added angrily. "They hoped the horse would kill you rather than dirtying their own hands with royal blood. We have to get you away from here."

"Away? I'm going back to the palace right now to—"

"To be killed," Pilo cut across Lute's words with a growl. "I suspect it's already too late. Your uncle said as much. Janko obviously had this planned. If you go back to the palace now, you will be dealt with. Right now they're trying to make it appear as an accident, hoping that an out-of-control horse kills you, or injures you sufficiently that you're out of the picture for a while. And if you're injured it also means you're vulnerable, can be finished off at any time on his orders. Your only chance of staying alive is to get away from here and to hide."

"Hide? I'm the heir to the throne."

"All the more reason. Listen to me, Your Highness, the Duke wants you dead or at the very least incapacitated. He has already admitted to your face that he sees himself as heir rather than you."

"But my parents. What about the King?"

At this Pilo felt a tremendous surge of pity for Lute. "I imagine the Duke made sure of their inability to act before he dealt with you."

Lute looked shocked. "Do you mean he's killed them?" he asked in a small voice.

Pilo shook his head, uncertain. "I think we can safely assume that if they are alive, they are now incarcerated. I think we can also assume that the palace is under his control. The only person he doesn't control is you. And you are his greatest threat, for you are the true heir."

The Prince stared back, fury in his dark eyes. "Well, then he should have done a better job of finishing me off, shouldn't he?" Lute growled. "Now he's got me as an enemy and by Lo's light I'll see him dead and on show to all our people if he's touched a hair of my mother's head or so much as forgotten to bow to my father."

His head on a spike it shall be, then, Pilo thought, for he was sure the King would not be permitted to live. Instead, he nodded. "That's the spirit, Highness. You are a threat to Duke Janko. He will send his henchmen soon to find you injured or unconscious somewhere, or better still, your lifeless body. When you can't be found, it will throw him into confusion. We have to get away from here. Will you trust me?"

"Always."

Pilo climbed up on the stallion again. "Then mount up, Highness. We shall take only Bruno. Let them find Tirell, still disturbed and shaky. They'll assume she's thrown you off somewhere and it will buy us valuable time."

Lute nodded, reached for Pilo's hand and nimbly hauled himself up behind his servant. Pilo wasted no time pushing the stallion into a canter, and once they'd hit the open moors heading north, he let the horse steadily gain speed.

"By the way," he said over his shoulder, before they were into a flat-out gallop, "the whistle worked. I heard it even if you did not." If they'd been riding under happier circumstances, he might have grinned at Lute's astonished face.

12

Griff awoke to find his brothers looming over him. "What happened?" he asked blearily.

"You tell us," Phineas replied, grinning.

"You fainted, like a swooning lady who'd just caught sight of Wolfboy," Matthias mocked.

Wolfboy was a young man who roamed on all fours, and with soft downy hair covering all of his body, he really did look like a wolf. He was one of their major attractions, particularly as he never uttered a word, simply barked and growled, doglike. Tyren had found him caged in the northernmost point of the realm. His father claimed a starved wolf had stolen him as food for his brood but that the baby—Tyren didn't even know his name—was taken pity upon by the she-wolf and the family ended up raising him as one of their cubs.

Tess shouldered through and shooed the jeering brothers out of the way. She looked flushed, worried even. "Davren carried you here to the wagon."

"Davren? But he was tied up."

She gave a sheepish shrug. "He can untie himself, and Elph has sharp teeth. They were worried about you."

"Don't worry, Tyren didn't see. In fact, few of the show-folk did . . . we're lucky. The centaur is back in the copse, apparently secured again," Phineas assured him.

"How are you feeling?" Tess asked, taking his hand.

Griff was uncomfortable with all of this attention. He sat up. "I'm fine. I really don't know what happened. Fainted, you said?"

"Out cold," Mat replied, making a swooning noise again and earning himself a glare from Tess.

"What do you remember?" she pressed.

Griff shook his head. "One moment I was stroking Elph and then everything went dark." He didn't want to mention he'd been talking to Davren.

The door opened without anyone knocking and a familiar portly figure was outlined in the sunlight.

"Hello, Griff. I hear you're not well. Feeling better?" the showmaster asked.

"Er, yes, Master Tyren, much." He tried to stand but felt shaky and remained where he was.

"Good. Because I've put you on the bill for tonight."

"Is that a wise idea? He's been—" Tess began.

But Tyren cut her off with a glower. "I decide on the show's lineup and we've already put the word out that the Great Griffin will be using his natural skills to read minds tonight. So hurry up, lad, look lively. Madam Tyren wants to kit you out with a costume. Don't dillydally," he ordered, and left the wagon.

The boys turned, looked at Griff and exclaimed in unison, "What?" wearing identical expressions of disbelief.

Griff groaned. "I haven't had a chance to tell you yet. He's got me in the show."

"Surely you didn't tell him? I thought you were always going to keep that secret," Mat said.

"He discovered it by accident. I had to tell him," Griff said, skirting the truth. "I didn't have a choice."

"But, Griff . . . ," Phineas began.

"What's done is done, Phin. I can't change it." He shrugged, not ready to tell them anything yet. He needed a plan first. "I'd better go. I'll see you both later. Go practice."

Tess grabbed a shawl. "I'll come with you."

On the way over to see Madam Tyren she glanced at him. "You weren't saying everything back there, were you?"

"No."

"Why?"

"Because Phin and Mat are too trusting. They're happy because they have each other, full bellies and big crowds who clap at their act. They reckon that their lives are simple, and that's fine and how they want them. And I don't want to be the one to tell them it's about to get a lot more complicated."

"What do you mean?"

He told her about Tyren and his threats.

"Why didn't you come and find me this morning?" she asked, aghast at the news.

"It was still dark, Tess. How do you think that would have looked with me knocking on your wagon in the small hours? It would have started tongues wagging. I didn't even plan to go to the copse—I just found myself there." He smiled.

"The creatures were lovely. . . . Helys is green but she flashed orange—that's good, right?"

"Yes, orange is great, but this fainting spell of yours is not."

"Can you keep a secret?" he asked, pulling her suddenly behind one of the wagons.

"Of course I can," she said earnestly.

Griff bit his lip. He remembered the sound he'd heard and then the frightened voice. "I didn't faint for no reason. I think I passed out because I was touched by magic."

"Touched by magic?"

He nodded, his thoughts spilling over each other. "Listen to me. When I'm in the copse with Davren, Elph and Helys, even Rix, all the voices that normally interrupt my thoughts and rattle around in my head stop."

Tess looked at him, puzzled. "But isn't that helpful?"

"Very. It was wonderful to hear only silence beyond my private thoughts."

"So?"

"Well, I think the peace came as a result of being around your friends. I think their magical presence somehow protected me, or at least canceled out all of the thoughts that normally flood into my mind from outside. Their magic forms a sort of barrier."

She beamed. "But that's marvelous. Doesn't that make you happy?"

"Yes, of course," Griff said eagerly. "And everything was fine for a while but then suddenly I heard this terrible scream in my mind. It was like . . . like . . ."

"What?" she queried, frowning.

"Well, it sounded shrill, like a whistle, but so much more

fierce. It was as though someone was blowing this loud, panicked whistle directly into my head."

"They say when you faint you hear ringing in your ears, perhaps . . ."

"No, it wasn't like that. This was definitely a whistle being blown. And that wasn't all. I heard someone call to me. A voice I don't know. If I were to guess, I'd think it was a boy. He sounded as though he was whispering."

"What did he say?"

"'Help me.' That was it. Just two words."

"Then you fainted?"

"Yes. It wasn't like the other voices I hear. Those are thoughts. I can't be certain, but this felt as though he was speaking to me. I'm not saying he knew he was doing it, or that he was calling to me specifically, but it was a voice, not a thought. There is a difference."

Tess looked at him with curiosity. "Only you can tell, I suppose. Perhaps he *was* speaking directly to you. Perhaps this talent of yours is not as simple or unimportant as you think. Perhaps you can communicate with people in the same way that I talk with my creatures and they talk back."

Griff looked at her doubtfully. "I don't think so," he said. "I don't talk with people through my mind."

She shrugged. "Maybe you should try it. Come on."

"Tess, there's something else I need to tell you."

"Not now, Griff. Let's not get into trouble. Later?"

He nodded but he was anxious now. Suddenly he felt responsible for Tess, her creatures, his brothers, his father; and he was worried—very worried. He had to formulate a plan and escape before Tyren made good on his threats.

And now this boy, the Whisperer. Who was he?

They had been traveling in silence for some time now and all the while Pilo had steered Bruno carefully alongside the ravine. But with the initial shock of what had happened wearing off, Lute was thinking more clearly.

"What do you mean, it worked?" he asked.

Pilo obviously didn't need reminding of what he meant. "I heard the whistle. What I didn't mention to you earlier is that this piece you wear around your neck was crafted by a silversmith who was said to be a wizard. He laced it with magic."

Lute opened his mouth to say something, then shut it again. This was not news he'd anticipated.

Pilo didn't seem to notice and continued talking. "I had it made for my daughter."

"Your daughter?" Lute asked, his voice filled with surprise. "But—"

"She died before I could give it to her. She and her mother were killed in an accident. It was a long time ago," he said as a way of steering Lute away from the topic, but Lute heard the pain in his friend's voice. This was not a wound that had healed. "I want you to have it."

"I couldn't keep it now that I know—"

"I want you to. It is fitting that it is used for its purpose and I can't think of anyone I'd rather see wear it than the future king of Drestonia."

Lute felt a pain knife through his heart at Pilo's words. "Thank you. I will treasure it, keep it safe."

"And make use of it. As long as I'm alive, I am yours to command, Highness. I should add that its sound has been fashioned with magic to reach my ears alone. No one else can hear its call but me."

"But that's amazing."

"Magic usually is," Pilo said dryly.

"I've never believed in magic."

"Until now, perhaps? I have always believed in magic."

Lute nodded quietly behind Pilo's broad back. He realized he actually knew very little about this man. Oh, he knew he was loyal, of good heart and, above all, someone he trusted. He knew he was tall and that his lean frame fooled people into thinking he was weak because he was not fleshy, but even now, leaning against Pilo's body, he could feel how hard it was. He liked that he shared similar color hair with his friend, but where his own eyes were as dark as the black marble from the Florian quarries, Pilo's eyes were light and usually filled with amusement and sparkle. He knew Pilo's features were angular with hollowish cheeks and he had a dark beard he kept very closely cropped. He'd overheard his mother describe Pilo's face as closed. It had taken him a while to work out what she meant but he understood now; Pilo rarely offered any change in his expression. The truth was he did carry a serious countenance and the man always seemed to be thinking. That said, it would be a mistake to assume he was not hearing and noticing everything. Pilo was extremely sharp and had worked hard to teach Lute those keen observational skills: how to use not only his eyes but also his other senses to pick up information about people. Most important was being a good listener because people, Pilo advised, often offer a lot more information than they mean to if you remain quiet. Yes, Lute knew all these aspects of Pilo and yet he had never known, never even suspected, that Pilo might have had a family. The fact that his friend had offered an insight into his life prior to joining the palace staff was a shock, but it made Lute realize he now wanted to know everything about Pilo. This, however, was not the time to ask.

Instead, Lute voiced the other matter that was troubling him. "This is slow-going sharing a horse, and why are we heading toward Billygoat Beacon?"

"Because that's precisely the direction they won't think to look in," Pilo replied. "By now the Duke will have sent his men to find your body and they'll head down the hill, not up it. Soon we'll have the cover of those trees ahead, although everything will start to thin out shortly. We just have to buy some time."

"But where are we going?"

"It's a place called Cave's End."

"I don't know it."

"Nor should you. It's used by thieves and highwaymen."

"What?"

"If we get separated—"

"We're not going to be separated, we're going—"

"I said if, Your Highness. We must be prepared for all events. If, for any reason at all, we are separated, I want you to get yourself up to that rocky crag that you can see about two miles away." He pointed into the distance. "There, can you see where I mean?"

"Yes," Lute admitted reluctantly. He didn't like where this was going.

"Beyond that crag you will follow the river. Stick close to

the trees. Travel at night if you must, no matter how scared you are. But keep out of sight."

Lute frowned. "That would take me toward Tarrow's Landing, wouldn't it?"

"Good boy. Yes indeed. Get to the landing and take the ferry. Here, keep this pouch of money in case you need it."

"Pilo, I don't want to—"

"You must, Lute! You must. Your survival is all that matters right now, to all of us who are faithful to your father."

Lute swallowed. This was already sounding like a farewell. "All right. Take the ferry and then what?"

"On the other side head away from the town and on that road you'll find an inn. It's called the Shepherd's Rest—can you remember that?"

Lute nodded.

"Good. Take a room and don't take any notice of what anyone thinks. Keep your money hidden and keep Bruno stabled. He's far too fine a horse to be tied to a post."

"He'll draw attention, you mean?"

"Exactly."

"Well, how do I explain him away?"

"Tell anyone who is rude enough to inquire that you are a stablehand from the palace and that you are transferring this horse from Floris to Copley on behalf of Pilo."

"And that will give me protection?" Lute asked.

"In those parts it will," Pilo answered, but revealed no more. "I want you to ask around for a man called Bitter Olof."

Lute couldn't believe the name. A nervous laugh fluttered into his throat. "Bitter Olof?" he repeated. "How did he get that name?"

"You'll see. And don't worry, just dropping his name around means he'll find you before you find him. When he does find you, tell him what's happened but not who you are unless it's unavoidable. Tell him I need you to have his full protection and that you're to be kept at Cave's End."

"And then?"

"I'll find you."

"Do you promise?"

Pilo nodded solemnly. "I give you my word." To prove his point he dragged a dagger from his boot and drew the blade swiftly across his palm. "There. Shake hands." Lute did so. "I give you a blood promise." Pilo pointed to Lute's jacket. "Now get that off."

"Too royal?" Lute asked.

"Yes, you need to look like a stablehand. Your breeches are fine quality, as are your boots, but they'll pass. The jacket, unfortunately, marks you as a person of rank. We need to make your shirt look dirty, too."

Lute didn't know what to say but Pilo filled the pause while he helped remove the boy's jacket and pulled away the soft lace at his neck. "I should probably tell you now that a moment ago we were spotted."

"What?" Lute responded, swiveling in the saddle, his alarm spiraling again.

"Don't be afraid, Highness. You know what to do," Pilo said, shocking the Prince further by leaping nimbly from the horse. He drew his sword. "Get going. Kick Bruno into a gallop. He'll scare you, but he does like you and he'll do as he's told if you let him know who's in charge. I've taught you well—you know what to do. Be firm."

"Pilo, what are you doing?" Lute's voice came out as a squeak.

"Buying you precious time. Go, Your Highness! Ride like the wind."

"Pilo, no!"

The royal servant slapped the rump of Bruno so hard the sound echoed around the foothills. "I said go!" he yelled. "Remember my instructions. Remember who you are!"

"Remember your promise!" Lute yelled, fighting back his emotion as he kicked Bruno's girth and spurred the horse into action.

He dared only one look behind him and saw to his horror that Pilo was being descended upon by two riders. He gritted his teeth, biting back the howl of anger in his throat, and gave Bruno the rein to gallop as fast as his big, brave heart would carry him.

13

The town had been buzzing with excitement about the show, and the Beracca was packed to near overflowing. Each panel of the tent was a different color, which during daylight hours looked dirty and worn. By night, however, it took on a carnival atmosphere as the rainbow-colored panels began to glow from the lamplight within. The various smells of the gathered people began to warm up and then radiate their aromas. Griff had cautioned Tess. *The hair oil is the worst,* he'd warned. It had made her giggle, but she understood now. One woman's scent was overwhelming in its floral potency as the perfume of too many different flowers and fruits jostled and clashed with each other in the concentrate that she'd obviously puffed all over herself before her big night out at the Traveling Show. It threatened to give Tess a headache, so she moved to the back of the big tent, where Griff stood wearing a grimace.

From this vantage she watched with horrified fascination as Matthias bent himself backward, grabbed his own ankles and then somehow miraculously used his arms to pull himself into a tight circle of strangely angled limbs. It was hard to tell where he began and ended.

"How does he do that?" she squealed in a whisper of disbelief to Griff at her side.

"They've both always been bendy," he said, frowning. "But they practice morning, noon and night to keep improving their suppleness."

"I can't even bend forward and touch the ground, let alone do that!" she exclaimed, her eyes shining with her enthrallment.

"Oh, they've hardly begun," Griff said, not in a bored voice, but certainly in a tone that said he had seen it all before. "Watch."

The burly Chauncey and his equally beefy friend Jasper arrived to pick up Matthias, who was now recognizable only as a ball of flesh, his face grinning out from somewhere between his knees, although Tess couldn't work out how his legs were ever in such a position. To her delight, mixed with a sort of horrified thrill, they threw the ball that was Mat, still smiling, toward his elder brother, who was also in the oddest of positions. Phineas was on his chest but his legs were curled behind him so his toes were above his head. His feet were pumping in the air in a circular motion but they deftly caught Mat the Ball of Flesh, and Phineas began to spin his brother frantically. Mat hilariously began to sing from within the mound, and the crowd erupted into cheers and then joined in the chorus of the song. It was a showstopper. But each new move of dexterity claimed even louder applause. To finish they both passed their bodies through a large embroidery hoop at the same time.

"That's impossible," Tess breathed.

Griff laughed. "They do it every night."

"How?"

"I'm not sure you want to know."

"I do," she said, eyes shining with a ghoulish wonder as she watched the two boys seemingly change shape.

"Well," he began, with a wicked glint in his eye, "right now they're dislocating their arms from their shoulders." He reveled in her soft squeal.

"Ugh." She shuddered, staring at Griff with disbelief and revulsion.

He grinned. "How else could anyone fit through an embroidery hoop that small?"

"Please don't tell me they move their hips out of their sockets?"

"They might," he said, shrugging, and laughed aloud at how his friend cringed. "Come on, you can see the rest of their show another night. We'd better go and get the creatures."

"They're going to be so nervous," she said.

"They're going to be fine. You've explained everything?" She nodded seriously as they walked. "They know why you need them to do this?" Again she nodded. "Then Davren will reassure Elph and Helys. What about Rix?"

"Rix obeys no one, not even me if I demand. But he will cooperate if I can give him a satisfactory reason. He will agree, especially if I've asked him nicely a dozen times."

"Is it a good idea to bring him into the tent?" Griff asked, remembering how nervous the veercat had been.

"No, it's not, but Tyren's not giving me a choice. I have to do as I'm told because he said he won't pay for their food if they don't perform. They're just lucky I don't have Gaston with me." She found a small smile.

"You know you always smile when you talk about your gryphon."

"He's so fearsome. But I love him. I spoke to him today."

"What?"

She nodded. "Just a brief chat. He doesn't like me interrupting his life. He's quite happy to drop in on me, of course, when he's missing me. But he's a loner. He likes his own time, his own peace."

"Is he all right?"

"He's unhappy at what's happening to us, although I've told him nothing about Master Tyren and his threats. But I've told him we're with friends now." She squeezed Griff's arm.

Griff scowled. "Tyren has no right to threaten you like this."

She sighed. "He has every right, Griff. He's the one who paid to keep me out of the orphanages and workhouses. I'm just lucky to have found a friend in you."

"I've been trying to talk to you about this," Griff said, looking around. "I'm planning to leave."

Tess stopped in her tracks and stared at him, saying nothing, her expression filled with accusation.

"I've got to get away, Tess. He's threatened me over this mind-reading lark that he's onto. He's planning to make piles of money from me. I don't care about the money. I'm not someone who performs and I'm certainly not going to let him use, for his fun and his gain, something I keep secret for very good reason. I don't want to stay here any longer. I've got to leave."

Her eyes narrowed. "So you're running away—is that it? You're going to desert me and the others," she hurled at him, pointing at the copse where the creatures lurked.

Griff scanned the area nervously. "Shush, Tess! Someone will hear us."

"I thought we were friends. I trusted you. I allowed the creatures to trust you." Her voice was wavering.

"Wait! You're getting this wrong. I'm not running away from you. In fact, I'm not leaving without you."

Now Tess stared at him as though he were truly mad, but he also glimpsed the flare of relief in her eyes. "Without me?"

"Without you or our friends," he finished. "We go together."

"How?"

Griff shrugged. "That's what I have to work out. We can't just run away. They would find us too easily."

"The Night Forest! We could go back there," she offered, eyes shining now.

"No, Tess. It's too obvious—they'll hunt us. And we can't go back to my home either, for the same reason. We'll have to think a plan through, and that's another reason we don't rush into this. Come on, call Davren. We have to hurry."

Lute rode in grim silence. He didn't dare think about what Janko's men were doing to Pilo, although his friend was arguably the best swordsman in the palace. Still, three against one seemed like an impossible task. Would they kill him? He wanted to tell himself that there was no chance of this happening, but fear had him in its grip and demons seemed to whisper to him that Pilo would not survive. Janko would not let him live. If Janko was prepared to overthrow the King, even stoop so low as to threaten the life of the Prince, then he was surely not worried in the slightest about taking the life of a mere servant. No, Pilo could not survive this, and Lute realized that his friend would have known this and still he had sacrificed himself for the Crown.

He stopped Bruno, slipped from the saddle and retched. Hot liquid shot from his mouth as his eyes squeezed tightly on the tears that arrived at the same time. He was crying for his parents, too, but Pilo was more than a servant, more than a simple aide. He was the person Lute was closest to, the person Lute loved most in his life.

And riding away from him was the hardest thing Lute believed he'd ever have to do—even if he lived to be as old as his father, older even! It was Pilo's brave voice and Pilo's courageous face that had given him the valor he'd needed to leave. His only friend was likely dead because he gave his life to save Lute's. The Prince's twisting belly began to unclench and he knew it would be wise to drink some water from the flask that hung off Bruno. As he straightened, he noticed the whistle dangling from his neck, and as he reached to grip it, he was reminded of the magic pulsing through it. If magic existed in this world, then surely other miracles could occur. Lute set his chin and without realizing that he was balling his fists, he urged himself not to abandon hope that Pilo might miraculously survive Janko's betrayal.

And if he did not, then Lute would not allow Pilo's life to be given cheaply. He made a promise to himself as he proceeded on that terribly lonely journey toward Tarrow's Landing that he would avenge all the wrongs that Janko had committed this day. His thoughts turned to his parents, and he remembered Pilo's careful avoidance of discussing the King and Queen. Perhaps he believed they were already dead. Lute realized his wandering, sorrowful thoughts had permitted Bruno to slow to the point where they were all but strolling. This would not do. He had given his word to Pilo that he would get himself as fast as he could to the ferry. Janko's men had found them, so they knew roughly the direction he was headed in and would surely give chase. There was no more time to dwell on those he loved. Right now it was all about speed and escape.

He could see Tarrow's Landing in the distance. Little plumes of smoke rose from the chimneys of the town that had sprung up around the landing point. This was one of the narrowest parts of the very large River Caravo, which flowed around Floris and virtually down the middle of the realm. It was here that people could cross the Caravo from east to west of the realm for trade, to visit relatives and to find work. As a result it was one of the busiest spots in the kingdom for travelers, and this also meant a certain amount of anonymity. A great many people moved to and fro across Tarrow's Landing, using either the public rowboats that plied the river at a fee or the bigger public ferry that was essentially a large canoe that could hold more people. To transport animals there was a raftlike structure that was hauled by horses at either end. This was the method Lute would have to use to cross with Bruno.

As Lute gazed out across the picturesque scene—already

lively with activity on the river, where a small flotilla of both public and private boats crossed back and forth—he imagined that, should he ever be King of Drestonia, he would build a bridge at this point. And it would be free. He would charge no toll for people to cross the Caravo to see their families or to better their lives by finding work or selling the fruits of their labors in the field. He nodded.

"This is a good plan," he murmured. "But come on, Bruno. Right now we have to cross the great river ourselves and find a man called Bitter Olof."

14

M aster Tyren called the excited audience to order. They'd all paid their five jaks to enter a small tent, where both Tess and Griff would show their skills. Its size meant the spectators could get much closer to the performers but Griff knew it was not for that reason that Tyren had dreamed up this special "elite" tent, or Beracc, as he called it. Tyren had introduced it in order to charge showgoers twice. They paid to go into the main Beracca to see all the acts but a few performers were held back to present their talents in the Beracc, and people had to pay again if they wanted to see these very special acts. He was cunning indeed.

"And now, folks, we would like to show you some creatures that some of you have likely never seen before and probably never will again, as well as some you may never have heard of."

Griff peeked out from a slit in the curtains. "Packed to the rafters, Tess."

"Well, at least Tyren will be happy," she replied, grimacing.

"That's right and that's all you need. Him happy and not giving you another thought. That's how we'll slip away," Griff murmured for her hearing only. "We have to make him feel very secure and convinced that you are cooperating and offering people a hugely popular performance."

"Here I go," she said as they heard Tyren introducing her. "Wish me luck."

"Ladies, gentlemen, children, may I present Miss Tess and her very own Marvels of Nature," Tyren roared with a flourish of his hands.

Applause went up and Griff gave her a reassuring smile as the curtains were pulled back and Tess entered the arena. Initially there was a gasp from the audience as they laid eyes on the beasts. Davren followed last, and by the time he entered the ring the silence was palpable, like a glue holding the audience together as one in a hushed, awed moment of wonder. Davren's arrival stifled all the odd coughs or sneezes. A pin could drop and anyone would have heard it.

Griff noticed that most of the showfolk had also crowded around the rim of the Beracc. They'd all heard about the amazing creatures that had joined the show and yet so few people had laid eyes on them. No one was going to miss this opening performance.

Tess's part of the show was very simple. She introduced each of the creatures, telling the audience about their living habits but not revealing that each had a name. Davren and Rix predictably continued to draw the most interest, people pointing and staring, and while Rix won cheers for his acrobatics in gliding and his obvious strangeness, it was Davren who made the watchers once again fall silent in awe.

Griff had to admit that Davren looked very beautiful. He was an extremely handsome centaur anyway with his dark wavy hair, bright blue eyes and thick, dark lashes. But tonight he stood especially tall and strong despite his youth and gave everyone a glimpse of the powerful creature he was yet to become.

"And if that's not enough to impress you, let me now demonstrate why Miss Tess here is rather special herself." Tyren turned to Tess and nodded, wearing a contrived smile of sincerity. Griff felt ill. It was only hours ago that Tyren had been threatening her life.

Tess turned to her audience. "Um, well, I can speak with my creature friends using my mind."

A sound of astonishment rippled through the crowd.

"Prove it!" someone called.

"Er, yes, all right," Tess said. She frowned, looked toward Rix, and suddenly he leaped from the timber struts at the very top of the tent where he had escaped to and glided expertly down to land in Tess's arms. "I, er, I called him to me."

Griff noted the crowd didn't appear especially impressed.

"You could have trained him to do that," someone grumbled at the front.

Griff shook his head slightly with disappointment. Already the awe of moments earlier at these magnificent and strange creatures was wearing off. What was the world coming to if it couldn't remain impressed by Tess's companions?

Tyren glared at her to do something.

Elph and Helys suddenly pulled themselves up onto two feet and spun around awkwardly. "Well, I just asked them to do what you just saw . . . and they did."

No one applauded; someone even muttered that they might be asking for their money back. Griff was appalled at their rudeness but also at where this might leave Tess, and going by the scowl on Tyren's face, it didn't take much imagination to guess.

He had to do something to rescue the act, to keep Tyren happy and thus Tess and her creatures safe. Against his own better sense and looking smart in his new performer's outfit—dark breeches and a white shirt with a black kerchief tied around his neck—Griff stepped out.

"Good evening, folks. If the audience would like to ask a favor of Miss Tess very politely, I'm sure she will oblige and ask it of her friends. That way you can see that no amount of training could prepare them for the randomness of your requests. Keep them simple, please, but let them be your own."

"But you may have your own carnival folk in the audience. You could be fibbing."

"And who are you, sir?" Tyren said, nodding appreciatively at Griff for his help and gesturing with a small wave that he would take over from here.

"I'm Councilor Ord," the man answered, and people nodded their heads politely as he threw a severe glance around the tent. "I say you ask this request of the mayor. We all trust him and we all know him."

"Very good," Tyren said confidently. "Is the mayor present?"

"I'm Mayor Whitten," a silver-haired man said, pushing through the crowd. He looked slightly embarrassed.

"All right, Mayor Whitten. Ask something of one of the creatures and we shall have Miss Tess request it of them."

The mayor frowned in thought but it was the councilor

who spoke up again. "Ask the centaur to bow to our mayor," he yelled out.

Tess immediately shook her head. "He doesn't bow to our kind. Please, we must respect his ways."

A murmuring of displeasure moved through the crowd and Tyren rounded on Tess, his own expression suddenly thunderous again.

"Er, I'm sure he will bow to Miss Tess, however," Griff offered above the murmurings. He gave Tess an encouraging nod. "Ask him," he urged.

She looked over at Davren, who was frowning. He had heard what they wanted of him but for the purposes of the show it was best that Tess made the request. Griff had already cautioned him not to let on that he could understand anyone but Tess. It was a secret Griff advised they should protect. Tess must have asked him because he smiled and without hesitation executed the most perfect bow to his friend, which had the audience exploding into wondrous applause.

"As you can see, ladies and gentlemen, she really can talk to her creatures without saying a word," said Tyren triumphantly. "Oh, wait, the centaur is moving . . . er, Tess."

"He's fine, Master Tyren, he will not hurt anyone. I think he wishes to pay special salutations of a different kind to the mayor."

Everyone watched Davren saunter across the arena, his hooves making the softest thud on the dirt floor, until he stood before Mayor Whitten. Then solemnly he placed a hand across his chest and nodded his head.

"That, Mayor Whitten, is a formal noble greeting in centaur language. I thought it more appropriate than to ask this proud creature to communicate in our gestures," Tess said politely. And then added, "He asked me to say a very warm hello and thanks to all gathered here this evening."

The mayor looked to be speechless but the crowd erupted into wild applause, loving the drama of the moment.

Tyren obviously decided that they'd all enjoyed enough for their five jaks and if they wanted to see more of the centaur or any of Tess's strange creatures, they could see the show they would put on the next night.

"Thank you, folks," he said, wrapping her act up for the evening. "Come again, please. We'll be at Monkton Green tomorrow night and I promise another eye-opening show. Now, for those who are holding blue tickets—who have already paid to see our next jaw-dropping performance—please remain where you are. Those holding red tickets should now leave the tent. Mr. Chauncey will be checking. . . . Thank you, ladies and gentlemen."

It was Griff's moment to feel nervous. Tess slipped back behind the cover of the curtains and Matthias arrived as well, with Phineas not far behind.

"We thought we'd come and see your first show," Matthias said unhappily.

"I thought you were both amazing," Tess said.

At this the boys grinned.

"Listen, can you escort Tess and her friends back to the copse?" Griff asked. "I don't think they should linger here."

"Of course," Phineas said.

"And miss you?" Tess exclaimed. "No chance. I want to see you in action, Griff. My creatures won't mind waiting."

"I don't even know what I'm supposed to do," he said, groaning. "This isn't going to work."

They heard Tyren announcing him with the usual theatrics.

"Welcome, ladies, gentlemen, children—oh, and Mayor Whitten again. Nice to see you, sir. I'd now like to give you what I believe is the most astounding act we have ever had the privilege to present. This is magic at its most potent, gentle folk. It will astonish and amaze you. . . ."

Griff groaned louder. "He can't be serious."

"I'll get the creatures back to the copse for Tess. Just do what you do, Griff," Phineas reassured, laying a hand on his little brother's shoulder. "Be yourself. Your curious skill *is* magic. Let it speak for itself."

He was so sincere that Griff could do nothing but nod and agree. He hated this. He hated Tyren most of all.

". . . the Great Griffin and his Mind-Reading Magicks," Tyren announced with a huge yell, encouraging everyone to cheer and applaud as Tess gave Griff a gentle push.

He lurched into the arena, terrified that all eyes were now upon him. It became quiet, and then silent enough that Griff was sure he would hear himself breathing. A few low coughs could be heard intermittently, but what everyone didn't know was that although the room was virtually noiseless, Griff felt himself assaulted by a barrage of thoughts as he let down his mind shield.

He could hardly think straight for the deluge of information streaming so hard at him. He knew there was always the safety shield that Davren and his companions seemed to offer, but for the purposes of keeping Tyren happy he knew that for now he had to press ahead with the act.

Griff cleared his throat and tried to shake his head clear

momentarily. "Er, good evening, everyone. I, er, I am Griffin and I can hear your thoughts."

People began to mumble to each other, some laughed softly, but almost everyone smiled at his words, not necessarily kindly, though. Their expressions were more filled with amused doubt.

"No, really I can," he said. "Mrs. Partridge, I know you're worrying about Mr. Partridge's bad knee and whether he's going to be able to get to market tomorrow. Widow Best, your daughter is seeing Master John—he asked her to marry him and she's nervous to tell you." A shriek went up somewhere in the audience and Griff had no time to apologize to the girl, who was clearly the daughter. "Er, Farmer Gyles, you need to return that money pouch you found in the pasture two days ago. It belongs to Councilor Ord." He had no idea who all these people were but their names and thoughts were flying at him. "But wait, Councilor Ord, that money doesn't actually belong to you at all. It was skimmed off the top of everyone's taxes."

"What?" Ord roared. "How dare you!" People looked around, unsure of whether to trust Griff or be as horrified as the councilor. Either way, there was a look of mistrust on their faces.

"Er, I'm sorry, everyone," Tyren leaped in. "Forgive us. The boy has no control, I suspect."

Griff's lips thinned. "I can only tell you the truth of what I hear. You all paid to hear this. Jayn Meak is thinking about whether to kiss Dan Farnby; Mayor Whitten is experiencing a lot of pain due to gout but doesn't want to complain to his wife because the mayoress is not very well herself these days with her weak heart." The mayor looked astonished. "John Coe at the Sleepy Badger Inn is watering down his ale and is worried that you all suspect as much." The murmuring intensified, and then a squabble broke out.

Griff continued, sensing immediately that this might be his way out of ever having to do this public performance again. He sped up, throwing into the open every negative thought he could find out. "Ellen Brenner is not using soap to launder the clothes you pay her to do; Spinster Jen is making love potions against the advice of Constable Drew—in fact, the constable has asked the night watch to keep a close eye on you, Jen. Beware. Tandy Forster is responsible for the theft of the crystal ornament from Mr. and Mrs. Beckwith's house and she has it hidden in her attic. She plans to sell it over at Neame at the annual traders' fair. Mr. Beckwith is extremely worried that—"

"Stop!" roared Mayor Whitten. "Stop this boy at once!"

"Griffin!" Master Tyren said, scurrying across the arena as fast as his heavy body would allow. "This is not what I meant."

"But this is what I hear!" Griff replied innocently. "I did warn you it wasn't a good idea."

The Beracc was in pandemonium. Squabbles had escalated to full-blown arguments amongst the crowd as the various offenders answered to their victims. Tyren looked lost as to what to do.

"Give them their money back," Griff suggested, sensing the showmaster's worry. "I can tell you now the mayor is already considering taking away your permit to perform in this town again."

"What?" Tyren roared, aghast. He glared at Griff, then rushed over to Mayor Whitten and began stuttering apologies.

Griff glanced over his shoulder to where Tess and his brother were working very hard but with little success to stifle their amusement. Mat raised a thumb at him, but then Griff knew Mat possessed a wicked streak that enjoyed stirring up people whenever he could. He would be most impressed with his young brother's effort today. And as Griff felt a helpless smile stretch hesitantly, crookedly, across his own face at their laughter, he heard another voice. It seemed to cut through the babble of thoughts that were still swirling around his mind, hurled at him by the angry crowd. The voice once again was barely above a whisper but it was as clear in his head as if the voice were shouting. It was the boy again, and Griff's grin froze and his body felt icy fear.

It was a groan of pain followed by a call of *Bruno*. Griff couldn't be sure but he thought he heard the name *Pilo* whispered.

15

Lute had led Bruno onto the special raft and tied him to the timber railings as the man in charge had instructed. He'd counted his blessings that he'd worn such ordinary riding clothes today in a deliberate attempt to play down his princely role in front of the Duke and that Pilo had rid him of his jacket. With all the frantic action his clothes now looked appropriately grubby and he could pass as another dusty, weary traveler.

His other piece of luck was that he was riding Bruno, who bore no emblems on his saddle or blankets. Pilo could, of course, wear all those signatures in his capacity as Prince's Aide but he was always one to prefer anonymity. He was a secretive man and clearly wanted no one scrutinizing his life. Lute fingered the silver whistle that he'd hidden beneath his shirt, wondering sorrowfully what had become of Pilo.

Someone had interrupted his thoughts. "That's a mighty fine horse you've got there, lad."

Lute had turned to look into the face of a bearded man, minus several front teeth, who was grinning at him.

He'd swallowed his surprise and nodded. "Just transferring it across the river to my master."

"And who would he be?"

"A very important man," Lute had said firmly, adding, "who answers to the King."

"The King?" the man had responded, but Lute had heard the mocking tone in his voice. "And who are you, then?"

"None of your business," he'd replied, unable to hide his indignance. "I'll ask you to leave me alone." He had known it was a mistake as soon as the words were uttered; his language was far too courtly for these men.

"Ooh," the man had mocked, clearly not planning to leave Lute alone. "Did you hear that, Brog?" A tall young man standing next to him had grinned. "This little toad's too high-and-mighty to share with us what he does for his very important master, who works for the King."

"I would think it's obvious if I'm in charge of his stallion." He'd tried to sound less high-handed but still he'd shuddered inwardly at the regal manner he wasn't successfully hiding. He would need to be very careful from now on if he was to survive in the world beyond the protection of the palace. He'd softened his tone. "Please, I have a job to do and I don't want any trouble."

"Who said anything about trouble, lad?" the man had replied in an injured tone. "I was just admiring the stallion, that's all." The man had then turned away, hands raised in a gesture of innocence, but Lute hadn't for a moment believed that was the last he'd hear from this fellow. He had moved away to stand by Bruno's head, stroking the stallion's velvety muzzle and soothing the horse with a stream of softly spoken words. He couldn't imagine that Bruno had traveled across water before and the last thing he needed was for the big horse to become spooked or agitated. Bruno had seemed decidedly mellow, however, and had waited patiently as the raft filled with various animals, from goats to pigs and even a cage of chickens, as well as a few huge sacks of wheat. These were traveling without their owners but Lute had no intention of leaving Bruno unattended.

Finally, the raft master had rung a bell that signaled to the man on the other side of the riverbank to begin driving the horses, which he did, and with a loud creak the raft had lurched forward and begun its slow trek across the river.

After arriving on the far bank, Lute had deliberately waited until everyone else had come aboard and unloaded their wares from the raft before he'd led Bruno off and paid the ferryman with the spare jaks he had taken the precaution to put in his pocket. He hadn't wanted anyone to glimpse the pouch of Pilo's money that he had slung around his waist, inside his breeches.

He'd looked around for the gap-toothed man and his lanky companion but there was no sign of them. Lute had sighed with relief and expertly hauled himself up onto Bruno's back. Urging the horse forward, he'd led him steadily away from the busy riverbank, with its crowds of people going about their equally busy lives, and down the road in the direction of the inn that Pilo had insisted he find.

The road had narrowed and it had become dark beneath the canopy of trees. Lute had looked up then, acknowledging how late it had become. Already the sun had dipped low and that meant light was fading fast. He'd hoped the

Shepherd's Rest was not far away. He had passed a cart with a family on it who waved to him; then another three travelers on donkeys had come by, all of them greeting him with nods or friendly smiles. He had become alarmed when he'd heard the gallop of hooves and a rider had come thundering past him at one point, but he'd looked like a messenger on an urgent errand and was gone from Lute's sight almost as soon as he'd seen him. Then there had been no one and the journey had fallen silent for him other than the soft twitter of birds settling down to roost and a few lone crickets chirruping in the grass.

His mistake had been not remaining fully alert. He'd allowed himself to fall into a thoughtful mood, lulled into it by the rhythmic movement of the horse beneath him and the quiet surrounding him. It had been a long, eventful day and fatigue had begun to make him careless. Lute hadn't noticed that daylight had diffused into dusk, nor had he seen the shadows moving stealthily alongside him in the trees flanking the road. By the time he'd registered the gap-toothed man and his companion, it had been too late. The lanky sidekick had hauled Lute down from Bruno and flung him into the undergrowth. Lute had felt something crack inside and he'd groaned Bruno's name, frightened that the horse might bolt. And then all he could think about was how he had let Pilo down barely hours after making his vow.

Now, above his pain and fright, Lute noticed that the man with few teeth was calming Bruno down. Meanwhile, his own attacker was blowing fetid breath in his face with a knife near his throat.

"Just give me a reason to use this knife on you," he sneered.

Lute shoved the young man's hand away, noticing in the dim light that he had a drooping eyelid.

"What do you want?" he demanded, careful to speak with as much of an unrefined accent as he could, based on how the stableboys at the palace spoke.

"Well, we've already taken yer horse," Lanky said. "And now we want yer money."

Lute dug in his pocket. "This is it. This is all I have," he said, showing the few coins he'd had the presence of mind to keep handy, including one gold coin so it wasn't obvious that he was hiding more. He prayed they didn't search him and find Pilo's pouch of money.

"How much?" Gap-tooth asked.

"A gold shard, a few silver kerrets and the rest are jaks and copper," Lanky answered.

"I hear horses in the distance," the older man suddenly said. "It will have to do."

"Well, this stallion is worth a pretty penny," Lanky said, whistling his appreciation. "It's even more refined than we initially thought, eh, Brutus?"

"That horse belongs to the palace," Lute warned. "Steal it and you steal from King Rodin."

Brutus smiled his ugly smile. "Not from what the rumors say. We hear that Duke Janko might have inherited the throne."

"Inherited?" Lute all but screeched.

"King's dead, or so the royal messengers have said. How come you don't know if you're in charge of a royal horse?"

"Dead?" Lute said, a pain hitting his heart as effectively as if he'd been punched. "I . . . I'm just a stableboy. I've been moving this horse to its destination."

"Which is?" Lanky demanded.

He had to think quickly, sound convincing. "Delivering it to Master Pilo, the Prince's Aide."

It was Lanky's turn to grin. "Well, the Prince won't need no aide no longer."

Lute frowned. "Why?"

"Because he's dead, too. News is flying around the realm that he was killed in a riding accident. King died of a heart quake, probably brought on by the news. Anyways, Janko is the only surviving heir, so looks like your precious Master Pilo is out of a job and won't mind us making best use of his horse." He laughed, enjoying his own jest. His amusement died as he scowled, a new thought obviously hitting him. "Are you sure you don't have more money on you?"

Lute was too shocked at the news to speak. He looked at the attacker blankly, shook his head.

"Yeah, well, I might just check that, you being a royal stablehand and all."

"Aw, leave him," his friend said. "I can hear the riders approaching. They'll be on us in moments. Let's clear off with the horse. His gold's enough to buy us a warm bed and dinner with plenty of ale. The horse we can get rid of up north for a good price. We've done fine here."

Lanky, who had Lute's collar bunched in his fist, let go. "You'd want to stay quiet an' all. Or we'll come looking for yer."

Lute said nothing, watched them leave with Bruno. His side was aching; it was hard to breathe, in fact, although he wasn't sure if that was from the rough handling by his attackers or the news of his father. And Pilo had been right.

Already Janko was spreading news that the Crown Prince had been killed in a riding accident. How convenient! He crawled deeper into the undergrowth and buried his face in his hands, determined not to cry. Pilo had always told him it was important that a man—especially the King—remain stoic about everything. He was never to show his emotions too nakedly. But even so, Lute could not prevent the tears that brimmed and then streaked down his cheeks.

Griff felt himself letting go. He was sure he was going to black out again and the only thing that stopped him from falling to the ground was that he was being hurried out of the arena by Tess. Mat was no help, still shaking with laughter at his younger brother's lack of tact during his revealing performance. They left Master Tyren to face the music of the angry mayor and his mob. Griff fell to his knees, once behind the curtain.

"Griff?" Tess began.

"I'll be fine," he said, dragging in lungfuls of air to stop himself from bringing up his dinner. Who was this boy? He didn't know how to help him, but whoever he was, clearly he was in trouble. "Can we get away from here?"

They sneaked a still-unsteady Griff away to the copse, where the creatures waited. He revealed to no one how his head was hurting or how nauseous he suddenly felt. His three companions were still sniggering and sharing stories about the various people's faces at their secrets being given up, although Griff was obviously not joining in the fun. But soon the fresh air and the change of scenery, as well as the quiet in his mind brought on by the presence of the creatures, ensured that he felt much better. He was frowning, thinking about the boy who was in trouble, wondering still if he was imagining this.

"Well, I think you've just sealed your fate as a grunter for the rest of your life," Phineas said, grinning, slapping Griff on the back.

"Very funny, Griff," Mat agreed. "It was a brilliant performance."

Tess nodded. "Inspired. I'm amazed at your courage. I wish I'd thought to do something like that."

They kept talking around him, no one really noticing that he wasn't responding.

". . . no way that Tyren will allow you to do that again," he heard Tess say above his own rambling thoughts. "Do you?"

"What?" he replied, shaking his head slightly in query.

"He's not even listening," Phineas said. "Listen, little brother. We're doing a second show tonight, so we have to go. How about you, Tess?"

She shook her head. "Once a night only. Tyren said he wants to build the intrigue around the creatures, let word start roaming ahead of us to the villages and towns we're yet to get to."

Mat whistled through his teeth. "Very cunning. We must go. See you both later. Thanks for the laughs, Griff." He meant it kindly and squeezed his brother's shoulder before he and Phineas dashed back to the Beracca.

Tess turned to Griff. Twilight was giving way to dusk. Stars twinkled overhead in a clear night sky. "You're very quiet," she said, a query in her voice. "Are you all right?"

"I feel sick."

"Well, I can understand that after what just happened."
She grinned.

"No, not that kind of sick. I mean I feel ill, dizzy."

"What is it?"

He sighed. "I heard him again."

"Who?"

"The Whisperer." She smiled slightly, but he could tell
she didn't understand. "The voice that talks to me," he added
as explanation.

"Oh, right. The boy?"

"Mmm, yes, him. He's in trouble."

"How can you be sure? It may be that—"

"Tess, I just know! I feel connected to him. And I could
hear the fear in him. Last time his presence made me faint.
This time I was stronger, I recognized it, so I didn't pass out
but I feel so unsteady. It's magic, I tell you."

"All right," Tess said carefully. "Tell me what he said this
time?"

"It was brief. He was under threat, I think. I don't know
how I know, but I think he's injured."

"That's it?"

Griff nodded unhappily. "I've got to help him."

"What?" Tess exclaimed. "You don't even know who he
is. Or where he is!" She put a hand on his arm. "Griff, you
don't even know if this is something in your imagination."

His gaze narrowed as he looked at her.

She had the grace to look embarrassed. "I'm sorry I said
that. Davren said it was very unfair of me, too."

Griff glanced at Davren, who nodded encouragement.
"He's in trouble. He seems terribly alone . . . and now he's

hurt." This boy, the Whisperer. Who was he? He wanted to know. It was suddenly very important to him.

"And that's your problem? Don't you think you've got enough problems of your own?" She looked embarrassed again.

"Is Davren cross?"

"Yes," she admitted again. "He's ashamed of me but you were just talking about escape and I got so excited and now this."

"But, Tess, this doesn't affect whether we leave here or not. It just adds another reason for leaving."

"What are you going to do?"

"Well, I have to find him."

"Griff, listen to yourself. None of this is making sense."

"Come with me, Tess."

She stared at him as though he were sliding into madness.

Griff tried again. "We want to leave anyway. I hated what I had to do tonight and I refuse to do it again. You've got to understand I have no control over what I hear. I don't have time to try to find people's thoughts that are nice thoughts. Very few of them are, to be honest."

"Tyren won't want a repeat performance," she tried to assure him.

"Who knows what he'll want? He has no idea of how this skill works. He doesn't seem to grasp that I can't pick and choose what people think. The only thing I can do is block it out as best I can. He wants me to open myself up to it. I swear it will kill me and if he persists, it could well destroy his business."

"So you're running away, using this stranger as your excuse."

"No, I was going to leave anyway and I offered to take you

with me. I want you and the creatures to come. The Whisperer just gives me purpose now. I need to know who he is. I can't explain this, but it feels important. He feels important . . . to me."

That came out badly and he could see how it hurt Tess to hear his words.

"Tess. I won't leave without you. Come with me. I have to leave but you have no reason to remain."

"Other than staying out of the orphanage, you mean?"

"If we keep on the move, he can't find us."

"What makes you think he won't set the Stalkers on us? He's losing two of his newest and what he believes will be his most popular acts. Do you really think Tyren isn't going to give chase?"

Griff knew she was right. "How much did you cost him?"

"Five gold shards."

"Five?" Griff blew out his cheeks. It was not a significant amount of money, in truth, but it was not the sort of money he could hope to earn in a hurry. Short of stealing it, he couldn't imagine how to lay his hands on that much.

"Still want me running away with you?" she asked, and he couldn't miss the bitter note in her voice.

"We go together and we're taking the creatures with us," Griff assured her.

"How?"

Before he could say anything more, a young lad came scurrying up. He was one of the many five- and six-year-olds that were too young to work other than doing routine fetching and carrying and delivering general messages. This was one of Tyren's runners.

"Pak, are you looking for me?" Griff asked.

The small, wide-eyed boy nodded. "Master Tyren wants to see you," he said. "You have to come now."

"Here we go," Griff said to Tess, looking miserable.

"I'll wait here," she said. "Don't let him even get an inkling of what you're thinking," she whispered.

Even without magic Griff could hear the worry in her mind that she wasn't sharing with him.

He grinned at her words in an effort to reassure his friend. "The magic fortunately doesn't work both ways. Explain everything to Davren. Listen to what he has to say. Trust him."

She nodded. "I always do."

"Come on, Pak, I'll race you back," Griff said.

16

Lute was too frightened to pick his way to the Shepherd's Rest, figuring that this was likely to be the inn where his attackers would head with his gold for the comfortable beds they were boasting about. He hated this feeling of fear and despised himself for behaving so helplessly.

But he was injured and couldn't remain here for the night. Mercifully, the pain had lessened and he didn't think he'd broken anything, although he suspected a rib was cracked and that would slow him down. But that pain was nothing in comparison to the deep agony he felt over losing Bruno. He fully intended to get the horse back—even if he had to buy him—but right now he needed shelter, a place to think.

An owl hooted mournfully overhead in the trees and reminded him this was now the time for nocturnal creatures to be abroad and not thirteen-year-olds, alone and injured. Lute pulled himself to his feet, grimacing at the sharp pain that knifed through his side again. It still hurt to breathe.

His father's kind face swam into his thoughts, and then he imagined his mother's worried expression. But it was Pilo's voice in his mind that made him rally his courage. It didn't take much for him to know precisely what Pilo would want of him now. Pilo was strong, always brave. He would urge Lute to ignore the pain, banish the fear, act like the son of a king.

Lute nodded. *I'm a royal,* he thought. He imagined how Pilo would respond. . . . *So start acting like one.*

Griff was standing in Master Tyren's spacious wagon, awaiting the showmaster's attention, which was currently focused on counting out coins in front of Chauncey.

"Here, give it all to them!" he said with disgust. "They'll be back for more, I guarantee it, and we'll charge twice as much." He sneered at Chauncey to be on his way.

Tyren turned and regarded Griff, who was doing his utmost not to fidget. He could sense the showmaster's anger but, curiously, it was not directed at him. The thoughts he was picking up were more about the aggravation of having to give anyone their money back.

"Evening, Griff," the man said, and threw down a shot glass of curaj.

Griff nodded. "Master Tyren. You asked to see me."

"I did and I'm sure you know why."

"Yes, sir, I do." Suddenly he found himself gabbling. "I'm sorry for what happened earlier. I did try to warn you, Master Tyren, and it's not that I want to upset your customers or yourself, but you need to understand that this strange skill of mine—"

"Stop!"

He did, unsure of what to do. Griff stared blankly at Tyren and in that second of silence, where his mind felt suddenly empty, he heard a voice whisper through his mind and it said: *I'm a royal.*

The dizziness was back. He was sure he was swaying on his feet but Tyren clearly wasn't noticing. Griff took a steadying breath.

"Just stop talking at me, boy," Tyren roared. "I'm not sorry at all about what happened."

Caught in the shock of the Whisperer's words and Tyren's, Griff blinked twice, slowly, not at all sure that he had heard anything right. He was fighting the feeling of light-headedness and the lack of sense in Tyren's words.

"P-p-pardon?" he stammered.

"What happened was amazing, Griff my boy."

Now Griff was confused. Thoughts crowded in and voices were back to muddle him. He could no longer hear the Whisperer and he had to throw up the familiar guards around his mind to do his best to block out all the usual noise.

"I don't understand," he managed.

"Let me spell it out for you, boy. You are going to make us a lot of money. We won't be doing any more public shows, though—no, lad, too dangerous, as we discovered to our cost. Instead, you'll give private audiences only, but we'll still make a handsome profit. I plan to charge a silver for someone to have you sit with them—in your own tent, mind—and tell them what they're thinking." He tapped his nose, a cunning smile stretching across his mouth. "Or what someone else is thinking."

Griff felt freshly sickened. Was this really happening? "Master Tyren," he spluttered, "we can't do this anymore. It's not fair—"

"Not fair to whom?" the showmaster bellowed. "To you?"

Griff nodded, panic-stricken.

Tyren laughed. A full-throated, belly-wobbling laugh. "I don't care," he finally said, and the tone of his voice assured Griff that he should make no mistake about this. "It is of no matter to me whether you like what you do. Your job is to work for me. I paid your father for you three boys on the understanding that you would all perform publicly if and when I chose. He accepted that term on your behalf. I'm afraid he effectively sold you to me."

It was like a slap in the face to Griff. He had never seen it this way. Encouraging the boys to join the Traveling Show was his father's way of giving his sons a future, a chance to make something of themselves or at least earn a living from an honest day's work.

"Now, you can either pay me back the money I gave your father—and it is no small sum—or you can work for your keep, young Griff. And I decide how you work. Until yesterday it was as a grunter, but now I want you to put that magical mind of yours to good use and earn gold for us. I've already said I shall increase your wages to reflect my appreciation of your talents."

"How much did you pay our father, Master Tyren?" Griff asked.

This seemed to surprise the showmaster. "Well, I shall

have to check my records but I seem to recall I paid a gold piece for you and three each for your brothers. Your father must be living like a king! That's seven shards, in case you can't add, Griff."

"I can count," he said coldly, hating Tyren now for making him feel like a bought slave and his father a greedy profiteer.

"Then you'll know that's a large sum of money."

"How much do you plan to pay me for this new job?" Griff asked.

That seemed to stop Tyren in his tracks. His chins shook. "Well, I haven't considered that yet."

"You'll need to think about it, Master Tyren, because I plan to earn my freedom."

At this the showmaster scoffed. "That will take a long time."

"Not if you pay me properly, and I won't do it unless you pay properly. You can't make me do this."

"Well," Tyren began, scratching his chin. "I can make your life miserable in the meantime. I can certainly find ways to punish your brothers for your lack of cooperation, and that friendship that you've so rapidly developed with young Tess, that could all come crashing down if I start to make life difficult for her."

There was the threat again. Now Griff knew he had to get away from here . . . tonight.

"I understand," he said, adding, "When is my next performance, Master Tyren?" He was careful to keep his voice even.

The man smiled. "I knew you'd see reason. Tomorrow

night. We'll be at Monkton Green. Word will spread ahead of us of your amazing powers. I'm expecting quite a crowd."

Griff nodded. There was nothing else to say. He would have to escape immediately and think about his family later.

Lute hobbled along through the night, gingerly picking his way toward the inn but keeping off the main road. There was a deer track of sorts that seemed to follow the road near enough and he was using that to ease his careful way through. It hurt madly doing it this way because the path was so uneven and had lots of obstacles to deal with in the dark, from tree stumps to a surprised badger, but he had to press on. Pilo had given him instructions and Lute knew he had to find Bitter Olof.

This time he heard nothing; not even the starlings that were roosting in the trees gave him a clue that he was being stalked by dark shadows. And once again, by the time his pursuers were upon him, it was too late for him to do much except yell.

He yelled so loudly this time that the starlings screeched their own fright and one of the trees above him seemed to erupt in activity as the small birds took to the air, angry to be disturbed.

Griff was making his unhappy way back to the copse to explain to Tess their predicament when he tripped in his fright, falling and banging his knees painfully on the ground.

As he did so, his mind exploded with the sound of the boy yelling. Griff called him the Whisperer but there was nothing quiet about his voice at this moment. The boy was in serious trouble and Griff saw sparkles behind his eyelids from the intensity. And then the voice just stopped and was gone from his mind and he couldn't explain the feeling other than it felt painful to lose him . . . not just physically, though; it felt like a bruise to his emotions. Why did he feel so close to the Whisperer?

Lute felt a meaty hand clamp across his mouth. He continued to struggle but it felt pointless, considering the size and strength of the man holding him. It also pained him a lot more than his efforts hurt his captor. He finally fell slack.

"You would have injured yourself more if you'd let that continue," a deep voice rumbled behind him. "Now, are you done with struggling?"

Lute growled from behind the man's hand.

"Answer me. Are you finished?"

Lute nodded.

"All right, then, lad. I'm going to release you but if you make a sound, my friend here has a fist twice the size of my own and he likes nothing better than to connect it with someone's chin. Any idea how long you'll be unconscious if I let him do that?"

Lute shook his head. He still couldn't see anyone and his side was on fire.

"Ages. And a mighty headache you'll have for days afterward. I speak from experience, lad, don't I, Mungo?"

Whoever Mungo was, he laughed from somewhere in the bushes.

Lute was finally released, the hand removed from his mouth. He turned slowly to be confronted by two huge men.

"Who are you?" he asked.

"We might ask the same of you and why you're creeping through the undergrowth and not taking the road like normal folk."

"I'm staying out of sight," Lute hissed.

"Nothing like stating the bleeding obvious. I think I can work that out, boy. What I want to know is why."

Despairing at being set upon for the third time today, furious at the pain in his side and the loss of his horse, and still to grieve properly at the news that his father may or may not be dead and that Pilo was almost certainly dead, Lute was no longer in any mood for anyone else to make a jest at his expense.

"Well, who are you that I'm answerable to you?" he demanded, surprised by how angry he sounded.

The muted moonlight from behind streaky clouds revealed both men were amused.

"Well, this is Mungo and I'm Little Thom."

Lute stared at the pair of them, more like bears than men. "Little?"

At this both men laughed softly.

Thom shrugged. "A name my mam gave me when I was a wee babe. It stuck."

Lute hung on to his fury. "If you knew what I've been through today, you'd know that I have lost all my sense of humor."

"Is that so?"

"Yes. And so if you'll forgive my rudeness, I'd like to be on my way."

"Look out, Mungo, we've got someone who's swallowed the palace silver."

It was an old saying and casually meant but Lute was reminded once again that he had to be so very careful around strangers. If anyone had even a sniff of an idea of who he was, it could mean terrible problems, not just for him but for his parents and the palace officials . . . and perhaps most importantly, it could alert Janko that he had survived Tirell's bolting. Right now it was best that his traitorous uncle was still searching for his body.

Little Thom cocked his head to one side. "Why are you bent over like that?"

"I fell over," Lute lied, feeling a flutter of panic that he hadn't concocted a story for himself yet. Everything could go horribly wrong before he knew it.

"Fell over, eh?" Thom frowned. "You look hurt."

"I'll be fine."

The man nodded. "You haven't given us a name yet."

"Name?" Lute knew he was hesitating too long, especially given the way Thom's gaze had narrowed. "Er, my name is Peat—at least, that's what Master Pilo calls me."

"Pilo?" Thom straightened. "What's he to you?"

Lute had hoped mentioning Pilo would work and he thanked his lucky stars that he'd remembered how his old friend had told him his name carried some weight in these parts. "He's my master," he said carefully. It was time to tell part of the truth. If these men were going to rob him, they would have done so by now. And if Thom recognized Pilo's name, then it was unlikely he would dare touch a friend of his. He took a breath. "Forgive me for being so careful, but I'm from the palace."

"Is that right?" Mungo replied, seemingly impressed. "Do you know the King personally?" This next was asked dryly, meant as a jest.

Lute gave a sad grin. "I've met him on occasion."

"And what's your position at the palace?" Little Thom asked, much more direct now.

"I'm one of the stablehands. But I particularly look after Master Pilo's beasts."

"What are you doing here, then, creeping along the road out of Tarrow's Landing?"

Lute sighed. "I was transferring a horse from Floris to an inn called the Shepherd's Rest and I was set upon."

"They stole your horse?"

He nodded glumly. "Worse. They stole Master Pilo's horse."

"And money?" Mungo chimed in.

Lute shrugged. "I didn't have much to steal," he lied . . . just in case, although perhaps to them it would have been plenty.

"I presume the horse is no small loss to your master?" Thom added.

"Bruno is a fine stallion. Master Pilo's going to use my guts for garters after this."

Thom scratched at his beard. "Why he'd let a skinny runt like you be in charge of a palace horse without anyone to accompany you seems strange. Pilo is cautious to a fault."

"You know my master, then?"

"Perhaps I do. I know you won't be able to sit down for a week when he learns of what you've lost."

"I didn't lose Bruno, Little Thom, I was ambushed and he was stolen. I was attacked, thrown to the ground, and the horse was taken by a pair of thieves that I hope look over their shoulders for the rest of their lives."

Both men laughed at his bravado. "Are you going to deal with them, young Peat?"

"You can be sure of that," Lute said sincerely. "And they can pay for the gold they stole from me with a hefty stint in the palace jail."

Thom grinned. "I wouldn't want you for an enemy, Peat. Come on, then."

"Where?" Lute asked, fresh alarm spreading through his body.

"With us."

"Look, it's good of you to—"

"I'm not being good, Peat. I'm telling you that you're coming with us." Thom's words were firm and if it hadn't been for the kindly way they were said, Lute might have tried to make a dash for it, frightened by what they might mean.

Thom seemed to read his mind. "No point running. You won't get far and looks to me like you need some attention to those ribs and perhaps a decent meal. I'll see to both for you."

"Why?"

"Well, because I don't care for thugs who steal from helpless young people," Thom answered, although Lute believed it was more to do with the fact that Pilo's name had come up. "Come on."

There was no alternative. Lute had to follow the two giants of men, marveling at their stealth as they moved silently through the trees and undergrowth that flanked the roadside. It occurred to him to try to learn precisely what they were doing there, too.

17

"You're sure about this?" Tess asked, lips pursed.

Griff nodded. "Never been more sure about anything in my life. He is threatening me and my brothers . . . and you . . . if I don't do exactly what he wants."

"Then do what Tyren wants!"

"No. I refuse. And before you ask me why, it's dangerous. Telling one person what another might be thinking about them sounds innocent enough, possibly even amusing. But it's not, Tess. I could stumble across someone who's going to commit a robbery, or hear the thoughts of a person plotting against someone else."

"So what? It's not your business, is it?"

"But I'm making it my business by interfering. Can you imagine the consequences if people acted on what I share with them? And keep in mind that I'm only hearing people's *thoughts* at that time. They could change their mind a day later and I wouldn't know. So suddenly you've got an angry person accusing someone of a robbery they haven't committed. No, it's too ugly, too fraught with danger. Someone could get hurt, or killed."

"What about this boy?"

"I heard him again. He's definitely hurt," he admitted, not yet ready to share what else he'd heard. It sounded too far-fetched, even to him. He had to find him and help him.

"But how can you help him?" Tess persisted as though she could guess his thoughts.

"I don't know but I have to try. There's something about this Whisperer. If I allow it, I am open to thoughts all day and all night long, but this is a voice directed at me. He doesn't realize it, but that's exactly what's happening."

"Griff, he could be around the corner or he could be on the other side of the realm, for all you know. Where do you begin to look for him?"

"Well, I'm going to take your advice."

"Which is?"

"Next time he speaks I'm going to reply."

Tess stared at him, momentarily speechless. "All right, that's a good plan. But, Griff, I can't come with you."

"Shh," he warned.

"What?" Tess mouthed.

"Chauncey and Jasper are coming."

"How do you know?"

"I can hear their thoughts from quite a distance. Listen, they'll be here in a moment. Be sure about this decision because I'm leaving tonight. I don't want to leave without you but"—he shrugged—"I can't force you."

Tess looked dumbstruck at the news. "I'm sure," she said, and he could hear her devastated thoughts contemplating how lonely it was going to be without his friendship.

The two hulking figures ambled into the clearing, carrying torches and thick ropes.

"Hello, Jasper, Chauncey," Griff began brightly. "What's happening?" He eyed the ropes uncertainly.

"We've come to collect the creatures."

"The c-c-creatures," Tess stammered. "Whatever for? They're safe and tethered for the night."

"Sorry, Miss Tess," Chauncey said. "Tyren's orders. He wants them safer still."

Griff frowned. Jasper's mouth hung open in surprise. He'd obviously not clapped eyes on Tess's companions prior to this. Griff looked back at Chauncey. "What does that mean?" But he could hear the thought rattling around the man's mind. Chauncey obviously didn't want to say it, so Griff said it for him. "You're going to cage them?"

Chauncey gave a sheepish grin. "That's clever, Griff, real clever. I thought you were faking it but that's good."

"You are *not* going to cage my friends," Tess challenged.

"Tyren's orders," Jasper echoed, finally able to tear his gaze from a scowling Davren.

And without further discussion the men set to securing the ropes around the necks of the squirming creatures, who couldn't escape their attention due to the thin lines that bound them to their trees.

Griff looked anxiously at Davren and shook his head briefly, telling the centaur not to struggle. Tess must have been doing the same thing because Davren, Elph and Helys gave in and meekly permitted the men to lead them away. Griff could see that Tess was only just holding on to her tears of despair to see Davren, in particular, with a rope around his neck and wrists, being led away like a dumb beast.

"You'd best bring that veercat yourself, Miss Tess," Chauncey suggested, and walked past her, Elph and Helys in tow.

"He lied to me!" Tess raged once the two men were out of earshot. "He promised me, no cages."

"Now you know what you're dealing with. Tyren is two-faced. I've learned that the hard way myself."

"Why can't people just leave us alone? All my life I've only wanted to be left in peace."

"You never will be, as long as you're part of this show."

"What can I do?" she begged. "Rix won't survive being caged and Davren will pine until his heart breaks."

"We're going to get them out, Tess, I promise you, and then we're going to leave here tonight."

"How?"

"Leave that to me," he said. "Tess, this is all the more reason for you to come with me. You can't trust Tyren."

Tess paused. "Yes, I'll go with you, Griff."

"Good. You're allowed to be angry. Let Tyren see that you are but don't let him get an inkling of our plan."

X❀X

Little Thom and Mungo had horses tethered about a mile across country. Lute had never been so glad to see a horse in his life. With the men's help he had been placed on the back of one with Little Thom up front, traveling in a westerly direction, the pain in his ribs screaming loudly with each bump and grind of the huge horse that took them further from Tarrow's Landing.

"Where are we going, Thom?" Lute asked. They had been leading the horses for an hour or so.

"Somewhere safe, I promise. No one will hurt you."

That didn't answer his question. He tried a different approach. "I'm actually looking for someone. I promised I would get a message to him."

"Oh yes, who would that be?"

He had nothing to lose. "He goes by the name of Bitter Olof."

The horse was brought to a stop and Thom swung around in the saddle. "Bitter Olof? Where did you hear that name?"

"From Master Pilo," he said, glad it won the reaction he needed. "Do you know where I can find him?"

"Are you sure you want to?"

"What does that mean?"

"He's a scary sort. Doesn't suffer fools gladly and suffers children only under great despair."

"I'm not that young and I have to see him."

"Why?"

"To tell him something important."

"Fair enough. See that torchlight in the distance?"

Lute squinted. He could see it, just. "Yes."

"I suppose you could call that home. We'll be there soon."

As they drew closer, Mungo began making a series of noises that sounded like a vallica beetle, loud and rasping. The sound carried effortlessly over the meadow they were crossing. It was met with the haunting call of the carun bird—not quite the hoot of an owl, more like a groan but just as spooky.

"Righto, they know it's us," Thom said. "Now they won't shoot us full of arrows."

"That's reassuring," Lute said, and Thom chuckled in front of him.

⚜

"What are you going to do?" Tess asked, shock still shaking her body. She had watched with distress as her precious friends were herded into two cages. If they hadn't let her take Rix in herself—and spend time in the cage soothing him through their mindlink—she was sure he would have attacked Chauncey or Jasper. He had threatened to, but she begged him in their silent manner of communication to trust her and to trust Griff.

Griff had promised her the creatures would be released by tonight but she honestly couldn't see how, given that they were now locked up, and the key was attached to Chauncey's belt. She looked toward Davren, whose face reflected the despair she was feeling. She felt so responsible for him, having persuaded him to trust her and to come with her to Master Tyren's Marvels of Nature Traveling Show. She had sworn he would never be tethered and she'd already broken that promise, and now the firm oath that he would definitely not be imprisoned by a cage was shattered. He had said little, refusing to communicate with her now, but he didn't have to say anything for her to know just how much Davren was hurting. For a creature of the forest, particularly with his sharp mind and almost-human traits, the bars of the cage were pure torture. She had to get him out of there. Had to rescue them all.

Gaston? she called through her mind.

Again? Already?

I'm sorry.

Don't be, the gryphon said across the miles from the Mountains of Marrh, where he preferred to live. *You sound sad.*

He's caged our friends.

There was a silence. Then Gaston growled. *How's Davren?*

Not speaking to me.

I'm not surprised. I'll talk to him.

Thank you.

But it's temporary, I hope?

Yes. We're leaving tonight.

All of you?

All of us. Plus our friend Griff.

Can you trust him?

Without any doubt.

Where are you going?

I don't know, Tess sighed as she watched Griff stroke Helys through the bars. She refused to change color. *But I'll let you know.*

It doesn't matter that we are not together, Tess. You are in my thoughts each day.

I know. You don't have to explain. I know your kind lives quietly and remotely.

You couldn't survive here in the mountains.

I have always understood your ways and, be assured, there are times when I am certain I can sense you thinking about me. Our bonds are strong, Gaston, but I have to live near people.

Distance means nothing. We are always together. We are family, despite our physical differences.

You will like Griff, I promise. It may be that he becomes part of our family, too. The silence across their link felt tense. She pressed her point. *He will not hurt any of us and he is keen to protect me.*

I trust your judgment, Gaston finally said.

Thank you. I promise to let you know more as soon as I can.

Then I shall not go hunting until I hear from you.

She knew how remote Gaston could become when hunting. *All right. I'll speak to you in the next couple of days. You won't go hungry, will you?*

She heard a rumbly laugh. *No, Tess. Be safe.*

"Helys has turned gray, Tess," Griff mumbled.

"I expected as much," she replied, feeling Gaston's mind pull away from hers.

Griff held up the lamp. Even by its poor light the califa looked to be sickening. "You have to talk to her, reassure her and calm down Rix somehow. He's going to hurt himself and the others with those sharp claws."

"But what am I supposed to say?"

"Tell them they'll be freed during the night. I'm working on something."

"Where are you going?" she asked, watching him with deepening anxiety as he walked away.

He turned briefly. "I'm going to speak with my brothers. Stay with the creatures and be sure you're polite to Tyren. Give him no clue that this does any more than disappoint you. He'll be suspicious if you don't look a little distressed but don't overdo it, Tess. He mustn't think you're ready to take silly risks."

"But I am!" she groaned softly.

"I know," he said, and his eyes begged her to call on all her courage to act her part now.

She still had no idea what Griff had in mind but she had

to trust him now. He was her only hope and his handsome face looked grim with worry.

She sat quietly with the creatures, Davren still refusing to talk with her, Elph deeply unhappy and anxious. Rix allowed her to stroke him but she could feel his muscles were tensed, bunched up at his shoulders as though he was ready to pounce at any moment. Helys she worried about most of all. Her grayness was worsening and the shy creature moaned softly in the corner of the cage she shared with Rix.

She's going to die, Rix told her, his voice bitter in her mind.

I think you're right, she said, her own voice heavy with sorrow. *I can't do anything yet, Rix. We have to pretend that we're going along with this for now.*

Why? It was Davren. His voice was filled with anger.

She felt a flutter of relief that he was at least speaking again but she didn't show it. Perhaps Gaston had already spoken with him. *Griff's planning something. He won't tell me what yet. He just wants us all to play along with Tyren's new cage idea. We don't have to be happy about it but we have to give the impression that we're a bit helpless, I think,* she explained. *We have to look as though we have no choice.*

Before more could be said, Tyren appeared and strode toward them.

She cast a glance that begged Davren to help her. *Please talk to Helys. Keep her occupied. Don't let her slip further from us. And, Elph, I promise you won't be in here much longer.*

You gave that same promise to me before we came to this wretched Traveling Show, Davren said, shooting a look of fury at her.

Not now, Davren, please.

"Oh dear, I see the scowl on your centaur's face, which

probably means all is not well in your camp, young Tess," Tyren said, looking smug.

"Did you expect caging the creatures would please them or me, Master Tyren?" she asked, not looking at him.

"Er, no. I didn't think it would make any of you especially happy, but I do have to protect my investment."

"What did you think we might do?"

He gave a snort. "Flee, I imagine. It's obvious to all of us that you don't mix easily with people, Tess. And your creatures are timid; they obviously prefer solitude over performing and are only doing this to keep you from the orphanage."

"It was their choice, too, Master Tyren," she said, more for Davren's benefit than the showmaster's. "You would never have so much as seen them had they not agreed."

"But then you would never have come had they not agreed to be with you."

She shrugged, showing Tyren she didn't care what he thought.

"I thought you'd be happy that they've been housed on the fringe of all the public areas. They can see the copse and are roped off from all prying eyes.

"I'm not happy at all that they're behind bars, Master Tyren. That was not our agreement and I don't know what I've done wrong for you to go back on what we settled."

"Ah well, in this you're right, young Tess. It actually has nothing to do with you or the creatures."

"Then why?"

"Griff is very angry about his new role as a performer and, unlike you, he can't see beyond his nose, for all the fame and fortune it could bring him."

"I'm not interested in fame and fortune either, Master Tyren," she said firmly.

"Oh, I know that. But you are interested in freedom and that's what fame and fortune can bring you. Now, Griff is fighting me on this and I sense he may be prepared to do something reckless."

"Like what?" she asked, deliberately creasing her face into a frown.

"Like running away. It would be a most unwise act."

"Why's that, Master Tyren?"

"Oh, he already knows why. But the consequences of that sort of unwise decision on his part would ultimately involve you."

"Me? Why?"

"Because you're his friend. You've not known each other long but I can see he's fond of you and your companions. And you see, Tess, the best way to get anyone to cooperate is to focus one's attention on those they like most. I doubt that Griff will risk any more limitation of your pets because he doesn't want to upset you any further."

"They are *not* my pets, Master Tyren."

"However you choose to describe them, young lady, is entirely up to you. But I know they're hurting and so are you. I imagine this is causing Griff concern and the best way for him to solve this is to get on with pleasing me and performing to the best of his abilities."

"And so you'll let my companions go if Griff cooperates?"

"In time, yes. Both of you will need to earn my trust. Especially Griff. You might like to tell him that."

"I will, Master Tyren, thank you for explaining it to me,"

she said evenly, not showing him that she spoke through gritted teeth. "I plan to earn your trust as soon as I can because I want my friends to be out amongst the grasses and trees."

"I'm sure you do. You know how to achieve that." He raised his dirt-brown cap to Tess in a mockingly polite gesture and left.

It was all Tess could do to prevent herself from growling aloud at his back.

He's lying, Davren said.

I know. He can make more money out of Griff than we could ever make him. Griff is where he sees his greatest potential but we are Griff's weakness.

I believe we can trust Griff.

I know we can. Just do your best to reassure the others, Davren, because none of them are listening to me.

18

It was only as they drew close to the soft lantern light that Lute noticed it was not a dwelling they were approaching. It was a series of interconnecting cavelike structures: some natural, some obviously dug out of the range of hills.

"What is this place?" he asked, a little overawed. He could see people moving about in the muted light.

"I told you, as close to home as I can give you for now," Little Thom said.

"But who are these people?"

"Friends," he replied.

Within moments they were met by boys who skipped out to take the horses and Lute was suddenly being ushered deep into a tiny, shallow valley surrounded by a cluster of hills. They crossed the valley on foot—it took barely a couple of minutes to do so—and then they were entering one of the hill chambers. Lute noted that Thom knocked, while Mungo had disappeared at some point.

"Come," a voice boomed.

Thom opened the door, reassured Lute with a soft grin and whispered, "Be humble, Peat, whoever you are."

Inside, a tiny brazier burned, warming the surprisingly spacious chamber with its rocky ceiling. The smoke was cunningly fed through a flue at the back of the hill. Lute was amazed by the ingenuity of the architecture.

Sitting before the fire warming his toes was a dwarf. His beard was luxuriant, dark and peppered with streaks of silver. For his short stature it was clear this man was bound with muscles, his shirt drawn tight against his chest and his bared arms thick, strong and covered with an array of beautiful designs that Lute recognized as the result of painful inking needles. He'd only seen someone with an "ink" once before and it was a very small mark at the back of the neck. The dwarf's true skin color was lost beneath the maze of art in wild colors, rich and almost with a light source all of their own. The pictures seemed to pulse, they were so intense.

The dwarf turned from the flames. "Aha, what have we here, Little Thom?"

"I found him skirting the road leading out of Tarrow's Landing. He's hurt: set upon by road thieves—probably that pair who prey on unsuspecting strangers using the ferry," Thom said.

"Come closer, boy. You're giving me a crick in my neck, making me twist it like this." A fat forefinger beckoned him.

Lute obeyed, glancing quickly at Thom, who nodded.

"Well, you look healthy enough."

"I am, thank you."

The dwarf regarded him gravely. "And well mannered, too."

"I was raised to be polite to my elders," Lute said, not sure what was the right thing to say.

"Indeed. And what name did your gracious parents give you?"

"I'm called Peat."

"Peat? That's a common name of our farm folk."

"And I'm from common stock."

"Is that so?" The dwarf regarded him steadily.

Lute nodded, mesmerized by the dwarf's enormously bulbous nose and by the beady charcoal-colored eyes that flashed both intelligence and mischief beneath the bushy brows.

"And so, Peat, are you hungry?"

"A little."

"We can remedy that." The dwarf glanced over at Thom, who opened the door and muttered to someone who must have been guarding outside. "I hope you like rabbit stew. It's what's on offer at our fine establishment tonight."

Lute was taken aback, completely uncertain of how to take this strange little man, and yet he had no reason to mistrust him—other than Pilo's warning to mistrust everyone. "Er, thank you. I can pay."

"Good. Now, apparently, you're hurt?"

Lute shrugged, kept to the same story. "I took a fall when I was attacked."

"How bad?"

"We think his rib's broke," Thom answered.

The dwarf made a tsking sound. "And we shall have that seen to as well. Thom, you'd better ask Nanny to bring her salves and bandages." He returned his attention to Lute. "So, young Peat. You seem to be taking a keen interest in my inks. Like them?"

"They're fascinating."

"Each tells a story that occurred in my life."

Lute's eyes widened. He pointed to a spot near the dwarf's left elbow where a huge eagle was carrying a child. "I'd like to hear that one," he said with no little awe. "Does it hurt to have it done?"

"Mightily!" the dwarf exclaimed. "Here we are. Nanny's here, and the food won't be far away," he said, nodding at the guard who ushered in an old woman.

Lute nodded. "Thank you, er . . ." He suddenly realized he didn't know what the dwarf was called. "I'm sorry, I don't know your name."

At this the dwarf grinned widely. "I go by the name of Bitter Olof, child."

⬨⬨⬨

Griff had waited for his brothers to finish their second performance and was now watching them wash off their painted faces for the night.

"That went well," he said.

Phineas rubbed his cheeks with a flannel. "That's because we were good tonight. Although, Mat, you're leaning too far to the right when we do the Crab."

"No, brother," Mat said, flicking Phineas with a towel, "you are positioning yourself too far to the left."

"What rot!" Phineas replied, and this set off a tall debate between the brothers.

Griff butted in. "Listen, I need to speak to you both." His brothers stopped their playful arguing and looked at him. He shrugged. "It's important."

"We're all ears," Phineas said, casting a troubled glance at Mat.

Griff had already checked that no one else was around, but Mat assured him. "What's on your mind, Griff? I imagine your skill already tells you that everyone else has gone to sit around the fires for the night."

Griff nodded. His brothers were the final act for the evening and thus always the last to clean up and reappear for the late toddy around the campfires. "Have you got any of that Dragonjuice left?"

Phineas looked at him, puzzled. "Almost the whole bottle."

Mat threw a mock glare at his elder brother. "You lied! You promised me old Chauncey had found it and drunk it."

Phineas shrugged. "Why, Griff?"

"I need you to use it to get Chauncey and Jasper drunk."

"What?" the boys exclaimed together.

Griff hushed them, then proceeded to tell his brothers everything he knew.

"Tyren threatened us?" Mat asked, disbelief in his voice.

Griff nodded. "It's his way of keeping control of me, Mat, that's all. It's nothing personal. You and Phineas have done nothing wrong. Your act is perfect."

"Don't defend him," Phineas said, scowling. "What a slime he is."

Mat arched his eyebrows at his brother with a sigh. "But you're not telling us this for idle reasons, are you, Griff? You've obviously got something more on your mind."

Griff bit his lip. This would be the hard part. He took a soft breath of courage. "I'm leaving, Mat." The boys stared at him as though they hadn't heard him properly. He filled the silence hastily. "It's the only way to stop Tyren. He'll never let up. And he's going to keep using you two and Tess to blackmail me. I can't do it." He shook his head. "I just can't do this because it's like a pain. It's hard to explain, but to hear what all the people just in the Traveling Show alone consider important to think about is overwhelming. It's endless noise in my head and often despair."

"I thought you could block it," Phineas said softly, frowning.

"To a point I can, and it's helpful when I'm doing the grunt work because I'm usually too busy to think, to focus on anything but my work. But Tyren's going to change all of that and I swear I'll just die from the intensity of everyone's thoughts in my head."

"We said we'd stick together. Da—"

"I know what Da wanted. But he wouldn't want me to be this miserable . . . or cowardly."

"Where are you going?" Phineas pressed.

"I don't know. I know you two are happy here and won't leave, but I'm taking Tess."

"Now I know you've gone mad," Mat responded. "That is plain stupidity."

"Why?"

"One person running away is bad enough. Two of you, and I presume a host of strange galloping beasts, is hardly going to be an invisible party that moves easily, is it?"

"Just stay, Griff. Don't risk it. You belong here with us," Phineas tried.

Griff gave Phineas a sad smile. "I love you both, you know that, but I don't belong here. I never have. I know that you both love being with the Traveling Show and I understand why, with you both being such excellent performers. Father was just glad we were sticking together and that was why he agreed to me leaving, too. But I was never cut out to be in front of audiences. And Tyren is going to want me to do more and more of it."

Mat stood, looking angry. "I don't agree to this."

"You don't have to," Griff challenged reluctantly. "This is my decision, not yours."

Phineas looked unhappy but he nodded. "I'll miss you, little brother."

"So you're just going to let him run away to who knows where?" Mat said to Phineas, astonished.

Phineas shook his head. "I can't stop him, won't stop him. I think Tyren's being cruel."

"But why risk Tess?" Mat urged.

Griff explained. "She hates it here. She is less suited to the Traveling Show than I am. And she has no choice but to perform—that's what he bought her for and he can always punish her creatures if she doesn't earn enough for him or do what he wants. No, it's a bad situation for Tess and I'm going to help her get away."

"But to where, Griff?"

He didn't want to say anything about the Whisperer, and as he thought about the boy he remembered what his most recent words had been: *I'm a royal,* he had said. What did that mean? If he was royal, Griff felt an added burden of duty to help him. "I don't know where we'll go but perhaps it's best we have no plan and that you have no idea. Then Tyren can't use you any further."

"So why involve us at all? Why not just sneak off into the night?" Mat growled, and Griff knew his big brother was upset, worried for him.

"Because I need your help . . . both of you."

"What can we do?" Phineas asked, throwing down his towel and pulling his shirt back on. "I'll help in any way I can, Griff."

Griff could hear his eldest brother's angry thoughts, his fear that something might happen to Griff and that he would never forgive himself if something did.

"You mustn't worry about me, either of you. I'll get word to you somehow that we are safe. Just be patient and I'll find a way to put your minds at ease."

"Our father put me in charge of us," Phineas added.

"I know. But he doesn't have to know that you were ever told. As far as anyone's concerned, I just sneaked off into the night, but I have to release the creatures first and to do that I have to get to the keys on Chauncey's belt."

"Ah, the Dragonjuice liquor; now I get it," Mat said, eyes gleaming with mischief.

"Except to make it work you not only have to get Chauncey drunk but you two have to get drunk as well—or Tyren will suspect you did it deliberately. You have to look blameless. I'll steal the keys when you're all too far gone on Dragonjuice to care."

Mat laughed sadly. "Count me in."

Phineas frowned, uncertain. "Griff . . ."

"Please, Phin. Don't say anything more. Just say yes. But remember, you can't act, you have to genuinely drink the stuff and be ill with it if necessary. We cannot risk that Tyren doesn't believe I took advantage of you."

196

"Where?" Phineas finally said, as though all the fight had gone out of him.

"Build your own fire somewhere away from the others and near that line of bushes. I'll hide in there," Griff said, pointing. "Chauncey won't be able to resist coming for a nose around and you can say you didn't want to share the bottle with anyone. Offer him some to stay quiet. You know he won't leave. Try to drink less than him. I need him out cold as fast as possible, but you two definitely need to swallow enough to convince Tyren you were not involved."

"Leave it to us," Mat said with seemingly unshakable confidence.

Griff didn't think Phineas looked quite so convinced. "So you'll promise to get word to us?"

"I promise. I'm not going to hug you just in case anyone's watching from afar. Laugh, Mat, as though I've said something funny." His brother obliged. "I love you both. Stay safe."

"Griff!" Phineas called to his back. Griff turned. "There's some money in our wagon in the tea caddy—"

"No, Phin, I—"

"Take it!" Mat said. "We don't need it," he added generously, smiling first at his elder brother and then at Griff. "You might."

19

The old woman introduced as Nanny had arrived to daub his bruises with a harsh-smelling balm, and then proceeded to wordlessly but expertly bind his ribs tightly with lengths of linen. Lute was fascinated at the way she sucked her toothless gums during the entire procedure.

"Thank you," he said to her as she prepared to leave, but Nanny remained silent.

Her bandages didn't take the pain away completely but they lessened the discomfort when he moved.

The dwarf opened a small chest that he kept on the crudely fashioned mantelpiece and from it withdrew a small vial full of liquid. "Sip this," he said, handing Lute the tiny, narrow glass bottle. "A few drops, that's all," he warned.

Lute did so and miraculously the pain dissipated to the point where it no longer troubled him, other than a soft reminding ache. He could handle that, and in the meantime a huge bowl of a darkly delicious stew had been placed in front of him and he could smell the fragrant spices and herbs that had gone into the dish. A hunk of bread was provided, thickly smeared with bright yellow butter.

"That's watered cider in that cup," Bitter Olof added as Nanny silently left. "Get some down you."

Lute did as he was told, swallowing half the glass of the cool, sweetened liquid. He noticed a small pot of purple-colored granules by his glass. His expression must have formed a question because Bitter Olof explained, "They're vaygo seeds. You chew them."

"Why?"

"They'll deaden the pain for you, boy."

"But the liquid . . . ," he began.

The dwarf reached for the vial. "That's very potent stuff. I can't have you taking too much of it. These are less speedy in their relief, I'll grant you, but safer and effective enough."

Lute stared at them and then back at the dwarf.

"Go ahead, don't you trust me?"

"Does Pilo?" Lute asked, but he was not referring to the seeds.

"Why do you ask that?"

"Well, he's why I'm here, isn't he? If I hadn't mentioned his name, I suspect Little Thom would have left me by the side of the road."

"Perhaps."

"So Pilo's name was a password of sorts."

"Pilo and I go back a long way, lad."

"Are you friends?"

"Not exactly."

"What, then?"

"We have an understanding."

"That doesn't sound terribly friendly."

"It isn't."

"Are you going to hurt me?"

"Have I so far?"

Lute shook his head. "You've been most gracious," he admitted.

"Then eat my stew, drink my cider and later chew the seeds and get some relief from your injured rib. It will hurt even more in a few hours."

Lute put the seeds into his pocket.

"They should last you. Chew them twenty-five times at least and then spit out the husk. We'll practice after you've eaten." Lute nodded. "So talk to me about Pilo. Where is he?"

"First you must tell me who you are to him."

"So you *don't* trust me?"

"Bitter Olof, I have to tell you that over the past day I've come to realize I can't trust anyone, least of all someone who seems to have offered me kind hospitality but in truth has abducted me."

Lute heard a low rumble and only realized as it became a little louder that it was the dwarf chuckling.

He was astonished. "Well, it's true, isn't it? If I wanted to leave right now, you wouldn't let me, would you?"

Bitter Olof shrugged. "Little Thom would shadow your every move."

"Exactly. So first tell me what you are to Pilo."

"I'm his sworn enemy."

"What?" Lute nearly fell off the chair he was sitting on.

"It's true. He despises me."

"But . . . but he told me to ask only for you."

"Did he now?" the dwarf said, more amusement in his voice. "I wonder why."

"He didn't say. He simply told me to find the Shepherd's Rest and to ask for you."

The dwarf looked at him thoughtfully, frowning. "Who are you?"

Lute remembered Pilo's warning not to give the truth of his identity if he could help it. "I told you, I'm Peat, a stable-hand, I—"

"I don't believe you," Bitter Olof said, cutting across his words.

"Why not?"

"I've just told you that Pilo and I are hardly friends. Ask yourself why he would entrust the life of someone he cares enough about to lend his horse to, to the person he considers his lifelong enemy. It doesn't add up. So who are you? The truth now!"

The dwarf was clever. Lute felt cornered. "I have nothing to say on that."

"But you can tell me who you are."

"I did."

"No, you told me what Pilo told you to tell me, or at the very least you've told me what you think I might believe. I'm tired of being thought of as dumb. I'm actually much smarter than I look," the dwarf said testily.

Lute blinked, unsure of what to say. He wasn't ready to tell Bitter Olof his true status. He bought himself some time. "Why are you enemies?"

"Ah, now, that is the right question, young Peat. How is your side?"

"The clear liquid worked. There is no pain. I'm numb in my ribs."

The dwarf grinned. "Numb everywhere else, too, I imagine. It won't last, so when it begins to hurt again, chew the seeds."

"You were about to tell me why Pilo would suggest you as the best person to count on when clearly it would seem to be quite the opposite."

"I suspect your friend has told you to seek me out because he values your life too much to risk it with anyone else. I can offer you the protection that he can't—that no one else can, in fact."

"But why would he believe you would offer that protection to your enemy's friend?"

"Probably because I owe him a blood debt."

Lute gave a low whistle. He had not expected anything like this. "A blood debt. That's expensive."

"Indeed, and so he must think incredibly highly of his mere stablehand to use up that debt on your head. What can you possibly mean to him?"

Lute shrugged.

"I warned you earlier that I am smarter than I appear. It pains me constantly that people make risky judgments about me based on my looks and short stature. Do not make that mistake."

"I . . . I'm not."

"Those who don't know me think I must be dull because I'm not as tall, not as handsome, not as lean or as desirable. It makes me feel very bitter indeed."

So that's how he came by his name, Lute realized. Bitter Olof!

"Finish your stew, Peat," the dwarf said sourly. "And then we'll talk some more."

※❈※

Griff found Tess at her wagon. He gave her a look of inquiry; he didn't need to say anything.

"It was easier to leave them alone," she said. "None of the creatures are happy with me," she added sadly.

"It's not you, Tess. It's Tyren. Davren knows this. He just can't get past his frustration, his anger at being caged. He will forgive you anything."

"And Helys has turned so pale she's almost white. Rix says we're going to lose her."

"We're not going to lose her. We're going to leave. You have to trust me. Now go to bed as normal but be ready. I'll come for you in the early hours. Take only what you can carry easily."

She looked uncertain. "But what . . ."

Griff took Tess by her shoulders. "Listen to me," he said, his eyes imploring her to trust him. He opened his mouth to tell her his plan but instead a sharp pain hit him that felt like someone was cutting a slice into his mind. And what came out of his mouth were the words *Bitter Olof!*

He staggered, dizzy.

"Bitter what?" Tess asked, frowning in surprise.

"I don't know," Griff said, holding his head now. "I don't know why I said that."

"What does it mean?"

"No idea."

"Someone thought it, then?"

Griff nodded. "Perhaps it came through with great force." Then he shook his head.

"Was it the Whisperer?"

He frowned. "It has his signature."

"What does that mean?"

"Well"—he shrugged, unsure how to explain it—"I know what *your* thoughts feel like in my mind. I can tell it's you immediately. Most of the time I don't concentrate on any of the information coming to me, or how the people it's coming from feel or even how they look in my mind's eye. But for people I care about, I do. I recognize the Whisperer now. It was definitely him."

Tess nodded, her brow creasing in thought. "Is that all that came through?"

"Yes, in a sort of blinding flash of thought," Griff said, then pulled a face of disappointment, adding, "I was too late to hang on to the connection with him."

"Well, he seems to be in your head quite often now. I imagine the next time is not far away."

Explaining his plan could wait. "Go to bed, Tess. Just act as normally as you can. I'll see you in a few hours." Griff strode away before she could ask any further questions.

20

Although the pain was presently just a dull ache, the dwarf suggested Lute try the seeds and keep the relief as topped up as he could. He did so, chewing twenty-five times before moving to the fire to expel the sticky mass that the seeds had become. The globule hit the flames and exploded into a purple flare, burning brightly for a few moments.

"Feel anything?" Bitter Olof asked.

"My tongue and cheeks have gone numb."

The dwarf nodded. "That's good—that's how it begins. Give it a short time and everywhere will be numb. But you can still talk," he warned.

Soon Lute felt as though his entire body was devoid of any feeling. The remains of his meal had been cleared and the cider was drained.

Now Bitter Olof regarded him with a baleful stare, finally sighing. "We can sit here all night, if necessary, but I am not prepared to help anyone unless they're being honest with me. I have told you the truth."

Lute crossed his arms to mimic the dwarf. "First you must tell me about the blood debt between you and Pilo. Then I shall tell you all that I know."

The dwarf nodded, took a sip of wine from the clay goblet he cradled in his pudgy fingers. "It is because of me that Pilo's family is dead." Lute hadn't expected anything quite so direct. His mouth opened in shock but Bitter Olof prevented him from saying anything, raising his hand. "Or that's how he sees it."

"What happened?" Lute urged.

Again the dwarf sighed. "What do I look like to you, Peat? What do you think I do for a living? Be honest."

Lute shrugged, hesitated, before he decided to be truthful. "A bandit?"

Bitter Olof clapped his hands with disgust. "You see! Everyone has a bad opinion of me. It's because I'm a dwarf, isn't it?"

"Well—"

The little man didn't wait for Lute to finish, continuing to rant. "I tried to be honest. I was a clever and profitable merchant for many years and yet no one trusted me and I know it's because of how I look. No wonder I'm bitter!"

"I'm guessing that Pilo did trust you, though?" Lute asked, hopeful to win back some trust and get the dwarf back on track with his explanation.

"That's right, he did. He was one of the few people in the realm who truly understood that looks can be deceiving." The dwarf's tone was filled with loathing.

"And?"

"He and I became partners of sorts. He was bodyguard to

various merchants and I became a sort of middle merchant, who supplied the goods for sale. I became invisible, you could say. The merchants bought the produce that I secured and sold it on at a higher price. We were a successful partnership."

Lute stood. It was no longer painful to do so and he poured another goblet of wine for the dwarf, who was clearly surprised by the gesture, but nodded his thanks, adding, "Pilo and I were very good friends."

"How were you involved with his family's death?"

"Pilo was unexpectedly called away to the north with a rich merchant who needed his protection. He had made a promise to his wife that he would not leave her alone until their child was walking. I think she'd had enough of his realm-roaming ways. She was young and very beautiful, and didn't like to be alone."

"Did she not have family?"

"Odele came from a wealthy family, who disowned her when she married Pilo. He wasn't good enough for her, according to her parents. But she ignored their threats and went ahead with the marriage all the same, and so they cut her off from her fortune. Neither she nor Pilo cared, for their love was strong, but her beauty and people's belief that she brought wealth with a dowry made her vulnerable to others who wished to take advantage of both. So once tiny Ellin was born, Odele made Pilo promise he'd stay close until the little one was a bit older."

"Why did he say yes to this job, then?"

"The man was very rich and offered Pilo four times what he would normally earn and for just a brief trip away. It was too good to resist. Pilo had wanted to move his family from the town they were living in to another, more prosperous town closer to Floris. He took the job but he asked me to provide his family with protection."

Lute frowned. "Wait a minute, I understood that Pilo's family was killed in an accident."

Bitter Olof shook his head. "It was made to look that way, but our enemies—the people who hated that he and I were enjoying such success with our business—decided to bring him down a peg or two. They watched his movements, saw that he was away and . . . well," he sighed, "the worst occurred."

"They were murdered?" Lute asked, both astonished and horrified.

The dwarf nodded.

"But what about your people? Where were they?"

At this question Bitter Olof looked down into his goblet, studying its contents for a while. The silence lengthened and Lute felt as though he were holding his breath in anticipation. Finally, the dwarf answered, his voice solemn and even more bitter than Lute had heard him sound previously. "I had no idea that the threat was so real. I thought Pilo was being overprotective, to tell the truth. He was just a bodyguard, not that important."

"Sounds to me like he was far more than a bodyguard, Bitter Olof. In fact, it seems that he and you were prosperous enough to come to the attention of all the wrong people."

"We were," he sighed.

"Pilo never tracked them down?"

"Well, if he has, I don't know about it. Pilo, as you probably know, is quite a secretive fellow."

Lute nodded. "How tragic this is to learn."

"I blame myself. I thought I had it all covered, though. I was stupid enough to believe that if they ever acted on those jealousies, it would be against Pilo or myself."

Lute grunted. "No. Not at all. If you want to get someone's attention and make sure they do as you want, you threaten those they love the most."

"You sound as though you speak from experience, Peat," the dwarf said, intrigued.

"Perhaps I do. Go on, please tell me the rest."

"Not much more to tell," Bitter Olof admitted, shrugging slightly. "If I'm being honest, I think it was meant to be only a warning. Odele and the child were not meant to die. But things went wrong and no one was there to protect her. I didn't think she needed such close supervision and so I took Little Thom off her guard when I needed his help elsewhere. That's when it happened."

"And Pilo has never forgiven you."

The dwarf shook his great head. "Worse. I fled when it happened but he has threatened to kill me if he so much as lays eyes on me."

"But he knows where you are."

"No. I live here now, in secret. Very few know about it. But Pilo knows that other people are always listening and that word will get back to me. He would have known that if you asked for me at the inn, someone would let me know a boy was looking for me and that it would take my interest enough that I would try to find out more."

"Except Little Thom stumbled onto me."

"That's right. I know Pilo won't forgive me, but I'm

hoping that time will make him forget the potency of his threat. Perhaps life at the palace has softened him slightly."

Lute gave the dwarf a sympathetic look. "I don't think so. There is nothing soft about Pilo, Bitter Olof. But I also don't think you have to worry about him hunting you down." Lute heard the catch in his voice. He was determined he wouldn't shed another tear. He needed to act in a manner that would make his father—and Pilo—proud.

"Why not?"

Lute took a deep breath. "I think he might be dead."

At this Bitter Olof dropped his goblet, which shattered on the stone floor, dark wine spilling like blood beneath his dangling feet. He stared at Lute through hooded eyes, his mouth set in a grim line. "You think?"

"I can't be sure," Lute admitted. "But it looked that way to me the last time I saw him."

"So you were not transferring a horse for your master at all—because he is dead."

"No. That was a lie."

"What else is a lie?"

Lute hesitated. Bitter Olof ignored the mess below him as he dropped to the floor and angrily pointed a finger at Lute. "Listen to me now. Whatever our differences of recent years, there never were two closer friends. Yes, I would be forced to try to kill him if he attacked me and I had half the chance. And Lo knows, Pilo could easily kill me if he found me. But you need to understand that this news you bring breaks my heart. I loved Pilo. Tell me everything." He poured himself some more wine.

Lute hesitated.

Bitter Olof pressed harder. "I told you, I won't help you if I can't trust you. Pilo hates me but he trusted me enough to send you to my care. Now tell me who you are, and what this is about. I've told you my story."

It was Lute's turn to tell his sorry tale. "My name is not Peat. It is Lute."

"Ah," Bitter Olof said, nodding now. "Like the Crown Prince."

"Indeed," Lute said, swallowing hard.

The dwarf raised his wine. "Long live the Crown!" And then it suddenly dawned on him. "Lo strike me, you're him, aren't you?"

"I am," Lute said, embarrassed.

He watched as another goblet shattered on the stone floor.

Griff was hiding in the bushes watching his brothers laughing with Chauncey and Jasper. How they'd persuaded both men to join them remained a mystery but Griff felt a surge of affection for Phineas and Matthias, who were performing a daring and seemingly drunken new balancing act. If he didn't know better, he would imagine both of his brothers were so intoxicated they could barely focus, but having watched from his dark hiding spot for the past two hours, he knew that it was not Phin or Mat that was doing the drinking but the two men. The four of them were lit up brightly around a small campfire they'd set up.

He'd had to stifle his own amusement watching Mat

accidentally on purpose miss his own mouth and spill a glass of the strong brew down his shirt, then his brother exploded into manic, apparently liquor-fueled laughter at his own stupidity when he did precisely the same thing with his next glass. Phin, he noticed, continuously had the glass to his mouth, but Griff could see his eldest brother was swallowing little, and whenever the men looked away he'd tip the contents of his cup into the grass beneath him.

Chauncey and Jasper meanwhile were roaring drunk: laughing, arguing, bellowing, drifting into and out of dozes. Phin kept shushing them for fear of bringing Master Tyren from his wagon but there had been no interruptions so far and Griff held his breath, knowing it couldn't be long now before Chauncey collapsed.

He watched Mat stagger over, giggling, trying to shush himself, to refill Chauncey's cup. He challenged Chauncey to tip it down his throat in a single gulp.

"You get the rest of this bottle, Chauncey, if you can do it."

"Do it, boy? I was drinking the famous Drestonian Dragonjuice before you were born. That stuff will set your body on fire. I've drunk a whole bottle of it in one sitting," he boasted. Griff didn't believe him. Dragonjuice was famous throughout the realm for its powerfully intoxicating qualities, which often resulted in nightmares. Most people had never tasted it because it was so incredibly expensive, distilled from the rare grebble berry that grew in the mountainous north, which was sweet for just a short time—twenty-six days, he'd heard—and then it turned sour. Griff listened to Chauncey's bragging, which was rapidly deteriorating into a slur of words that made little sense.

"*Harr!*" Mat said, giving the roar that meant "good health" and which people called out when having a drink together. "One gulp, remember, Chauncey, and it's all yours."

Griff smiled. Mat hadn't realized he was suddenly speaking perfectly good Drestonian—his own pretense at being drunk forgotten—as he watched the show's manager tip back his head and pour the liquor down his throat.

"*Vashi!*" Chauncey said, the traditional response to "*Harr!*" Then he fell backward into a drunken sleep. Beside him Jasper was already snoring loudly, his lips vibrating as each loud roar was produced.

Mat poked Chauncey. The man didn't stir.

Phin, suddenly alert, gave a whistle. "He's out cold."

Mat carefully reached for the key that hung at the fat manager's hip, and as his fingers touched the metal, Chauncey grunted and turned on his side.

Griff, watching, could barely breathe for the tension.

Mat signaled to Phin. "You do it," he mouthed silently.

Phin nodded, raised himself and tiptoed around Jasper until he could squat near Chauncey. He glanced at Mat, who nodded. Griff knew they were both probably thinking about what sort of trouble this was going to lead to. Nevertheless, he saw Phin unhook the ring of keys slowly from Chauncey's belt before he turned and hurled them toward the bushes. Griff deftly caught them, then mimicked drinking from a bottle and acting tipsy. The boys understood. They nodded and gave him soft smiles that made his heart ache, especially as he realized he could not hug them farewell. He hadn't imagined he would leave without saying goodbye properly but that was exactly what he had to do. He lifted a hand into the air and his brothers did the same.

"Be safe," he saw Phin mouth, and he tried to look brave by sticking his thumb in the air.

There was nothing else to say or do but turn and leave. So he did, casting a prayer to Lo that he would protect Phin and Mat from Tyren's wrath.

Griff broke into a jog and very soon was running as silently as he could back to the wagon, where he hoped Tess was awake and alert, ready for their escape.

21

The dwarf eyed Lute with a baleful stare. "Now look what you've made me do," he said, shaking his head at the second broken goblet. "Tell me I made an error or that I misheard you, boy."

Lute swallowed. "You made no error, Bitter Olof. I am the Crown Prince."

He wasn't sure what to expect but he didn't expect a roar of laughter. The dwarf was instantly seized by high amusement, which raged for several seconds. The mirth only quieted as the dwarf watched Lute's expression turn from serious to grave. Gradually his hilarity lessened until he too was as poker-faced as his guest.

"This is a jest, surely?" he asked.

"No jest," Lute said, holding the dwarf's intense stare. "My name is Lute. Prince Lute, if you care to address me politely. Or"—he smiled crookedly—"Your Majesty, if you prefer to be formal."

Lute watched the dwarf's face turn pale.

"Prove it!" Bitter Olof demanded, jumping down from his chair by the fire again and pacing.

Lute shrugged. "I can't. I have nothing to show but myself. I have no birthmarks that confirm my royal blood; I carry no papers that pronounce my title. I deliberately removed the more obvious of my fine clothes so I could travel relatively unnoticed."

"Little Thom!" the dwarf bellowed, and the door opened, its space suddenly filled by the bulk of the man he had summoned.

"Yes, Bitter Olof?"

"Have we heard news from our runners yet?"

"They're just arriving now. Jhen leads. Bran is a few minutes behind."

"Send them straight in. I would hear their reports immediately."

Little Thom dipped his head to the dwarf but glanced Lute's way. Lute knew the big man wondered what had upset his master. He closed the door as he left.

"We'll soon know the truth of your outrageous claim," the dwarf promised.

"I have no reason to lie about this, Bitter Olof. I have withheld who I am until now, but I am telling you the truth. I gain nothing by lying to you. Can I fetch you another goblet of wine?"

"Ha!" the dwarf yelled, pointing a pudgy finger at Lute. "No true prince of the realm would be so subservient."

Lute replied calmly. "I am a prince, yes, but that doesn't mean I don't respect my elders. I can offer to pour you a wine, can I not? Surely good manners do not brand me an impostor."

"We shall see," Bitter Olof said grumpily.

There was a bang on the door.

"Come!" the dwarf bellowed.

Little Thom arrived and behind him came a man whom Lute had not seen previously. He looked disheveled and still wore his traveling cloak; tiny rain droplets glistened on his shoulders. He pulled off his hat and cloak before bowing to his master.

"What news from Floris?" the dwarf demanded.

The man nodded; he was not very old, Lute noticed. "Rumors only, sir, nothing we can confirm yet."

The dwarf's gaze narrowed. "Go on."

"There is word amongst the soldiers that King Rodin is dead as a result of his weak heart."

Lute leaped down from where he had been seated in the corner of the cave. "Rumor only, you say," he urged the man, his voice breaking on the last word.

The young man stepped back, his expression one of surprise that this boy would talk to him so directly, cutting across whatever his master might have said at this point.

"It is all right, Jhen. Speak freely before the boy."

Jhen glanced Lute's way again but continued to talk to Bitter Olof. "We have not been able to confirm the King's passing."

"Where is the Queen?" Lute demanded.

Again the man hesitated, waited for the tiny gesture from the dwarf that Lute noted. "We have not seen or heard anything about the Queen or the rest of the royal family. Word has got around in the city that Duke Janko was about to make a statement on behalf of the family but no one knew what it was about."

"How does anyone know such a thing?" Lute asked.

The dwarf answered. "Ordinary people work in the palace. They aren't all tight-lipped about what they see and hear in and around the royal family. Perhaps someone has heard something and mentioned it. Doesn't take long for word to spread." He returned his attention to Jhen. "What else?"

"Again, I can't confirm this, Bitter Olof, but there is frenzied talk that Crown Prince Lute was killed during a freak riding accident not long before King Rodin passed away from a heart quake."

Lute glared at Bitter Olof, who held up a hand. "My, my, a most dramatic day for our royal family. Anything more?"

"Only that the army seems to have a larger than normal presence in and around the city, sir."

"How, exactly?"

"Well . . ."

"Er, let me answer that," Lute said, looking at the dwarf. Bitter Olof gave a gesture with his hand that Lute could continue. "The royal army had essentially surrounded the city. Every entry point into Floris and each exit from it was covered by the Duke's men."

Bitter Olof frowned. "Is this true?" he asked Jhen.

The man nodded. "We only discovered that this morning." Jhen looked confused and Lute knew he was wondering how a boy would know this information—especially one already in the "care" of his master. One glance at Bitter Olof told him that the dwarf was considering the same question.

A bang on the door prevented further discussion.

Bitter Olof signaled to Little Thom. "Jhen, go and fetch yourself a meal, lad." He turned to Thom. "Quick, hide Peat behind you." Little Thom frowned but did as he was asked. "Not a word, Lute," said Bitter Olof. "Pass this test and you have my help. Come!" the dwarf called as Jhen left.

"This will be Bran," Little Thom whispered to Lute, hidden behind his huge bulk and in the shadows. He was invisible to anyone coming into the chamber. Peeking beneath his protector's great arm, he watched the door open and in breezed a man that struck Lute to be almost as old as his father.

He banged off the rain from his cloak, stomped his boots for good measure, grumbling the whole time.

"Hello, Bran," the dwarf said good-naturedly. Bitter Olof liked this fellow, Lute decided.

"Ah, my aching joints. I'm getting too old for this, Olof!"

"Nonsense," the dwarf replied. "No one spies as well as you do. We are blind without you, Bran."

"Ha!" the man grumbled again. "What does a man have to do to get a cup of something warming in his belly on a cold night like tonight?"

"He just has to ask," the dwarf replied, signaling to the warmed, spiced ale that sat in a jug near the fire. "Help yourself."

Bran sidestepped the mess on the floor, not even flinching at it, and poured himself a large cup of the ale.

"What news from the capital?" Bitter Olof asked again, his tone deliberately casual.

"All grave, my friend," Bran said, wiping away the rain from his whiskery beard as he found a seat and sat down before draining the cup in a single draft. "Ah, that's good."

Lute's ears pricked up but he moved deeper into the

shadows of the cave. He had a deep sense of foreboding. There was something about Bran that told him he didn't want to hear any of the news coming out of this spy's mouth.

"Tell us, Bran," Bitter Olof finally said.

"King Rodin is dead," he said bluntly.

Lute froze in the background.

"Do we have proof?" Bitter Olof asked quickly, no doubt trying to stop Lute from saying anything that might reveal himself yet, or his identity.

"I've seen his body. It was lying in state in the Royal Chapel." He held up a hand. "Don't even ask. I have my ways."

Lute felt as though all his blood had drained into his feet. He could no longer move, couldn't speak either; he hoped this was a nightmare he would wake from in a moment. He leaned against Little Thom's solid bulk.

"The Queen?" the dwarf prompted.

"She was keeping a mourning vigil. I noticed something strange, though."

"What?"

"She was surrounded by soldiers."

"Is that unusual? They were protecting the King's body, presumably."

"No, Olof. They faced inward, not outward. They were watching her, not guarding the corpse of their King. And I'll tell you something else that my big nose sniffs at and assures me smells bad."

"Go on," the dwarf said.

"They aren't the King's army."

"What?"

"They look like the regular army—I mean, they wear the uniform of the royal guard—but my instincts tell me they're hired. There's no pride in that uniform and their accents are strange. I reckon they're mercenaries who are guarding the Queen for some reason . . . and not in a good way."

Lute was fighting back the anger, the bile, the tears all at once but he still found himself rooted to the spot. He was sure his blood had turned to ice listening to Bran discuss his mother.

Olof was nodding. "Very strange. Tell me, Bran, what of the Crown Prince?"

At this Bran shook his head. "Nowhere to be seen. And that doesn't make sense either. He's young, yes, but he's not an infant. For the sake of the Florians—for the whole realm in fact—you'd think we'd have seen the boy. He should have been grieving by his mother's side. He should have been the one to take the public outpouring of sympathy over the King's death at the palace balcony on behalf of his mother if she was too sad to face it. There's more. Rumors abound that the boy was killed in a riding accident. Strange how it's all happened in the same day. I smell deceit somewhere."

"So who did?"

"Did what?" Bran asked.

Bitter Olof remained patient. "Who met the people on the balcony? Who accepted their grief?"

"Duke Janko did."

On hearing this, Lute let out a strangled cry that sounded more like a growl, his anger overwhelming whatever had made him become so still and drained of energy, and he leaped forward, out of the shadows. Quick as a blink, Little Thom, for all his bulk, grabbed him from behind. Lute realized that Thom must have thought he was going to hurt the dwarf; he found his hands pinned behind his back.

"Who's this?" Bran queried.

"No one important, not yet," Bitter Olof soothed. "Trust me, Bran. Tell me everything first. Do you remember Pilo?"

Bran smirked. "Who could forget him?"

"The boy is a friend of Pilo's," Bitter Olof said, revealing little.

Bran nodded. "Then I have bad news for him. There is a price on Pilo's head, according to the rumors around the city."

Lute felt sick.

"What do you know?" the dwarf prompted.

"Very little," Bran admitted. "Although it's all very strange. The word on the street is that this horse-riding accident that may or may not have claimed the life of the Prince is being blamed on Pilo—apparently this is coming from the Duke's people—but I don't know a better horseman than Pilo, do you?"

Bitter Olof shook his head.

"I left before any formal announcement but our final runner, Liam, should have news. We think the Duke will offer King Rodin's body to lie in state at the cathedral and confirm Crown Prince Lute's death. It's too strange and far too co-incidental for my big nose," Bran continued. "Pilo was the Prince's closest companion. If something happened to his charge, Pilo would have been at his side until they put the boy's body in the ground. And yet Pilo has disappeared. And after greasing the palm of one of the stablehands, I've learned that his prized stallion is nowhere to be found."

"That's because it's here," Little Thom chipped in. "I would recognize that horse anywhere."

"Here?" Bran repeated, surprised. "According to my sources, he was riding it today, so why and how would it be here?"

Lute stepped to the side but his face was still hidden by the shadows in the dimly candlelit cave. "I brought it, I am—" Lute said from behind Little Thom.

"Wait!" Bitter Olof interrupted. "Bran. Tell me what you know of Prince Lute."

Bran shrugged. "Thirteen summers, dark-haired, very dark eyes. Used to be sickly, a fragile sort, but since Pilo took on such a close role alongside the Prince, the boy has matured very noticeably. He is popular and people say he emulates the best of both his parents. He should make a fine king one day."

"And yet," Bitter Olof said, a wicked glint in his eye, "he doesn't seem to look at all like his parents, according to your description. I have only seen them once but neverthe-less . . ." His voice trailed off.

Bran blew his cheeks out as he considered this pointed remark. "Well, you're right, Olof. Rumors persist that he is not of the royal blood."

"How dare you!" Lute said, emerging fully from the shadows and advancing angrily as Bran stood up, alarmed. The man's face visibly drained from ruddy to almost gray as he realized who was in the room with him. Despite his shock Bran still had the presence of mind to go down on one knee.

"Crown Prince Lute. Your Majesty."

Bitter Olof was off his chair in a blink. "This is him? Is this really Prince Lute?"

Bran nodded. "Of course. I've seen him many times. What is he doing here?"

Bitter Olof turned to Lute, his small eyes blazing with intrigue. "Well, Your Majesty," he said, loading the title with scorn, "now you are going to tell us everything."

22

The lock turned with only the barest squeak, and with Tess gently hushing an eager Elph and Helys, Griff and Davren led the way out of the cage. Rix soon ran ahead, delighting in his freedom. Helys was too weak to walk, so Griff picked her up and, cradling her in his arms, they tiptoed soundlessly from the camp.

In the copse they all breathed again, their whispers blending with the sound of the crickets and the odd haunting hoot from an owl.

"So far so good," Tess whispered, still anxious. "And I think Helys looks a bit pink, don't you?"

Griff nodded even though he could barely see a change— not in this light.

"Davren says it's because you're holding her. She's very fond of you."

Griff grinned in the moonlight. "I'll hold her all night if it means she'll blaze orange again soon."

"Where are we going?" Tess asked.

"We're going to follow the forest line. We need it for cover, and when Tyren sends his people after us—and he will, Tess—the creatures will at least know how to use the forest to hide."

"Follow the forest line to where?" Tess asked.

He shrugged. "I don't know yet. I have a feeling it's to Floris but—"

"Floris!" Tess hissed. "Are you mad? I'm not taking the creatures there."

"I'm not suggesting you will. That's the direction I sense we are headed in. Don't worry, I won't put you or them in danger."

She pinned him with a stare. "You've said that to me once before and yet here I am off on some strange journey that definitely means danger for all of us. Is Floris where the Whisperer is?"

"I don't know, Tess," Griff said, sighing. "I really don't. But I'm going to talk to him soon, once I can clear my head of all of its worry. Let's just put some distance between us and the Traveling Show tonight; then we'll make plans, all right?"

Davren trotted up to Griff and put a hand on his shoulder, a finger to his own lips.

"Someone's coming!" Tess whispered, her face frozen in fear.

"Go!" Griff mouthed, and pointed. No one moved. "Davren, lead them. Go!"

Tess turned back, worried. "What about you?"

"I need to see we're not being followed. I'll keep Helys. Run, Tess, but silently." He flicked a hand, didn't look at her,

226

his eyes riveted on the person approaching. He had no idea who it was. All he did know was that it wasn't Tyren, which was a small measure of comfort. He would know that man's silhouette anywhere.

He sensed Tess's departure and then deliberately let down the shield in his mind and instantly felt a barrage of thoughts. Not as many as he'd anticipated but he realized that was because it was the small hours of the morning. Most people were asleep and dreaming. Mercifully, he was not subjected to thoughts from their dreams, only those when they were awake.

He began to search through the messages pummeling his mind until he found him. It was Mad Dog Merl. *Of course,* Griff thought, looking up and noticing it was almost a full moon. The wolf was rising. Mad Dog Merl was one of their strangest performers—if you could call him a performer. Normally, he was brought out onto the stage caged and chained. Each full moon triggered a horrible change in what was otherwise a mellow young man. He became enraged, dangerous to everyone, including himself. The showfolk had got used to the routine of each full moon, helping Mad Dog Merl to shackle himself and prepare for the onslaught that would last for a few days while he raged and howled as a wolf might. Left uncaged, he would attack people. Griff had heard that Merl had killed a donkey once when the showfolk had not made it in time with the chains. Now Master Tyren kept a very close watch on the tides calendar and knew precisely when to make a move. It was probably going to happen in the morning, but the fact that Mad Dog Merl was moving around at this time, and in that twitchy, almost-drunken manner, suggested to Griff that the rising was on its way. He was not dangerous, not yet, but it was so close it was not worth taking a risk, and if Griff moved now he couldn't be sure that he was safe.

He remained still in the copse, willing the monster that lurked inside Mad Dog Merl not to rise fully for a few more hours.

Merl was almost upon him. He would walk into him if Griff didn't say something.

Griff took a step, clutching Helys tight, and holding his breath gave a tight grin to the young man, who stopped abruptly before him. "Er, hello, Merl." He tried to make it sound as casual and friendly as possible.

"Is that you, Griff?" Merl slurred.

The wolf was coming; Griff could almost smell it but he could also hear the deranged thoughts in Merl's mind warring with all the gentle, kind thoughts that normally marked this man.

"Yes." He froze to see Merl lick his lips at the sight of Helys, who flashed red momentarily. Fear. She knew. "Er, are you all right?" he tried.

"It's happening," he groaned. "We're late."

There was no point in pretending any longer. "We're not too late, Merl. We can get you back to the wagon and do what we have to do right now. I'll help. Come on."

Merl pushed his hand away. "No!" he snarled. Then relaxed. "Sorry, Griff."

Griff nodded. This felt dangerous. The wolf thoughts were dark and angry. He wanted to eat Helys.

"That califa looks tasty."

"Not as tasty as the hunk of ox I could fetch you right now, Merl. Shall we go and find it? I know where the food is stored. You can eat everything."

"I think I want some califa tonight. Perhaps even some sagar," he said slyly.

"I can't let you do that. Surely you wouldn't hurt me, would you, Merl?"

"I don't want to," he slurred. "You know how it is."

Griff nodded, looked around nervously.

"You might as well give her to me," Merl said, his mouth salivating. "Or you may get hurt when I have to take her from you."

"I can't, Merl," Griff repeated, his voice filled with fear but nonetheless firm. "She's my friend and I'm her protector. I can't let you touch her. She's small and helpless and truly not much of a meal."

"But she's tasty and here, and I'm famished." Merl's voice seemed to have dropped an octave lower. There was cunning in his body language now. Suddenly Griff felt Merl was huge as well as menacing. He was still slow, though, and Griff could hear that his thoughts remained muddled. The wolf had not yet fully emerged.

"You'll have to get past me, then, Merl, because I'm not giving her to you." Griff pointed anxiously. "Merl, look! They're after you!" he yelled, and as the young man-dog turned, frowning and confused, Griff ran headlong in the opposite direction, gripping Helys tightly, who was pulsing red now.

He ran as hard as he could but soon enough heard the growl and lunging footsteps behind him. Merl was slow but he would be strong and Griff would be no match for him. He paused, unsure of whether to hide Helys, tell her to run on alone while he faced Merl or hang on to her while he tried reasoning again. He was just about to bend down and tell her to run for it when Merl blundered into the clearing.

"That wasn't a good idea to trick me," Merl snarled.

"I had to do something," Griff said, desperately keen to keep the man-dog talking while he strained to think of another diversion, something to buy just a few more moments.

"Now I'm going to take her!" the man-dog promised, and then he howled to the moon. It sent a shiver of terror through Griff, who could feel Helys trembling in his arms, and he hated feeling so helpless.

Just as Merl was lowering his head, his gaze narrowed and fixed on Helys, no doubt preparing to pounce and rip out both their throats, Griff felt the presence of someone new.

Next to him stood Davren. Taller than Merl and looking very strong, his muscles outlined clearly in the moonlight, he was wearing a look of such loathing that Griff stepped back.

"Davren . . . ," he began.

"Let him be." It was Tess. "He refused to leave you. Now he'll fight for you and Helys . . . for all of us."

"But this is Mad Dog Merl. The man-dog is—"

"No match for the centaur," Tess cut across his words. She sounded calm behind him. "Trust Davren, Griff. You have no idea how strong he is. He comes from a warrior line, I know that much. He would fight to the death."

"I don't want him to die for me!"

"He has just told me he won't have to."

Griff watched confusion flit once again across Merl's face.

"Davren's talking to him," Tess explained. "He can reach the animal side of this man. He's suggesting that this meal is not worth pursuing."

"I can't be sure that Merl is hearing him, though."

"No, that's probably true, but Davren wants us to move now. He wants us to go."

"I won't leave Davren."

"I thought you'd say that. Give me Helys."

Griff did so.

"I'm going to take the others. Davren tells me Merl wants to fight."

"And I was afraid you'd say that. Go, Tess."

And then in a blur of snarls and fur and rage, before Griff could say another word, the man-dog lunged at the centaur.

But Davren was fleet of foot on his four legs and danced out of the way, landing a blow with his fists that Griff was sure must have made Merl see stars. Without giving the man-dog a chance to recover, Davren reared up and bashed him in the chest with his front hooves.

Merl doubled over, but though hurt he was not finished yet. Still bent over, he ran at Davren and tried to ram the centaur. He made heavy contact but Davren's fists were large and as firm as stones, and they boxed Merl so hard that the man-dog fell to his knees.

Griff hated to watch the beating. He had always liked gentle Merl, but Mad Dog Merl was capable of harming anyone and had no ability, it seemed, to reason through his moon-calling. He watched with horrified fascination as Davren turned and, using one back leg, kicked viciously and precisely at Merl's large chin. As soon as he connected, the man-dog went down—for the last time—and lay heavily, unconscious.

Tess crept out. "He's not dead," she reassured Griff, who was now kneeling beside Merl, looking appalled.

"Are you sure?" he asked.

"Davren is. He was careful to just hit him in the right spot to knock him out. He'll sleep for a while I suspect and wake with a fearful headache."

"By which time, hopefully, Tyren will have found him and secured him." Griff stood up from the prone Merl and regarded Davren. "You're magnificent," he said helplessly.

Davren smiled gently.

The crickets began to sing again. "We have to go," Griff said. "I hate leaving him here but he's strong and fit, and breathing properly."

Tess looked up. "It will be dawn in about two hours, I reckon."

"How do you know?"

She sighed but there was pleasure in it. "I know the open skies, I know how the forest feels at all times of the day or night. We should travel as far as we can while we still have the cover of darkness. And you need to know I brought only some bread and a small flask of water."

"We'll be fine. Let's go. Tell the creatures we have to move as fast as possible."

"Let's strap Helys to Davren's back. He doesn't mind. She's as light as a feather anyway. Elph is generally the slowest, but if he knows what we're up against, he'll move surprisingly swiftly."

"Go ahead; that's a good idea. And Rix is safe?" he said, pointing at the veercat high in the trees.

She smiled. "He's loving being free. Yes, he's safe. He'll glide from now on probably—he won't want to touch the ground for fear of being trapped."

"Who could blame him," Griff muttered, and then he froze.

How dare you! Griff heard in his mind.

He knew it was the Whisperer and instantly raised his shields to every other sound so that he was a receptacle only for this boy, wherever he was. He wasn't going to lose him this time, no matter what. He had never done this before but somehow he understood that he must try, and equally startling was the knowledge that he seemed to know how. The Whisperer's trace was there and Griff realized all he had to do was follow it. And so, as though reeling in thread, Griff wound in the Whisperer's trace until he felt like he'd arrived at a point where the boy was near him.

He was blind and deaf, though, to everything but this strange sort of silver void he was suddenly standing in. He could no longer see the woodland or Tess. His pulse quickened. Was he dying?

With relief he noticed a soft blaze of color glow momentarily on the fringe of his mind. It reassured him that he wasn't dying, nor was he blinded in the traditional sense but there was actually just nothing to see. The sense of deafness passed the moment he heard a familiar voice.

Don't be alarmed, Griff, it's Davren.

What . . . what's happened?

I can't say for sure but you seem to have tapped into a vein of magic that has brought us into your mind. We are in a new plane, one I don't understand but have heard about.

You'll have to explain that.

Although Griff couldn't see Davren, he was sure he could sense him smiling. *I recall my grandfather talking about this once. If I'm right, it's called the Silvering.*

You seem very knowledgeable for a young centaur.

Griff heard a sigh. *By centaur standards I am still very young, Griff. But in comparison to you or Tess, I'm really quite old.*

That made sense to Griff because Davren seemed to speak with maturity, even though he had been led to believe by what Tess had said that Davren was almost childlike. It was reassuring to know he was in the company of someone with knowledge, for he was now entering pathways he had no understanding of, and it was unnerving. *All right. So what happens in the Silvering? I should tell you, now that you mention it, that whenever I'm hearing thoughts, my mind is rimmed by a sort of sparkling quality. It's hard to explain.*

That's interesting. Davren frowned. *You know, it might be that our magicks are connected. It's not easy to explain the Silvering but let me try. According to my grandfather, it is a place in the mind that is locked away to most people. Very few can find it, and for most, if they stumble across it, they don't recognize it, rarely have any inkling of how to use it, or even how to find it again.*

What am I doing here?

Is this the first time you've found this place?

Yes.

Then you must remember how it feels. Lock all of your senses into it so you can always find it again with ease.

Why do I need to?

Because, Griff, this is a magical place. This is no ordinary part of your mind. It is a place where you can be touched by gods, where the extraordinary can happen, and I think your gift of hearing people's thoughts gives you a special entry to the Silvering. It is silent in here. You let in only the people you want. Perhaps you haven't realized it yet but you let me in. Your mind reached out and found us. You are using the Silvering without realizing it.

You say "us." Are the others here, too?

Elph, Helys, even Rix are all present and listening but they are remaining quiet. They do not want to startle or crowd you.

Was that Helys I sensed glowing just now?

Yes.

Tell her I'm pleased she is feeling brighter and turning pink.

She hears you.

It is you, then. It is because of you creatures that I can hear him.

Griff, you are welcome to whatever magic you can draw from us.

Thank you.

But, Griff, I think you will find that the magic is all yours. Perhaps our "otherness" has simply helped you to navigate your way to the Silvering.

How long have I been here?

I cannot measure time in the way of people. Long enough, shall we say.

Is Tess all right?

She's fine, worried at first when you wouldn't respond, but I've assured her you're not unwell and that she must be patient. She knows I'm speaking to you and that you are safe. Are you trying to reach this person that Tess has told me about?

Yes. I am near enough now that I feel as though I can touch him.

You can, with your voice. Are you going to try?

I'm scared.

Don't be. Speak to him now.

23

In the cavern three people stared at Lute, their mouths slightly open, their expressions ones of disbelief.

"Are you saying that Duke Janko is taking the Crown by force?" Bitter Olof demanded.

Lute nodded. "As I explained, he tried to have me killed and I watched his men advance on Pilo. I know for a fact that everything Bran says about the army is true and that if my father is no longer alive, then, natural or not, his death was helped along by my treacherous uncle. Janko knows my father had a weak heart—perhaps he also knew that a big shock would threaten the King's life. His betrayal of his brother stretched to attempting to murder me. What's more, he must have sent riders ahead long before he attacked me, for people at Tarrow's Landing to have heard of my father's heart quake and my supposed death before I arrived. I've been traveling all day. They couldn't have gotten here first unless they left before I did."

The dwarf began to pace, his activity making the inks on

his arms appear to be moving and telling their stories. "Janko is dangerous. I have no respect for him."

Bran nodded. "Not that he cares what you think, Olof, for you are an outlaw of the realm with a very high price on your head, but I agree that Janko is all bad news for Drestonia. He may be a good general but his methods do not suit kingship. And your father's death aside, if he's tried to kill you, Majesty, then he's already a criminal."

"The problem is," Lute said, "right now he's very popular. The people don't know the ruthless side of him. They see him only as a hero."

Bitter Olof banged his fist on the table. "But he plans to tell the realm that their Crown Prince died in a riding accident, am I right, Bran?"

The man nodded. "I believe that's what is occurring. Liam will be here soon with the news."

The dwarf continued pacing. "Assuming he does, then we know for sure that his heart is black. I've always liked our King and Queen, even though some would argue I work against them. I prefer to think I simply work on the other side of their law. It's nothing personal."

Little Thom grinned, then glanced at Lute. And Lute felt his spirits soar. Suddenly the men who had been his captors felt like his friends. For it seemed they alone knew the secret of his survival and he could rely on their support to reclaim his throne.

"What can be done?" he asked into the quiet that had suddenly surrounded them, and then deliberately added, "For although my parents were relatively patient with the realm's bandits, I doubt very much that Janko will be. I suspect he will hunt down known offenders."

The dwarf stopped his pacing and swung around to face Lute. In that moment they seemed to share an understanding. Lute knew that if the dwarf helped him, then a debt was owed. "We have no choice. We must show the people the real Janko," Bitter Olof said. "We alone know the secret of his deeds because we have you alive and well. We must protect your identity until such time as it is helpful to reveal it."

Lute nodded. "That's precisely how Pilo saw it and likely why he sent me to find you. He knew you'd hide me."

"What are you cooking up now?" Bran asked his leader.

The dwarf tapped his big nose. "Just hatching a plan to bring down our murdering Duke."

"If they have killed Pilo as well, then it would make their deaths count for something if we expose Janko for the evil man he is."

"And what's in this for us, Prince Lute, should we be able to help you restore your throne?" Bitter Olof asked directly now. "Or should I address you as King Lute?"

A fresh, tense silence descended around the cave as all of them, including Lute, accepted for the first time that he was no longer the heir, but the monarch.

He'd only known the dwarf a short while, but the story of Pilo's connection assured Lute that although he was dealing with a known bandit of the realm, this was someone he could trust. And suddenly Lute realized he had very few people he could count on.

He swallowed, the weight of responsibility and title so very heavy on his young shoulders. "Help me restore the throne to its correct bloodline and I will restore your good name and declare a pardon for you, Bitter Olof, and for all of those in your clan who assist me."

Bitter Olof's mouth widened into a beaming, gap-toothed smile. "Gentlemen, pay homage to our new King."

And in his shock at watching the dwarf, Little Thom and Bran all bowing low to him, Lute hardly noticed the curious sensation, as though someone was slicing into his thoughts. But the voice certainly snapped him from his shock into fresh alarm.

Hello? it said hesitantly into his mind. *This is Griff. Are you there?*

Then chaos descended. The door to the cave burst open and Mungo charged in, clearly stunned to see the three men bowing to the boy. He stood there, momentarily speechless, until Little Thom growled at him.

"Mungo! What's the meaning of this?"

"Riders. Lots of them. All soldiers. They've brought dogs."

Suddenly everyone's attention was riveted on the huge man blocking the doorway.

"How long have we got?" Little Thom asked.

Mungo shook his head. "Minutes at best."

"Go!" Bitter Olof said, taking charge. "Bran, get out of here. Mungo, round up everyone. I presume they're already on the move?"

Mungo nodded. "Fleeing as we speak, sir."

"Good. Cover your tracks as best you can and we'll re-group at the Devil's Smile. Got that?"

"Devil's Smile, got it," Mungo said. "I'll spread the word."

"Everyone be careful," the dwarf warned. "These are Janko's men."

Mungo ran back out. Bran squeezed Bitter Olof's fist.

"You be safe, Olof."

"I have Little Thom. I couldn't be safer," the dwarf said, grinning.

"What about the boy?" Bran asked, jutting his chin toward where Lute stood, swaying slightly.

"His Majesty stays with me. The Devil's Smile, remember. Make no move until I get there."

Bran left the cave.

"Ready?" Little Thom asked, pulling on a strange sling.

"I'll be sad to leave this place," Bitter Olof admitted, a hint of genuine regret in his voice. "It's really rather comfortable."

"We always move on," the huge man said in reply. He glanced at Lute, nudged the dwarf. "Is something wrong?"

"Majesty?"

"Wh-what's going on?" Lute stammered, his words slurring slightly. He felt confused, as though his mind had just been twisted upside down.

"What's wrong with you?" Little Thom queried.

Lute shook his head. "Something just happened that I don't understand."

"Are you all right to move?"

"I think so. It's just—"

"Listen!" Bitter Olof cautioned. The three of them froze. "Too late. Hide him, Thom; you know where," he growled.

Before Lute could make another move, he had been scooped up roughly in the big man's arms and instantly felt himself hauled backward, once again, into the shadows of the cave.

"There's a secret entrance that I had tunneled for this very purpose," Bitter Olof explained over his shoulder as he ran to the door to peek out. "So glad now that we took the precaution, eh, Little Thom?"

"Mind your head," the big man growled at Lute as he pushed him up into an inky, cold blackness. "Hush now. Absolute silence. If anything untoward happens, or we're carted off, you head upward, but not yet, all right? Wait until you know what's going on. There's a peephole, can you see it?"

"Yes, I—"

"Good. Now stay very still."

"But what if—"

"Too late, they're here! Silence, Majesty—your life depends upon it." And then Little Thom left him and went to stand by the dwarf's side. He held his breath as the door burst open again.

"Gentlemen," Bitter Olof said in calm welcome as several burly men—though none as large as Little Thom—piled in through the doorway to the cavern.

And then from his hiding spot, and despite the muffled level of sound, Lute felt a knife of fear as a familiar voice spoke. "Ah, Bitter Olof, at last we meet."

"Duke Janko, I presume?"

"Well, actually," Janko said, smiling that mirthless smile of his as he slowly removed his riding gloves, "it's King Janko now."

"King? So the rumors are true?"

"News obviously travels fast," Janko replied. "And what have you heard, dwarf?"

"I've heard that King Rodin died of his fragile-heart complaint and that our young heir might have been killed during a freak riding accident."

"Excellent. You must pay your spies extremely well."

"My spies are loyal, not rich."

"Well, they inform you truly."

"And the Queen?"

"She is, as you can appreciate, indisposed through grief."

"Of course. And you, sir, loyal brother and indeed brother-in-law, on top of taking the burden of kingship and consoling the grief-stricken wife of the former monarch and mother of the true heir, still find time to come after a minor outlaw . . . in person. I'm impressed."

"Indeed. Rodin spoke to me about you. I'm sure he'd be pleased that I have finally hunted down the infamous Bitter Olof and his gang."

"Are my people dead?" the dwarf asked. It was the first time Lute had heard Bitter Olof's voice lose its composure.

"You obviously post good lookouts. Most got away. You, however, are the prize, not them."

Lute saw the dwarf nod. "I'm flattered that I feature so highly on your list of important things to do after killing a king, murdering his heir and taking the Crown."

Janko laughed and looked to one of his henchmen. "Put an arrow in that big sidekick of his, would you? Don't kill him, though. I'm sure he'll make for good sport in the torture chamber."

Lute felt as though his heart had stopped when he saw the soldier raise a crossbow. He saw Little Thom take a step back in alarm but he didn't beg for mercy.

"Wait!" Bitter Olof urged. "You came here for a reason and we both know it wasn't because you'd lose sleep just yet over an outlaw. What is it you want?"

Janko raised a hand to stay the bow. "I want my nephew," Janko replied, as calmly as if they were all good friends.

"Nephew? How should I know where he is? By all reports he's dead, isn't he?"

"By all reports, yes. But we both know he's not."

"Do we?"

"I have spies too, Bitter Olof. And I happen to know he made his way to Tarrow's Landing. I know he was ambushed and that his horse was stolen. The offenders—a couple of opportunists and well-known bandits—very helpfully explained that they left him at the side of the road. They were even kind enough, despite their . . . er . . . injuries, to show us precisely where. Tracking dogs did the rest—I'm sure you heard them." He held up a red scarf. "This is Lute's. The dogs found it helpful and his scent led us right here to your hideout."

"How can you kill him, having already killed his father? Your men can aid you to take the throne. He doesn't need to die." Bitter Olof sounded truly aghast.

"Oh, but he does. Boys grow into men and he will always be a threat. Just for the record, I didn't kill Rodin. He genuinely died of his weak heart, but I'll admit my actions likely brought his heart quake on. I'll make you a promise. I'll make it swift. The boy will feel nothing."

"You're incredible, Janko," Bitter Olof responded.

"Thank you, I know," the false king replied, ignoring what was meant as an insult. "Now, where is the boy? I can even make it worth your while, dwarf. Not one of your rabble has to die here. How does five thousand gold shards sound to you, and perhaps a ship of your own so you can go anywhere you like and I will not send a single soldier after you? You can become a pirate, an outlaw on the high seas rather than in my realm. Sound good?"

"Sounds very good," Bitter Olof replied. Lute felt his stomach clench at the dwarf's new tone. "How do I know you're not lying?"

"Bring it in," Janko said over his shoulder to one of the men.

Moments later a small chest was carried in. When Janko opened it, Lute saw through his peephole the unmistakable glint of gold.

"It's all there. I knew we could find something in common, Bitter Olof. It's all yours."

"And the ship?"

"She's called *Sea Star*. Her papers are already signed over to you and she's fully crewed, awaiting your private instructions as to where they should sail her and meet you. I don't give a damn. All I want is the boy."

"And you plan to kill him?"

"What I plan is none of your concern, Bitter Olof. Do we have a fair exchange? You have no reason to protect him, especially when you already have my favor."

"Better we die proud. His word is worth nothing, Olof," Little Thom finally growled from the back.

Janko ignored him. "Do we have a deal, dwarf?"

Bitter Olof licked his lips. Lute saw him nod his head and his heart sank. *Traitor!* He heard the dwarf agree. "We have a deal. Get your men out of here."

Janko signaled and all but one filed out. "Where is he?"

"Don't," Little Thom warned.

"Shut up!" Janko pointed at the big man. "You are nothing."

"Neither are you, usurper!" Little Thom spat back.

Janko regained his calm. "Hurry up, dwarf, I tire of you and your sidekick."

"There's a huge oak as you approach our hideout."

"I saw it," Janko replied evenly.

"Look high into its branches. There's a tiny tree house built cunningly out of its own wood. He's hiding in there."

"I curse you, Bitter Olof," Little Thom said, stepping right away from the dwarf. "You'll die rich, but lonely."

Janko laughed. "What did Lute promise you?"

Bitter Olof shrugged. "A knighthood."

Their enemy exploded into genuine mirth. "You fool. I'm far more generous. But you should have listened to your friend here. My word is only worth something when I want it to count. Shoot the giant in the shoulder; that should quiet down his insults."

An arrow was loosed, zipping hideously across the cavern and landing with a sickening thud into Little Thom, who went down with a groan. Bitter Olof shouted in shock and Lute nearly lost his footing but held on grimly, terrified to see what would happen next.

⬦⬦⬦

What happened? Davren asked into the silence.

Whatever link we had was suddenly broken, Griff replied.

It's likely you startled him.

I'm sure I did. I can remember how it terrified me the first time he spoke into my mind.

You will have to try again later but right now I fear you must reassure Tess. She is anxious and keen for us to be on our way.

Yes, she's right. Griff blinked, felt the cocoon that the Silvering provided burst like a bubble, and suddenly he was staring at Tess and hearing once again the sounds of the night forest—crickets chirruping, an owl hooting softly somewhere, Elph snuffling in the undergrowth for seeds.

"Griff!" Tess exclaimed, relief clearing her worried expression.

"I'm sorry. Did Davren explain?"

"As best he could. Did you speak with the Whisperer?"

Griff shook his head. "I think I made it through to him but we lost each other."

"Did you scare him?"

"That's what we think must have happened. I'll try again, but for now we should move."

"Still heading west?"

"Yes." He smiled at Helys, who was nestled into a sling on Davren's back and glowing a soft pink. "She's mending," he said, his own relief obvious.

"Cages are really bad for my creatures," Tess replied. "Come on. How much of a head start do you think we have?"

"Two hours at most. Tyren will discover the creatures gone just before dawn, depending on how badly his bladder needs emptying. But if he's genuinely forgotten about Mad Dog Merl and remembers suddenly, he could be upon us within minutes."

"We'd better make those hours count, then," Tess said. And the band of six set off once again with Rix remaining amongst the tallest trees.

24

"Lock them in here," Janko ordered the guard. "Post four men outside. No one is to speak to them. Do not open this door until I return. I'm going to find the boy."

And a moment later, the door barred and guarded on the outside, Lute realized the three of them were alone. He didn't move, though, remembering Little Thom's warning.

He watched Bitter Olof scuttle across to his companion. "Oh, my dear friend, I'm so sorry."

And impossibly, Little Thom laughed. Lute couldn't believe it. "I had it coming. I would have been surprised if he didn't carry through on his threat. Lo, but it hurts!"

"Tell me you can still move," Bitter Olof pleaded.

"I'm not dying, Bitter Olof, I'm injured and I'm angry because it hurts. Get everything. Let's go. That mad story about the tree house will be discovered false in minutes."

"Well, it's a fair walk to that oak. At least we have those minutes. Let me help you up."

Little Thom knocked away the small man's arm and

groaned as he rose. "Let's at least take his money," he said, the pain driving his poor manners.

"I intend to. You've earned it!" the dwarf said. "Where can we leave it?"

"We'll hide it once we get clear. Here, climb onto my back."

"But—"

"Just do it!" Little Thom ordered beneath his breath, grimacing through the pain.

"The bleeding!" Bitter Olof whispered angrily.

"There's no time!" And Little Thom all but dragged the dwarf onto his back, grabbed the chest and, with what seemed inhuman strength, hauled himself and his cargo into the secret tunnel.

"Head up, quickly and silently; our voices carry," he growled to the astonished Lute, who, although he wanted to, thought it best not to say anything about the wound that was bleeding at an alarming rate.

He got a foothold and began to scramble, further astonished by the realization that Bitter Olof was nestled comfortably on Little Thom's back in a sling contraption. Footholds were cunningly carved into the tunnel, and although it was by no means easy work, with concentration and determination it was simply a matter of time before they would leave their would-be captors far behind and no doubt angrily scratching their heads for a while as to how their prisoners had escaped.

"Ingenious," Lute whispered to himself, not realizing his voice carried to his friends.

"We like to be prepared," the dwarf chuckled from behind; and then all three fell silent as they began their ascent in earnest. Lute lost track of time as they climbed with only the sound of their grunts in the semi-darkness and the scuttle of insects to be heard. Gradually the light increased, and finally they emerged, breathing hard and smeared with grime from the damp, challenging journey.

Lute found himself balanced on a high plateau, the nip of the night's air a cold shock on his face after so long in the vertical tunnel. His fingers ached from supporting himself and his legs were weak from the strain but he could feel an energy pulsing through him. Pilo had once told him that pounding of the heart and throb of blood were driven by fear—but that it was a good thing.

Your body puts itself into a state of fear so that it is ready either to run from its hunters or to turn and fight. It is no different in the animal kingdom, he had explained. *That energy puts all your senses on high alert and you can achieve extraordinary feats in that heightened state—but only for a short time, so never waste it.*

What do you mean? Lute remembered asking his friend.

Well, it's a time to make a decision. This is often based on instinct. But make it and then follow it. Don't dither. If you dither, you are lost.

Lute would have felt lost now if not for the huge comforting presence of Little Thom, who was just emerging from the tunnel.

"All right?" Little Thom murmured to Lute as he emerged, struggling to drag his enormous bulk over the lip of the tunnel's exit, Bitter Olof still clinging to his back in the safety of his sling.

"Yes, you?"

"I'm managing. We made good time."

"It's obviously safe to speak, then."

"For them to get to us here they'd need to travel around the caves—an extra day at least, although there is another way up, if you know the entrance through the forest. They won't."

"Why can't they just climb the tunnel as we did?" Lute asked, watching the man stride over to a huge boulder. He struggled to lift it and roared with evident pain as it came loose in his hands.

"They could, if they could find it," Little Thom replied, staggering slightly to the lip of the hole. Blood was still seeping through his shirt. "But even if they did, they would have to shift this," he said, and dropped the boulder down the mouth of the tunnel.

Lute listened until he heard a screeching crunch. "Aha, now I realize why the top two-thirds were roomier than the first."

"Clever, aren't we, Your Majesty?" Bitter Olof commented. "We're teaching you all our secrets."

"Er, listen. I'm not used to my title being used constantly. Can we just stick with Lute, or Peat if we're unsure of our company?"

The dwarf nodded and Little Thom grinned.

"Lute it is," Bitter Olof agreed. "Let's go, Thom. We'll hide the money in the hollow."

"Do you two always travel like this?" Lute asked, impressed.

"Only when it's dangerous," the dwarf replied. "I feel safest on Little Thom's back."

"So now we go to this place called the Devil's Smile? Where is it?"

"Hard to explain," Little Thom answered.

Lute decided the big man was being deliberately vague. It didn't matter. The fact was they'd given Janko's men the slip. He nodded and finally asked what had been on his mind since they first climbed into the tunnel. "Don't you think it's a bit of a coincidence that you've obviously lived here in secret quite successfully for a while and then suddenly the Duke's men are able to track you down?"

"I've been having the same thought myself," Bitter Olof agreed.

Little Thom frowned in the moonlight. "Someone has betrayed us."

The dwarf sighed. "There's no love lost between me and Janko, as you know. The price on my head is enough to tempt most, and although he said he used tracking dogs, I think he had some extra help. They got here too fast."

Little Thom's frown deepened. "One of the younger ones, perhaps someone new."

"Jhen!" They both said it together.

Little Thom sighed. "Never fully trusted him."

The dwarf grimaced. "But Bran did and I trust Bran."

Little Thom shrugged. "Jhen is new to us. Doesn't hold the same sense of loyalty."

Lute looked between the two men anxiously. "But he could be showing them the secret way up here. Have you considered that?"

"Not until you just mentioned it, no," the dwarf said testily, although Lute felt sure he must have. "Which is why I think we should stop chatting and get on with fleeing."

"We don't have horses, Lute. Are you able to run with your injury?"

"Don't worry about me," Lute said, although he was lying. The pain was back, but knowing the soldiers were all but upon them helped to deaden it.

"Chew some more seeds," Bitter Olof suggested. "We know your rib isn't broken. But it is likely cracked and it's going to hurt. Now, what about you, my friend?" he asked, tapping Little Thom on the shoulder. "Yes, I can see you're not dying immediately, but who's to say you aren't going to bleed to death slowly?"

"I'll rip the tails of my shirt and pack the wound for now. We'll worry about it later."

Lute felt Little Thom was being far too casual about his wound. There was a lot of blood loss, but their situation was precarious, and he hoped once they could get far enough away, something could be done to help the big man. And so while Bitter Olof muttered to himself and went about the business of binding Little Thom's shoulder, Lute chewed on his seeds. He spat out the husk, feeling the familiar tingle of numbness in his mouth, knowing it would soon begin to spread through his body.

"Let's go," Little Thom finally said.

They ran. Little Thom led the way and Lute put his head down and followed. They fell into silence, losing themselves in their thoughts and the rhythm and pace that the big man set. It gave Lute the opportunity to think about what had happened.

Had he imagined that voice in his head? No! He wasn't going mad. He had clearly heard a boy say hello and he'd also said a name, hadn't he? Lute searched his memory. It took him several minutes of concentration before he remembered it. *"Griff!"* he exclaimed beneath his breath. That was it. He'd actually introduced himself, and then he was gone. Or the truth was they'd been interrupted by the arrival of Janko's men. Why had the voice sounded in his head? How odd it was. Having discovered the mystery of El-lin's whistle, he was certain magic existed. Now he had to accept it was being used on him by a boy called Griff. Lute had no idea who Griff might be but he felt both frightened and excited by this new event. He couldn't imagine what it meant, but he hoped the boy would try again.

After what must have been three, perhaps four hours of trekking along the plateau's ridge, they caught sight of the first few riders.

Bitter Olof spat a curse. "They're too quick for us."

Lute was exhausted. He felt close to dropping, although he was grateful that regular chewing of the seeds kept him numbed from the pain in his side. "If it were not for me, he'd not have bothered about you."

"Perhaps you flatter yourself, my King," Bitter Olof said with a sad smile. "But I suspect you're right," he added.

"Then leave me. Just go! I'll try to outwit them. Why risk them catching three of us?"

"Your courage is admirable, but firstly, do you hear the dogs?" Lute nodded. "They will not only hunt you down with ease but they now have our scent, too. What's more, Janko is known for his ruthless nature. We tricked him. He will want to make us pay with our lives, so Little Thom and I will not be spared his wrath. Finally, you are the key to our lives now. Your presence offers us the only protection we possess for harboring you in the first place. You are the King. You command the army. Those were mercenaries who ambushed us today. I'd bet my big nose that the regular army has little idea of what is actually going on. If we can get you to Floris, show you to the senior officers, tell your story, then I imagine we have a chance at saving not only our lives, Majesty, but making Janko pay for—"

He never finished. Little Thom collapsed and Bitter Olof fell with him.

25

They had been on the move for hours now. Tess stopped first. "I need to rest and I'm sure Elph does, too. He can't keep up this pace."

Griff pulled the rucksack off his back and put down Helys, whom he'd carried for the past hour. As light as she was, even Helys became a burden after that long. He sighed and looked around. "All right. We rest here but not for long, Tess. Just enough for a brief doze, perhaps something to eat."

"We've put enough distance between us and them, surely?" she asked.

Davren must have said something to her because Griff noticed her stop and listen.

She nodded somberly. "Davren is convinced the Stalkers will come."

"He's right. We have to be realistic about this. Tyren is not going to allow you to just disappear without a fight."

She snorted. "It's you, Griff, not me, who is his prize."

He shrugged, already missing his brothers and realizing

he might never see any of his family again. "Either way, we're together, so we make his hunt easier."

"What are you saying?"

"I think we're making it too easy for them. Hunting us through woodland and forest is hard but not hard enough. We may well be able to hide ourselves, Tess, but it will mean being on the run constantly. Every night we'll have to sleep in a new hollow, beneath a different bush, in a fresh cave."

"And so you have a better plan?" she asked, irritation creeping into her tone.

Griff's dark gaze dropped. "The city," he said, and before she could protest, he added, "It's our only chance."

"Are you forgetting something, Griff? How do you imagine Davren or any of the creatures will survive in the city? And how long do you imagine they'll go unnoticed? A minute, perhaps?"

"I do realize all of that but I overheard some of the others talking. I think this year Tyren was planning to go to Floris. The show hasn't visited it in many years, apparently. There is some forest surrounding the city and Blind Pippin told me—because no one else would listen—that when he was a boy and had his eyesight, he and his father used to poach in the royal woodland. The palace has its own parklands and this is private land that only the King uses for his hunting."

"You think we can hide in the King's hunting woodland?" Tess asked, her voice loaded with disbelief.

"Why not? We won't be poaching. If we're seen, we'll say we're lost or just using it to get from one part of the realm to another. We carry no weapons. We have no traps. We look too young to be of any threat anyway. The creatures know how to hide and it's their preferred countryside. You can't imagine the Stalkers are going to tramp all over the royal parklands . . . they wouldn't be allowed. But we can sneak in. And best of all, I don't think Tyren or the Stalkers would think we'd move toward the city. They'd assume, if anything, that we'd head east toward the Night Forest and where I come from . . . where you were first found."

"Davren agrees with you," she said, a little sulkily.

"It's a good plan." He shrugged again. "Just until we can work out something more permanent."

"How far away are we?"

"If we move steadily, perhaps three days. Tyren has brought us in a northeasterly direction, from what I can tell. We were going to do shows in Shepton, followed by Weston Four Fields and then Tarrow's Landing for a week, I think, before we did the summer in and around Floris proper."

"And the royal parklands?"

"I'm not sure. I have a feeling that they reach almost as far as Tarrow's Landing."

She sighed. "Right. So we can doze now? My feet ache."

He smiled sympathetically. "Everyone should sleep."

"Davren says he'll keep watch, he's not tired."

Griff yawned as he nodded, and closed his eyes before he could offer his gratitude to the centaur.

He dreamed.

In the dream he was walking, very tired, and he recognized that he was dreaming about what was happening in his life. Except, in the dream, he didn't recognize the landscape. He seemed to be on a high ridge, looking down into a valley presumably—it was too dark to see. He thought a river glinted in the distance as it snaked its way around what looked to be a busy township; twinkling lights told him as much. And not much further west he could see the sea. He was worried about something but not about the same thing that was frightening him. His fright revolved around being pursued. That made sense but his worry was over someone who was hurt. And, oh, how his own body ached. His side was on fire!

He is here, said a voice.

Davren?

Yes.

Am I awake?

The centaur chuckled softly in his mind. *I believe so.*

I thought I was dreaming.

Not unless you're dreaming me, and I am very much here. So is he.

He?

Your friend. The one you're trying to reach. He's here, he just doesn't realize it, I don't think.

Why?

Why is he here? I think you're bringing him, Griff.

Griff frowned. He was awake, he realized, but he was back in the familiar silver void, which no longer felt unnerving. In fact, it felt safe. *And he doesn't know?*

If he did, I think he might say something to us, don't you?

Perhaps I should talk to him?

You should. Remember, he'll be alarmed.

He can't hurt you. It was a different voice.

Who's that? Griff asked, looking around the Silvering.

It's Rix.

Rix! Griff laughed.

What's funny? What's wrong with my voice?

Nothing. It's just—

Rix, Davren said softly, *he's not used to hearing us speak. Everyone should give salutations.*

Hello, Griff, said a shy voice.

Helys. Is that you?

She giggled and Griff saw the flare of an orangey glow on the fringe of his mind. He smiled.

Elph, where are you? he asked.

Here, said a deep voice, slow and mellow.

Tess is so lucky to be able to talk to you all. I feel as though I could never be lonely if I could always have this.

You can, Davren said. *You can reach the Silvering at any time.*

It's not us, Griff, Helys urged.

Rix joined in. *The magic is all yours. It's you who called us here.*

I don't understand, Griff replied.

Davren tried to help. *What we're saying is that perhaps we've helped you discover your own true magic because our presence helps to block out everyone else's thoughts in your mind. If you're right, then we bring calm, but the magic to talk, to find the Silvering, to bring us all together in your mind, to reach out and speak across distances is your special gift.*

Griff thought about this, noticing as he did how the silver void he thought was still actually pulsed gently. *So when Tess talks to you, it's not like this?*

It was Elph who answered. *No, she just talks in our minds. This place does not exist for her—at least, I've never seen it with her,* he said.

Elph's right, Davren said. *Tess has the ability to link minds with us but not with the Silvering.* There was a pause. *And one more thing,* Davren added carefully.

Yes?

You were not dreaming just now. You had already arrived at the Silvering and without knowing it you were calling to me. You were obviously scared and didn't realize you'd reached out to me. It's why I'm here now . . . why we're all here.

Not dreaming? How could I be awake and see what I did?

Davren hesitated again. Griff could hear his reluctance.

Tell me, he urged.

Griff, I think you have the ability not only to reach the Silvering and bring people to it and talk to them, but I think you can see what they are seeing, too, no matter where they are.

What?

I could be wrong, but as this boy is on your mind so much, I have a feeling that you might have, without realizing it, tapped into him and seen through his eyes. Your connection to him is so strong. It's why I said earlier that I felt he was present. You've got to speak to him, especially as you think he's in trouble. You said there was pain and he was frightened of being pursued.

I told you that?

Yes, as you were calling to me you were describing what you were looking at.

Except I thought it was me. We're being pursued, I just—

I know. But your side doesn't pain and you're not worried about someone being injured either. You've got to speak to him. Just try to remember how it felt a moment ago and reach out. He was here; you can bring him back.

Lute had to help free Bitter Olof before rolling Little Thom onto his back. The dwarf was cursing but Lute knew it was from the terror that his great friend was in trouble. It was nearing dawn, and in that murky light of night giving way to morning, Little Thom's face looked pale, almost gray. His shirt was soaked with blood and Lute thought the worst. As Bitter Olof put his head to his friend's chest to listen for his heart, Lute stood, unable to bear the thought that Little Thom had died. He looked across the landscape in despair, and as he did so, Lute felt as though his mind was being tugged at, and then suddenly, momentarily, everything disappeared and he was in a silvery void. He was aware of another's presence but he was too startled to focus on much beyond his own fear.

And then the sensation was gone almost as swiftly as it had come upon him and he was back in reality, looking down on Bitter Olof's ashen face.

"He's alive," the dwarf said. "Quickly, dig in that sack I was carrying. There should be a small porcelain flask."

Lute found it. "What is it?" he asked, turning the flask over in his hand.

"A revival remedy. It doesn't last long but it's so powerful it works like magic. It will buy us time to get help for him."

Lute gave it to the dwarf, who dropped some of its contents past the lips of Little Thom. The big man groaned almost immediately. "What's happened?"

"You fainted," Lute said.

"Because you're too weak," Bitter Olof added as they helped Little Thom to sit up. He sipped some more of the revival remedy.

"Never thought I'd need this," he admitted.

Bitter Olof nodded. "We need to face facts, my friend. They're not taking any rest either. I can hear the dogs." Lute couldn't hear anything but presumed the dwarf had especially sensitive hearing, helped by his enormous ears.

Bitter Olof continued. "They'll be upon us sometime during the morning. We can't outrun them even if we could make it to the Devil's Smile."

Little Thom's face looked grim. "We can't give them the boy. I'd rather drop dead trying to get him away."

Lute swallowed hard, touched by the loyalty, and he knew it was to him personally rather than the Crown itself. He loved Little Thom for that solid friendship and he loved Bitter Olof for what he said next.

"Janko will get Lute only over our dead bodies, old friend, I promise you that."

"I'm feeling good enough. How long will this last?"

The dwarf shrugged. "Three hours, perhaps. Not long enough."

Lute looked anxiously between his companions. "What are we going to do? Again, I say—"

"Don't repeat it, we have no intention of splitting up," Bitter Olof said gruffly.

"Where can we get to in three hours, then?" Lute asked.

"Not even close to the rendezvous. I suppose there are several towns. Places like Timpton Willow or Weston Four Fields."

"Nowhere to hide, though," Little Thom admitted. "It's not as though we both blend easily into the crowd," he added, and smiled sympathetically at his friend, who returned the sad expression.

"We can't stay here," Lute said. "Think! There has to be somewhere we can hide out for a day or so."

"It's not just a matter of hiding, Majesty," Bitter Olof counseled. "Thom needs help from a healer."

"There is somewhere," Little Thom said softly.

"Where?" Lute asked, his voice eager. He could hear the dogs in the far distance now and they'd been here for too long already.

"The sea."

"No!" Bitter Olof snapped. "That's not an alternative."

"It's our only alternative if you don't want me to die."

"I don't!" Bitter Olof spat, cursing under his breath.

"What's at the sea?" Lute asked, baffled, glancing toward the ocean that the dawn was now lighting in the distance.

"Not what, but who," Little Thom replied, and winked.

Lute smiled despite his anxiety.

"You know what will happen," Bitter Olof said, disgust in his voice.

"I think it's worth my life, don't you?" Little Thom replied, slowly pulling himself to his feet. "We can be at the cove in an hour if we hurry."

"What cove?" Lute asked as they began to move, Bitter Olof walking now.

"It's called Shearwater. Very few know about it," Bitter Olof answered, still apparently disgusted that they were headed there.

"And who is at Shearwater who can help us?" Lute persisted.

Little Thom grinned over his shoulder. "That would be Calico Grace."

26

Griff took a deep breath and then, opening up his mind to the trace he had been following, he searched for it again. He found it easily this time.

Do it, Davren encouraged on the edge of his mind. *We will give you some privacy.* And then Davren and his companions were gone.

There was no point in hesitating any longer. Griff intensified his focus, and suddenly he could see a new scene. This time he knew for sure that he was observing through someone else's eyes. It was a shock but he didn't recoil. The boy whom he presumed he'd reached was following someone huge who had blood, bright and wet, staining his shirt. The injury didn't seem to be on his back, but the blood had crept over his shoulder and beneath his arms. No one was talking. They seemed to be traveling downhill, concentrating hard on their footfall, not tripping or stumbling. The boy was clearly anxious. Griff could feel the tension in him.

And then suddenly, *Who is this?* the voice he recognized said. Movement stopped.

There was a third person because Griff heard a voice as the owner obviously crashed into the boy's back.

"Lute!" it said, and Griff could hear the exasperation.

"Sorry," the boy called Lute said.

"What's wrong?" The big man in front turned and Griff reeled back as he saw that all the front of his shirt was soaked in blood. He saw a hand go up in the air.

"Give me a moment," Lute said.

"What's the matter?" This came from the second voice, which Griff now realized belonged to a strange-looking dwarf of a man.

"It's . . . it's nothing, let's go, I just stumbled," Griff heard Lute say.

This is Griff, he said, determined now to make proper contact.

Lute finally answered across the mindlink, and Griff was relieved to see that his new friend kept moving, although he stumbled slightly. *I . . . I hear you, but who are you? I mean, I know your name is Griff, but—*

Don't be alarmed. I can see you're in trouble. Look, I know this is incredibly strange—it is for me, too—but I've been hearing your voice in my mind for a couple of days.

I don't understand.

It's a long story, so let me just explain that I've got the magical ability to hear people's thoughts. And I've heard your anxiety. You've been calling out for help.

First tell me exactly who you are, where you are and why I find myself talking to you in this extraordinary way.

Griff thought that was fair. *I'll tell you everything I can.* Griff proceeded to tell his astonished listener his story, pleased to see that the deeper he got into his own tale, the more assured Lute's movement became. He could sense his mind-companion's alarm dissipating. He felt an instant friendship toward him as he had for Tess.

At the end of it he heard Lute give a soft sound of awe. *You can hear what I'm thinking when it's important enough? That's amazing.*

I'm glad you see it that way.

So we're the same age and you seem to be in almost as much trouble as I am. Looks like our lives are running next to one another, even though I have no idea what you look like. They shared a smile across the miles that separated them, and Griff wondered if this was how Phin and Mat felt at times, so connected to each other in their closeness as brothers. *I'm going to tell you something very secret, but first I have to ask you, what do you know about Duke Janko?*

Janko? Griff asked, surprised. *Nothing, other than what I hear around the show's campfires. I've never been to Floris so I know nothing of the royals, never seen him in person, but I hear things about him.*

Like what? Lute asked.

Well, some people think he's a hero. Others are more careful. Our showmaster thinks there will be trouble once he returns to the capital.

In what way?

I'm not sure. I think he was suggesting that his presence might cause trouble for the King, although I don't know why. I'm just a grunter; I don't understand politics.

The fact that you're talking to me through magic tells us you're far more than a mere grunter, Griff. And if the Stalkers really are hunting you, then you are a lot more important than you think. In a different situation I would be able to help you with those Stalkers. He sighed.

Help? How?

And it was Griff's turn to be astonished as he listened to the horrid tale of his new friend. When Lute finished talking, he was momentarily silent.

You mean I'm talking to Crown Prince Lute? he asked, still finding it hard to believe.

Er, well, no, that's not absolutely true. It's King Lute now, and the Stalkers answer to the Crown. In normal circumstances I could stop them. However, they seem to be following their own orders. Lute sounded angry.

Griff's mind reeled. *King! And you think Janko will kill you if he catches you?*

Not think. I know he will. He's very determined to steal the throne, and as long as I'm alive, I'm in his way.

That's very scary. So you and your friends are running to the ocean in a bid to escape. But you're hurt, another is seriously injured and the dwarf is . . . well, on very short legs.

Lute laughed, and it was a nice sound in Griff's head. *That's the sum of it, I'm afraid. But we can't sit around and wait for them to catch us. There's someone at Shearwater Cove who we're hoping will offer aid called—*

Griff! Davren's voice was urgent.

Who's that? Lute asked, alarmed.

He's a friend. What's wrong, Davren?

They're onto us much faster than we thought. Hurry, we have to run. They've got a dog and it sounds like plenty of men.

Lute, I have to—

I heard. Run, Griff. We'll talk whenever you can reach me. Be safe.

You too.

Griff cut the mindlink, the silver floated away from his vision and suddenly he was back in the woodland, gazing at the terrified face of Tess.

It appeared that Davren had told her everything, so she wasn't asking any questions of him. "They're close," she said.

"Tyren must have known, otherwise he couldn't have caught up with us so quickly. But I don't understand how he'd have dogs."

"Stalkers," she said, as though tasting something bad. "Tyren must have guessed we'd try to escape and already taken precautions by calling in the Stalkers." She sounded disgusted.

"We're as good as captured, then," he said bitterly.

She looked at him, eyes blazing in the early dawn. "No, I'm not giving myself to them as meekly as I did last time. I was frightened for the creatures, but this time everyone agrees that we should take our chances and flee."

Griff nodded. It wasn't as though they had much choice. And he was reminded of what his new friend, Lute, was up against and took courage from his determination. "Come on, Helys. What about Elph?"

"Don't worry about him," Tess said, a fierce look on her face. "Elph's strong. He can keep up for a while . . . until we lose them," she said as confidently as she could. "Rix will guide us from the trees and keep a lookout for our pursuers. He says there's a stream not far from here. We can lose the dog, perhaps."

Griff nodded. They continued on their way, Tess and Davren leading, no one speaking, everyone frightened but trying hard to remain calm.

⚜

They'd paused for a few moments so Little Thom could sip more of the revival remedy. "It's less effective already," he grumbled.

"It will be," Bitter Olof said. "But we knew that." He turned to watch Lute spit out the husk of the painkilling seeds. "You're quiet."

"Worried, that's all."

"How come you ignored us talking to you, then?"

"What? Er, sorry. I didn't hear you."

"That was obvious," Bitter Olof replied.

"My mind is all over the place—I'm sure you understand. Who is Calico Grace?" he asked, deliberately changing the subject. He was still feeling unnerved by Griff's appearance in his mind, but he liked the sound of his voice and needed time to think about what he'd said. It was such a curiosity, and although he didn't understand it, he was glad of it.

Bitter Olof grimaced. "We'll tell you when we hit the beach. Let's go," he said sourly.

"I'm not feeling too good," Little Thom told them.

Lute could see that as the morning lightened, Little Thom's face was ghostly gray and glistening with sweat. Thom sank to his knees and gave a sad glance toward Lute. "I'm sorry, Your Majesty."

"We can't carry you, Thom, old friend," Bitter Olof said,

his voice suddenly gentle. "Be strong now. I need you to be as strong as you've ever been; snap to your feet and help us get to Grace."

"You don't even want to see her," the big man groaned.

"No, that's true, I don't, because we both know what it's going to mean. But she can offer us help, and she can offer it quickly. And the person standing behind me is no ordinary child. This is our King. I'm no friend of the royals, you know that, but I'll be damned if I sit by and watch that black-hearted brother steal this boy's crown, especially when I know Lute is our friend and therefore more likely to be . . . well, shall we say, understanding when the need arises. Janko has already put an arrow into your shoulder. The next one will be aimed to kill, not to maim you or slow you down."

Little Thom looked up at Lute through glazed eyes. He swayed slightly.

"He's just a boy," Bitter Olof added softly.

"Never known you to be so sentimental," Little Thom muttered, and his focus seemed to clear. Lute could see it took a mighty effort for the giant of a man to haul himself back to his feet. He looked fully spent, and yet he found a grin. "I'm sorry about that weak moment, Your Majesty. Shall we try again?"

Bitter Olof nodded. "Indeed."

Lute could hear that the dogs were close now. "I think we should run."

"I think you should," Little Thom replied. "Lead the way, friend," he said to Bitter Olof. "I'll bring up the rear this time."

And then they were running, Lute's mind empty of everything except the need to follow the dwarf's footsteps.

⌘

Not so far away, Griff was running, too. "Tell me more about the Stalkers," he asked Tess, catching up with her. "I need to know as much as you do if we're going to avoid them."

"They're a force unto themselves."

"They're not run by the Crown?" Griff said, surprised.

She scoffed. "Not likely. Duke Janko set them up years ago as a sort of constabulary. They keep an eye on affairs at a very local level, so he can focus the army's attention on the realm's borders and any outside threat."

"How do you know this?"

"I made it my business to learn as much as I could about my captors," she replied, anger in her tone. "They should answer to the King, but they ignore that line of command. They're puppets to the Duke, as I understand it."

"But why does he have so much authority?"

She frowned at Griff. "You really are quite ignorant of our realm's politics, aren't you?" He found it hard to shrug as he ran, but he managed to convey the same message of indifference. "I'm no expert," she admitted, "but the Duke runs the army, and his role is to keep the realm secure. Unfortunately, he's forgotten that he—and the army—answers to the King. The Stalkers were formed to hunt down individual undesirables and should also answer to the Crown, but somehow over the reign of Lute's father they've turned themselves into mercenaries and hire out their services to people like Tyren."

"I'm sure if the King knew this was going on, he'd stamp it out."

It was Tess's turn to shrug awkwardly. "That's how it is. They hunt down everyone from criminals to people like me—and for a hefty price."

Hearing this made Griff even more determined to beat them.

"We can't keep this pace up for much longer," Tess urged. He knew she was right. "Can you hear what they're thinking?"

"What?"

"Use your skill, Griff. Try to listen in on their thoughts. Perhaps you can hear something that will help us."

He'd never tried or wanted to use his skill to deliberately find someone, but he'd been able to with Lute. Perhaps he could do the same thing with the Stalkers.

"I'm not sure I can do it while we run."

"Then we'll stop," she said, and did so, breathing deeply. They all were. "Try now. Whatever you can do, Griff, just try."

He nodded and glanced at Davren, who'd heard the conversation and now trotted back to where they'd stopped.

Griff reached out with his mind and instantly was in the silver void. *Well done,* Davren said. *That was fast. No dreaming or half sleep. You've done that with skill.*

Thanks, Griff said self-consciously. *I'm glad you're here with me.*

You brought me with you, Griff. I had nothing to do with it. But time is short. See if you can find Tyren; perhaps he can lead you to the Stalkers.

I know his trace well. Here goes, Griff said, and without

really understanding what he was doing, Griff recalled Tyren's "signature," as he thought of it. It was a familiar trace and he found it relatively easily. *I've got it!* he yelled across the mindlink.

Again, well done. Now follow it and see where it leads you. I can't help.

Griff followed it and at lightning speed found himself hearing Tyren's thoughts, which were, predictably, a mess of anger connected with the loss of Tess and her creatures, and amidst the ranting he heard thoughts of how the creatures would be branded with Tyren's name and chained permanently, even when on show. Tess would no longer be in charge of them. They would have a keeper who would answer to Tyren. Tess would be locked into her wagon at night, and she too would be living with a keeper. Griff shuddered as Tyren's thoughts revealed that he'd already chosen Widow Klenk for the role. The widow was in charge of all the sewing for the show, and she was a sour, bad-tempered sort on a good day. Tess and her feisty personality wouldn't survive long under Widow Klenk. But Tyren's most savage thoughts were about the loss of Griff, and Griff learned that he would be in leg-irons from now on, released only for shows but with minders surrounding him during showtime. Tyren planned to make it look like protection, when in fact it was imprisonment. He too would be locked in at night but also chained to a metal bar that Tyren was planning to install in a special reinforced wagon. Griff would be under guard constantly and, as punishment, kept apart from not only Tess but also his brothers. He reeled backward to hear his own name being raged about with such poison, pulling away from Tyren as fast as he could.

Davren guessed what had happened. *Do it again*, he said gently, *but hurry*.

Griff tried again, this time ignoring Tyren's bitter thoughts and searching through them for anything that might lead him to the Stalkers. It was strange to be invading someone's thoughts and seeking something specific. He identified his goal within moments, a man called Snark. Using Tyren as a curious sort of leaping platform, Griff did something he never imagined he was capable of and diverted his skills, linking to a new trace and following it. He found himself hearing Snark's thoughts in seconds.

We've got you cornered now, you curs. Once my men come around from the sides, you'll have nowhere to run but deeper into the forest, and we'll just keep closing the circle—

Griff snapped back, and found himself meeting Tess's troubled expression.

"What?" she asked, searching his face for clues.

He couldn't tell her everything he'd heard. It would break her. What he did choose to say was bad enough. "We're surrounded," he gasped. "The Stalkers are closing in from several directions. They're deliberately trying to drive us deeper into the forest."

"Wait," she said urgently, "let me check with Rix."

Moments later she looked back at Griff. "He's been gliding at lower levels, trying to keep us in sight. That's why he missed what they're up to. But you're right. There's three separate groups."

"How long?" Griff asked.

"Just minutes, I think," she replied, ashen.

"There's only three groups. Ask him if he can guide us through a narrow route—a way to slip through them."

She shook her head helplessly but tried anyway. "There is a wider opening in this direction," she said, pointing. "But they've got a dog, Griff; they can just keep on tracking."

"Well . . ."

"Then we go deeper. We'll have to figure out what to do as we run. If we wait here a moment longer, they'll be upon us—"

He held up his hand to stop her speaking. "Just run, Tess!"

27

It felt to Griff as though the dog was all but snapping at their heels. He scooped up Helys, threw a sympathetic glance at Elph, who rallied once again, and they all ran for their lives.

But it was Elph who gave up first.

"He can't go any further," Tess said sadly, flopping on the ground next to the deeply panting sagar, she herself barely able to speak. "His heart will give out."

Griff was bent, breathing hard. He'd put Helys down and she went to Elph to comfort him, her color turning paler by the moment in her anxiety. Even Rix came down lower to watch from midway in the trees, while Davren, the least breathless, arrived to stand next to Griff. He placed his fist on his chest. Griff understood the centaur was telling him to be strong, have heart. But Griff didn't know how to find that hope, not without a weapon and with so many to protect from men, the dog and no doubt plenty of arms.

"They won't hurt us, Tess, I promise," Griff said. "We're his prize acts, remember?"

"I don't care about me, Griff, but he may hurt one of the creatures to remind me he owns me! That punishment will be too much to bear and you know he's capable of it."

Griff nodded forlornly. "Tell Davren, and Rix especially, not to fight back. I'll say it was my idea and I'll take the blame. But they mustn't anger him. Promise me." He waited while she used her mindlink to talk with her friends and felt a knot of fear tighten as her eyes began to water. "What is it?"

"Rix," she said, fighting back her sorrow. "He's not coming with us. He says he can't go back into a cage, says he'll die if he's imprisoned. I understand, don't blame him. Veercats need space and need to use their wings; otherwise they lose the will to live. I've told Davren to go but he refuses to leave me and the others."

"Listen to me, Tess. I can talk to Rix using the Silvering. I can always find him for you, I promise."

She looked at him as though he were speaking gibberish.

"I've got a lot to explain to you—what the Silvering is, who I found there."

"I know you've been speaking to the Whisperer because Davren told me."

"And I haven't had a chance to tell you what I discovered, but right now I just want you to know that Rix is not lost to you. I'm glad at least one of the creatures is getting away and I promise you that I'll keep you in touch with him. Tell him to go and not be caught." He looked at Davren. "You shouldn't stay but I understand why you will. Just don't fight them. I know you refused to be scared by Tyren, and after watching you deal with Mad Dog Merl, I know that you're strong enough to fight back, but right now being meek and acting scared is our best protection."

Davren gave a small smile of understanding, and it broke Griff's heart to see the fine, proud creature of the forest accepting that he must appear humbled by a greedy, cruel man. But Griff knew it was the only way that they might come out of this without any of them being physically hurt.

They gathered under a huge old oak and anxiously awaited their pursuers, chilled by cool shadows beneath great branches where the sun could not penetrate. There was no point in running any longer. Their pursuers were getting closer by the minute.

In his nervousness at what was about to occur, Griff's thoughts fled to Lute. He was still shaken that the Whisperer had turned out to be the Crown Prince, now apparently King. He hoped Lute was faring better right now than they were. His mind was dragged toward the sounds of riders. They were upon them.

Into the clearing they came, and in no particular hurry—not that the horses could travel quickly through this dense part of the forest. But the dog traveled with ease and suddenly Griff and Tess and the creatures were faced by the snarling, panting beast. It nipped at Davren's hooves and he kicked out at the animal.

"Call it off!" Tess screamed as the men came into view.

Griff saw Tyren. He was surprised the fat showman had bothered to come along. He expected Tyren to leave his dirty work to be done by others. "There's no point in hurting your prize, Tyren," Griff yelled, no longer paying the man any politeness.

"Oh, but *you* are my prize, Griffin," Tyren replied, unhurried. "I might even let the dog have the centaur. It's ready to rip him to shreds on command of Master Snark here."

Griff swallowed. "Why lose two acts to prove a point? You've caught us. The creatures are not to blame for the escape."

Three more riders arrived. There were eleven Stalkers in total, wearing the telltale red riding gloves, red feathers in their hats and dark capes. Griff picked out the leader, Snark, because his cape was lined with a deep red, while the rest had black linings in their capes.

"Where's Glosh?" Snark asked one of his men.

"Just coming; he backtracked because he heard something."

Snark nodded. "Well, we're all here bar one. Are these all you seek, Master Tyren?" he asked, staring at Griff and his companions as though they were vermin.

"One missing. The veercat," Tyren answered.

"And you'll never have him in your possession again," Tess hurled at him.

He shrugged. "Not much of a loss. With luck he'll likely die out here alone anyway. Veercats need packs to hunt successfully, don't they?"

She ignored him but Griff could feel her pain.

"Thank you for your work, Master Snark," Tyren said appreciatively. "I hope this is the final time I need to employ your men for the task of tracking Miss Tess and her creatures."

"I take it you will keep them chained permanently from now on?"

"And guarded constantly," Tyren replied. "Well, as I'm paying you for the extra help, I think we should do the branding here, don't you?"

"Messy business and usually filled with the wretches'

screeches. Best now where no one else can hear their screams. We'll get a fire started; shouldn't take long to heat up the branding irons. You said a large *T* is sufficient, didn't you?"

"That would be perfect. And I shall have it inked onto the boy and girl, too."

"We can do that for you as well."

"Does it hurt?" Tyren asked innocently.

"I'm afraid it does," Snark answered, and got on with the business of organizing his men.

"Oh, good," Tyren replied, and Griff heard a note of glee in his voice.

Most of the men climbed down from their horses and tethered them, and then as an added precaution—not that their prisoners were planning to run—Snark had one of his men train a bow and arrow on them. The remainder untied their weapons, stretched and took advantage of this time to rest and eat. A couple of them quickly built a fire and watered their mounts. Meanwhile, a horrible silence was held until Tyren broke it.

"Hungry?" he asked Griff and Tess.

"A little," Griff admitted. There was no point in taking Tess's attitude and ignoring the man, because it was only going to make it worse in the long run.

"Good. You can stay that way. And I hope the branding really hurts your creature friends, Tess. If you think that califa looks pale now, wait until the Stalkers have finished burning my mark into her flesh," he said with genuine cruelty in his voice.

"We'll do the centaur first," Snark said, poking an iron into the fire that had already begun crackling.

Griff wanted to go into the Silvering and talk directly to Davren, who appeared suddenly skittish, and understandably so.

"Is this beast going to give us trouble?" Snark demanded.

"What do you think?" Tess replied, refusing to back down. Griff admired her pluck but he didn't think it was helping their cause.

"We'll soon fix that," Snark replied, smiling nastily. "You did say it was all right, didn't you, Master Tyren?"

"Injure but not kill were my orders."

Griff felt his stomach clench with fear, and then before anyone could say anything further, a silent signal was given and one of the men loosed an arrow into Davren's side. The centaur reared up in pain, howling his anger, and Tess screamed but she begged her creatures not to run or risk being injured. Davren was bleeding, his hide streaked with bright blood. Bravely he reached around and pulled the arrow out.

"Ah, good, just a simple flesh wound. No real danger but it should quiet him down," Tyren said appreciatively to Snark. "And if he gives you any further problem, put another one in him—"

He was interrupted by the arrival of a final Stalker. He was leading a horse.

Snark looked up from heating his branding iron.

"I found this tethered to a tree not far away, Master Snark," the man called Glosh said.

"Well, whose is it?" Snark demanded.

Everyone looked around, baffled. Griff heard rustling and looked up into the tree.

"Well, it has to be owned by someone. It hardly tied itself

to the damn tree. Find who it belongs to!" Snark ordered angrily. He'd barely finished speaking when three arrows whizzed by. Within a few blinks of the eye three men went down screaming, with arrowheads in their thighs.

"No need," said a fresh voice before its owner dropped with grace and agility from a branch above. He landed lightly near Griff, turning to stare at him with even more astonishment than Griff felt staring back at him.

"I can't believe it," the man said. "It was only when you looked up I realized it was you," he murmured. With daunting speed, before anyone could react to him, the man loosed arrows into two more individuals. Five men were now writhing on the ground and cursing.

Griff frowned but then chaos erupted and he had no time to ask the obvious question.

"And who in Lo's name are you?" Snark snarled.

"Let's not bring our god into the unholy scene I look upon here, shall we?" the man replied. "And never mind my name, sir. I don't share it with bullies, let alone criminals, and what you are about here is criminal business. Now call your dog off immediately." When no order was given, he sighed. "I can kill him or, better still," he said, shocking everyone at the speed with which he could retrieve an arrow and nock it, "I could kill you." He aimed the weapon at Tyren, drawing his bow tightly.

Griff watched Tyren bristle. "How dare you! I'll have you know I own—"

"No one owns anyone in our realm, Master Tyren. Only you seem to think so. You and your thuggish sidekicks here. This is the last time the Stalkers will walk this land with any authority. Call off the beast or take the arrow, Tyren. Put the dog on its leash and tie it to a tree."

"Do it!" Tyren ordered. "Now!" he yelled at Snark.

Snark sneered. "My men have the authority of the Crown." He gave the signal and the dog was tied up.

The newcomer shook his head. "No, sir, they do not. Now that the Crown knows of your dark work, you will be disbanded and I don't doubt your nasty group here will be rounded up and soundly punished. I see some solid floggings and lengthy jail sentences coming up. As for you, Master Tyren, you will not escape heavy punishment for the brutal treatment I have witnessed."

Snark laughed again. "Er, whoever you are, apart from the obvious fact that you are seriously outnumbered, we're the ones with weapons," he said, glancing at the man holding the bow. The others, Griff noted, wore swords at their sides.

The stranger seemed untroubled. "In the time it takes your man over there to nock a single arrow, I will not only have killed him but likely you as well, Snark. Don't risk it."

Snark laughed. "Shoot him!" he ordered. "But don't kill him."

But the Stalker got no further than reaching behind for an arrow. A knife whizzed through the air and landed dully in the Stalker's shoulder. Meanwhile, Snark screamed and put a hand to his ear, blood suddenly pumping from the side of his head.

"But I hadn't forgotten about my knives," the stranger said. "Or these," he added, crossing his hands over his shoulders and retrieving two hidden swords from the cunningly concealed scabbards he wore at his back that Griff had seen the moment the man landed. Griff stole a glance at Tess, who was wide-eyed, her gaze shining with pleasure as much as disbelief. Even Davren wore a sly grin, his wound ignored for now. He nodded with obvious glee at Griff. No one knew who this man was but none of them cared. He was their savior.

"My ear!" Snark shrieked, pulling his hand away to reveal a bloodied mass where his ear had been.

"Rest assured it doesn't spoil your good looks, although I'll be happy to balance up your head and cut off the other one," the man said.

Griff felt a thrill to see Tyren's eyes filled with fear. Tyren was fine when he felt in control and was pushing people around with his threats. But now he was scared.

The stranger must have sensed the same. "Don't move, Master Tyren, I can throw a knife hard and fast and very accurately over long distances. I can fell you before you even get out of this clearing. Now get off your horse, you oversized bully; it surely needs a rest from your big arse weighing it down."

Tyren blinked. He struggled down from the saddle.

"Quickly, boy," the stranger said quietly, "get their swords—count that you have twelve—and lay the hilts in the fire. They won't be picking those up in a hurry. And be careful that they don't grab you, use you as bargaining power. Be wary."

None of the men were inclined to risk further injury or loss of life and stayed still. Griff moved swiftly to do as he was told, quietly marveling at the ingenuity of the man's idea. Snark was still clutching the side of his head and wailing at the pain of his lost ear. Griff had to stop himself from laughing.

"I'll have your hide for this, Griff," Tyren muttered, for his hearing only, as he passed. The showmaster carried no weapon to Griff's knowledge and the boy could easily dodge the podgy man, so he didn't feel nearly so threatened anymore. He wished he could speak to Lute right now and explain with glee the seemingly magical arrival of a gifted stranger.

"Capes off, gentlemen, please," their new friend continued. "All remaining weapons into the fire and no one else will get hurt," the as-yet-unnamed individual ordered. He pulled off his own hat, which had been pulled low over his face.

"He's outnumbered!" Tyren yelled at the bleeding Snark. "Why don't you tell your men to overwhelm him?"

Griff laid the last of the weapons into the fire and noticed as he did so that the bravado had gone out of Snark. It was obvious he was in pain and feeling sorry for himself; the leader of the Stalkers seemed to have lost all sense of authority or ability to intimidate. Now he just looked like a hurt, ugly little man with no courage . . . only a vestige of the sort that comes with being in large groups and with someone at his mercy.

"What's wrong with you?" Tyren raged, his face as red as a ripe cherry.

"I know who this is now," the head Stalker snarled, filled with bitterness, "and I know it's not worth my life to challenge him. He can take us all on and not one of us would be left standing . . . and the worst part is, he wouldn't kill us but we'd lose arms, legs, bits of ourselves. You've seen what he's done to my ear. That's nothing to what he's capable of. No, I know this man and his reputation too well."

Griff returned to stand by the man's side. He grinned up at him and the stranger frowned momentarily. He shook his head. "Take your friend, whoever she is, and scare off the horses as best you can, but first save one for each of you. Let the Stalkers at least have to look for their mounts. Quickly, Lute," he added.

It was Griff's turn to frown but the stranger had already looked away. *Did he call me Lute?* he wondered. *How odd.*

"I demand to know your name," the showmaster said, filled with frustration.

"It seems I've been recognized anyway, so it's of little matter. You can ask your companion later. But you should know now that I am a servant of the Crown—just as Master Snark is—except his idea of service has become a little skewed."

"I don't know anyone from the palace, so your name would be meaningless to me anyway," Tyren spat.

"But not to these men, it seems," the man replied evenly. "You have made a wise decision, Snark, especially as it would have given me immense pleasure to hurt more of you for what you have done to this magnificent creature here and for what you planned to do. Sadly, I don't have time to care about you, so you may now go and look for your horses. These two we shall keep," he said, his chin pointing at the pair that Tess and Griff held the reins to.

"That's theft," Snark threw back.

"Go and complain to the King," the stranger replied, untroubled by the accusation. "Mount up," he continued, turning to Tess and Griff. "What about the centaur?"

"He says he'll manage," Tess answered.

"He's as brave as he is magnificent," the stranger said, looking at the centaur.

To Griff's surprise, and he knew Tess was taken aback, too, Davren bowed low to the mystery man.

Tess couldn't hide her shock.

Whether the stranger knew that a centaur bowing to a man was not done, Griff couldn't tell, but he was pleased when the stranger returned the gesture, bowing equally low to the forest creature.

"I'll carry that one, shall I?" he said, straightening and pointing at the sagar.

"Hopefully, he'll let you," Tess said, smiling shyly, and the man returned her smile.

"Let's see, shall we? Does he have a name?"

"It's Elph."

"Fancy a ride, Elph? Come on, big fellow, you look dead on your feet." No one was surprised when the exhausted Elph obliged to being handled by a stranger, and once sitting on the horse's back, cradled by the man's arms, he looked almost comfortable, and curiously small, against the tall newcomer.

Griff picked up Helys, who was once again a soft pink. She was feeling safer already, he was pleased to see.

"Was that a veercat I saw in the trees above me?" Pilo asked.

Griff grinned. "His name's Rix."

"I can't wait to hear your tales, my boy," the man said. "But for now ride like the wind."

28

They'd somehow reached the tiny beach; the cove that Bitter Olof spoke about was just around the tip of land that jutted out a short way into the sea. But their pursuers had also reached the beach, barely moments later, and right at the front of them was a smug Duke Janko, with three armed mercenaries and two dogs growling at their handlers to let them off their leashes.

Lute wasn't worried by the dogs. They were not fighting animals, simply trackers, and were unlikely to attack them. He was, however, swallowing hard over the arrows trained on them. There weren't that many men, in truth—just the four—but there might as well have been four hundred because they were armed, and not only were his companions unarmed but one was badly injured, and the other would be ineffective against these hardened fighters.

"Hello, Lute," Janko said, and his tone was syrupy. It made Lute's flesh crawl. "My, my. When we found your red scarf, I thought you were dead. . . ."

Ignoring the Duke, Bitter Olof turned to Lute with a look of great apology. "We were so close," he murmured. "I'm so sorry, Your Highness."

Lute took the dwarf's lead and ignored Janko as obviously as Bitter Olof had. He knew his uncle wanted him dead and gone and he had no intention of listening to the man's feigned simpering for a moment longer. He would be stoic and he would die as bravely as Pilo had. He looked at the dwarf. "Don't be sorry. This is not your fault. It wasn't even your fight. You've done everything you could to help me. No one could ever question your loyalty to the Crown, Bitter Olof. I feel proud to have known you and if I had a sword I would knight you here and now for services to your King."

The dwarf gave him a bow.

"What are you doing?" Janko snarled.

At this Bitter Olof turned, his face a sneer. "I'm bowing to my King, you dolt." Lute was cheered to see the triumph on the dwarf's face.

Janko's expression darkened and his smugly smiling face turned angry as his lips thinned. "King? Here is your King!" he yelled, jabbing himself in the chest. "You bow to me alone from here on. You!" he said, pointing to Little Thom. "Bow to me!"

Little Thom looked up, letting out a tired sigh at the pompous, snarling man on the horse, and without saying a word simply shook his head.

"You dare to defy me?" Janko howled.

"Olof," Little Thom said wearily under his breath. "Stand behind me. You may have a chance to save our King if I take the punishment first and win a few more moments."

The little man paused and then looked at Lute with sad resignation. "Then this truly is farewell."

"I'm sure we'll get up to no good together in the next life," Little Thom replied, not taking his gaze off the riders, but in a voice tinged with sadness. "Be quick, his patience has ended, for there is no further sport in this for him."

"What are you doing?" Janko asked.

"Run, Lute, straight into the sea but head for the point. Swim beneath the surface if you can," Bitter Olof urged. "And don't look behind. Go!"

Lute ran and heard Janko give the fearful orders.

"Kill them!"

Splashing into the sea, he ran as hard as his legs could possibly propel him. Just before he dived into the waters, he disobeyed Bitter Olof and glanced behind.

And what he saw was Little Thom, in an effort that seemed beyond human capability, shielding his and Olof's progress with his great frame for as long as he could stand, while the Duke's men fired arrows into his back.

"No-ooooo!" Lute screamed, and then the salty waters swallowed him.

❧❀❧

They'd ridden west on the fringe of the forest as fast as they could go. Tess assured them that Rix had faithfully followed high in the trees, and it was nearing midday after a lot of hard, silent riding before the man had slowed them and led them deeper into the woods to a narrow brook that gurgled with a comforting sound.

"We can water the horses here," he said, "and we could probably all use a rest. I'm presuming none of you have slept in hours."

"Or eaten," Griff admitted, sliding off his horse and helping Helys down. She and Elph instantly began to forage, whereas Davren and the horses moved directly to the water. Davren drank greedily and Tess followed suit, kneeling down to cup water in her hands and gulp it down. Her beautiful golden hair was wet from trailing in the brook and she looked bedraggled and weary. But her eyes were shining and he guessed it was with the pleasure of freedom.

The man's first thought, apart from unsaddling and tethering the horses, was Davren.

"Let's have a look at this wound, shall we?" he asked, looking to Tess for permission.

She nodded. "He trusts you."

"Good, because I need to see if it's worse than it looks." He glanced at Griff and his gaze softened. "What? Not even so much as a hug, eh?"

"Er . . ." Griff looked baffled. "Forgive me, er, sir, but everything's happened so fast. Tess and I, well, I don't know what we'd have done if you hadn't come along when you did, but I do know that right now we'd be in chains and being led back to Master Tyren's Traveling Show."

"Is that where you've been?" the man asked, looking completely confused now. "Why didn't you go where you were supposed to?" His tone was suddenly abrupt. "You can't take chances like that. You are too important!"

Now Griff was mystified. "Look, er, sir, I'm not sure what—"

"And why do you keep calling me 'sir,' for Lo's sake? If

you can't hug an old friend hello, the least you can do is use my name."

Tess sidled up to Griff. He knew she was feeling just as bewildered and also suddenly frightened again for both of them—all of them. Surely the kind stranger wasn't going to turn into some crazed captor himself?

Griff bit his lip. "I would, sir, if I knew it."

The man was tethering the last of the horses but he rounded on Griff now. "This is a jest, is it? Am I supposed to be laughing with you or is it some joke I don't understand?"

Griff took a deep breath. This was turning odder by the moment. "My name is Griff, sir. This is Tess. We've told you the names of the creatures. . . ."

The man looked back at him as though he had said something very daft. "Griff?" he repeated.

"Yes?"

"No, I mean, you said your name is Griff?"

"Yes, sir. Is something wrong?"

"I'll say! I don't understand. What's happened?" he said, frowning. "You're acting as though you don't even know me."

"I don't think he does," Tess said, trying to help. "Who are you?"

"Lute," the man replied, his tone filled with injury now. "Lute, it's Pilo."

Griff stared back, none the wiser for that information. "Master Pilo, I—"

"No, just Pilo. That's how you know me," the man corrected, his expression sagging.

"I've never seen you before in my life, er, Pilo. I honestly don't know you."

The man looked as though Griff had just slapped him.

"And his name's not Lute. This is Griff," Tess said.

"What have they done to you?" Pilo asked. He turned to glare at Tess. "What have you done to him?" he demanded.

"Nothing!" she hurled back at him. She shook her head. "We're friends. I hardly know him, to have done anything to him."

"I have to get you help," Pilo said, advancing on Griff. "A healer needs to see you. Have you banged your head? Taken a fall? Have those men brainwashed you?" He grabbed Griff's arm.

"Wait!" Griff yelled. "None of those things have happened. You're mistaken. I'm not who you think I am."

"I think I know the Crown Prince Lute when I see him!" Pilo said, indignant.

"Crown Prince?" said Griff and Tess together, dismayed.

"Well, actually, King, if I have anything to do with it, Your Highness." Pilo glared at his young companions. "Why are you staring at me like that?"

Tess started to explain but Griff stopped her. "No, wait. Master Pilo. Please listen to me. I am not who you think I am, but I do know who you're talking about. And I know him because I've just been speaking to him and he's in trouble."

Now Pilo looked at Griff as though he really had slid into madness.

"I can prove what I'm saying," Griff added.

"I'll humor you, but I realize I have to get you some help. You've obviously lost your mind."

Tess sat down. "If you have any food in those saddlebags, Master Pilo, I would appreciate even a small hunk of bread, but either way, you are going to be still and listen to what Griff has to say. Please."

Pilo tossed her the saddlebag he was holding. "Help yourself." He turned his disbelieving, now-angry gaze on Griff. "I'm listening."

Griff gathered his thoughts. This wasn't going to be easy. "You're Pilo, aide to Crown Prince Lute. He thinks you're dead; he's sure you were killed by Duke Janko on the morning the Duke's men deliberately startled Lute's filly . . . er, I think her name is Tirell. You saved Lute and the horse before anything bad could happen and you forced him to leave you, to take Bruno, your horse, and go to a place called Tarrow's Landing. Is that right?"

Pilo nodded. "But—"

"There is more you should know," Griff said, cutting across whatever Pilo was going to say. "He was attacked by bandits and your horse was stolen." Pilo's eyes clouded. "Lute was hurt, too, but not badly enough that he couldn't move. He was found by some other men and taken to a place where he met a dwarf who goes by the name of Bitter Olof."

Tension left Pilo's face at the mention of the dwarf's name. He looked relieved. Griff continued, telling Pilo everything. But now came the hard part. "Master Pilo, Lute is in trouble now. The last time we spoke Duke Janko was hot on the heels of Lute and his friends. The man called Little Thom was seriously injured with an arrow wound and they couldn't make it to a place called the Devil's Smile."

All the while he'd been talking, Griff had watched Pilo's expression change into what he could only describe as silent awe. He stopped talking and waited.

Pilo said nothing initially, just gawked at him.

"Aren't you impressed?" Tess demanded, munching on some bread. She laid a hand on Griff's arm and smiled encouragingly at him. "I am."

Griff grinned his thanks.

"How can you possibly know this?" Pilo finally asked. "You must be Lute; only Lute could know of my horse's name or the fact that I'd told him to find Bitter Olof."

"Your enemy," Griff added for good measure.

Pilo nodded. "Yes, my sworn enemy."

"Except he wishes he could make amends, Master Pilo. Er, I hear that Bitter Olof has never forgiven himself and that if not for him and the blood debt he owed you, Lute would likely already be dead."

Griff watched Pilo's jaw grind.

"Do you believe me now?"

He shook his head with wonder. "I don't know what to think. I have to believe you. But until now I thought I was talking to Lute."

"Well," Tess said, frowning. "If you know all that he has said is true, then if he were Lute, he would be with Bitter Olof now. He can't be in two places at once."

"Exactly," Pilo replied, his tone now filled with awe. "And yet you cannot know all of this unless Lute is with Bitter Olof."

"Which proves I'm Griff and here with you, while Lute right now is trying to shake off the Duke's men."

"How do you talk with Lute?" Pilo asked, frowning.

Griff took a deep breath. "I can eavesdrop on people's thoughts. I hate having this talent but I can't do much about it. I was born with the skill. And it's through this magic, I suppose you'd call it, I first heard Lute's call for help. I can now link to him and talk to him through our minds."

Pilo stared at Griff, his expression a mix of confusion as much as wonder. "I've never heard of such a thing, yet I have no choice but to believe this because all the evidence suggests you have been talking to Lute. But how much do you know about your own family, Griff, because now it's my turn to stun you." He reached into a pocket, pulled out a palm-sized disk of porcelain. "I lost my family a few years ago. The royal family became my new kin, you could say, and Prince Lute filled the terrible gap that came when I lost my own child. He's a great fellow, will make a fine king if we can help him to outwit Janko. Here," he said, offering it to Tess, who was closest to him. "The palace artist was doing some portraits for the King and Queen and this was something spare he did on a whim. The likeness to the Prince is accurate. See for yourself."

Tess stared at the disk in silence. She handed it to Griff without a word but her face told him that something had shocked her. He took the portrait sketch and stared at it. There had to be a mistake.

Pilo cleared his throat. "I say again, how much do you know about your family, Griff?"

Griff looked up, his throat turning dry as his gaze met Pilo's. They were both thinking the same thing.

29

Lute thought he was drowning and it was only when he began to fight the pull downward and push himself to the surface that he noticed he was being unnaturally weighted down. He began to struggle, kicking his legs furiously. He heard a muffled gasp and it was only then he realized that he was not alone in his struggle but that Bitter Olof had his arms wrapped around Lute's neck.

"You'll kill us both!" Lute yelled, gasping for air as his head broke through a wave.

"I can't swim," the dwarf screeched, clearly terrified, gulping water.

"I can see that! Here," Lute said, still panting hard, "hold my hand. You have to stay calm. I promise I will not let you go. Just trust me."

Lute kicked around to look back to the water's edge and felt instantly numb. He could see Janko and his men standing over the fallen shape of Little Thom. Three arrows protruded from his back. The men were reloading their weapons and

Janko was pointing at Lute and Bitter Olof. It was their turn to die.

A wave rolled over them and the shore was blocked out. Lute dragged Bitter Olof lower, although the dwarf fought him in his fear, and Lute waited for the arrows to come fizzing through the water to impale him. When his lungs felt fit to burst and he had no choice but to surface again, coughing and spluttering, he instinctively looked to the beach and was stunned to see several bodies slumped around Little Thom's.

And then an unfamiliar voice spoke from above.

"Are you happy to drown, then, or do you want a hand?"

He looked directly up into the weather-beaten face of a short, stocky person—manlike but with what he was convinced was a woman's voice. But before he could work it out for sure, strong hands dragged him and a near-drowned Bitter Olof out of the waves and onto the rocky crag. As the dwarf coughed up the sea, Lute tried to catch his breath. He was shocked to count more than a dozen people.

"Who are you?" he groaned, but he was ignored as the man-woman bent down and with a huge fist wrenched Bitter Olof easily to his feet.

"You stupid old fool! Whatever possessed you to cross my path again?"

Bitter Olof couldn't speak, could barely breathe yet.

"Hey!" Lute yelled. "Don't treat him like that."

"Oh, I'll treat him how I please, laddie. And if you don't want a cuff around your stupid ears, you'll watch your tongue with me."

Lute stepped back. The person definitely spoke with a woman's voice but was dressed like a man in loose pants and shirt. There were inkings on her forearms, and out of the corner of her mouth hung a crooked pipe. It wasn't lit and it bobbed around as she spoke in her curious gruff voice. Her silver hair was pulled back tightly into a pigtail and the men around her definitely gave her respect.

Lute decided it was a woman looming over him. He was bent over, dragging in air, dripping and still spitting salty water. "Listen, that man on the beach, the big one—" Lute began.

"Looks dead to me," the woman cut across his words. "Forget him."

Lute looked horrified. "Forget him! Are you insane? He's a loyal friend. Did your men deal with the Duke?"

"Duke? Is that who he was, eh?" She cackled a laugh. "Well, he turned tail as soon as our hail of arrows started. I'm sorry we missed him."

"You've heard then that he has stolen the throne," Lute continued, his gaze on Little Thom.

"No. Nor do I care. I hate the royals. Oy! Dwarf! What have you got to say for yourself?"

Bitter Olof groaned and held his arm out for Lute to help hold him up. He was breathing hard and definitely looked worse for the wear of his past day. But he set his jaw firmly. "We go and get Little Thom."

"He's dead, fool. Can't you see that? You have both had that coming for a long time. And I don't doubt you'll be the next one squirming around with an arrow in yer back."

"So be it." Bitter Olof stepped to the edge of the crag.

"Wait!" Lute yelled, grabbing for him.

Bitter Olof turned and Lute looked deep into his eyes for

the first time. In there, all of the dwarf's gruffness was gone and what he saw was grief and love. "He's my friend, Your Majesty. Whether they're alive or not, I don't leave friends behind and I have never had a more loyal friend."

Lute nodded, laid a hand on the dwarf's shoulder. "Now you have two. I shall go with you."

The woman spat on the rock near their feet. "So we did all that for nothing. Killed a pile of soldiers, scared off the throne-stealing Duke, saved your sorry backsides from drowning and not even so much as a nod of thanks."

"Forgive my manners. Thank you, er . . . madam, for dragging us from the sea." Lute held out a hand.

She stared at Lute long and hard, her eyes narrowing, while the pipe's stem roamed around her mouth, making a clacking sound as it did so. She didn't take Lute's hand. Instead, she rounded on Bitter Olof, who was still blinking from the stinging sea salt. "And why in Lo's name are you calling him Majesty?"

Bitter Olof sighed and looked at Lute again. "I'd like you to meet Calico Grace—she's an old, er, acquaintance."

Lute recalled the feminine name, although it certainly didn't match up to this terrifying vision that loomed before them. "Pleased to—"

"Acquaintance! Why, you old rogue. I'll give you acquaintance!" She lifted a beefy fist as though she was going to belt Bitter Olof, and Lute instantly saw that the dwarf would be biffed not only into the sea but into the next realm if she connected with his jaw. She was a fierce, strong sort. She looked as though she wrestled bulls for a hobby. Her forearms were as thick as his own thighs, he was sure.

"And this, Grace," Bitter Olof continued, seemingly untroubled by her threat, "is His Majesty, formerly our Crown Prince, now King Lute."

Her huge fist remained bunched in the air but her thinned lips slackened and shock claimed her expression.

"It's a pleasure to meet you, Madam Grace," Lute continued when he could tell nothing much was coming from that gaping mouth for the moment. "Er, Bitter Olof mentioned how charming you are." He didn't dare look at the dwarf, although he knew his friend was staring at him sideways with not-very-well-concealed amusement. He smiled.

"We have to go, Gracie," Olof said softly. "My heart is breaking just to see him fallen. I couldn't live with myself if I left Little Thom like that."

"I know you saved our lives, Madam Grace," Lute added, unsure how to address this curious person. "But Little Thom saved them just moments prior. Those arrows were meant for us. He shielded us with his body and took all the punishment. He was brave and selfless. I too cannot leave him."

Finally, her fist lowered and her pipe began moving around her mouth again. She scowled. "Would you not call me madam, Yer Highness. I don't really hate the royals. I'm just on the wrong side of their law. The name is Calico Grace, and if your thickheaded friend here had told you everything, you'd know how he has treated his so-called *friends* in the past." Her tone was scathing. She turned to the dwarf, spat again, the spittle somehow emerging easily from between her lips, the pipe not even shifting position, and the gob landing directly between Bitter Olof's feet. "And you will stay right here. You are going nowhere!" She called orders to her men, who instantly leaped into the water on the other side of the crag, where a small craft was anchored. They rowed expertly around the point and back to the beach. The eldest, and presumably the most senior in rank, yelled something but Lute couldn't hear what was said. The wind carried the man's words away.

They watched in silence as the men hefted Little Thom's body into the boat and rowed him back against an increasingly fierce breeze that was whipping up.

"What did you say?" Calico Grace called to them as they approached, her hand cupped to her ear.

The man was standing in the boat as it neared. "I said he's still alive," he yelled.

⬨⬨⬨

Tess gawked at both Griff and Pilo. "Let me understand this," she said to Pilo. "You think Griff has a twin brother and that his twin is the new King?"

"I don't think it, I know it," Pilo replied. "I've known Lute for most of his life. And although now I am aware this is not Lute sitting opposite me, I can assure you I would have lost all my money and the very clothes off my back if I'd been asked to wager against it. They look identical. You don't move the same as Lute, Griff—I see that now—but your voice, mannerisms, even your smile . . . it's as though I am with Lute."

Griff threw down his apple core. "But how can this be, Pilo? I've told you everything I can. I grew up on the other side of the realm. I have a family—my brothers behave as

303

twins, although they're not, but I've never known anyone else. No other brothers or sisters."

Pilo considered this, chewing on a square of hard cheese. "You said your mother died when you were young. How young?"

Griff looked down. "She died the day after I was born."

"So you never knew her," Pilo said.

Griff shook his head. "And we didn't speak about her either. My brothers are just a few years older than me and they were sent away, apparently, so they have no memories of my birth, but they can recall that everything had changed when they returned."

"What do you mean?" Tess asked.

"I don't really know. You'd have to ask them but they said there was a new feeling around the house. It wasn't just the sadness of our mother's death; our father had changed. He had become suspicious, very careful of strangers. We moved from the town, beyond the villages that surrounded it. We lived alone, kept ourselves to ourselves."

"What is your father's line of work, Griff?" Pilo prompted.

"He's a falconer."

Pilo grinned. "Oh, excellent. I always wanted to train hawks."

Griff shrugged. "He loved his birds but they didn't make him very much money."

"And still he was able to build you a house, feed you three growing boys." Pilo scratched at his beard, deep in thought.

"We never wanted for much. What are you—"

"Nothing, I just imagine it would have been hard to do that on the little he'd earn as a falconer. I know how tightly the nobles keep their purses shut when it comes to paying for necessary services like training falcons. They don't want to live without those services, but they also don't like paying fair wages to the men who work hard to provide them and have families to feed, clothe and put roofs over their heads."

Griff stared at him quizzically.

Tess interpreted for him. "Pilo's wondering whether your father might have had an income from somewhere else."

He shook his head. "No. I was with him all the time. He only worked the birds."

"Then he either had money given to him or earned a sum of money to afford what he did for you boys."

"What are you saying?" Griff asked, feeling a tide of indignation move through him.

"Calm down, Griff, I'm not insulting your father or saying he did anything bad. Listen, your mother died when you were born. Your brothers had already been sent away. Presumably, the only witness to your birth was your father and perhaps a woman from the local village who helped with the birthing."

"And another woman, but she wasn't local," Griff answered, almost by reflex.

"Well, how do you know that?" Tess asked, intrigued. "You were newborn."

Griff frowned. "Well, my skill developed early, and from the time I was walking I was tapping into my father's thoughts without realizing it."

"And?" Pilo prompted gently.

"He would try not to think about the woman—and not because of me, but because it upset him. She was very beautiful, very sad. She was brought to the house in a cart with a single driver. She wore a pale hooded cloak and always kept her face covered outside." Griff's frown deepened. "My father was nervous around her."

"Why would she scare him?" Tess pondered.

But Pilo's eyes were shining. "He wasn't scared of her, but of who she was. Isn't that so, Griff?"

Griff spoke as though his mind was far away. He was delving back into distant memories of his father and they were carrying him to a time in his early childhood that he had buried long ago. "She only came to us twice. We never saw her again after the day I was born. My mother died the next morning. And my father's grief became a permanent companion. After he buried my mother, he locked her away in his mind and very rarely allowed himself to think of her. I only know what my mother looked like because he sometimes told me that I reminded him of her, and when he did, I could see her in his mind. She was dark and pretty."

"Did your father know you could listen to his thoughts?" Pilo asked.

"Yes. I think he realized what I could do before I did, to be honest. After that his mind became a vault. He learned how to shut himself off from me."

"That's strange, don't you think?" Tess said to Pilo.

Pilo shook his head slowly. "No, not if he was hiding something."

Griff stared at Pilo, barely breathing.

"I know you hate me saying that; I can see the anger in your eyes, Griff. But I need to say this and I think you already know what's coming."

Griff looked at the ground between his feet, dropped his head. "You must be mistaken. You have to be."

"Griff and Lute were born and Lute was taken away?" Tess asked for both of them, her voice barely above a whisper, filled with disbelief.

Pilo took over. "I think the woman you speak of is our Queen." He held a hand up. "No, hear me out, Griff. King Rodin and Queen Miralda were childless for years. They badly wanted an heir, but knowing our Queen, she really just wanted a child to love—girl or boy, she would have adored it. But Lo didn't bless them with a son or a daughter. As I understand it, it was all but taken for granted that Rodin's only brother, Duke Janko, would succeed to the throne upon Rodin's death. In return Janko threw himself wholeheartedly into supporting the throne by commanding its army, which he did with great courage, never holding back from any battle, leading his men from the front. He has become quite a hero for the realm. The people love him. But the people don't know the true Janko. The real Janko is cruel and loves power and wealth. He craves kingship and when an heir miraculously came along, many years after most had given up the notion of Rodin and Miralda producing one, Janko was not prepared to give up his dreams of kingship. Instead, he pretended loyalty, all the while putting together a small army of mercenaries who would fight for anyone who put up sufficient money—and Rodin had ensured Janko was a rich man. He certainly had the means to pay these hired soldiers. He also made a couple of attempts on the Crown Prince's life, if I'm reading the situation correctly."

"What?" Griff said, looking up in amazement. "Were you there?"

Pilo shook his head. "No, but it's why I was hired. Miralda suspected that the fall that Janko claimed the baby prince had suffered was not so innocent. She had suspicions about Janko from early on. And it was confirmed that there were grounds for her fears when Lute was permitted to join a hunt with his father and had another fall, this time from his horse—also the result of some interference from Duke Janko."

Tess looked astonished. "What happened?"

"Oh, the detail is not important. The fall occurred and looked like an innocent accident, but the boy could have easily died. I was one of the royal trackers then; it was pure coincidence that I happened along at the right time and was able to hasten the injured Prince's return to the palace. Janko claimed he had ridden as fast as he could back to the palace for help, but the physicians arrived long after I'd carried Lute to safety. Curiously, Duke Janko was not seen again for several years—he headed north and continued his heroics on the mountainous borders that are always under threat from King Besler. Once again years clouded everyone's memories and he rose to near-legendary status for the way he kept our realm so safe, and Rodin learned to rely heavily on his brother's might."

"But the Queen wasn't fooled," Tess guessed, eyes shining.

"Correct," Pilo said. "The truth is that she never liked or trusted the King's brother and she decided to put in place a permanent bodyguard for the Crown Prince. She chose me and made up a title called Prince's Aide, but neither I, nor Janko it seems, had any misconceptions about my role. I was there to protect Lute from harm, especially from his conniving uncle."

"Why couldn't the King see his brother for what he is?"

Pilo shrugged. "Rodin is a fine king. He loves his family,

loves his people; he makes very good decisions. His weakness is his brother. He seems to be blinded by his brother's strength and courage. Rodin is no warrior and if you met them you would see an enormous difference between the two men. One is small and really quite gentle, very amusing. The other is tall, broad, handsome, loud and entertaining. Janko impresses most people he meets."

"And then he made yet another attempt," Griff continued.

"That's right, and that was the closest he's come to succeeding."

"Well, he so nearly got Lute again, and if not for Bitter Olof, the Duke might have finally realized his wish."

"He's taken the throne anyway," Pilo said bitterly, "but we have to return it. And your magical skills will help us, Griff." He squeezed the boy's shoulder.

"What about Davren?" Tess reminded them.

"Yes," Pilo said, rousing himself from his thoughts. "Come on," he said. "I need to look at Davren's wound, and while I do so, Griff, tell me everything you can about Lute's whereabouts. He's going to a beach, you say?"

Griff nodded. "They've been on the move since the early hours and are headed to the sea."

"I think I know what Olof's plan is."

"What?"

Pilo actually laughed but it was mirthless. "He must be desperate because I think he's trying to find Calico Grace."

Griff and Tess shared a glance. It didn't seem as though Pilo was going to explain, nor did it look like he was especially amused any longer.

30

They were all in the boat, rowing out to what Lute could now see was a large ship anchored in the distance. In their panic earlier he hadn't noticed it, but obviously Bitter Olof had known exactly where he might find Calico Grace and her men. Lute watched him now, the dwarf's expression flitting between resentment at being here and relief and concern for Little Thom.

The captain—as her men called her—studied him with a gaze that had narrowed to slits in the morning glare, puffing quietly on the pipe that she had finally lit. Behind the stare, though, he had already noticed that Calico Grace had the bluest of eyes, and he wondered if and when he ever saw her smile, whether her plain looks might brighten, because right now she was terrifying.

"King, eh?" she said suddenly.

Lute flinched, unprepared for any attack she was intending.

"Now, Grace. There is no mileage to be gained from him," Bitter Olof warned, stabbing a finger toward Lute.

"You're jesting with me, dwarf, surely? Perhaps you have finally brought something worthwhile into my life. Do you hear this, men? You are rowing the King."

There was a murmur from the rowers and Lute didn't think they looked at all impressed to have a royal on board. Nor did he think Calico Grace had his best interests at heart.

"Are you listening to me, Grace, I—"

Calico Grace pulled the smoldering pipe angrily from her mouth. "No, Olof, you pay close attention to what I'm about to say." It was her turn to jab a finger in his direction. "You owe me!"

"But, Gracie—"

"No. Don't you dare 'Gracie' me, you old rogue. You have an enormous debt to repay me from your previous visit. And here you are, in trouble once again, and who do you come running to? Ah yes, good old Calico Grace. And no, dwarf, don't even think about adopting that innocent expression, as though it were pure coincidence that you happened to be at Ghost Beach just when I happened to be anchored off it. You came seeking me. We saw you coming a way off, crashing down through that undergrowth and onto the beach. And you knew I was there, too. You counted on me interfering. I should have let that stupid Duke just kill you and be damned. Now the Crown's got a genuine beef with me for helping one of its enemies, and just to keep it all nice and spicy I've got the damn King about to board *Silver Wind*. It's always trouble with you, Olof."

Bitter Olof sighed. "And still you help me."

She shook her head helplessly. "There's no accounting for love," she said in a scarcely audible voice.

Lute's ears pricked up, but when he glanced around,

Calico Grace was staring out to sea, Bitter Olof was studying his drenched boots, Little Thom was groaning softly by their feet and the rest of the men were focused only on rowing to the glittering schooner that appeared closer by the moment. No one but Lute seemed interested in the turn of the conversation, so he stored it away and fixed his gaze on the ship awaiting them.

She was a beauty. She seemed to shine beneath the kiss of the sun and from the reflection of the glittering ocean.

"Your schooner is magnificent, Calico Grace. She really suits her name."

The captain turned to regard him. "She can outrun any ship you pitch against her, Yer Majesty."

Lute whistled softly and nodded. "She looks fast. Where was she built?"

Calico Grace tapped her huge nose. "Never you mind, Yer Highness." Now she winked at him.

Lute frowned. It took him a few moments for all of it to fall into place, and as they drew up beneath the shadow of the sleek vessel, he noted that her pale color made her look ghostly this close, and where a ship normally had brass, the *Silver Wind* had curious silver fittings, which only added to her strangeness.

"Calico Grace, may I ask, is this a pirate ship?"

She tapped out her pipe on the side of the boat as she stood. "The best on the high seas, Majesty," she said proudly.

⋈⊰⊱⋈

Pilo daubed some salve from a small pot he was carrying onto Davren's wound. The centaur was grimacing.

"Sorry, friend, I know that hurt," Pilo said.

Tess looked anxious. "Will the bleeding stop?"

"Yes. I know it looks bad and it hurts but it's not deep or life-threatening. I have to tell you that your friend is brave. I couldn't have gritted my teeth for as long as he did. He should remain still."

"Still?" Griff interrupted. "But we need to go and help Lute now."

"We?" Pilo laughed. "No, I have to go and help Lute. You are going to continue on your merry way."

"You're leaving us?" Griff looked at Pilo as though he were a stranger to him again.

Pilo had the grace to look uncomfortable. "Well, I have a king whose life might need saving. I'm sorry that—"

"If you're right, then that king is my brother. My twin brother, and I'll be damned if you think you're going off to find him without me!"

Pilo stared at Griff, who was breathing heavily, clearly angry. "And leave Tess? Is that your plan? Leave Tess, whom you had planned to save from Master Tyren and his Stalkers?" Griff swallowed. "And not just Tess, but Davren, who is wounded, and Helys, who is frightened, and Elph, who is too slow to move with us?"

"If we stick together, then everyone's safer," Griff tried, looking around at all of them, feeling desperate.

"No, Griff!" Pilo said, shaking his head and walking toward his horse. "I travel faster alone."

"So that's all we are to you? A burden?"

"You know that's not right."

"Well, it's obvious you only care for my *brother*."

"Griff, he's the King," Pilo said softly, appealing to Griff's sense of loyalty. "And he's being hunted down by a madman who plans to kill him."

Griff nodded and turned away. "So am I. Come on, Tess, we'll head this way," he said. He glanced at Pilo, his gaze suddenly hard. "Farewell, Pilo. Thank you for your help today and good luck with everything." He shrugged. "Say hello to my brother for me."

Even Davren scowled at Pilo as the centaur picked up Helys and limped away after Griff.

It left only Tess to be polite. She gave Pilo an embarrassed look. "We'll be going, then."

"What did Davren say? He looked at me just then as though I shot the arrow."

She looked down momentarily, then answered. "He said to tell you not to bother about saying hello to Lute for Griff. Griff can do it himself using his magic. And then he can tell the King, er . . . well . . . about you leaving us."

"Look, Tess . . ."

She shook her head, smiled awkwardly. "You don't have anything to explain to me. At least Griff is the King's brother. I'm no one." She turned. "Take care, Pilo. Thanks for saving us earlier." And then she too turned her back on him and walked away. "Come on, Elph. We're moving at your pace now because of Davren."

They got as far as the edge of the clearing before Griff heard the sound of hooves. He turned. "Master Pilo?"

"All right, you win. We go together." He looked beaten.

Tess glanced at Griff and grinned, then said to Pilo, "Davren said you wouldn't leave us."

"Did he, indeed?"

She nodded. "He assured me that you would not let us get beyond the fringe of this part of the wood."

Pilo gave a sound of disgust. "That predictable, eh?"

She smiled. "Afraid so. He said you are far too honorable to desert us, even though your King needs you."

Pilo bowed from his saddle to Tess. "I'm flattered," he said, although Griff noticed the sly look he also threw toward the centaur. Something akin to respect seemed to pass between Pilo and Davren at that moment and it warmed Griff's heart.

Pilo got off his horse. "It occurred to me that if we stitch Davren's wound, although he's not going to enjoy the experience, I can assure you, then perhaps—"

"He says yes, Master Pilo. He will bear whatever he has to if it means we stay together."

"Right. I wish I could communicate with Davren like that, or anyone." He looked awestruck.

"You can, as a matter of fact," Griff said. "You just have to ask me and I can allow you to talk to Davren anytime you wish."

"Truly?"

"Truly," Griff confirmed. "But there is a catch. I'll be blinded. If I'm in the Silvering, I'm not aware of anything going on around me."

"That sounds dangerous," Pilo admitted.

"It is. But Davren seems to be able to talk to me in the Silvering and keep his five senses working outside of it. It's another reason why I think we need to stay together. We can help you to reach Lute."

"I hadn't thought of that. It seems once again I must rely on magic."

Griff shrugged. "Lute told me you entrusted his life to your daughter's magic whistle."

Pilo looked up sharply. "Now I know you're not lying about your abilities. He is the only person to whom I've told that story."

"I'm sorry, I don't mean to—"

"It's all right. Ellin's whistle did save his life." He looked suddenly sad. "I just wish it could have saved hers." He turned away, clearing his throat. "I suggest we stay on the move. Let's put some distance between ourselves and the Stalkers, though I suspect you will no longer be followed, and if Davren can stand the pace and keep up, then I think by tonight he can have some rest."

Everyone was in agreement on this plan. Soon they were all focused on the needle and thread that Pilo managed to find in his saddlebags. Neither Griff nor Tess wanted to do the stitching, so Pilo asked permission of the centaur and it was granted. Davren bore up bravely, making no sound, simply grimacing now and then. Before long they were saddled up and moving in a northwesterly direction again, with Elph and Helys happily riding with Pilo and Griff. Tess kept Davren close at her side, although Griff didn't believe the centaur needed nursing. He could see the gleam of adventure in his friend's eye and instinctively knew that, despite the arrow wound, he had never had such fun. In years to come he imagined the centaur would wear that scar as one of honor.

"How long will it take to reach where Lute is?" Griff asked.

"If we ride all day at this pace, I should be able to get us to Ghost Beach by nightfall. It's one of Calico Grace's favorite haunts and we just have to hope they're still there once we arrive. That's assuming they've found her, of course."

31

Lute stood aboard the gleaming schooner. This wasn't how he'd imagined a pirate ship would look. He'd always thought they'd be grubby places with a nasty-looking crew and dark timber that creaked and groaned.

"I know what you are thinking, Majesty," Grace said, tapping her nose again.

They were watching Little Thom being hauled up the rope ladder from the rowboat. It seemed to require the help of a dozen men that Bitter Olof had taken charge of for the time being. He was calling out orders, fussing and flapping his arms around.

Grace shook her head and pointed at the dwarf. "He's worried they may hurt him." She snorted. "I can assure you that the giant can't feel a thing. He's nearly dead as it is."

"Don't say that, Calico Grace. We have to save his life. We have to."

"Take him below," she yelled at her men, once she'd seen them finally get him on board. "Olof, you go with them and see to it that Dash attends to him."

She returned her gaze to Lute.

"What is it that I'm thinking?" he asked. It was an awkward moment and he was tired of Calico Grace's scrutiny, which felt as though she was plotting and planning as to how to make the best of having a royal at her mercy.

She smiled and he stepped back. It was the first time she'd done that and he could see now that she was missing teeth. Calico Grace really was a most plain woman and yet her clothes were crisply ironed and they didn't look at all tatty. She was obviously wealthy. "You're wondering how come this schooner looks so shiny and new, aren't you?"

"Yes, you are indeed a mind reader, as well as a successful pirate," he said, looking around.

She cackled a laugh, barked an order to pull anchor. "No, my King. It's true I've had my wins here and there. But the greatest win of all was my schooner here."

"She must have cost a fortune to build."

"She didn't cost me a single copper." And Grace laughed again but in it he heard sorrow.

"Nothing? How . . . how come?"

"Ah, well now, that's a long story, Majesty."

Before he could reply, Bitter Olof came running out onto the deck, dragging a man with him.

"Tell her what you told me," Bitter Olof said, his breath coming in short gasps.

"Yes, Dash?" Calico Grace responded.

"Captain, er, well, that wounded man is dying before us. We have but minutes, I would say. There's nothing I can do for him. He's too far gone."

"Gracie, please, I beg you," Olof said.

"What? If Dash can't save him, there's nothing more I can do, dwarf. I've already done more than I should have by interfering in your matters with the Duke."

"You can do more, you know it."

"No, I refuse. Why should I?" She looked away.

Lute looked between them. There was a fresh tension he didn't understand. Bitter Olof looked desperate.

"What's going on? How can Calico Grace help? She's not a healer."

Calico Grace turned back, triumph gleaming in her eyes. "There, dwarf, even your own King knows it's a lost cause."

"But why does he think you can still do something?" Lute wondered aloud.

Calico Grace glared at them both before making a sound of disgust and stomping away belowdecks.

Bitter Olof sighed.

"Tell me what's going on," Lute implored.

"It's not my place," the dwarf said sadly. "She must tell you."

"Right," Lute said, tired of all this. There was a man's life ebbing away as these two bickered. "Let's sort this out now."

Bitter Olof forlornly followed as Lute marched below-decks, asking directions to the captain's quarters. He knocked on the curious pale wood of her door, the silver doorknob gleaming. "Calico Grace, may I come in?"

She pulled the door open. "There's nothing to say!" she yelled, but she stepped aside and let Lute enter. She even allowed Bitter Olof to follow.

The chamber was tastefully furnished in pale silk and velvets and it smelled sweetly of old tobacco from Grace's pipe.

She sat down heavily in a magnificent brocade armchair in the palest of blue fabric.

"Go on—say it!" she said.

Lute wasn't sure what she wanted him to say but he said what was on his mind. "How on earth does this chamber manage to look so fresh and clean . . . and, well, beautiful?"

"Are you saying I'm too dirty for it?" she accused.

"Not at all. In fact, you're so clean and tidy as well. Come to think of it, for pirates your crew is very smartly kitted out. I don't think I saw a single stain on any of their shirts or trousers."

Calico Grace looked indignant. "I run a tight ship here, Majesty."

"Tell the truth, Gracie," Bitter Olof growled. "Tell him all of it. He's going to find out one way or another."

※

They had to follow the line of the forest so that Davren could remain hidden by a thin veil of trees, but their horses were finally out on open road and that would make the going much swifter.

Pilo decided that the creatures made them too noticeable. If Davren cut through the woods and headed north, he reasoned, he would come out on the other side of the river at Tarrow's Landing, where they would also be.

"He can carry Helys and they'll both stay safe in the forest. We'll keep Elph covered under my cloak because he can't move fast and Davren can't carry them both. Rix looks fine to follow Davren."

"But you said we'd stick together," Tess appealed.

"We're parting for very good reasons of safety, Tess, and only for a few hours. We'll be reunited sooner than you think, I promise. This keeps your creatures safer than if they were out and about in open country. They attract too much attention. You have to trust me. We can't keep them hidden unless we do it my way."

Tess was quiet for a moment and then nodded. "Davren says you're right and I have to agree that, much as I don't want us to split up, I do want them to be safe."

"Good girl," Pilo said.

He spent several long minutes explaining to Davren how to reach Tarrow's Landing. The centaur looked confident and Tess checked several times with him that the pain wasn't too bad at the top of his back leg. He shook his head as though it were merely a scratch. They all knew it was more than that but he certainly looked quite capable of making the journey.

"It will be around midafternoon when we all find each other again. Don't emerge from the forest until then. Perhaps you and Tess, using your mindlink, can work out exactly where we'll meet."

Davren grinned.

"Go. Be safe. Talk to us constantly so we know you're all right."

And then they were gone, bounding off, Davren clearly enjoying the freedom of independence, and even Helys was a beautiful warm golden pink as she sat comfortably in his arms.

They rode hard for several hours, no one talking. It was a few hours later when Griff looked over at Tess.

"You're very quiet," he said. "Are you worried about Davren and Helys?"

She shook her head. "Davren can actually take very good care of himself so long as he's in the forest. I think most of the time he's been taking care of me rather than the other way around."

"So why so silent?"

"Well, I've been thinking," she said, frowning. "I believe I know how you can beat the Duke, Master Pilo."

Pilo glanced at her. "I'm listening."

"You say that Griff is the walking image of the real King."

"He is. I guess I can tell the difference now, but it's so subtle that someone who doesn't know Lute as well as I do couldn't pick them. And frankly, even I was taken in."

"Exactly. So I'm thinking that you could pretend that Griff is the King."

Pilo stared at her and Griff began to feel uncomfortable as the silence lengthened. Finally, Pilo spoke. "How do you see that working, Tess?" There was no disbelief in his tone. He was clearly taking her seriously.

She took a breath and her words came out in a rush.

"Well, it's not very nice, Pilo, I know, but you'll have to use Griff as bait. You need to swap him with Lute, clothes and all. Get Bitter Olof—is that his name?—anyway, Griff and the dwarf have to be seen by the Duke or his men. The Duke is hunting Bitter Olof and he knows with him goes the King. Once they're spotted and fleeing, the Duke and his thugs will give chase, thinking they're hunting down the King. Meanwhile, Pilo, you take Lute back to the palace and ensure the army knows that their true King is alive and ready to take command of his realm. The army is loyal, you said. I'm right, aren't I?" she asked, worried. Pilo nodded, his jaw slack. "And then Lute will have his army hunt down Janko and his mercenaries. The Duke's men won't know what's happening back at the palace, so they're not going to expect an attack from within, if you know what I mean . . . especially as they'll be convinced they're already chasing the King."

Pilo stared back at her, a smile forming. "Inspired, Tess! What are you, some sort of military strategist?"

She laughed. "Years of trying to dodge the Stalkers. But they finally caught up with me, so I'm not that clever."

"No, truly. That is a cunning plan, young lady. And you know Janko is so blinded by his own cleverness that it wouldn't even occur to him that he's being tricked."

Tess nodded. "He doesn't know about Griff, so it won't enter his mind, I'm sure. The main thing is that you get Lute quickly back to the palace, onto the throne and seen by the army and everyone else who counts."

Pilo agreed. "You're absolutely right. When I stole this horse from the stables, I heard that the Duke was preparing to pronounce himself King, but I knew he'd need to await Rodin's funeral before he produced the body of the Crown Prince—"

"He'd just lie," Tess cut in. "He'd place an empty coffin into the royal tomb. No one would be any wiser."

Pilo looked crestfallen. "Right again. That's exactly how he'd work. But he hadn't been crowned King when I left the palace grounds last night and I doubt he's King yet, especially as he is giving chase himself to Lute. No, he wants to be sure Lute is dead. We still have time to put your plan into action."

They had been talking around Griff for all of this time, not noticing how quiet he had become. They turned now and regarded him.

"Of course, you would have to agree to being bait for Janko, Griff," Tess said, obviously only now realizing what they were asking of him.

He didn't hesitate. "I agree. It's a clever plan."

Pilo frowned. "Griff, it will be incredibly dangerous. Janko is unpredictable."

"Lute is the King. That's what this is all about, isn't it? We're trying to save the Crown, save the realm from a madman?" Pilo nodded. "And if you're right, he's also my brother. I can't let my brother be killed in cold blood without trying to stop it."

"I can't believe how brave you are, and you're so young. I'm very sorry I ever doubted you or suggested you would slow me down." Griff felt himself blush. "You're quite sure, Griff? I feel ashamed even asking this of you. It's putting your own life on the line."

"My life's not worth much. Lute's is. And I couldn't live with myself anyway if I didn't do this."

Pilo nodded. "I salute you. So now we have to get to Ghost Beach as fast as possible. We have to stop Calico Grace from pulling anchor."

"Well, that's easy," Griff said, grinning. "I'd better have a chat with my brother."

32

Lute looked at Calico Grace and Bitter Olof with astonishment. "A magic ship?"

They nodded.

"Who gave it to you?"

Calico Grace sneered. "The Witch Grevilya."

"Why would she give you such a beautiful vessel for nothing?"

"It wasn't for nothing. It just wasn't for money," Bitter Olof said, and he certainly sounded bitter to Lute.

"Well, tell me, will you? I can't guess what you could possibly exchange that is worth a magic schooner."

Calico Grace made them both sit down. She called for Dash, who arrived looking nervous. They watched Calico Grace go to a small chest that she unlocked, and from it withdrew a dark-green bottle. She lifted the glass stopper and sniffed the contents.

"I'm always amazed that it smells so sweet and enticing."

Lute glanced at Olof but the dwarf shook his head slightly, telling him to say nothing.

Dash looked unsure. "There's so little left, Captain."

Calico Grace sighed. "I know. But you know what to do with it—all of it if you have to."

"But—"

"Do it, Dash."

The man took the bottle and departed, throwing an angry glance Bitter Olof's way. The dwarf looked humbled; Lute remained quiet. He had no understanding of what was going on here.

"Happy, dwarf?" Calico Grace asked Bitter Olof.

"Thank you, Gracie. I can see that's all you have left and that you're about to use it for our benefit. I owe you even more now."

"And you will pay, I shall see to it." She turned haughtily to Lute. "I'm going to tell you everything and let you decide whether you think I'm justified in feeling angry."

Lute nodded.

She began.

"A long time ago there was a handsome couple. It's true they were thieves and they were very, very good at it. But they made every effort to steal only from the wealthy—er, especially the King." She grinned apologetically. "They were very much in love and decided once they had enough money they would marry, buy a ship and sail the high seas as famous pirates. Except one day they stole from a very wealthy noble, who used the services of a witch to track them down. They offered to give back the money and jewels but she said it was too late. The noble was so aggrieved, because it was the third time the couple had robbed him, that he wanted them punished properly—"

"By hanging," Bitter Olof interrupted.

Lute's eyes widened.

Calico Grace continued. "The young couple begged the witch to tell them if there was any possible way she could spare their lives and keep their identity secret but take back all that belonged to the noble. She thought about it for a while. And then she said there was a way to avoid the hanging, and give the loot back, and get away safely. Naturally, the handsome couple agreed instantly to whatever the terms were. But the Witch Grevilya told them to be very careful and to be very sure they understood what they would have to give up.

"'Anything,' they cried."

"Everything," Bitter Olof chimed in bitterly, "except their lives."

Calico Grace ignored him. "The Witch Grevilya said in return for the woman's beauty, she would keep their secret. And in return for the man's handsome looks and proud figure, she would give them a very special ship to sail away on."

Lute stared at the pair as it all fell into place. "You were that couple?"

"Isn't it obvious?" Bitter Olof growled back. "If you'd known me, Majesty, you'd have seen a tall, strong-limbed, dashing man."

"They said I was not only the most beautiful thief to ever have walked the realm," Calico Grace said in a forlorn voice, "but I had a face and figure that would enchant even a king." She turned to Bitter Olof. "Except I loved him, Your Highness. He promised to marry me, no matter how we looked. He promised to stay with me, on our ship, and sail the high seas."

"And the ship is magic, you say?"

"Oh yes," Calico Grace replied. "The Witch Grevilya only dealt with magical things. *Silver Wind* never needs cleaning or polishing. She changes color to suit her surrounds. She can blend to almost invisible, Your Highness. *Silver Wind* clothes us and feeds us. As you can see, we are a healthy and neatly dressed crew. No one can catch her. She can pull into the shallowest of waters, and if there is no wind and she has to pull out of those waters quickly, then she can create her own." She looked around the chamber. "She's pale and silver today because from far away on this very sunny day you can't see her easily. If it's overcast tomorrow, she'll turn gray, and at night she turns black."

Lute gave a low whistle. "That's amazing." Then he turned to Bitter Olof. "So what happened? You deserted Calico Grace?"

The dwarf looked appropriately embarrassed. "I couldn't do it, Your Highness. We were both so ugly. I felt like we'd sold our souls. And I knew that every time I would look at Gracie or wake up aboard this ship, I'd be reminded of what we'd given up."

"But you would have had to give up your lives!"

He shrugged. "We could have run, given ourselves up to the King, appealed to him. Rodin was known for his generous ways. I think we took the coward's way and we have been paying for it ever since. Neither of us is happy. And safety was only ever guaranteed aboard the ship—we're both as vulnerable as anyone else when we're away from it."

"You should have married me as you promised. Instead, you blamed me!" Gracie accused.

"I never blamed you, Gracie. I just couldn't bear for us to look upon each other like this. And you changed, not just outwardly but inwardly, too. You were just as unhappy. You've become hard, even cruel, while I've become bitter and uncaring."

"Well, we're on our way now. I've pulled anchor and you're stuck on board the ship you hate and with the woman you despise."

"Oh, Gracie, I don't despise you."

As Calico Grace continued hurling insults at Bitter Olof, Lute felt a familiar tingling tug in his mind and suddenly he was in a silvery cloud with a familiar voice in his head.

Lute, it's Griff. Where are you?

I'll never get used to this, Lute replied. He could see his companions arguing but he couldn't hear them. *Are you out of danger?*

Never mind that now. The main question is: are you safe?

For the time being. I'm on board the Silver Wind, which belongs to a pirate called Calico Grace. We've just pulled anchor and I don't know where we're heading, but yes, we're safe—

Lute, you have to remain anchored.

What?

You must convince the pirate to stay where she is. We're coming.

Who's coming?

I have some good news. Pilo is with me.

Pilo! He's alive?

He's riding alongside me. But listen, there's no time now—we're all safe and heading toward Ghost Beach.

Wait, Griff. What about the Stalkers?

They've been dealt with. Now listen carefully. I can't explain it all now because it would take too long but we're on horses, making for Ghost Beach as fast as we can. Trust me, we have a plan and we will help. But you have to drop anchor now!

I don't know if Calico Grace—

I don't care what she says. This is your life at stake and we think we know how to save it. By the way, I've got someone with me who'd like to say hello.

Lute heard Griff say "Go ahead and speak." Then a new voice entered his mind, one that made his eyes blur with salty tears.

Er, Majesty. It's Pilo.

Pilo? he whispered. *Truly?*

It's me, Lute. I know what you think you saw, but I can handle myself against a few men. He laughed. *Fate has thrown me together with Griff. We have a lot to tell you and, well, show you. But he's right. You've got to stop Grace taking that ship any further out to sea.*

I'll try.

We have to go. It was Griff again. *If we're going to make it by nightfall, we need to hit a gallop right now.*

Lute didn't know what else to say, let alone think, about all this. His mind was reeling with relief that Pilo was alive. *See you tonight.*

The silvery mist cleared and Bitter Olof was shaking him. "What's up with you, boy . . . er, Majesty?"

"Bitter Olof, we have to stay here."

"What?"

"Captain Grace, you must stop. We have to stay at Ghost Beach."

She looked at him as though he had lost his mind, and he believed she could be forgiven for that, considering how he must have appeared to them both moments earlier.

"Please," he continued. "Bitter Olof, Pilo is coming. Apparently, they've got a plan and they insist we remain at Ghost Beach."

"You said Pilo was dead."

"I thought he was," Lute said, shaking his head. "It certainly looked that way."

"Well, how can you know any different?"

"Because I just spoke to him." The words were out before Lute could phrase them in a way that would make more sense.

Bitter Olof and Calico Grace took a step back and regarded him as one might look at a strange insect.

Lute stood, hands in the air in a gesture of apology. "All right, I know that sounds odd."

"Odd?" Calico Grace repeated. "More like barmy. Are you sure this is the King and not some lunatic you've brought on board my ship, Olof?"

The dwarf made a hissing sound at Calico Grace. "Tsk! Watch your words, woman. He could order your head chopped off!"

In return she made a huffing sound, filled with indignation. "You are hearing what I'm hearing, aren't you? Does it make sense to you?"

"No. King Lute, what do you mean by what you just said?"

Lute sighed. "Perhaps it's now time I told you a story, but you have to trust me and stop *Silver Wind*. It's important, I promise you."

Bitter Olof stared at him for a few long moments, then made a gruff sound of resignation. He turned and nodded at Calico Grace.

She shrugged, opened the door and yelled, "Drop anchor!"

Lute could hear the order being forwarded via several of her sailors until they heard the unmistakable sound of the anchor uncoiling on its thick rope, plummeting again toward the seabed.

"You're fortunate we hadn't actually hoisted sails and moved too far from where we were," Calico Grace said to him in the weary voice that adults adopt with children.

"We're all ears, Majesty," Bitter Olof said, making himself comfortable.

And Lute told them everything he knew about Griff.

33

"And he's going to try," Griff said as he finished explaining to Pilo and Tess what had occurred in his conversation with Lute. "And I checked in with Davren. All goes well. He's holding up fine and Helys is a healthy pink. They're making good ground. Rix is flying with them for the time being."

Tess nodded, relieved. Pilo didn't look quite so content.

"So we don't know yet whether Calico Grace is going to weigh anchor or not?"

Griff shook his head. "I think we just have to believe in Lute—that he can persuade Bitter Olof and Calico Grace to trust him. I imagine he's going to have to tell the truth about me and how we speak."

"And he's going to sound less like a king and more like the village idiot," Pilo growled, more to himself than to Griff.

"If Bitter Olof trusts the story of Ellin's whistle, then he should trust the story of our magical mindlink. It's hardly likely that Lute is going to lie about this to him."

Pilo seemed to accept this. "In light of the vessel they're currently aboard, he should believe him."

"What do you mean?" Tess asked.

"It's a ship built from magic."

Pilo watched as their mouths opened and then a flurry of questions flew at him.

"No time now," Pilo said. "We have to ride hard. Come on. I hope you both know how to ride a horse at a gallop?"

They nodded.

"I learned to ride almost as soon as I could walk," Griff remarked.

"I doubt I ride as well as Griff, but I'm not scared of any animal. I rode wild horses bareback when I was very young," said Tess.

Pilo looked impressed. "Let's go," he said, and nudged his horse forward with his heels.

Unbeknownst to Pilo, Tess and Griff, they arrived not far from where Lute had been set upon by the thugs who stole Bruno. They walked their horses carefully along the deserted road, waiting for some signal that would tell them that Davren was near.

"Check," Pilo urged Tess, stopping his horse.

Griff followed suit, thinking Pilo looked worried. But as Tess didn't seem alarmed, he took his lead from her: after all, she was the one who could reach Davren at will and with ease.

"He's all right," she assured them. Within moments

they heard hushed footfalls near where they were stopped, and then a beloved head poked through the bushes. Davren smiled at them. Tess squealed softly. "There you are, you clever fellow!"

Relief coursed through Griff, and he was sure, going by the expression on Pilo's face, that their friend was also letting out a long-held breath. It had been Pilo's idea for them to split up, so Griff could forgive him for feeling so nervous about whether they could meet up again easily. It seemed Pilo had underestimated the centaur's impeccable sense of direction as well as his resilience.

"You look tired, Davren," Griff said, grinning at his friend.

"He says that after a few hours Helys feels like she weighs as much as a herd of sagars!" Tess said.

Helys flashed an angry red.

"I'm just glad everyone's safe," Pilo said. "Well done, Davren. You're a warrior."

The centaur banged his fist to his chest, and that needed no interpretation.

"Are you well enough to continue?" Pilo asked.

"He says let's go," Tess answered for Davren.

"Right. It's going to take another few hours to get around to where they are. Davren can keep us in his sights because this light woodland continues for many miles."

Finally, they reached the coast and led their horses down to Ghost Beach just on nightfall as Pilo had predicted. Everyone was tired, yawning as they picked their way down, but as they finally hit the soft sand, they all became a lot more alert. They were here and, with luck, so too would be Lute and his companions.

"There!" Griff said, pointing.

At the shoreline they could see a light blinking on and off.

"Ah," Pilo said. "That's definitely them."

"How can you be sure?" Tess asked.

"Olof and I always used a blanket over a lantern. You see? It's happened three times. That's his call." He ran forward. "Olof!"

Suddenly everyone began to hurry, both parties running toward each other. Pilo reached Olof first, swung the little man easily up into his arms, and Griff heard a flood of words from each, both trying to apologize for their own actions and the silence that had festered into such enmity over the years.

"So you're not going to kill me, then?" Bitter Olof asked when he was finally put back down on the sand.

Pilo shook his head. "There've been enough years passed for me to fully accept that I shouldn't hold you responsible." He sighed. "Even if you had been guarding her, you might not have been able to stop it from occurring. I've blamed you for too long for my family's death. But now you have saved the life of someone most precious to me. You have redeemed yourself in my eyes. Where is Lute?" He turned to see Griff and Lute staring at each other silently. "Ah, I should have said something earlier."

Bitter Olof turned to regard them as well.

"What the—"

In the eerie glow of the lamplight it was impossible to tell the boys apart. Griff looked uncomprehendingly at Lute, but at least he had been somewhat prepared for this revelation. He realized Lute had had no warning and he could all but feel the shock of what Lute was seeing, coming in waves of confusion at him.

"Majesty," Pilo began awkwardly. He looked up briefly at Calico Grace and nodded but said nothing, his attention immediately back on the boys.

Lute shifted his stunned gaze from the person standing opposite him, who seemed to be a mirror image of himself. The clothes were different and the hair was longer but the likeness was unmistakable. He looked now at Pilo.

Pilo, Griff and Tess bowed. "My King," Pilo began, "forgive how this must feel. I . . ." He shook his head. "There was no time to say more. Let me now. Fate crossed my path with Griff's and I have no explanation for you other than this is a twin brother no one has ever known about."

Lute heard Bitter Olof whistle and was surprised but reassured to feel Calico Grace lay her hand on his shoulder. "What in Lo's name possesses you to shock the boy like this, Pilo? Have you gone soft in the head? Does it occur to you that this could be magic being wielded?"

It was Pilo's turn to look shocked. He swung around to Griff. "No, such a thought had not occurred to me. *Is* this a trick, Griff?"

"A trick?" Tess squealed. "How dare you! Griff's put his life at risk to get here. Why would he trick anyone?" She rounded on her audience. "Ask yourself, what's in it for him to risk Master Tyren's wrath and then his own life and limb against the Stalkers?" She turned back toward Lute, a sour look on her face. "Your Majesty," she added, though it was far from polite. "Shouldn't you be wondering why you look like Griff? It works both ways, you know." Tess's chest was

337

heaving with her anger. "We should all be asking whether these are twins."

Everyone fell silent at the shock of that suggestion.

Pilo cleared his throat. "We will get to the bottom of this. And I know who can clear this up for us." He gave Griff a reassuring glance.

Griff shrugged, embarrassed, before he said, "It's all right, Pilo. It's a shock for me, so I imagine it's a real fright for you, Lute, er, Your Highness."

Lute was yet to say anything; his throat felt suddenly dry and his tongue felt as though it were stuck in his mouth. "So this is why I don't look like either of my parents?" he finally croaked. Pilo began to say something but Lute cut him off. "No, wait. Janko made some accusations that reminded me of all my childhood anxieties. It's always worried me that I don't resemble either of them. Janko said I would lay false claim to the throne and he's right. I'm no heir. I'm an impostor," he said, his voice breaking with anger. "Janko can have the throne!" He turned and strode away from them all. Everyone looked helpless, but Griff followed. "And stop calling me by a title until this is all done. Until we're rid of Janko, I'm just Lute!"

"Make it right in his mind, Pilo," Bitter Olof said, "or we're all doomed."

But it was Tess who moved first. She ran after Lute and Griff.

"Lute," she said softly.

He didn't take offense to her ignoring manners, and anyway, this was no longer about kingship or politics. Suddenly all that seemed to matter at this moment was finding out the truth behind his birth. He was reeling from the shock of learning the mother he loves was most likely not the mother who had given birth to him. He stopped walking away.

"I'm Tess, Griff's friend." When he didn't say anything, she continued awkwardly. "You know, I think Griff has been suffering all of his life from hearing voices in his head. Everyone else's thoughts invade his own. Imagine how hard that is!"

"Yes, he told me," Lute said.

"Well, I was there when he first heard your call for help. You came to him not as a thought but as a clear voice, as though you had picked him out to give your cry of help to." Lute kicked at the sand but he was listening carefully. "Since that moment, although I know Griff has done everything he can to help me and my creature friends to make a run for safety, his risks have actually been taken for you. He felt an immediate link to you that was so much more than the random connections he makes with people all day, every day of his life. He hates it; I'm sure he told you that, too. He spends his time climbing around scaffolding to avoid them. Anyway, none of that matters. What matters is that you reached out and you found your twin brother. I know this changes everything you know about your family, but, Lute, your twin hasn't had a mother for all of his life. And he's had to give up the father he loves in order to earn a living traveling with strangers and being pushed around by nasty people like Master Tyren. You got the good life, Lute. You've been raised as a crown prince by parents who I imagine worshipped the very ground you walked upon."

"They loved me, and I them, but—"

"No buts. You have no idea what it is to be without loving parents in your life. Griff and I do. You should be counting your blessings, not blaming them for loving you, giving you such a special life. And now you've found your twin brother—and there are two more brothers in your life as well. How lucky are you? Even Pilo survived. And everyone is here now to try to save your life; they're all prepared to risk their own lives, while you get upset because you've just discovered you're not the true heir. Lute, you are the King because Rodin has named you his heir, whether or not you're his real son, and that's why Janko will do anything to get you out of the way. But *you* are King, not Janko, and you'd want to start behaving like it because I haven't galloped all over the realm and watched my beloved centaur take an arrow or risked the others' well-being for anyone other than my King." She finished her long speech breathlessly, then turned to stomp off back to the others.

"Wait!" Lute called after her. Tess was right. As much as it hurt him to learn about his mother not being the woman who birthed him, he could never say he was unloved or ever felt he was anything but a real son to the King and Queen. "Yes, indeed," he muttered to himself, "Janko might be an heir but he is not the King!" He caught up with Tess. "Only Pilo talks to me like that."

"Well, I suppose I have nothing much more to lose, so I don't care that you're King and could probably have me swinging from the highest tree. I'm tired of being on the run. This at least gave me purpose, and I hoped by you being the new ruler, you might be able to change things."

"I can," he said.

"But will you?"

"Yes!"

"Good." She stopped and gave an awkward curtsy that made them both smile. "Then come, Your Majesty. Listen to the plan that we've come up with to restore the throne to its rightful owner."

34

They were all crowded into Calico Grace's suite. She'd insisted that everyone eat and get some much-needed sleep so they'd all have enough energy to do whatever they planned to do. And while they ate, Dash had done a pretty good job of patching up Davren, whose stitches had torn open.

"That's very neat," Tess said to him.

"Years of mending sails, young Tess, not to mention I'm using a needle and thread created with magic." He winked. "And I've stitched men many times before today but never an animal and never, even in my wildest dreams, a creature so handsome as your centaur."

She hugged Dash. "Thank you. He'll be fine, won't he?"

"As good as new. He can wear that as a war wound."

She nodded. "Yes, he's already quite proud of it."

It had been decided that the creatures they had laboriously rowed back to the *Silver Wind* would remain on the ship and out of harm's way. Tess, however, had refused, with steadfast determination, to remain behind with Calico Grace when the conversation turned to who would be heading to the shore again.

"No offense," she insisted, "but I began this journey with Griff and I plan to end it with him." Before anyone could put up more excuses, she'd raised her hands. "No, save your breath. We're sticking together come what may. Rix and Davren are coming with us, too."

"You don't suppose Janko might think it slightly odd that I've somehow found myself a girl, a veercat and a centaur?" Bitter Olof asked, his tone dry.

"I don't care what the murdering Duke thinks. But I guarantee that all he'll really be paying attention to is the fact that Lute has been spotted. How you came by us will be irrelevant to him, as I imagine he plans to kill us all anyway."

That brought a horrible silence to the room.

"I like this girl," Calico Grace finally said into the silence, puffing on her pipe. "She's one after my own heart."

"No one's killing any of us while I'm around," boomed a new voice from the open doorway.

Bitter Olof and Lute exploded into action, running toward the huge figure, who scooped them both up with ease.

"Little Thom, you made it!" Lute shouted, delight in his eyes.

"Good as new, like that strange animal Dash was just stitching in my chamber. What a fine creature. I have no idea how he came to be here." He looked around. "Or why we have so many people . . . or two King Lutes."

Laughter erupted. Bitter Olof explained everything as Little Thom looked with wonder over the two brothers. He shook his head at the tale before shaking hands with and then bear-hugging Pilo.

"I'm glad that's all over," he said to his old friend.

"Me too," Pilo admitted, having heard about the magical elixir. "And I'm even more glad you're fit to be alongside Bitter Olof and Griff. What was in that stuff?"

Calico Grace gave a mock sneer. "Bah! You owe me, Little Thom. I used on your wounds all of the reawakening potion that the Witch Grevilya put on the ship! Now you too are in my debt."

Griff had enjoyed listening to all the happy conversation around him but he knew it was a false happiness. Everyone, including him, sensed the tremendous danger that he, the dwarf and now this giant of a man were putting themselves into. He had been tempted to talk to Lute privately via the mindlink, but he was enjoying the freedom from voices in his head that Davren and the creatures offered him; and also, because he could talk to Lute openly, he preferred it that way. He walked over to Lute, frankly still rather amazed by their likeness, and couldn't help but grin as he stared at his twin, who was now dressed in his clothes. "I'm sorry they're so battered," he offered, slightly embarrassed.

"And I'm sorry mine are so damp," Lute responded. "We nearly drowned." Then his expression grew more serious. "Griff, are you sure about this?"

"Tess came up with a good plan." He shrugged. "He's never going to suspect that I'm not you."

"But you could be ki—"

"No. Let's not think like that. You're going to send the army and hunt down Janko before anything like that could happen to us. We'll be cautious, I promise. All we have to do is stay out of sight long enough for your men to rescue us."

"I can't let you take all the risk by pretending to be me." Griff stared at him. "I'd do it for any of my brothers."

"That doesn't make it right!"

"It doesn't make it wrong either, brother. Listen, you were raised for this. You know how to be King. I don't. I can't do what you do. You can't do what I do, which, apart from looking like you, is to use magic to hear thoughts. This is not about bravery, Lute. We need you to survive and to go and claim the Crown from Janko. That's your duty. Standing up to him and, especially, tricking him is being brave and so much more. It's being smart."

"I'll beat him at his own low game!" Lute growled. Then the anger dissipated and he stared at Griff again. "Why did he give us away?"

Griff knew exactly what his brother referred to. "I've been thinking about that, too. Our father was so poor when we were coming along that the offer of gold from the Queen would have been impossible to turn down. It was a way to ensure the future of his family—and of the realm. Three of us could remain and he'd have money to look after us, and the one who had to go would have a life of privilege. Better that than starve. Then, when the Traveling Show made an offer to our elder brothers, and he could see they desperately wanted to get away from the tiny village and have a more exciting life as performers, he could not deny them." Griff shrugged. "When you meet Phineas and Matthias, you'll know why I love them so much, and Da knew he couldn't let us be parted. He knew my heart would break being left alone and he was probably all too mindful that he'd already ripped me away from one brother. He let me go with Phin and Mat. Master Tyren liked to tell me Da sold us but I think he accepted the money unhappily. In truth, he was letting us follow our own desires. We can all be reunited soon, but you should know that we would all put you first. . . . You are not only our family—you are our sovereign."

"I don't know what to say."

"Don't say anything more. Let's get this charade under way."

Tess had joined them quietly. "Do we know where Janko is? How do we ensure he spots us?"

Pilo glanced toward the brothers. "I think our amazing Griff can do that for us."

Griff nodded. "I'll need to take us into the Silvering, Lute, and once I look through your mind and get a picture of Janko and the sound of his voice, I'll be able to find him."

Calico Grace looked astonished. "Is this a jest?"

Pilo winked. "Not only you lay claim to magic with your ship, Gracie. Griff here has a talent that you can hardly imagine." He nodded. "Do it. We still have the cover of darkness. We need to get ashore to wherever Janko is."

"What if he's already back at the palace?" Lute queried.

At this Pilo frowned. "We have to pray he's not."

Griff returned from the Silvering and smiled secretively. "He's not at the palace. I've found him. He's at Tarrow's Landing. A place called the Shepherd's Rest. Bruno is stabled there, too. I could see him."

Lute threw a glance to Pilo, who smiled. "Yes, I know it well. I even hope he's stealing my horse back. It will give me great satisfaction to have another reason to hate Janko, not that I need one."

"All right, then. It's back to Tarrow's Landing for us," Bitter Olof said.

"It's a pity we have to take the longer way around," Pilo said. "If we could use the route through Tarrow's Landing, we could be there so much quicker."

"Master Pilo," Tess said, "I have another idea."

They all turned to look at her; she was holding Rix.

"It makes sense to dress Griff in Lute's clothes. But if you dressed the King very differently, perhaps you could slip through Tarrow's Landing unnoticed."

"What have you got in mind now, Tess?"

She smiled. "You're not going to like it much, Your Highness, but I think you should be in a dress."

"What?" Lute cried. "Absolutely not. No! No King of Drestonia wears women's clothes!"

Pilo laughed, scratching his head. "That's not such a bad thought, actually."

"No, I won't," Lute gasped.

"I think you'll have to," Pilo said. "It cuts another day from our journey. Come on, Majesty. Whatever it takes, we must do. Griff is putting his life at risk for you."

"Yes, the least you can do is wear a dress," Calico Grace cut in, but then added, "You too, Pilo. You'll have to shave, of course, but I think we can do better still. I'll search out something from my trunk for you. I'm sure I've kept a couple of lovely dresses from my days when I was much taller, much trimmer," she said, tapping her girth, with a wicked smile on her face.

"Er, no, that won't be n-necessary," Pilo stammered,

but he realized he had already lost the fight. Everyone but Lute and Pilo was laughing and Calico Grace had already signaled that the men should be ready to row back to the ship.

"We'll be back in a jiffy, Pilo," she said, and even Lute's face creased in a smile at Pilo's look of horror.

They were back on the shore watching as Calico Grace cheekily tied a bow beneath Pilo's chin. "There we are. Perfect," she cooed. "You can be Mistress Whatever-you-please for a day and this is your darling daughter, Miss Lucy."

King and aide gritted their teeth with displeasure beneath their bonnets. "This is not funny," Pilo growled, his skirts flouncing around him.

"Oh, but it is," Bitter Olof chortled. "That dress fits you rather well, Pilo."

"So help me, Pilo, I find you quite attractive," Little Thom teased, and blew him a kiss.

"All right, boys, enough joshing," Calico Grace said, suddenly taking charge. "I'm rowing back now to bring *Silver Wind* around to Deep Bay, which is where the royal brig is anchored. If you need me or my lovely silver cannons, we're at your disposal."

"Thanks, Gracie. I'm hoping it won't come to that," Pilo said. "Just keep Elph and Helys from harm." He glanced at Tess, who was nodding in agreement. "So Davren and Rix travel with Bitter Olof's party to Tarrow's Landing. I know I don't have to tell you," he said to Tess, "that your creatures are in serious danger. They should stay concealed within the fringe of woodland."

"I promise they will," she said.

"Then we ride now. Good luck, everyone. Griff, you will need to keep Lute informed of where you are at all times. We're deaf and blind to your plight, so we need your magical skills working hard."

Griff nodded. "Just get back to us fast. Who's going first?"

"You lot get going. We'll follow at a more sedate pace. We can't risk being seen too close. Remember, Olof, only allow yourselves to be glimpsed and then go for your life."

Bitter Olof tapped his nose. "I know you don't, but trust me, Pilo, I'll keep Griff safe. Initially I did this for you but now I'm doing it for our King. I've grown quite fond of Lute! Rest assured I won't let that swine touch a hair of Griff's head either."

"You do that." Only Tess caught any more of Pilo's muttered words: "For so help me, should anything happen to Griff I'll . . ."

Tess didn't listen anymore. She could guess what Pilo would do and she was sure the dwarf could as well.

35

Duke Janko was stirring a darkly golden sweet syrup into his bowl of porridge. He was privately seething and his fury kept him sour enough that he couldn't taste whether it was honey or treacle. Nor did he care. In fact, he was so distracted by his internal anger that he struggled to swallow, and the only reason he'd ordered anything to eat was that he knew it was going to be a long day ahead and an empty belly might weaken him.

And this was not a time to be weak. *No, by Lo's light!* he thought. *This is a time to be stronger than ever.* An old-timer had once counseled him that a soldier breaks bread before he fights. At first he had dismissed the words as blather, but as he'd matured he had grasped their wisdom. Consequently, he always forced himself to eat, even when, like now, he didn't feel hungry in the least. Unless one counted his hunger for power, that is, or his hunger for vengeance.

He threw down his spoon in disgust. Where those archers had suddenly emerged from at the beach he had no idea. One moment they'd had Lute and his wretched minders, the strange dwarf and equally strange giant of a man, and the next his own men were dead around him. It had just been a stroke of luck that he'd been mounted and able to gallop away down the beach, then pick his way back toward Tarrow's Landing.

At least he'd killed the large fellow. Now that Lute had lost his big warrior, he would be more vulnerable than ever. If anything the dwarf was a liability, not an asset, and Janko assumed that the pair would have to surface somewhere soon. They were in the sea, for Lo's sake. With luck their bloated bodies might turn up, drowned and no longer a threat, but even Janko believed that was too much to hope for. Whoever had come to their rescue from behind the point was obviously interfering, but still this was a group of strangers. Once they learned the truth—if Lute ever told it—it was unlikely they'd want any part of it. That sort of group, lurking in the shadows of a well-known pirating beach, would likely be thieves of some sort. He had made some inquiries. It was the haunt of many pirates and he had not spotted a ship, so presumably they were opportunists who happened to get involved because they were on hand. His gut told him that Lute and his dwarf friend would turn up somewhere soon, however. Lute could not stay hidden for long—not if he had any intention of claiming the throne.

Janko laughed bitterly, drained the ale in his mug and slammed it down, wiping his mouth with his sleeve. It would all be over soon. He still had some mercenaries traveling with him. Not many—not as many as he'd like—but they were eager to be paid and knew they'd get not a penny until the boy, alive or dead, was under his control.

His thoughts wandered as the serving girl drifted over,

and as he watched the pretty golden-haired maid top off his mug, he began to imagine whether Miralda would accept his terms. He'd already made it very clear to her. She had begged him to spare Lute's life, and the only way, he had sneered at her, that he might go along with such a thing would be if she agreed to marry him. He had always had a flame burning for Miralda, even though she made it obvious that she despised him. But he found her irresistible and had never been able to understand what she had seen in Rodin. At least, he had argued, she would still be Queen, and Lute could remain Crown Prince—after they'd made a big fanfare of his miraculous recovery . . . so long as he himself would be King.

She had said she would think about it, but he'd seen in her eyes that she was too proud, too angry, and even though she'd be risking her life and her son's life, he suspected she had no intention of agreeing to it; she'd simply promised to consider it as a means of buying time. She still had hopes that his nephew might surprise them all by doing something heroic like rallying loyal troops. Didn't she understand that the men of the army were loyal to Janko before any gold crown? He sighed. Such a pity, because Miralda would have to be shipped off immediately to some distant convent, where she could live out her days in silence and solitude and sorrow. What a waste of an opportunity! He allowed the daydream's bubble to burst. He was about to order a warm drink when one of his men barged in and hurried over to him.

"What is it?" he questioned testily.

The man didn't seem at all bothered by his tone or humbled by the person he was addressing.

Wretched mercenaries, Janko thought. *I'll have all of you dealt with as soon as I'm King.* "Well?" he prompted.

"We've sighted the dwarf and the boy with some others, including that huge man we thought was dead," the man replied lazily.

Janko was on his feet in a blink, his chair scraping back noisily on the flagstones. "Where?"

"Ah, now . . . that would be telling."

"What?" Janko growled, his eyes narrowing. "What are you saying? We have a deal," he said, but only loud enough for the man to hear.

"*Had* a deal," the man corrected, equally quietly. "The situation has changed. I've lost too many of my men on your folly. And you never told us we were murdering a royal."

"He's a boy!" Janko hissed.

"Well, by law he's King."

"He is *not* King!" Janko's voice had escalated in volume and he looked around at the disturbed drinkers and diners, who up until now had paid him little notice. He had deliberately dressed in very plain clothing, wore no insignia and carried nothing more than a common-looking sword. It was sharp enough to do its job, just not elegant enough to attract attention. Normally, he enjoyed being recognized, but right now Janko wanted to pass through this trading town unnoticed. He wanted to capture Lute with as little fuss as possible, although the royal wretch was proving to be as slippery as an eel.

"Hush now, you don't want to attract undue attention, do you?"

"You rogue."

The man shrugged. "Let's discuss terms and then we'll discuss where your prey were seen."

Janko took a long breath to calm his rage. It would not do

to lose his temper here. Later, when this was all done and Lute was in his possession, he would take great pleasure in dealing with this two-timing thief. Unfortunately, at the moment he needed the help of these men, and so, through gritted teeth and a voice he had wrested back under control, he said calmly, "All right, I'll double the wages I've already offered."

"And we'll have the wages of the men who have died for your cause."

"That's—"

"Uh-uh, Duke," the man said softly, careful not to be overheard as he used the title. "Those men, however much they irritated you to be in your employ, had families. You were quite happy to make use of their services. Now you'll pay for those services in full and their bereaved families will benefit . . . as they should."

Janko growled something unintelligible under his breath.

"Do we have a new deal? I'll need to see some gold to seal it," the man continued, not at all threatened.

Janko closed his eyes to calm his anger. Then opened them, smiled serenely at the man he intended to enjoy killing one day soon and nodded. "Deal. Outside before any money exchanges hands."

"No hurry. Enjoy breaking your fast," the mercenary said, and grinned at the Duke before he left him to his bowl of now-cold porridge.

Pilo and Lute kept the horses at a deliberately sedate canter as they approached the Shepherd's Rest.

"Hold your nerve now, boy. They have no idea who we are."

Lute nodded. "Lovely day, isn't it, Mama?" he said sweetly, in a higher than normal voice.

Pilo glared at him from beneath his big yellow bonnet.

Lute shrugged. "Just getting into character."

"Don't speak at all if you can help it."

Lute smiled beneath his own red bonnet, although deep down he was nervous. He could see some of the mercenaries leaning against posts and sitting on the ground, no doubt awaiting their next orders. Some were checking their bows, others were chewing on bread. They were close enough now that he could see that their bread was thickly smeared with blackberry jam. He felt his own belly grind with hunger, having only nibbled at the food offered on the ship, but the truth was he was more tired than he was hungry. Unfortunately, there was no time to sleep or feed. He wished they could simply hit a hard gallop, but he quashed that desire as quickly as it arose and continued at his dignified pace.

As they drew almost level with the inn, Lute saw with horror that his uncle was emerging from one of its doors. He looked to be in a hurry and seemed to have lost his normally very controlled, always vaguely amused expression. This morning he looked angry and seemed to be speaking tersely to the man who walked alongside him, cutting his hand through the air as if all patience was gone as he gave his instructions.

Pilo had seen him, too. "Steady, Lute. Just keep riding; smile if necessary but be shy, keep that bonnet low."

Lute felt a burst of nervous laughter erupt in his chest.

He'd only just noticed that Pilo had put on the long gloves that Calico Grace had suggested he wear to cover his hairy arms and hands. It took every ounce of willpower not to explode into giggles that would have attracted all the wrong attention.

Even so, the Duke noticed them. He had been reaching into his pocket for something when he stopped himself. It looked furtive even though he tried to cover his actions by smiling at the passersby. "Morning, ladies."

Lute dipped his head and presumed Pilo must have done the same.

"A lovely morning for a ride, isn't it?"

The Duke clearly expected more than just a nod and it would be impolite, certainly noticeable, if they didn't respond in the right manner. As Pilo couldn't risk using his deep voice, Lute had to fill what felt like a horrible silence, although it was only a momentary pause.

"It certainly is, sir," he said in his new higher voice.

He saw from the corner of his eye that Pilo had lifted a gloved hand and was waving politely.

"Enjoy your day, ladies," they heard him say as they passed by fully, before he muttered to his companion, "Here!" They heard the unmistakable chink of gold. "Now, where did you see the dwarf and my nephew?"

Lute glanced at Pilo and could see the cunning smile. "He's taken the bait," Pilo said, finally out of earshot of the Duke.

"I'm worried for the others," Lute said.

"That's why it's time to ride, my boy. Let's take these horses up to a trot and get across that river as soon as we can."

It was all straightforward. They met no other soldiers and it was still early enough that they could keep themselves to themselves and not be noticed for the impostors that they were. The man in charge of the ferry was barely awake and was too busy scratching his huge belly and yawning to take much notice of the newcomers boarding, a mother who paid from a daintily gloved hand, traveling with her daughter.

Lute was sure he held his breath for the entire crossing, and felt a surge of relief as they finally led their mounts off on the other side.

"Now we can gallop," Pilo whispered.

Lute chanced a look back. "Janko and his men are making the crossing, too."

Pilo nodded, looking at the Duke, who was impatiently waiting for the ferry to return to his side of the river. "Makes sense. I told Olof to be noticed on this side, getting a feed at the Old Wheatsheaf."

"It's worked."

"Are you ready?" Pilo asked as they both settled into their saddles.

"As I'll ever be."

"Ride hard, boy. We've got lives to save now."

36

"Hurry now. We've been seen. Now we must melt away into the woodland behind Tarrow's Landing," Bitter Olof encouraged.

"Where are we going?" Tess asked.

"Nowhere in particular. We have to hide. They're going to pursue us. I won't lie, Tess, it will get rather dangerous from here on."

Tess glanced at Griff. "We're going to stay well out of their sight—as best we can, Tess," he reassured. "Come on."

Little Thom had already swung the dwarf into a sling. "Follow me," he said, his long legs making huge strides up the hillside. "Stay in line with the buildings. Use them as cover for as long as possible."

"How long have we got?" Griff wondered aloud.

Bitter Olof replied from his position, watching Griff and Tess scramble along in Little Thom's wake. "We were noticed when your porridge was served."

"That long ago?" Griff said, clearly surprised.

"We couldn't let the man who was watching us know that we knew we'd been spotted. I had to wait until he'd left, and he seemed determined to finish his own bowl of porridge."

"So how much of a lead do we have?" Tess persisted, her breathing already erratic from her exertions.

"The mercenary had to cross the river, find his leader, who would then have had to advise the Duke, who would then furiously saddle up. He would have to make his way to the landing itself and then await the ferry and cross to this bank. I should imagine he'd be waiting impatiently to get on board the ferry by now."

"You'll probably be able to see them once we get to the top of this hill," Little Thom said, not even vaguely out of breath. He turned and hauled both Tess and Griff up a particularly hard part of the climb. "Come on, slow coaches. If you value your lives, you'll move faster."

"Tess, get a firm fix on where Davren is. We don't want to be searching for him once we round the hill," Griff said.

She nodded, and despite her climbing, Griff could see her concentrating as she sent a message.

They crested the hill.

"Stay low now," Little Thom urged. "We can be seen, so we mustn't attract too much attention." He put Bitter Olof down. "You two crowd Bitter Olof—his shape is too instantly recognizable, even from afar."

Bitter Olof grunted. "Just worry about your own strange shape, Little Thom."

"That's why I plan to run in this rather odd, crouched position you see me in," Little Thom responded.

Tess came back with a message. "Davren says he can see

us. We're to head for that stand of hazel trees. And some bad news. Rix can see our pursuers from the treetops. The Duke is already halfway across the river."

"All right, forget trying to mask who we are," Bitter Olof said. "Pick me up, Thom. We run for it. Our best chance is in the woodland."

"I agree," the big man said, and scooped up the dwarf. "Let's go." And the strange party of four began to run for the trees.

In the distance they heard a shout go up. They'd been spotted.

⊠⊹⊠

Lute had never ridden this hard or fast before. They said nothing to each other; couldn't even if they'd wanted to, such was the speed they were pushing their horses at. He dearly wished he had his brave Tirell beneath him. She was the fastest filly in the realm. He imagined Pilo sorely wished he had Bruno galloping beneath him, but their horses were doing their best and this was no time for wishing things could be different.

Pilo finally gave him the nod to slow the horses.

"Their hearts will give out if we ride them any harder," he explained when he saw Lute frowning.

"We're not going to make it, are we?" Lute asked, airing his fears. He didn't want to be so pessimistic but Pilo's face told him he was right.

"We're doing the best we can."

"No, Pilo. We're running away. You've got me to safety,

so in your mind that's all right. You're thinking the others may have to be sacrificed so long as the precious King is alive and can claim the throne."

"Your Majesty, I—"

"I can't do this." Lute dragged on the reins until his horse actually stopped.

"Lute!"

"No! You knew we wouldn't make it."

Pilo shook his head. "That's not true. I promise you I did not lie. This plot was not even my idea."

"That may well be but I know how your mind works, Pilo. I know you love me and you admire my parents and above all you are loyal to the Crown. So the royals have to come first in your eyes. You couldn't risk my life any further and Tess's plan gave you that wonderful chance to keep me safe . . . and let Griff take all the risk."

Pilo looked suddenly helpless. His mouth was open to say something but no words were coming out. He simply shook his head again.

"I can't let Griff die."

"And I can't let you die, Your Highness. I love you as my own. My child was lost to me. You can't imagine how that broke me or how long it took for me to even be able to live with myself again without loathing. She died because I didn't take care of her. And I'll be damned if I let you die because I allowed the same fate. I hardly shared Ellin's life but I have shared much of yours. I can't risk losing you."

"But you're risking Griff and Tess, Bitter Olof and Little Thom. They're all being so brave and all for my sake."

"They are, but who's to say they won't survive?"

"Me! Because I've ridden this journey before at speed and it took me a lot longer than we have to spare before the Duke catches up with them. He's ruthless, Pilo. He won't care about the others. He might spare me for his own reasons and manipulations but he will happily kill our friends. I don't know what I've been thinking allowing this to happen. I must have—"

"We are not going back. There is no point. It's already too late. By the time you catch up with them, it will—"

"At least I'll give my life for a good cause. Do you honestly think I can happily sit on that throne knowing my friends spilled their blood for it and I did absolutely nothing except run away and let them spill it?"

"You have no choice. If you don't want Janko running this realm, you *have* to claim that throne . . . and quickly."

"I understand. But, Pilo, you need to understand that I would rather stand alongside those brave people and face Janko than beat him with our clever trick but know in my heart that I lacked the courage."

"It's not about courage, Majesty. This is about—"

"Ladies?" inquired a voice, one that both Pilo and Lute recognized instantly.

They turned in their saddles, stunned to see Queen Miralda on a horse, standing on top of the rise not far from where they had stopped to argue. Next to her was the captain of the Drestonian Guard. They both looked stunned.

"Are you both all right?" she continued. "We could hear you arguing from—"

"Mother?" Lute said, pulling off his bonnet, and realizing that the male voices Miralda had heard would have been at odds with their appearance.

"Lute?" She stared dumbly at her son, unable to continue for a few long moments, during which time Pilo sheepishly untied his bonnet.

If this were any other situation than the dire circumstances they faced, Lute would have exploded into uncontrollable laughter to see Pilo's stubbly face emerge from beneath the frills and flounces that Calico Grace had insisted he wear to disguise the fact that he was clearly a man.

"Pilo?" she whispered, even more shocked, her hand moving to her throat.

"Your Highness," he answered, pulling angrily at his gloves and flinging them down to the ground.

"Am I seeing things?" she pleaded. "Tell me it truly is you two."

Lute leaped down from his horse and pulled off a dress to reveal Griff's old clothes beneath. "It's me, Mother."

Now her hand covered her mouth to prevent the cry of relief from making her look too undignified.

Pilo was also off his horse in a flash and bowing. "What are you doing here, Queen Miralda?"

She pointed behind her, laughing amidst the tears that flowed down her cheeks. "I'm bringing the army to your aid."

"What?" Lute said, and ran up the rise to look down into the small valley. "Pilo, look! The Guard is here."

Pilo strode up the rise to join him. "Lo save us, it is. How did you know? How did you escape?" he asked her, shaking his head in confusion. "The last I heard you were under mercenary guard."

"I was," she said, climbing down from her horse. "You'll never believe it but Lambert the cook was the one who mustered all the right people!"

"Lambert?" Lute questioned, astonished.

"Yes," she said. "He was the first to notice something was wrong, long before your father was told or was able to act. He managed to get out of the palace before the mercenaries took full control. He stole out via the herb garden and that creaky old side gate that no one seems to pay much attention to. Can you imagine it?" Lute shook his head. The Queen continued. "He took as many people with him as he could and got them all to find and brief the various army lieutenants on what they thought was happening. When Captain Drew was"—she glanced at Pilo—"well, shall we say, detained by your traitorous uncle, it was Lambert who found the next-in-command and, in secret, explained what was really going on in the palace."

"And they got you out," Pilo finished.

"It took a while. I was under very close guard. But as soon as the Duke was out of the palace, our own army struck and there were far too many of them, so the mercenaries were overwhelmed. Janko has no idea yet, I suspect."

"That's because he's too busy stalking me over at Tarrow's Landing."

"Yes," she said, hugging her son hard, stroking his hair. She looked at Pilo again. "You'd left the message with people you could trust that we should look there for you both."

Lute nodded. "Except Uncle Janko thought he saw me, or at least his hired thugs thought they saw me headed northwest out of Tarrow's Landing. He's giving chase as we stand here and discuss it." His voice held an edge and Pilo gave him a warning glance.

Miralda looked between them quizzically. "What is he talking about, Pilo? Is he not well?"

"Talk to me, Mother. Talk to me quickly about how I came to be your son. Time is short. I have to ride back now to save my twin brother, who is masquerading as me, tempting my treacherous uncle to kill him instead of me!"

Lute watched his mother's face turn pale and her mouth move with no words. She looked ready to faint.

"That was harsh, Majesty, and not very fair of you," Pilo cautioned.

"I'm sorry," he said to both of them, and meant it, "but—"

Lute got no further. The link was slicing open in his mind.

37

Griff had forced Tess to climb a tree, and with the help of Little Thom she was now hidden high amongst an oak's branches with Rix delighted and nearby. Unless she made a noise, their pursuers wouldn't think of looking for anyone up there. As far as Griff was concerned, she was safe and so were the creatures; he'd made Davren melt back even further into the woodland.

"He doesn't know you're here, he won't be looking for you, nor will he care. But I don't want you attracting his attention. Don't do anything heroic, Davren, all right?"

The centaur gave no indication that he was agreeing, other than to turn solemnly and head deeper into the trees. Griff sighed with relief.

"It's the right decision, boy. You and I are the ones he's interested in, and in truth he couldn't give a damn about us," Bitter Olof said, indicating himself and Thom. "You are the prize."

"We're just a nuisance to be dealt with," Little Thom agreed.

"So we're going to do our utmost to stay out of sight but we're not going to split up."

"Surely that would give us a better chance?" Griff reasoned.

"Perhaps, but we gave our word we would stick by you, Griff," Bitter Olof said. "And I'm not going to let Pilo down again."

"Shall I try to talk with Lute?" he asked. "Perhaps they'll have some news for us."

He saw the dwarf share a sad glance with his tall friend.

"Er, Griff. There probably was never going to be a good time to tell you this, but I suspect no one is coming back for us—not in enough time, anyway."

"What do you mean? Pilo has—"

"Got Lute to safety, yes," Bitter Olof said gravely. "I'm sorry, Griff."

He looked at Bitter Olof, then at Little Thom. He still said nothing as his gaze slid back again to the dwarf and understanding fell into place.

"I'm bait, nothing more."

Bitter Olof looked briefly at the ground, then faced Griff. "I wouldn't put it quite like that, but I'm sure that's how it's going to feel shortly."

Griff looked incredulous. "But that makes you bait also. And Little Thom."

The dwarf nodded.

"Why?" He shook his head. "I mean, whether or not I've been tricked, why would you do it?"

"I can only answer for myself. I owe Pilo this much. And beyond that debt, this is the King we are talking about."

"And where Bitter Olof goes, I go," Little Thom explained.

Bitter Olof looked up and smiled at his friend. "You're far too loyal."

Griff pushed past his shock. "You've got Lute all wrong. Perhaps Pilo, in his fear for the King's life, is prepared to let us sacrifice ourselves, but I don't believe Lute would knowingly agree to this."

"You don't know him at all."

"He's my twin, Bitter Olof. I know me. And I wouldn't let him walk into such danger without knowing I was going to do everything I could to help."

"And I'm sure His Majesty will try, but you need to understand that the distance is too far."

Griff began to pace, his shock crystallizing into anger. "Tess is not to know anything about this. Agreed?"

"Agreed," his two companions said solemnly.

"And the other thing we need to agree on is that we are not going to die here. Little Thom has already given his life once for Lute, and if not for magic, we would have been burying him at sea. Each of us has risked plenty. Lute knows that. He will not let us die here. We are going to stay alive until he can get us help. Agreed?"

"Agreed," they said, more slowly this time and with a lot more doubt in their voices.

"Right," Griff said, although he was back to pacing nervously again.

"So how do you propose we are going to stay alive?" Bitter Olof wondered.

"I'm going to start by finding out where my brother is. Give me a few moments."

He found the Silvering with ease. Within the silver void he tugged at Davren's mind. Davren was with him in the blink of an eye and Griff quickly told him what he'd learned.

I'm not sure Tess will accept this situation, Davren said.

You can be sure I'm not going to give her an inkling.

There was an awkward pause and Griff was about to ask what was wrong when Davren sighed and spoke before he could. *You'd better speak with Lute.*

It was easy to find Lute as well. It occurred to Griff how difficult he had found this initially and how Lute's voice had only ever sounded like a whisper in his mind. Now Lute sounded clear and as close as if they were standing next to one another.

Lute, it's us. Where are you?

Griff, I'm so relieved you've reached me. I wish I knew how to do this.

You did it first, remember?

I have some news.

I hope it's good, because all I've been hearing is bad news.

Oh?

Bitter Olof and Little Thom have just admitted that they don't think anyone's coming back for us, Griff said carefully.

Lute sounded excited when he replied. *Well, you can assure them that we certainly are coming back. In fact, we're already on our way and we're bringing the might of the Drestonian Guard with us.*

Are you serious?

Completely.

I knew you'd come.

Did you doubt me?

Never.

Griff, you just have to hold on now. Stay hidden until we arrive.

I'm not sure that's going to be so straightforward. The Duke is almost upon us. We've hidden Tess and the creatures are safe but . . . Griff trailed off. He didn't want to utter the words that were in his heart.

You make it happen—find somewhere to hide! You are not going to die, Griff. Do you hear? Stay safe. We have to ride.

Wait! What about your father?

I'm afraid he is dead, confirmed by my mother, who also rides with us.

I'm sorry to hear that.

There will be time to grieve but only when I have his murderer to answer for his death, Lute said grimly, his voice driven with emotion. *I must go, Griff. Please, be alive when we arrive.*

We'll do our best, Griff replied doubtfully. Still, it felt heartening to know his instincts about Lute were right, and he wasn't going to allow his companions to feel anything but pride for their new King. He snapped the link shut and shook his head clear of the silver void.

Bitter Olof and Little Thom waited expectantly. "Well?" the dwarf prompted.

"King Lute is riding hard, with the Drestonian Guard at his rear," Griff said triumphantly.

They could barely believe what they'd heard. Smiles stretched across their faces.

"Truly?" Bitter Olof asked.

Griff nodded. "We just have to hold on, he urged me."

"I'm too difficult to hide," Little Thom reminded them,

and he smiled regretfully. "But let's get you two hidden. Perhaps I can lead them away?"

"No!" They both said it together.

"We'll fall together if we have to," Bitter Olof told his friend. "But we must do everything to save Griff. He's got his life ahead of him and I'll be damned if I allow the murderous Duke the satisfaction—even for a few false minutes—of thinking he's destroyed the real heir."

"You can talk all you like between yourselves but it just soaks up more precious time and it doesn't alter the fact that I am standing alongside you," Griff said. "It's only when he sees me that this trick can work. We will have to face him, keep him talking, hope that he will want to prolong the pleasure of finally having me at his mercy."

"You're putting a lot of faith in his arrogance, son," Olof said. "He may just fill us all with arrows and be on his way back to the palace."

"Well, if he does that, he's going to meet the real King and the Guard flanking him. I'm sure Janko's hired soldiers will flee at the sight."

"It's true those sorts of mercenaries won't stick around. They're little more than a motley mob of paid thugs . . . not even proper soldiers for hire, from what I could see of them."

"So," Griff said, "we stand together."

"You're very brave, my boy," Bitter Olof said, shaking his head. "We're giving you a chance to live—both you and your brother can survive this."

"Bitter Olof, I've always been afraid. Afraid to be left behind by my elder brothers when they joined Master Tyren's Traveling Show, afraid of the skill I had that allowed the thoughts of others to storm my mind, afraid of being found out. I was afraid for Tess when she arrived and afraid of the Stalkers when they were pursuing us. But mostly I was afraid of the truth I felt deep down that there were secrets to my life—I knew this because of the way my father kept his mind so closed. And now I know part of the truth, and now that I don't feel so alone, with a twin brother and friends like yourselves and especially Tess and her creatures, I do believe it's time for me to be brave and face all those fears head-on. What we're doing this morning could save a lot of lives. That's worth being brave for."

Little Thom nodded. "Well said."

Bitter Olof smiled his sad agreement. "All right, Griff. But we are going to do our best to conceal ourselves. I reckon we've just got enough time, so let's not waste any more of it on chatter. Let's settle on a spot where we shall make our stand and hope your brother—the King—gets here very soon."

There was one more talent that Tess had not thought to mention to Griff before, mainly because she had always taken it for granted, as others might accept a talent for being good at sums or fast at running.

Tess had always enjoyed exceptionally fine hearing, and here in the almost-silent forest, and despite being high up, she had heard every word discussed by her three friends down below and she was both furious and frightened.

Davren!

He sighed. *I know what you're going to say. I didn't even bother explaining to Griff that you would have heard everything being discussed.*

They're all preparing to die. They're accepting it!

He said nothing.

Davren!

I hear you, Tess. I just don't know what to say to you other than don't even think about climbing down from that tree or I'll pick you up myself and drag you away from here. As it is, I'm concerned that you are present at all. This is not something you should watch.

I'm not going to sit by here, cowering in an oak, and watch Griff give his life meekly to that thieving, murderous—

Tess, listen to me—

NO! There has to be something we can do.

You and I? What use are we against weapons? If I had my way, I'd have nothing to do with men at all. They always bring my kind grief.

There has to be something we can divert the Duke's men with, she groaned.

Well, I suppose I could charge into the clearing and surprise them.

Don't be ridiculous; they'd just shoot you full of arrows and worry about how interesting you are later.

We could sing for them, he offered.

Davren, you're not taking me seriously.

Listen, Tess. There's nothing we can do. His voice was grave now and all the sarcasm had fled. *If I heard it right, then Bitter Olof and Little Thom have known from the outset of their journey that they were likely coming here to die. And so did Pilo.*

Well, I can assure you neither Griff nor Lute had any idea.

No, but that was the point. The men knew that if either Griff or Lute realized this, they would not agree to the plan.

It's all my fault. The plan was my idea. Griff is going to die because of me. Her voice began to tremble.

You heard that Lute is on his way back now with the Guard.

It's not over yet. Lute told Griff they just have to hang on for a little longer, stay out of sight, keep the Duke and his men searching for as long as possible.

We need a diversion, she repeated. *We have to throw the Duke off the scent or at least hold him up. What can I do? What can I do?* she muttered desperately.

I've got an idea, said a new voice.

Rix?

You know I don't care for any of these people. They're more trouble than they're worth in our lives.

I don't agree, Tess replied sadly.

I know. And because I love you, Tess, I agree that we should try to help.

What have you got in mind? Tess asked. *I'll go along with any idea if it's got the slightest chance of throwing the Duke off Griff's trail.*

Oh, it will do a lot more than that, Rix responded, and she could hear the sly tone in his voice. *I can't believe neither of you have thought of it. I just hope there's enough time.*

What? Tell us! Tess shrieked across their magical link.

And Rix did.

38

Griff peered from around a huge tree and glimpsed the Duke as he entered the area on foot. All of his men had needed to dismount because the trees were so dense and low in this part of the woodland.

He was surprised how calm he suddenly felt. It was as though this had always been his destiny. Fear was behind him now. He had a role to play and an important task to save the life of his brother . . . of a king. It felt absolutely right that he do this, and his only regret was that he might not live long enough to see Lute again, or to find out the truth of their birth.

He deeply wished he had insisted that Tess remain behind on the *Silver Wind*, but at the same time he knew she was safe and that Davren and Rix would protect her to the end. Hopefully, reinforcements would arrive before the Duke even noticed Tess. So long as she didn't get involved!

They'd decided not to run deeper into the wood because that's what the Duke would expect. Bitter Olof had reasoned that they should stay here in the shallow reaches of the trees because it kept them closer to where help might come from, but it also might just fool the Duke. He would not expect them to be so close but rather running for their lives, the dwarf had argued. And he and Little Thom had finally agreed.

So now they each watched, hidden behind the widest trees they could find, as the Duke approached with armed men.

Griff opened a link and reached Lute immediately. *He's here. I can see him. He's brought a dozen or so men, because we're obviously such a formidable trio, unarmed and helpless as we are.*

So much for the brave warrior of the north, Lute snarled back over the link. *I can see the landing, Griff. One more hill and we'll be galloping across country straight at you. You just have to hold on.*

Davren?

Yes, Griff.

Ask Tess to send Rix up. Lute needs to get a fix on where we are. But don't let him be seen. If they look up, they might put two and two together.

I doubt it, Davren replied. *However, if they look up, I think they'll get a much bigger surprise.*

What are you talking about?

I doubt that Lute will have any problem at all knowing where we are.

You're talking in riddles, Lute said, having listened to all this.

Griff shook his head. *I don't understand either, but I need to focus now. I've been blind for too long in here and I need to know where the Duke is. Hurry, Lute.*

He snapped shut the link, and just in time, it seemed, for the closest man was now mere yards away from where Bitter Olof hid. Griff held his breath as the dwarf instinctively stepped back further around the tree and, in doing so, snapped a twig underfoot. In any other situation it would have gone unnoticed, but it was as though a clash of cymbals had sounded.

Every man went on the alert; bows were pulled tight, their arrows loaded and ready to fire, while swords, already drawn, were lifted and ready to slash down.

"That was a mistake," Duke Janko drawled. "Now we know you're here and close."

He waited and the silence lengthened. Griff closed his eyes as he watched Bitter Olof's shoulders slump in defeat. The fight was over, yet it had hardly begun . . . and all because of a snapped twig.

"You might as well show yourselves now," Janko urged, and a sly smile stole across his face. "I might even be lenient with you, dwarf," he taunted, even though they remained hidden. "I'm really only after the boy."

Again he waited, and again his query was met with silence.

He seemed in no particular hurry, feeling so confident of his prize. "I'm even prepared to pay you for your trouble in keeping him safe for me. I'll offer the giant compensation for the arrows he took, and my somewhat amazed congratulations that he not only survived but is apparently fit enough to come back here, trying to hide my nephew and elude me." He took a few more steps and signaled to his men to spread out slightly. "Let's talk gold, dwarf, shall we? I'll let you keep the haul that I know you've already hidden somewhere around your cave. And I'm prepared to offer right now two hundred gold pieces to you and your big friend, in exchange for the boy and your silence. What's more, I'll grant you safe passage. I have no fight with you . . . unless you steal any more of my money, of course." He laughed. "Then I'll see you hang from the nearest tree." He grew serious again. "But right now I want my nephew, and there needn't be any bloodshed on your part—only profit. He is meaningless to you, and I'm going to put this behavior of yours down to some sort of misguided loyalty to the Crown. Fret not; you'll find me a most benevolent king. I'm going to ignore your previous black marks. We shall wipe the slate clean, and you may take yourself and your now-good name away from here. You can be rich, and you will have the protection of the new King."

Griff thought that if the Duke took another three steps, he'd all but tread on Bitter Olof. Their hiding time was over. Now he just had to keep the Duke talking and hope it gave them enough minutes for Lute to arrive.

He shocked Bitter Olof and Little Thom by stepping out from behind the tree and yelling, "He already has the protection of a king, you treacherous sod! The true King!"

Janko swung around and Griff could see the man's eyes glittering with joy.

"There you are, Lute. Tsk, tsk. Did you really think you could outwit me?"

"I have, several times," Griff said.

"Brave talk," Janko sneered.

Immediately Bitter Olof and Little Thom showed themselves.

"Train your weapons on them," the Duke ordered. "If they run, cut them down and make it permanent this time."

"So much for trusting you," Bitter Olof said indignantly.

Janko ignored him, turning his attention back to Griff. "Yes, brave talk, indeed, but your tricks and turns have led you nowhere but here . . . at my mercy."

"Is that so? Somehow, I feel my best trick is yet to come, dear *uncle*."

Janko laughed with high amusement. "Really? I have you cornered and helpless, and I'm going to kill you because I suspect your mother has only pretended to consider my offer of marriage." He frowned. "Oh, did I mention your father is dead, by the way? His poor weak heart. Anyhow, your narrow-minded mother will not agree to being my wife, so I can't possibly agree to keeping you alive as she begged. No, Lute, you must die. But first, would you like to know the truth of your birth? Let me at least send you off to Lo knowing the real story, because I fear I rattled you during our morning ride. My word, that seems such a long time ago now, doesn't it?"

Griff remained silent.

"We were discussing how you didn't look like either of your parents. You see, I did some digging and greased all the right palms. I've learned that you were born on the eastern coast on the fringe of a village. Your real father is a lowly falconer. And your mother?" He laughed. "Your mother was born to peasants and remained a peasant for the whole of her short, hard life."

Griff's teeth clenched, along with his fists.

Janko must have noticed because he smiled his evil smile. "She died, Lute, giving birth to you. You killed her. She bled out within hours of her peasant son's arrival. But wait, the plot thickens. The very poor falconer father, unable to feed his first two sons, let alone another one, agreed to sell you." The Duke loaded his voice with astonishment. "Sell you!" He clicked his tongue in sad amazement. "What a rogue. He sold his newborn son. What he didn't know was that the highborn woman who offered him gold for his child and for his silence was no less than Queen Miralda herself, who could not carry a child of her own." The Duke droned on: "And rather than face life without an heir, Rodin obviously agreed to her sinister plan to buy one. She could lavish all that unspent love on the son she craved and Rodin could parade you around Floris as the heir that finally blessed their marriage." He clapped his hands. "How convenient, don't you think, Lute?"

"How do I know you're not lying?" Griff stalled.

"You know I'm not," the Duke baited. "You know it in your heart. And if I had the time, I'd let you meet your real father. I've had him brought to Floris, you see. I didn't know whether I'd need him in this whole sorry sideshow of your life. But now I know I don't, so I'll likely kill him too, and then the secret of your birth remains safe and does not tarnish the Crown."

Griff felt fury rise and consume every inch of his body. He imagined his father locked up in some dungeon, cold and confused, unsure of whether his three sons lived or died— probably unaware of who his fourth son had become.

"I'm going to see you punished," Griff snarled at the Duke.

Janko laughed uproariously. "Really? Well, that is frightening. So perhaps I'd better kill you first." Until now his sword had remained in its scabbard but he drew it with a chilling clang of metal.

"You're murdering a king," Bitter Olof warned, his voice filled with loathing.

Janko shrugged. "Oh well, it won't be my first," he said, his tone as uncaring as he could make it. "Right, then, Lute. Be brave now, unlike your pretend father, Rodin." He raised his sword.

"Duke Janko!" cried a new voice.

"Tess!" Griff yelled. "I told you not to—"

"Ah," Janko said, turning to one of the men. "You did say something about a girl with them." He glanced at Bitter Olof. "You have collected some strange hangers-on, haven't you, dwarf?"

"Leave her alone, Janko!" Griff snarled.

Janko grinned. "I'm not sure you're in a position to do anything about it even if I defied you, Lute."

"No, but I am," Tess said. "Duke Janko. I'd like you and your men to meet a friend of mine. His name is Gaston, and he's very angry that he's been disturbed."

As she said this, all the horses reared as one, whinnying with fear, and bolted. Everyone looked startled except Tess. And then, impossibly, a huge shape loomed into view, its shadow darkening the area where they stood. It broke branches as it smashed its way into the clearing.

Duke Janko's jaw fell open. "What in Lo's name is that?"

Gaston spread his enormous wings, each tipped with a vicious and clearly sharp claw, then opened his equally threatening hooked beak and let out a savage roar.

"I don't think he's taken kindly to you threatening me or any of my friends. I'm going to talk to him now; can I suggest you all remain very still?"

A moment later the gryphon moved in a sort of swooping

motion, and immediately they heard the creak of branches, which suddenly crashed to the undergrowth.

Duke Janko looked horrified. "What just happened?" he asked, swiveling to take in the fact that half a dozen large branches lay near the terrifying beast.

"That was Gaston's little demonstration of what his sharp claws can do. As you saw for yourselves, it took little effort. Imagine what it might do to flesh. Actually, don't, it's far too scary. And as I said, he's angry and I could lose control of him if you don't put down those weapons this second!"

Every man but the Duke threw down his weapon.

Again Gaston let out a loud roar.

The hired men turned and ran for their lives, their leader yelling over his shoulder, "We didn't agree to any of this. You're on your own, Duke!"

Janko let out a roar of his own, filled with frustration.

Bitter Olof laughed. "That's a fine creature you've got there, Tess."

"Beautiful, isn't he?" she replied, her voice filled with pride. "He lives in the mountains to the north of here. A stroke of luck that he was foraging close enough to be here so fast."

The initial shock had passed, but none of the fear or awe had left Duke Janko's voice when he tried to sound his usual controlled, dry self. "How convenient."

Tess laughed at him. "A word from me, Duke, and your whole body could be easily sliced in half. And don't think I wouldn't give that command. I hate bullies, and you are so much worse. Bullies, I've found, are usually cowards. And yet you have nothing to be cowardly about. You are adored by the people for your strength and courage."

"And that's why I would make a great king," he spat at her.

He threw down his sword, but despite that moment of relief for all, they were astounded by the speed at which he dragged a dagger from a small scabbard at his waist. "And why," he said, shocking them as he leaped at Griff and grabbed him, "he wouldn't."

A tense silence ensued. Tess had obviously told Gaston to do nothing, although a low growl was coming from the gryphon.

"Call off your . . . your . . . thing," Janko yelled at her.

Griff linked. *Lute?* he asked into the silver void.

Moments away, brother. Unless we're mistaken, there's some strange winged beast that we've just watched land. I'm assuming he's one more of Tess's oddities.

You've guessed right, but hurry; Janko's about to slice my throat open. He cut the link.

"I said call your creature off," Janko bellowed.

"Or what?" Griff hurled at him, twisting in his grip.

"Take a guess," Janko replied nastily. "I don't feel squeamish about killing a king, I've already told you that."

"No king here, you fool," Griff jeered.

"Did you hear that, Janko?" Bitter Olof asked angrily. "There is no king here."

"I'm glad you finally see it my way," Janko sneered.

"No," Little Thom joined in. "You're not getting it, Duke. There is no king amongst us."

Janko hesitated, frowning. "What are you going on about?"

The group had arrived soundlessly on foot and now one of the new party joined the conversation.

"That is not Lute," said a familiar voice.

Janko's head jerked up and he stared with bewilderment at Pilo, and then into the face of a boy identical to the one struggling in his grip. He let Griff go in his astonishment at seeing them and, standing nearby, Queen Miralda and five archers, all with their bows drawn tightly, arrows trained on Janko.

"A word from me, Janko, and you're full of holes," Lute said calmly.

Janko pushed Griff to the ground. "What's going on here?" he growled.

"You've been tricked, Janko," Miralda explained, her satisfaction obvious.

"Outwitted by children, in fact," Pilo added with a sneer.

Griff stood and threw a soft glance of thanks to Tess, who grinned back at him.

Little Thom strode over and, with great ease, yanked the dagger from Janko's grip. "Don't think of bolting or we'll set the gryphon on you," he warned the man, and smiled close to his face.

Lute took up the story. "You see, Uncle Janko, I have learned the truth behind my birth."

Griff grinned. "He's just been explaining it to me with great pleasure."

"Is that so?" Miralda chimed in, everyone enjoying watching Janko's head swiveling from person to person, each of whom seemed to be in on the plot.

"Yes, except that poor peasant falconer you took such delight in sneering at played you at your own game, Janko. He told you as little as he could, no doubt under threat of death to himself or, more likely, to his sons."

Janko's confusion deepened. "I don't understand."

"Let me enlighten you, Uncle," Lute said with glee, "as I

can see you are far too muddled by our presence to work it out for yourself. There were two of us. Our mother gave birth to identical twins. Our father kept one of us, who happened to be Griff. The other he agreed to give to the mysterious noblewoman, who promised his son a better, more prosperous life than my father could offer. He didn't sell me. He gave me to my royal parents. The Queen insisted, however, on building him a home, giving him some money with which to follow his dream to rear and train falcons."

"Boys, your father was a modest man, but he was noble in his heart," said Queen Miralda. "He just wanted to give you a chance, Lute, but, Griff, he couldn't bear to part with you both. I hope you'll forgive him."

"Twins!" Janko hissed, his countenance darkening. "I have been duped! I haven't been pursuing Rodin's heir?"

Everyone smiled slyly. "I'm afraid not," Pilo said, "and we can all thank young Tess for the brilliant plan that has deceived the great Duke Janko."

Tess smiled shyly, and Griff could wait no longer to go to her side. "Thank you" was all he could manage. He would say to her all that he wanted to later.

Davren walked into the circle of people and joined Gaston, who made a new noise in greeting.

"What is this? A misfit's circus?" Janko spat.

"I see no misfits here, Uncle, but there is no place for a traitor like you."

Griff sought the Silvering. *Lute, death is too easy for him. You don't want blood on your hands to commence your reign.*

He's right, Davren counseled. *Lute, there are other ways to make him suffer.*

How? I want him to pay.

I think I know, Griff said. *Let's not keep them waiting; they'll all be wondering why we're staring at nothing.*

They all returned.

Lute nodded at Griff. "Janko, I somehow feel that death is really too good for you. My brother would like to share an idea."

Miralda and Pilo looked the most surprised. But they both obviously realized that Lute was now King and his word alone counted.

"Griff, go ahead," Lute said.

Griff took a breath. "Bitter Olof, I presume you're returning to Calico Grace and the *Silver Wind?*"

"I will be, for sure," Olof said.

"Then I think you should take Janko with you. Leave him far from here on some island of your choice."

Lute nodded his approval. "Take him to a place so far away that he can never return and where he has no means of travel: not ship, nor horse, nor money. Give him the means to build a dwelling for himself and seeds to sow for food to feed himself, perhaps a cow that he can milk. Let him learn about life as a simple person, fending for himself. And he can learn what it is to be solitary. He can learn how much it means to share his thoughts with someone, to hear someone else's voice, and he can appreciate all that he's given up in his greed for power and wealth."

Miralda nodded, impressed. "I have raised a benevolent, clear-thinking son, Janko. And you are such a fool, your wits so dulled by your selfishness and your ego, that you couldn't even see that you already had power, wealth and a good family. Now you will live without all of those things. Your title will be stripped, of course."

"You cannot do this to me!" Janko roared.

Pilo laughed. "I think King Lute just did." He whistled and more men arrived. "Master Janko is to be put under armed guard and escorted to Floris. He is to be taken to Deep Bay, where he will board the ship *Silver Wind*, under the command of Captain Calico Grace. Your King will give further orders in due course."

"Miralda!" Janko cried as guards began to put him into irons and chains.

"Oh, go away, Janko," she said wearily, and turned her back to him.

They heard him screech all the way down the hill, until his voice became nothing more than a groan in the distance.

Everyone sighed.

Pilo broke the quiet. "Well, boys . . . and Tess with her marvelous creatures. What a triumph!"

Relieved laughter broke out.

"I'm proud of you, Lute," the Queen said. "That was very well done."

"Be proud of Griff," Lute replied. "If it were left to me, Janko would already be dead. It was Griff and Davren who made me see a different way."

Griff could see in the Queen's face a question. He would let Lute explain someday how they used magic to communicate with such ease.

"What now, Majesty?" Bitter Olof said brightly.

"Well, I think we should all return to Floris, and bring Calico Grace and her crew up to the palace as well. After

I have mourned my father, we shall have a proper coronation."

"A feast?" Bitter Olof asked.

"A big one, in honor of my friends who gave me back the Crown," Lute confirmed, and everyone laughed when the dwarf began to do a small jig on his short legs.

EPILOGUE

Many years later . . .

King Lute's reign was a long and prosperous one. He continued his benevolent ways and became a much-loved leader.

Janko, meanwhile, lived as a captive on a place known as Black Isle. Calico Grace and Bitter Olof chose well. The island was buffeted by fierce winds and huge swells. No ship went near that region, which was fraught with danger from rocks and unpredictable winds. He was never seen again in Drestonia, but curiously, he corresponded with his nephew, and a seemingly impossible yet fragile bond developed between them. They never spoke in person, but their letters were exchanged as often as Lute cared to send a carrier pigeon. Lute would never forgive Janko, but he refused to forget him or the fact that he was a lonely man now, desperate for any word from anyone.

The King's mother remained in mourning garb for the rest of her life but took immense pleasure in watching her son mature into a fine ruler. Lute's champion, Pilo, remained at his side, while his kind and loyal counselor, Griff, was proclaimed the King's long-lost brother. Lute was honest with his people and explained his arrival into the lives of King Rodin and Queen Miralda by royal announcements all over the realm.

And his people gifted him their trust, scarcely troubled, it seemed, by the deception of his parents, such was their love for them. They were far more troubled, in fact, by the murderous ways of his uncle, and relieved that Janko had not taken the throne.

Lute was reunited with his real father and elder brothers, while Master Tyren's Traveling Show continued its merry way around the realm—but this time with royal minders ensuring that all traveling shows treated their folk fairly and no one was pressed into service as a performer.

The Stalkers were disbanded, and their leader, Snark, was duly punished with a long stay in the King's jail.

Tess married her childhood sweetheart, Griff, and at the King's insistence an area of the royal parklands was cordoned off and became the habitat of her creatures. Here, within the most beautiful forest, roamed a centaur, a sagar, a califa and a wild veercat . . . and their friends.

And on the high seas a magical ship crewed by Captain Calico Grace plied the salty oceans with her special guests, Bitter Olof and Little Thom. The *Silver Wind* was no longer a pirate ship. Now the sleek vessel was on a new adventure, searching realms both far and wide for a witch called Grevilya and the chance to give its captain and her beloved dwarf their lives back.

But that's another tale. . . .